me Moore grew up in Luton, in a very poli... ily. She read history at Aberystwyth university and law through the Open University. After working in a library, she moved to west Wales to set up a restaurant with her sister, and now runs a craft business and occasionally teaches family history in rural Pembrokeshire, the county where her mother's family were once farmers, carpenters, stonemasons and ministers.

She has a much-loved niece, part share in assorted cats and far too many woodpeckers.

Very grateful thanks to my editor, Janet Thomas, for her patience and perception, to my friend and fellow author, Catherine Marshall, for keeping me going, and to the unnamed girl in the newspaper article, for the inspiration.

A TIME FOR

SILENCE

by

Thorne Moore

HONNO MODERN FICTION

First published by Honno

'Ailsa Craig', Heol y Cawl, Dinas Powys,

Wales, CF64 4AH

2 3 4 5 6 7 8 9 10

ISBN 978-1-906784-45-4

Published with the financial support of the Welsh Books Council.

Cover image: Izzy Ashford

Cover design: Simon Hicks

Printed in Wales by Gomer

To everything there is a season and a time
to every purpose under the heaven:
A time to be born and a time to die...
A time to keep silence and a time to speak.

Ecclesiastes

A weak flicker of sun filtered down through naked branches, catching little by little the wreck of the cottage. It flashed on broken panes, shattered slates, crumbling stone, and then it was gone, leaving me staring into shadow. Picking my way past brambles, I pushed ivy aside to peer in through a blackened rotting window frame, and felt the dark breath of the house exhale around me. Echoes of a forgotten past. My past. All these years this cottage, Cwmderwen, had lain cradled in a tangle of thorns, like Sleeping Beauty's resting place, waiting for the kiss that would awaken the secret it held. All my life, all my mother's life.

Pure chance had brought me here, but I could believe deeper forces had been at work, drawing me to this spot. I hadn't planned it. That morning, setting off in the dark from my mother's door, I'd expected nothing but a long journey home. A week ago, seeing my fiancé off from Heathrow, I hadn't dreamed of finding myself in this part of the world. But all the time I had busied myself with other plans, this house had been here, waiting.

For me.

1

'That's my flight, baby.'

I could feel the satisfaction rippling through Marcus, so I released him and turned to look up at the board. BA0115 to New York. 'God, I'm going to miss you.'

'And I'll miss you.' He hugged me once more. I could tell it was the final parting. 'But it's only for three months. That's nothing.'

'Nothing for you!' I growled. 'You'll be wining and dining and showing off to all those corporate bigwigs, and I'll be advertising fudge bars. This is what Einstein meant by relativity, you know. Hey!' I brightened. 'I know. Take me with you. Smuggle me in your suitcase. We can run off to Las Vegas and tie the knot with an Elvis lookalike and a pink Cadillac.'

'Mm. Tempting... but no. Too late. Already booked my bags in.' He reached into his jacket for his passport and boarding pass as if to check, but really to gloat over them. He'd been angling for this trip for months. 'You be good, Sarah Peterson. No mischief while I'm away.'

'No Polish plumbers?'

'You won't have time for Polish plumbers. You'll be far too busy thrashing out the wedding details with Mumsy.'

3

I groaned. 'No pink Cadillac?'

'Pink rosebuds. Humour her. Go with the flow.'

I muttered, Muttley-style.

He laughed. 'Well. This is it. Take care, baby. Keep busy, be good.'

'Skype, text, email, every day, promise?'

'Twice a day.'

One more quick kiss, so distracted it almost missed, and I watched him walk away into the jaws of the security controls.

So. Where now? Out of Terminal 5, into a sharp March wind under a lowering grey sky, feeling deflated. Not grief and desperation, exactly, but a void was spreading under me, and it needed filling.

I found my car, slumped into the driving seat, and sat there. My phone, which I had left under the seat, gave its customary bleep. I fished it out, flicked through texts, looked at my messages. In just over an hour, I had missed three calls.

No point in ignoring them; see what the world wanted of me.

'Sarah. Yes. Um...' My boss, Trevor, slightly slurred as usual after lunch. 'Hope you are, um... anyway, sorry, looks like we've lost the Solar contract. Not sure what, um... Disappointing, eh? Anyway, speak to you about it when you come in. Are you coming in? Or tomorrow. Yes. Right. Okay?'

'Trevor!' I slammed the dashboard, ignoring anxious glances from a couple in the next car. I'd given everything to get that contract. If we'd lost it, it was down to Trevor. Probably messed up the paperwork. So, instead of a project that could have set us up among the serious players, I was left with a fudge bar. It was sitting on my desk waiting for me. The manufacturer, a friend of Trevor, wanted me to market it, please, with erotic overtones like Flake but a hint of homeliness like Hovis? No. I didn't want to market it at all. I'd told Trevor we should be concentrating on...

Oh, what was the point? It was just a job.

The next message kicked in, and my innards shrank. Marcus' mother. 'Sarah, darling. Caroline here. Did Marcus get off all right? I wanted to come and see him off too, but he said better not. We're all going to miss him, aren't we? Now you are going to come this Sunday, aren't you? Russell and I are expecting you. After all, you're practically our daughter already, so I hope you think of this as home. We've got such a lot to do before Marcus gets back. That wedding to arrange? Let's see if we can sort out that dress this time. See you soon.'

That wedding. *That* dress. Not mine; I was just the mannequin. Caroline was the mistress and commander of the project, wrapping her octopus tentacles around me. The thought of Sunday dinner at the Crawfords without Marcus as compensation was too much to bear. I needed time to ground myself. Time to mourn my beloved's absence without being tempted to murder his mother.

The last message: Freddie, of all people, out of the blue and out of the past. Freddie my one-time occasionally transvestite boyfriend, before I had traded him for Marcus and he had traded me for Japan. 'Hiya Sai, how you keeping? Keep meaning to ring. Listen, when are you performing next? Still doing Murphy's? There's a couple of guys here, I told them all about this fantastic singer I know and they're going to be over in England next month, itching to hear you. Any dates? Let me know. Love. Okay?'

Of course, I should have realised; Freddie still thought of me as a singer. How long ago was that?

I'd been in a band. We'd started it at college, got a taste for the sound of applause, and tried to keep it going in the big world, seriously convinced that the next gig, the next song, would be It. Fizzled out in the end, of course; once Sean had got himself arrested, and Jemma – Jemma had got herself killed. That had been a dark time and a dark place for me. Too dark to survive, I'd sometimes thought, as I'd begun to spiral into depression and alcohol. Freddie, my ardent fan, had tried to convince me I could make it as a solo act. He set me up as a regular at a local club, promising world stardom, while I'd staggered from one night to the next in a miserable haze of pot and vodka.

All behind me now. I'd come through all that, out into reality. My glittering adolescent fantasies may have been swept away in the process, but at least my black dog days had gone too. I'd emerged, miraculously, the right way up. My casual day jobs crystallised into a career with Frieman and Case Promotions, my anarchic private life morphed into an engagement to a sexy young solicitor. Pension plans, mortgages, kids were on their way. I hadn't sung in Murphy's bar for what? Two years at least. I hadn't sung anywhere except Sophie's wedding, when everyone, including me, was too drunk to notice.

Sorry, Freddie, I'd moved on. Like I should be doing now. No good sitting there, waiting for Marcus' plane to shoot away without me. Decisively, I started the engine. Now all I had to do was find the exit.

'Where the hell is it?' I asked the empty seat beside me, and felt another pang at the thought of three months without Marcus. Three months of weekend wedding planning with Caroline and the petty frustrations of a mediocre career in advertising. I needed him already. I relied on his granite certainties. Marcus would know the way out of here.

For God's sake, Sai Peterson, you can find your own way. Of course I could, and I did, laughing at my own sense of empowerment. Driving home, I decided I needed to break out a bit, treat myself to a tiny dose of rebellion.

Back in my Guildford flat I phoned my mother. I hadn't seen her since Christmas. 'Hi Mum.'

'Sarah.' Her voice echoed down the phone, set against the mellow drone of Irish radio. 'How are you?'

'Coming to see you.'

'Wonderful. When are you landing? I'll be at the airport to pick you up.'

'No need. I'm driving.'

'Oh you can't. Do you have any idea how far it is?'

'Nothing to it. See you Friday night.'

So once I'd balled out Trevor at the office, rescued another contract and given our perfectly adequate trainee, Maya, her wings, I treated myself to an extended weekend. A flight out to Kerry would have been too immediate, out of one set of issues straight into another. I wanted the solitude, the liberation of the drive, windows down, hair flying, singing my lungs out as I headed for an ever-receding horizon. I may not have sung for years, but I was going to sing now. Just once more.

I sang everything from Madam Butterfly to Postman Pat.

I sang across England and Wales. I sang onto the ferry at Fishguard. I sang across Ireland. By the time I arrived on the doorstep of my mother's cottage, buffeted by the Atlantic roar, I could barely croak a greeting. She nursed me with honey and whiskey.

We walked and, when I was capable, we talked, about nothing that mattered. She asked me, 'How are the arrangements going?' I said, 'Fine, missing Marcus.' She nodded understanding, and that was it.

Weddings were not a subject I felt I could discuss with my mother. Too sensitive. My parents had divorced, and my father had gone off to Another Woman. Mum had been left like a wounded bird, washing up eventually on this distant shore, with her whiskey bottle and her art.

She was bearing up, I decided, watching her critically. Or putting a good face on it, losing herself in her painting. I ought to come more often; I couldn't have her sinking into lonely depression out in County Kerry. But in the small hours of Monday, as I got ready to leave, I made a mental note to take the plane in future. I really hadn't grasped how long the journey would be.

I did sing a little, as far as the ferry, but the sea was far choppier this time and when I drove onto dry land I was sealed in nauseous silence, vowing never to go near a boat again.

The negativity of sea-sickness refused to wear off, so I stopped at the first town I came to, looking for a coffee and a chance to re-orientate.

As I walked, I caught my reflection in the plate glass window of an estate agent. Washed out, hair limp, bags under my eyes. Great. I tried a smile. Okay, a bit better.

Then I looked through the glass. We'd been pouring over property details in recent months, apartments in converted Regency houses, dockland developments, semi-rural residences with hot tubs and commuter connections. But we had idly day-dreamed about a little rural hideaway, far from the city. Marcus had this romantic idea of a turreted hunting lodge on wild Scottish moors. This was west Wales, not Scotland, but still Celtic. There were hills. I looked to see if there were any turrets among the adverts for modern bungalows and drab terraces.

An old rectory. Way too big. A converted mill. That sounded better. Interesting.

Then I saw it. The name. Cwmderwen.

Just a fly-blown sheet of paper, squeezed in among building plots and garage leases. No picture to tempt. It had been there for months, years maybe, slowly fading.

'Cwmderwen, Llanolwen, cottage with outbuildings, suitable for development.'

It was a shock to find a name I knew, here in the middle of nowhere. Except that, on second thoughts, here was exactly where it would be. My mother had once found Llanolwen for me on a map. I had been eight, nine maybe, working on a family tree for a school project, so she had produced her birth certificate.

Sîan Ellen Owen, born 23rd February 1948 at Cwmderwen, Llanolwen; father John Owen, farmer; mother Gwenllian Owen, formerly Lewis.

My mother had grown up in Peterborough with her aunt Dilys, so the Llanolwen farm had swirled into the ragbag of family myth, but here it was, staring at me though an estate agent's window. I couldn't just pass by. I had to have a look.

The girl at the desk, feeding details to another prospective client, gave me her partial attention and a share of the corporate smile. 'Can I help you?'

'You've got a place in the window. Cwmderwen, in Llanolwen. Any chance of seeing it?'

Her hopeful mask sagged as she swivelled to run off the information sheet. Even in the current climate, this was a sale barely worth pursuing. She handed me the sheet. 'You won't be able to go in. It's locked up.'

'That's all right. I just want to take a quick look.'

Twenty minutes later, I was in Llanolwen. Another twenty minutes, back and forth, and I still hadn't found the cottage. 'The lane to the property forks to the right shortly after the turning to Castell Mawr farm,' read the blurb. 'It is marked by a milestone.' What milestone? In the end, I stopped at the Castell Mawr entrance and got out.

I was in a broad lay-by, neat verges hedged by clipped conifers, with a white gate onto a concrete track clearly signposted to Castell Mawr. So far so good. At the far end the lay-by petered out into rough grass and bramble under a cluster of trees, and I finally unearthed the milestone, buried in the tangle of last year's weeds.

There was the lane, forking off through the undergrowth, slithering down into the woods. No tarmac, no concrete, no grit, no way my little Fiat could make it down there, so I walked. A pilgrimage into my family's lost past.

I wouldn't even have managed on foot if a tractor hadn't been that way recently, crushing and severing brambles, leaving glutinous mounds of mud and squelching pools in their place. I nearly lost a trainer, but I battled on down into a secret wooded dell, concealed from the outside world.

So this was Cwmderwen. Grandfather Owen's farm. 'Farm' to me, meant something like the farm near Dilys and Harry's retirement cottage in Buckinghamshire. Grand porch, big gables, immaculate lawns, enfolded in rolling wheat fields.

Not this. A cocoon of tangled trees, the smell of old mould and new wet grass, birdsong, and amid it all a small dark cottage.

Even in its heyday, it couldn't have been a serious farm. A smallholding maybe. According to the agent's details, it came with a yard, an overgrown garden and half an acre of woodland, that was all. A rusty gate, wired shut and engulfed in nettles and briar, giving a glimpse out onto rough empty pasture. Cwmderwen's land had passed into other hands.

But not the house. I'd thought 'suitable for development' meant 'cute convertible out-buildings' but it turned out it actually meant 'totally derelict'. Barns, pigsty, cowshed, whatever they were, had crumbled into rubble. Sculptures of rusted iron stood in the cobbled yard, under heaps of leaf mould. Slates had poured from the cottage roof and the beams were caving in.

The sun came and went and I shuddered. The door was padlocked, to keep chance visitors safe, but I could peer in through a window, and shapes materialised in the darkness. I could see a scaffolding pole, topped with a paint-splashed plank, supporting the sagging ceiling. Tucked beside a massive fireplace with a rusting range, outsized worm-eaten steps wound up into darkness, barred by a plank and yellow warning tape.

I stared at the ancestral hearth. Eternal twilight, the

11

stench of decay. Dry rot, wet rot, woodworm, all decomposing life was there. Withered leaves rustled on the black flagstones. Cobwebs, thick as rope with dust, dangled from painted beams and draped across mouldering wallpaper.

Then I saw the dresser. It was huge and sad, embarrassed by my intrusion, caught in a state of undress, no glimmer of its former polish and shine. The doors hung askew, the shelves bowed. It must have been my Nan's dresser.

I could remember Nan. Almost. I was three when I'd seen her last. At least, I'd seen polished linoleum, enamel bed frames, drooping flowers, and my favourite teddy bear... and somewhere in the midst of it, a faded wisp, tired of life, drowning in the smell of sickness and disinfectant. But I'd known she was my grandmother, Aunt Dilys' sister. Flesh and blood. And once upon a time she'd lived in this place. She'd stood on those slabs, arranging pretty gilded china on that rack.

That same rack. I'd swear no one had touched the place since she'd left, when my grandfather died. The world had moved on, but not this cottage, not for sixty empty years.

I saw it as it must have been, bright, fresh, lived in, the yard swept clean, pinks and hollyhocks in the garden, John Owen's cows grazing in the pasture, John Owen's young family running in through that doorway, John Owen's wife, round-bellied with my mother, shelling peas in that kitchen.

If it had just been abandoned, why couldn't my mother have grown up here, inheriting it maybe, to bequeath to me?

I stood for a moment listening for the voices of the past, the echo of forgotten laughter. There was a sense of life and hope continuing. Sun was filtering through naked branches onto celandines carpeting the steep valley side. Spring grass was beginning to glow green-gold in the meadow. In the back garden, a gnarled and mossy apple tree was struggling to produce a few sprigs of blossom. Still, after all those years, life welled up from this soil.

It was wrong that Nan had been forced to trade this for the crucifixion of cancer in the antiseptic loneliness of a hospital far away. All wrong.

I'd made my impulsive pilgrimage to the past. Curiosity satisfied. But Cwmderwen wouldn't let go. It followed me back to Guildford, whispering, nagging. I really knew very little about that side of my family, despite my closeness to my mother and Aunt Dilys. On my father's side, the Petersons were full of interest; the Oxford don, the bi-plane pilot, the dipso daughter of the Raj. A lot of make-believe, but at least people had bothered to fantasise. The Owens were just farmers from West Wales, with a shopkeeper thrown in for good measure. Enough said. Except that now I wanted more, because I had seen the farm, humble as it was.

Arriving home past midnight, I unearthed my old school project. There I was, Sarah Peterson, in my own family tree, writ so large my brother Sam was squeezed into the margin. Plenty on the colourful Petersons, but on my mother's side just faceless names. When I was adding her parents, I hadn't equated Gwenllian Lewis with the Nan who had withered away when I was three. As for John Owen, he was just a Methuselah who had died, as old men did. I'd been given his date of birth, 1901, which had seemed so impossibly distant I accepted his death without question. But thinking about it now, he couldn't have been so very old. He had died when my mother was a baby, so 1948? Not yet fifty. TB probably, or a farm accident.

On impulse I switched on my laptop to search. Amateur genealogist friends had assured me it was all online these days. It took a while to find my way around, but eventually death records popped up. So many John Owens, but only one in the right place, right age. John F. Owen, 1948, second quarter, aged 47. I could purchase the certificate if I wished. Why not? I had a week for the interest to fade, but I was still curious to see what the certificate said when the envelope finally dropped through my letterbox.

Staring out of the window, I pictured again that cottage, the place where my grandparents had loved and laughed and raised a family. An idyllic life cut short by this. This thing no one had told me, or even hinted at.

Cause of death, cerebral destruction by gunshot.

My grandfather had been shot.

2

1933

Not a bad day for a wedding, all things considered. The thunder has edged away over the hills, rain already drying on the slate steps of Beulah chapel, splashes of blue between the torn clouds. The wind has died down, but a gust snatches at a loose wisp of her hair as she emerges on his arm.

Mr and Mrs Owen. So simple, a little chapel solemnity, names scratched in a register, and Gwenllian Lewis has been raised to the status of married woman, absorbed with a word into a man's identity.

'Here we are, my good people.' The Reverend Harries is shepherding the bridal couple, a big strong man, straining his black cloth with solid flesh and certainty. He clasps their hands, Gwen's in a paternal way, John's in a supportive grip as he presents them to the world.

Surely she should feel something, sense some change in her bones?

Nothing. Nothing but the sharp sting of the storm's tail on her cheek.

A bride is supposed to feel happiness, but for Gwen that carries a suggestion of sin. Gratitude then. Yes, there can be no impropriety in gratitude. She takes her John's arm, grateful that in this random lottery of mating she has won someone she can be proud of.

A tall man, features gaunt and bony as a prophet. She glances at his profile, sharp against the washed sky, jaw firm like a warrior, deep-set eyes steady as an eagle's fixed on prey. There is nothing weak or servile about him. Yes, she can be proud.

She feels trepidation too. All brides are allowed that, and it is no wonder that she should feel it now, gazing with slight myopia on the assembled worthies of Llanolwen. So many faces, and so few whom she knows. Just her sister Dilys, supporting her father.

Dilys, eight years Gwen's junior, girl still within the emerging woman, is surveying the crowd jauntily, appraising the matrons with disparagement, the young men with an occasional flash of brazen approval. Irrepressible Dilys. She turns her head, bobbed hair swinging, and meets her sister's eye. In an instant, her air of critical evaluation vanishes, subsumed beneath a warm smile. She reaches out to Gwen.

'Bless you, Gwen.' Unconditional warmth and reassurance.

But Gwen has no time to respond, for the Reverend Harries' hand is directing her. A young man with a camera is preparing for the official dignified memento of this day, and Gwen must be manoeuvred, steered into position on the steps, her new neighbours ranged around her.

Then introductions. John plays his part with dignity, saying, 'My wife,' as if it slips naturally from his tongue already. Smiling nervously, Gwen greets face after face, desperate to remember names. Farmers, quarrymen, shopkeepers... so many to remember.

'Good luck, John.'

'God be with you, John.'

'The Lord's blessing on you, John.'

'And you, Mrs Owen. You have a fine man there.'

Wishes and prayers for John, but congratulations for her. The luck, they are saying, is all hers.

'Mrs George,' says John. 'Our neighbour at Castell Mawr.' He presents Gwen for inspection. 'My wife, Mrs Owen.'

Gwen will not easily forget Mrs George. Matriarch of the parish, taller than most of the men and built like Pembroke Castle, with something of the bullfrog about her, blooms nodding belligerently on her hat. She looms over Gwen, sharp eyes probing. unrelenting in their search for weakness.

'Well, Mrs Owen, you are very welcome. Lewis, was it? Hm. Lewis of Penbryn.' She speaks as if a heathen tribe had invaded the Christian sanctity of Llanolwen. Then she relents. 'Henry Lewis, is it?'

She turns her bulk in the direction of Gwen's father, where he leans on Dilys. Since his seizure, he has been all out of balance, left side drooping, mouth askew. Some of the younger people take him for a drunkard and sniff their disapproval.

But the older ones know better. Henry Lewis is a man of talent, hymn writer and crowned bard, once renowned throughout Wales, even if his fame has long faded. Gwen hears the murmur of a line from one of his best-known hymns, and the Reverend Harries is bending over him with respectful unction. Her father, who could once weave

17

words like a true druid, struggles to mouth a response. The minister beams understandingly.

Henry looks up to smile at his daughter, but his benediction only compounds her guilt. She should not be leaving him. It is wrong.

'A name we know,' says Mrs George, with grudging approval, nodding at the once great man before turning her scalpel gaze back on Gwen. 'And you are his daughter.'

'She is,' says John.

Mrs George nods again, lips pinched. 'From Howell's Groceries, they tell me. Well, you will not find life so easy here, Mrs Owen. You'll have no time for idle gossip over the counter with our John to care for and a farm to keep.'

'I know it,' says Gwen, fixing her smile with determination. It is no more than she had expected, this instant suspicion of the stranger. She could insist that she is well acquainted with hard work. For years, she has carried the Lewis household through the shame of bankruptcy, the struggles, bereavements, support to her father, mother to Dilys. And her mother's family were farmers over in Hebron, so she is no stranger to farm work either.

Gwen says no more. They will learn her metal soon enough.

'Hm,' says Mrs George again. Behind her, her son William, stiff in his finery as John's best man, smiles with provisional approval. An easy-going, friendly man, as far as she can tell, but even he is reserving judgement. He'll wait to see if Gwen does well by her man and then he'll smile whole-heartedly.

She draws a deep breath of relief as the Georges move

on, and another neighbour draws John away in earnest talk. More good wishes for him on this momentous day? She listens.

'...twin calves and the beast won't survive. It will be a sorry loss.'

Farming does not stop even for weddings.

Gwen's arm relinquished, she looks round, searching for an ally, aware how completely she has already been wrenched from her former life.

She should have wed in Seion, her own chapel in Penbryn, with her kindly Reverend Phillips to bless her and her fellow townsfolk to see her on her way, but another bride had elected the same day to wed and Seion is occupied with her lace and lilies.

John had not thought a change of date appropriate. Besides, this is his chapel, his spiritual home. *Thy people shall be my people, thy God my God.* So here she stands, in Llanolwen, alone and quiet, in her simple grey frock, for Gwen is ever quiet. A biddable woman.

A dozen pairs of eyes meet hers, summing her up. She must not wilt.

'My God, they're a suspicious lot.' Out of nowhere, Dilys is by her side, facing down the Llanolwen dames. 'You'll not get many laughs to the shilling out of them.'

'Hush!' Gwen bites down a laugh. 'Don't offend my new neighbours. These are John's people.'

'So they are,' says Dilys, with stout diplomacy. She does not value John as his new wife does. She likes her admirers noisy and brash, not sober and stately, but then Dilys, with her strapping good looks and shameless confidence, will always have her pick.

For Gwen it has been another story. Few boisterous young men appreciated her frail gentility, and since her mother's death, family duties have taken her from the contest. Dilys might not give the likes of John Owen a second glance on her own account, but for her sister's sake she'll respect a man who has resolutely set his hand to the plough. If Gwen is content, so is Dilys.

It is Dilys who will now return to Penbryn to tend their father. Another coil of familiar guilt knots itself in Gwen's belly. Dilys, of all people, should not be condemned to nursing spinsterhood.

'Dilys, about Dad. I hope—'

'Hush, don't be daft, girl,' interrupts Dilys, happily. 'Don't you go worrying about us. Dad and I will be just fine.'

'Perhaps when I am settled...' Could she bring her father to Llanolwen, to live with them? Would John permit it? She has not dared ask him yet, but soon perhaps.

'Don't fret yourself,' insists Dilys. 'You have enough to think about. And if any of these fine folk are a bother to you, you let me know and I'll sort them out.' She will too. She's already eying up one young man, prior to sorting him out, and he's returning the compliment.

'I'll do very well, thank you,' says Gwen with a smile, letting her sister take her arm.

'I've heard them muttering. Don't you let them think you are just some shop girl of no account.'

'Indeed not. I am Henry Lewis' daughter,' says Gwen, with self-deprecating mockery.

'Yes, let them remember that! And they owe you respect on your own account. I know they think John is such a mighty singer—'

'Indeed he is!'

'Yes, yes of course he is. But you have talents too. You tell them to ask at Seion who is the most accomplished harpist and pianist in the county. Tell them how Lady Richards complimented you, Christmas last.'

'I'll do no such thing.' Gwen is watching a young girl, a toddler, hiding behind her mother's skirts and summoning up courage to peep round at the new lady. When the child at last succeeds, Gwen smiles and the girl smiles back, a sunburst of innocence.

Dilys follows her gaze and the sisters exchange glances, an instant flash of understanding between them. Children. That is what marriage is about. The highest blessing. Neither gives voice to the sentimental thought, but they recognise it in each other, and Dilys squeezes Gwen's hand.

The fulfilment of motherhood. Is that at last a flutter of happiness she feels?

But the day is too much of a whirlwind for her to dwell on it. John is returning to claim her and Dilys steps back with a reassuring nudge, Gwen's bridal posy clasped in her white-gloved hand.

'The trap is waiting,' says John. His hand is firm on her elbow. No time for dawdling.

'Wait,' she pleads.

He relinquishes her reluctantly as she hurries across to receive one last kiss from her father.

'You be good now, girl.' Henry Lewis laughs. As if there could be the need to say that to his Gwen! He is pushing her away, reassuring her that all is well, that she is doing right in leaving him. Not for the world would he stand between his beloved daughter and the sanctified joy of marriage. A marriage that will free her from their cramped and sorry life in Penbryn.

She kisses his hand. She must not linger. Her husband is waiting.

The monstrous Mrs George is guarding the gate. 'Well, John. Mrs Owen. You know where we are if you need anything. Mind you take care of him, girl.'

'Indeed yes,' the Reverend Harries booms. 'We must keep our finest baritone in full working order.'

Gwen smiles her compliance.

Outside in the road, the pony and trap are waiting. Someone has threaded poppies and blue ribbons into the harness. It is an unexpectedly frivolous touch and no one owns up to it, a gesture not altogether appropriate for this very quiet affair. There is no cake and tea. It would not be seemly, with her father being so infirm, John having so many responsibilities and money being so tight. It is more fitting that they just drive away, newlyweds, to Cwmderwen.

John helps her into the trap, strong hands lifting her slight frame. Children in their Sunday best run around, being called to order by disapproving parents. The little girl who had found courage to smile at Gwen comes forward boldly, thrusting a handful of daisies up at her.

Gwen extends her hand to accept the miniscule gift. 'It's very pretty. Thank you.'

But John's hand reaches across to hers, pulling it back. The child looks into his face, her new-found courage drained, lip quivering. John's grip tighten on Gwen's arm, reminding her that all her care lies now with him. Obediently, she sinks back into her seat, heart pattering, eyes forward. The child runs back to her mother.

Panic. Sudden and overwhelming panic. It surges through Gwen. This is all too soon, everything has swept along too fast, she is not ready for this.

What does she want with marriage? She wants her old world back. She wants her old home, her two small rooms over the shop in Penbryn, surrounded by those who love her. She wants her work and her Sunday School duties, her quiet hours at the piano, and the greetings of everyday acquaintances. She was happy there, content with spinsterhood. Children – she could be aunt to Dilys's brood, wouldn't that be enough?

She should not be here. She must tell them it's all a mistake. In the rush, she's had no time to think.

But truthfully, there has been no rush. This wedding had been the sacred seal on a modestly temperate relationship, devoid of unseemly passion, arranged with calm decorum.

Her Reverend Phillips had set it all in motion, ferrying his pious music lovers from Seion to a mission concert at Pen-y-bont. The harp had been indifferent but the piano was passable and the singing excellent. Especially the baritone.

'A splendid performance, MrOwen. Our community is honoured. And here is an admirer, Miss Lewis of our Seion Chapel. An accomplished musician of some renown in our own small circle, I might add.'

She had been passed to John, almost like a bag of sugar over the counter, and Gwen had not resisted. Why should she? She never nursed impossible dreams of true love and romance. If there was passion in her, it was in the secret response of her viscera to John's splendid voice. Enough to justify her compliance, and after that she simply succumbed to the absolute taciturn possessiveness with which he marked her out as his. Weekly visits, never rushed, never untimely or improper; Mr John Owen coming to pay his respects to Miss Lewis.

Until this burst of panic, she has remained spellbound by his stateliness, the righteous dignity of a farmer of unimpeachable standing. Why doubt now? This is her duty, the world approves; she must be calm.

Still the urge rushes through her veins to jump down and run. But it is too late. John clicks. The horse trots forward, the trap sways and Gwen clutches at her hat, her heartbeat thundering in her ears.

There is a muffled comment from someone in the watching crowd, laughter hastily shushed. 'Mind your tongue now, Huw Morris. No call for that sort of talk. This is a solemn occasion.'

Solemn and irreversible. She breathes deeply, determined to master her nerves. There is no going back. Cwmderwen. So near, and yet so apart. The descent into the trees calms her, reminding her of her all-consuming duty. The past is over and this is to be her future.

She has never been here before. They courted at the Chapel or in Penbryn teashops. She gazes around, careful to mask any hint of disappointment. She had really expected no more. Though mercenary thoughts played no part in Gwen's decision to accept John, she had made a point of learning what she could of his situation, listening to the gossip of Penbryn tradesfolk.

A farm, but no treasure-trove. A precarious tenure that John's wastrel father Frank had nearly lost, squandering all in the Butcher's Arms and roaring home drunk each night to beat his wife and children, letting his land go to ruin, the rent unpaid, eviction and penury looming. Thank a merciful God, said the gossips, for dropping him, dead drunk, under the wheels of a cart.

But the same merciful God has cast the son in a different mould. John is honoured, a man of iron control and moral probity, holding fast through the lean years since the war by working himself to his knees, wasting nothing, surviving against odds that would have crushed a lesser man. Day and night he has fought to be what his father was not. Every inch of him has rejected the demons that destroyed his childhood and his reward is universal respect. Poverty is no matter. Cwmderwen is his patrimony, however humble and now it will be hers.

Never mind the gloom. The sun will make all the difference. There is a cosy little farmstead down here under the overhanging trees with a cow byre, a barn creaking on ancient timbers and a pigsty, its solitary resident paying her cursory attention before returning to snuffling among the litter. Cobbled yard, pump over the well, a few chickens pecking around. The cottage is solid enough, if dark. Without the gleam of sunlight, it looks dour and forbidding, but as with the human frame, it is the heart within that counts.

As John hands her over the dark threshold, she is determined to approve. There are no luxuries, no extravagances, but she asks for none. The house is a man's house, without softness. A thin worn cushion on the hard high-backed chair by the range is the only concession to comfort in the kitchen. The small parlour is immaculate in perpetual readiness but lacks the dainty trimmings a parlour needs. A religious text and a print of Queen Victoria, spotted by damp, are the only decorations.

She can add the woman's touch, the fresh curtains, embroidered fire screen, bright china on the heavy old dresser. No instrument. Unexpected, that. Even when her family had fallen on hard times, they had kept the old piano for her to play. Perhaps it can be brought here, if a cart can be spared. She has secretly dreamed of playing in her new home, accompanying John while he sings. Of course she is no concert performer like him, but it is an image she cherishes.

That may come, but she has other things to think about for now. There will be precious little time for music while she finds her feet. A new home, new duties, a new life. A husband. Wedded love. Marital obligations.

A stirring of panic again. There are things yet to face that she will not allow herself to think about for now. Be busy, girl.

Her trunk stands in the corner. John and his friend William came to fetch it yesterday. On the scrubbed table is a basket of provisions; tea, milk, butter, eggs, cheese, bacon, a loaf of bread.

Its brazen presence catches John by surprise and he frowns. Then his jaw relaxes, under orders. 'We have good neighbours. Mrs George and her daughters.' There is tight-lipped inhibition in his voice, clearly begrudging this gesture of good will. Is it on her behalf? Does he take the basket to imply that his neighbours doubt his new wife? They need not fear. She has coped for years.

'They are very kind.' There is a pride in her too, stiffening her resolve to conquer, sweeping away the last vestige of that foolish panic. She will prove to the doubters that she is no mere burden on her man, without dowry or sense. With her help and management, Cwmderwen will continue to thrive and John will not be robbed of one iota of the respect he has laboured so hard to earn. She will be a good wife, care for him, bear his children. None will ever accuse her of falling short.

John is watching her intently. With love? That is beyond her expectations. With possessiveness, yes. Respect, she hopes. That is all she truly craves. 'Well, Mrs Owen,' he says. 'Will it do?'

'Mr Owen, it will do very well.' She removes her hat with a shy smile and puts the kettle on to boil.

3

'We've decided it's going to be a Goth wedding.' I parked
my great-aunt's wheelchair beside a bench on Hove front,
and plumped down next to her, taking in a deep breath of
sea air. My arms were aching from manoeuvring the chair
round tourists and dog turds. 'The dress is going to be
black leather with crow feathers.'

'Black leather! Who ever heard of such a thing?!' said
Dilys on cue. 'The very idea!'

It was a game, me being outrageous, Dilys being
outraged. I was supposed to add something even more
shocking at this point; something about nose studs maybe.
But I was too busy nursing bruised resentment to enter
into the spirit properly, so I said nothing.

Dilys sniffed, rearranging the blanket that protected her
knees from the sea breeze and glanced at me askance.
'You're far too old for that sort of thing.'

She was trying to chivvy me into continuing the ritual,
but I could only think, Not old enough to be told the things
that matter.

'What does Caroline Crawford have to say about such
nonsense, I wonder?'

I couldn't help but smile, picturing Caroline's face if I

did turn up at the altar in black leather. Whereas my great-aunt, for all her lip service to propriety, would probably take it in her stride. She'd obviously taken plenty of other things in her stride. Like murder.

'What you need to do, girl, is set the day and get on with it.' Short and sharp.

She was right. Despite Caroline's endless fussing, Marcus and I still hadn't even fixed the date. 'It's not as easy as you think. There's a lot to juggle: Marcus' work and mine, and when the church is available and Lyngrove Manor and all sorts of things – including when Marcus' cousin Josie is due to have her brace removed, apparently.'

'Stuff and nonsense. If you two are committed, you should stop this shilly-shallying. I won't be around forever, you know.'

The prime purpose of my marriage, of course, was to bring peace to my great-aunt. I hadn't given her much to date. Despite all the piano and singing lessons she'd paid for, I had failed to pursue a career in opera. I had picked up and dropped a string of meaningless jobs while I was with the band, I had consorted with at least one convicted criminal, nearly got myself arrested, and my early boyfriends would have turned Dilys' white hairs tangerine. So, since she knew that the only true happiness lay in a wedding band, sensible footwear and Friday night bridge, she naturally regarded an ultra-respectable young lawyer like Marcus as the second coming. I could have told her that bridge and sensible shoes were not a part of Marcus' steamy and dynamic universe, but that would have been cruel.

'You want all the trimmings, don't you?' I demanded. 'All the ghastly ceremonial? It takes time.'

Dilys smacked my knuckles on the arm of her chair. 'Trimmings, stuff and nonsense. You don't need that high church rubbish. Get that boy to walk you to the nearest chapel before you get cold feet.'

'My feet are warm, Dilly! I'm finding it hard to get enthusiastic about all this wedding stuff, but that doesn't mean I'm having second thoughts about the marriage.'

She gave me her sideways call to judgement. I'd run out on Marcus once, two years earlier. I didn't exactly jilt him at the altar but it was near enough. Caroline's juggernaut had been rolling over me, suffocating me, so I'd done a bunk, taken a plane to India with an overnight bag and a scream in my heart. Coward.

But I came back, back to England and Marcus, who'd forgiven me, which was all that mattered; we'd gone on as we were, keeping quiet about the whole running away thing. I wasn't even sure if Dilys knew about it.

Her scrutiny told me she did.

'No second thoughts? Hmph. So what's this worm gnawing at you? You've been up to mischief, my girl.' Dilys' sharp eyes were fixed on me, uncannily perceptive, just as they had been all my life. She was well into her nineties, old and deaf. She tended to doze when she thought no one was watching, and sometimes her short-term memory lapsed. She couldn't manage a trip from her plush nursing home to the front without a wheelchair any more, thanks to arthritis. But a large part of her wits were as quick as ever.

And they were fixed on me by right, because whatever great-aunts normally were, Dilys was far more than that to me. As a child I had taken my family intricacies for granted. I had a Gran Peterson, Daddy's Mummy, who was a real

Gran, the sort who spoiled me to death and criticised the way I was brought up. I had Mummy's Mummy, Nan, who was more like a distant aunt, the sort to be visited and presented to once in a while. And I had a Great-Aunt, Dilys, who was like another proper Gran, always there, for my mother and for me.

My mother made it sound quite normal: when her mother, my Nan, was widowed, she and the children came to stay with her sister Dilys in Peterborough. Nan moved on to Leicester, taking the boys, and Dilys kept my mother, who was just a baby. Nothing official, no formal adoption, no change of names. As far as I knew, my mother never called Dilys anything other than Aunt, because Dilys would have frowned on unlicensed familiarity, but she grew up with Dilys and Uncle Harry as their own beloved daughter. Nothing odd about it at all.

So Dilys had the right to bully and tease my secrets out of me as if I were her granddaughter, and she could detect an uneasy conscience with unnerving accuracy. But if she had rights, surely I had some too. The right not to be kept in the dark. The right to know how Nan had come to be widowed in the first place. If I started hurling open doors, figuratively and literally, she had no right to be surprised.

'You've been up to something,' said Dilys.

'I've bought a house.' I sounded brazen, challenging. Challenging myself rather than Dilys perhaps. The day after I received my grandfather's death certificate, I'd rung the Welsh estate agents and put in an offer for Cwmderwen, driven by outraged certainty. The cottage had been snatched from us by a horrible event and I was an angel of vengeance redressing cruel injustice. As the impulse became a legal commitment, I was beginning to wonder what I was doing. I had told no one till now. Too embarrassed.

Dilys, with no suspicion of my impulsive idiocy, merely nodded satisfaction. 'Well that's a start. In the city, I suppose. Marcus will want that.'

'It's not that sort of house. Just a weekend place. Something to work on.' It was no good. However much I wanted to discuss it, I couldn't help prevaricating. Dilys had that effect on me. I was a child again, hiding my hands in my lap so she wouldn't see I hadn't washed properly before tea. 'Just a cottage.'

'What does Marcus think?' She knew there was some guilt at work and she was going to have it out. A well-aimed thrust on her part.

'Marcus is away for a few months, honing his expertise in American corporate law, so I'm handling it on my own.'

'A high flier, that one.' I couldn't tell from her sniff whether she approved of Marcus' driving ambition or not. 'I didn't ask where he was. I asked what he thought of the cottage. You do speak to him, don't you, on the telephone?'

I gave a laugh that didn't even convince me. 'Dilly, we've been planning on buying a weekend place for ages. He thinks it's out of this world.' I could feel my nose growing. Marcus would think Cwmderwen out of this world. If I had any power over him, he would. When I finally got round to telling him. Our transatlantic calls, texts and emails had been lengthy and numerous, but they had centred on American enterprise, the excitement of the Big Apple, the availability of St. Hugh's next spring, my professional trials in the world of advertising, and numerous intimacies that wouldn't bear repeating. My decision to spend my Peterson inheritance on a Welsh ruin was something I needed to explain face to face, when he got back. I needed time to do it properly, to make him understand how important it was, how much it meant to me.

'Hmm,' said Dilys, still eying me suspiciously. 'If he approves of you frittering away your money...'

'Approves! Dilly, this is the twenty-first century. I don't need permission to spend my own money.'

Dilys snorted again. 'That's not the way wives did things when I was young.'

'When Uncle Harry descended on your village in a raiding party and carried you off over his shoulder?' The other way round, more like. 'Changing times, Dilly. Women are different, these days. We have the vote. Sometimes they even let us sign our own cheques. Anyway, I'm not married yet.'

'Never will be at this rate. Not if you go behind his back.'

I bit my lip, tempted by the change of topic, but it wouldn't do. If I wanted questions answered, I had to get on with it. 'Marcus will understand why I have to have this cottage. It's Cwmderwen.'

Dilys looked blank, fingers fidgeting at her ear. Had her hearing aid gone dead again? It could have been the traffic noise rushing behind her or the raucous shrieks from the beach. Maybe she wasn't responding because the name no longer meant anything, forgotten after all these years. No, I knew what it was. She was choosing to be deaf. She could do that when she wanted. Some words seemed to be blotted out all altogether: divorce, gay, death, bowels. But I wasn't going to let her play that trick this time.

'Cwmderwen,' I repeated. 'The house where Nan used to live. In west Wales?'

She looked up, scowling, no longer feigning deafness. 'Now what did you have to do that for?' She said it with exasperation, as if she had warned me against that very thing at least a dozen times.

'It was our home. Ours by right.'

Dilys was unimpressed. 'Stuff and nonsense.'

'No, it's not stuff and nonsense. It was our property for generations.' When I'd laboured over my family tree all those years ago, my mother had phoned Uncle Jack in Canada and he remembered a family bible, recording the baptisms and marriages and burials of the Owens of Cwmderwen: fathers, sons, grandsons.

'They didn't own it,' snapped Dilys, as if that made all the difference.

'All right, so they were tenants, but they worked the land and that's what counts, and it was taken away from them. So I thought, since it was up for sale, I'd bloody well reclaim it.'

'Language!'

'Oh language. Right, this is the language of Justice!' If I'd had a sword in my hand I'd have plunged it into any dragon around – but this was Hove seafront. 'Simple justice,' I repeated, more moderately.

'Justice!' said Dilys. Her expression was full of scorn as she looked out to sea. Canute must have looked like that when ordering the tide back. 'Justice doesn't come in this world, girl, and you needn't sit waiting for it.'

Justice doesn't come in this world. Hadn't that point been made to me all too savagely once before? My best friend Jemma had been killed and I wasn't allowed to blame anyone. I was supposed to just let it pass. But not this time. Oh no. 'I'm not going to sit waiting for it, I'm going to go out and grab it.'

'You can't wave a magic wand, girl, and make everything right. Some things are just meant to be.'

'No!'

Dilys looked up, then laid her hand on mine, with something approaching sympathy in those piercing eyes. 'We never lived in Eden, girl, and we're not crawling on stony places now. Life has thorns and roses for everyone, for your Nan, for you, for everyone. You just learn to survive the bad times, and the good will take care of themselves. There are ups and down for everyone.'

Ups and downs. Was that how I should regard violent death? Cerebral destruction by gunshot? A bit of a down moment? I was not going to give in. 'Cwmderwen was Nan's home and it was just taken from her when...' I had to say it, but I couldn't. The thing that Dilys had never told me all these years stuck in my throat.

She turned in her chair to face me, her usual sternness etched into the grooves of her ancient face. But behind the sternness I could sense uncertainty. Dilys was never uncertain. She worked her lips.

'When my grandfather was shot.' Had I merely thought it or spoken it aloud? Barely aloud. The words, soft as a bat's wings, escaped into the sea air.

Dilys wasn't deaf now. She retorted sharply. 'We don't speak about that!'

'No, well that's obvious! I'm twenty-nine and I never even knew till now. Couldn't someone have told me?'

35

Dilys shifted her shoulders indignantly. 'Why? What good would that have done?'

'I want to know. I want to know how it happened.' The death certificate, acquired with such casual ease, had said enough with one stark phrase to turn my world upside down, but there was so much that it hadn't said and I had no idea how to find out more. Speaking to my mother on the phone, I'd been several times on the point of asking her, but I'd shied away. She'd been a babe in arms, so all knowledge would have to come from Dilys, who didn't speak about such things. My mother probably had no more idea of how he had died than I had and, considering the other disasters in her life, it wasn't my place to burden her further.

So Dilys was the only one I could ask. 'Did he shoot himself?'

'I don't want to talk about it!'

'But I need to know.' There was something far too emphatic about 'cerebral destruction' for the shooting to have been a careless accident, and that left suicide or murder. I still couldn't decide which was worse. 'Did he shoot himself?'

'No!' The word was torn out of Dilys and she shook, fighting to regain control.

'So he was murdered. Who did it?'

She munched on her false teeth, until the shaking ceased. 'Person or persons unknown, they said. Now. That's enough. You hear me?'

With the big question answered, or partly answered, the determination driving me began to fracture. Time to stop badgering her.

'Sorry,' I said. 'It was just a shock to find out, that was all. There was Cwmderwen and it opened up the past. Is it so wrong to want to have it back?'

'Let this thing go.' Dilys turned to me, glaring. Her anger was not the usual parade of harrumphing indignation about rates, good manners and the onslaught of multiculturalism. It was genuine. Her eyes burned. 'A bad place, that's what it is. Terrible gloomy place. Should have been pulled down. No one would want it, down there. Let it go.'

I began to realise how much this must hurt her. Of course. No justice in this world, she said. Person or persons unknown, meaning that no one had ever been convicted. My grandfather had been murdered and the law had failed, leaving Nan to suffer and Dilys to pick up the pieces, deal with the fallout, the grief and rage. Even sixty years on, it would still hurt. I assumed that to her generation any notoriety was a matter of shame, like being caught with dirty underwear. But this wasn't about social disgrace, it was about genuine trauma. I should never have raised it with her.

But if not with her, who could I ask? Nan was long gone and her sons were beyond reach too. Uncle Jack, whom I'd never actually met, had died in Canada a year ago of a heart attack. Uncle Robert was equally detached from life, out of his head, somewhere up north.

Whatever I did to find out more, it wasn't going to involve Dilys. Not now. I needed to appease her. 'It's just a cottage, Dilys. Not dreadful at all. Really cute, or it could be. It's a beautiful spot, surrounded by woods, you can't see or hear the outside world. Just birds and this deep deep silence. No noisy neighbours, no traffic. So peaceful. And totally unspoiled. I'm going to have electricity connected, of course, but they reckon I can use a pump for the well.'

Dilly was not going to be won round by pumps in wells. I hadn't really expected her to be, but there was no harm in trying. 'It's just something for me to work on. Us to work on. It's a project. If it weren't this house, it would be another, so why not this one?'

'Any house but this one. You're playing with fire, girl. Sell it. Find another.'

I could have argued on, but only at the cost of exhausting her, so I decided to surrender. 'Well, maybe. I'll think about it. Nothing's settled yet. It's just an offer, so far.' A bit more than that, but no need to say so. 'I'll probably let it go. So. What shall we do now? Home or shops?'

'Hm. So you're not going to leave me here catching my death of cold? Are you going to buy me a cup of tea, or do I have to get it myself?'

We found a place for tea, too weak she said, they can't make tea these days, and the scones were stale, which was true. We paraded as far as the pier and gazed out at sails on the horizon, and she complained happily about dogs and noise and poor service and the buses and Mr Barraclough's table manners, and we didn't mention Cwmderwen again.

We didn't mention it, but I thought about it. So, I knew, did she. Remembering it as she must have known it, all those years ago.

4

Dilys has come to visit, with her young man Harry Prothero. He is gingerly, naughtily, nudging his chair closer to hers as they sit round the scrubbed Cwmderwen table.

'See this, Gwen?' Dilys shows a photograph of Seion Chapel with the Reverend Phillips, and three of Gwen's former Sunday School students.

'How they have grown,' Gwen murmurs, peering at once well-known faces that have moved on without her.

'Marion's taking classes now,' chatters Dilys. 'She put Harry right on Nebuchadnezzar, didn't she, boy?' She hugs Harry's arm, mouthing a kiss as he grins fondly in reply.

Must be serious, this one, thinks Gwen with a pang, as she doles out more tea. Dilys has been walking out with Harry for over a year. Not as wild as some of the others either, and a far more sensible catch than most. A big, happy, handsome boy, with comfortable prospects and one irresistible asset. Harry has a motor car for his work, a shiny black Morris 10 and Gwen wonders if that might be part of his attraction.

But no, that is an unworthy thought, and anyway, who is she to scorn it? Harry's motor has brought her sister to Cwmderwen and it is a rare enough visit. Though the bus passes the end of their lane, Dilys doesn't come often. She has their father to care for, so she cannot go gallivanting at will, off on social jaunts. Besides, the sisters see each other regularly enough, when Gwen goes to Penbryn with John on market day, so no call for Dilys to come traipsing out here.

The truth is, Dilys does not care for Cwmderwen. It is obvious to Gwen, even though Dilys takes care to say not a word. She knows the silence and shade of this little valley, when the sun is low or the sky is clouded, can be oppressive to a town girl. Not that Gwen herself is oppressed. Heaven forbid. She is accustomed to it, and there is sun enough on occasion.

But there is more to Dilys' aversion than the physical gloom. It is the obvious penury of the place that she dislikes, the scraped, make-do-and-mend starkness that goes far beyond the genteel shabbiness of her old home. Dilys thinks that her Gwen deserves better than this.

Gwen feels a pang of anger. She owes loyalty to John and she has a pride of her own that will not permit regrets. Dilys doesn't appreciate how it is on farms these days, or at least how it is on this farm. They are on a knife-edge and, God knows, John can cut no slack, but he can be sure his wife will stand by him, no matter what. She really doesn't need the frills and fripperies that Dilys thinks she deserves. This is the life she has chosen and she will cut her cloth as she finds it.

An unfortunate phrase, she thinks, resuming her seat and staring again at the photograph of the chapel.

She did cut her cloth, the roll of bright fresh chintz that Mr and Mrs Prynne had given her, to make new curtains.

John had taken umbrage. No good her explaining that it was a wedding present, just as any bride might receive on marriage, a gift for her new home. To John it smacked of extravagance, or worse, of charity, a suggestion that he could not keep his own. She had learned then how tender his pride was, and how desperate the struggle to maintain it in the face of unending hardship. A struggle she must respect, and so the old curtains hang still, at John's command. No waste in this house.

Gwen recalls too vividly the bitterness of her father's bankruptcy. She understands John's iron determination never to slip into debt. He has a family to support and God knows, he loves his own, but the children have only added to the farm's burden, so she will certainly do nothing to increase it. Which is why she always puts on the bravest of faces, even with Dilys, terrified that word will get back, that the trades-folk of Penbryn will be nodding over their counters: *That Gwen Lewis, in a desperate way, she is. Poor as a church mouse, that man of hers has no business taking a wife if he can't put bread on the table. Better off back here, she'd be.*

But perhaps today the meanness of their hospitality and the gloom of their home have escaped Dilys' notice, thanks to Harry Prothero claiming the greater part of her attention. Harry and his smart clothes; Harry and his new toys – unfortunate here in a house where there is no money for toys. But Harry is an innocent boy, delighting in his gadgets, wanting to show the world his motor car, his watch, his camera, and it doesn't occur to him that others might not share his fascination with such exotic possessions.

Dilys fondly elbows him out of her light and leafs through more photographs. 'Here's the whole Sunday

School crowd. Oh and this is Mrs Prynne with that old grimalkin. You remember, Gwen? Soppy old thing.'

Dilys passes on the pictures her Harry has taken, and Gwen dutifully looks at them. Pictures of another world. A world that was once hers.

She smiles and nods, showing them to a curious Rosie, taking care to keep the toddler's greasy fingers off. 'That is your Mam's old neighbour, see, and the pussy cat?'

Gwen thinks better of passing them on to her husband. Life in Penbryn will be of no interest to him. He has more important matters to occupy his mind.

Still, John is doing his duty, sparing precious time to sit down to tea with them. Gwen can tell that under the forced smiles and the stilted conversation, he is grudging every moment he must devote to this foolish idleness. There is so much he wants to be doing, the hay to be turned, a calf to be fed, endless vermin to be exterminated.

Gwen has made Welsh cakes, sparing with the currants, hoping he will excuse the extravagance for guests. Harry laughs, a hugely boyish laugh as he munches thoughtlessly through the plateful.

They chatter on. Or Dilys and Harry chatter. 'Oh Gwen, you know Mr Parry, up St. Mary's Lane? Had the doctor in with this terrible cut over his eye, and Alfred says it was his wife did it with a frying pan. He told you that, didn't he, Harry?'

'True as I'm alive. And you'd have thought butter wouldn't melt in Mrs Parry's mouth. More hell fire in her than we gave her credit for, eh?'

They laugh, but Gwen dare not. On market days, she laps up the gossip, vicariously enjoying the thrills of Dilys' life, the scandals of the High Street, the tittle-tattle of Seion Chapel. But here at John's table she says little, painfully aware how Dilys and Harry's loud and unseemly babble is grating on John's impatient nerves.

Harry is one of the lucky ones, these days. He has a good job, money to put in the bank if he doesn't squander it all. He sells farm machinery. Especially tractors, the monstrous masters of a new age. Harry loves them and anything mechanical. It is as much his enthusiasm for the subject as the professional salesman in him that makes him try to sell the idea to John.

'I tell you, this is the future. Horses are all very well, but every farm is going to need a tractor. You have to see it as an investment. It will pay for itself in no time.'

His host sits, nods gravely and says nothing. What is Harry thinking of, the silly boy? All that modern machinery is not for the likes of them. Borrow money? Take on crippling debts for something so new-fangled and uncertain? The very suggestion of it is raising John's hackles. Can Harry not see the telltale signs?

But Harry does not see. A mechanic to his soul, no feel for the soil in his blood. His cousin has his own small engineering workshop away east, somewhere over in England, and Harry could join him if he wished, a perfect career for someone so insatiably delighted with machines and engines. What is keeping him? The answer is obvious. Her bonny beaming sister. Harry is far too serious in his courting of Dilys to allow career prospects to interfere. He will not leave without her.

And Dilys of course cannot leave. Their father, virtually bed-bound by another stroke, cannot manage without her and he'd never cope with a move to England, far away from his own home, his own people, his own language. Dilys must stay. Is she as eager to marry as Harry appears to be? Gwen cannot tell, Dilys is so good at hiding any discontent, but she suspects the longing is there.

Gwen's old anguish has subsided into a perpetual ache. She would gladly have her father here, but it is not possible. John has made that clear. Doesn't she have enough to do in the house, what with the babies and her chores, without finding food for an extra idle mouth? No matter how she might crave it, Gwen cannot offer it. But how to tell Dilys that, without betraying John?

Quickly, she whisks the cake plate from the table before its emptiness can make her look niggardly. There are crumbs on the floor under Harry's chair. She will have to brush them up before John begins to fret. He hates slovenliness and waste – as does she, never doubt that.

No time for sweeping now. Harry's grand new box camera must be put to work again. Dilys wants a photograph of the family.

John consents, his silence spelling out his irritation, if they would only notice.

They troop into the backyard and the family stand while Harry fusses and fiddles and makes jokes at which John does not laugh. When the photograph is taken at last, the master excuses himself with a few brief words and strides off. Work to do. Gwen sees him disappear into the barn, shaking off the folly of it all.

Is there an easing of the atmosphere? The sun is breaking through.

Dilys has turned to pick up little Rosie, planting a kiss

44

on the child's cheek, giving her a hug and whispering in her ear. The child laughs. Rosie is usually so quiet, dreaming in her own secret world. John doesn't like noise and disruption in the house, and with a new baby providing all the irritation he can bear, the girl has learned to keep her peace. It is good to hear her let loose that joyous childish laugh occasionally.

Gwen hoists Jack up from her hip so that Harry can dangle his watch for the baby, egging him on as the boy gurgles and reaches out. Harry beams as the podgy fingers close on the polished silver. 'There's a fine fellow!'

Gwen allows Harry to take the baby and in an instant he is involved in a complicated game of man and monster that he and little Jack understand perfectly. Galloping up and down the garden path, prowling round the apple tree, while the baby is reduced to hiccups with breathless glee.

Two boys together. Harry will always be a boy, but that won't matter. Dilys is strong-willed and competent enough for them both, and she has her lad secretly under control. She'll be the master in their house, managing him just as he will be content to be managed. Well, that works well enough in some households maybe, even if the traditional ways are observed religiously in Cwmderwen. They will make good parents one day if circumstances ever allow them to marry.

'Dilys, about Dad.'

Dilys squeezes her arm. 'I've told you a hundred times, you're not to go fretting about him. He and I are doing just fine. We got him out to Chapel yesterday, didn't we, Harry?'

'Oh, yes, he's no trouble,' says Harry, far too good-humoured to complain.

'And the Reverend calls once a week, and Mr Howell, and Mr and Mrs Prynne. We're getting along just fine. He has your visits to look forward to. You know he loves you coming to play to him.'

On her old piano. It is the only chance Gwen has to play. It has never proved possible to bring it here to Cwmderwen. There has been no time, no cart available, they have no room. And she has too many other duties here to think of music, so she must content herself with her market day visits, her father's face lighting up as the lid is raised and her fingers touch the keys.

'It's little enough,' she says.

Dilys snorts contempt, turns it hastily into a laugh. 'Indeed. We don't want you getting rusty.'

'I don't mean my playing. I mean I wish I could do more for Dad.'

Dilys brushes off the suggestion. 'With all that you have to do here? Nonsense, girl. You have a family to tend to. More than enough on your plate. You leave Dad to me. Now then, Harry Prothero, are you going to be tumbling about all afternoon? We need to be on our way.'

They amble round to the front of the house, gathering coats and hats and bags, ready for departure.

John emerges from the barn, ready, almost eager for the final act of courtesy in seeing them off his land. Gwen can be proud of the sight of him; he'd look the part of country squire if his clothes were less threadbare, so tall and upright and dignified, shotgun over his arm, his dog Jess at his heel. He is going off to shoot the pests that plague his land. Non-human pests, that is. Shooting his visitors is not allowed, but he can vent his impatience on the rest of creation: foxes, crows, kites, rabbits, badgers, otters. He is resolute in his war on them all. Gwen is far too sensible to be squeamish about the regular slaughter and rabbit pie makes the scant housekeeping stretch a little further.

Dilys has been searching in her bag and has furtively produced a bundle that she is offering to Rosie.

Instant alarm in Gwen, but the child's eyes light up with delight as she unfolds...

A rag doll. Nothing grand, but even so. Gwen must act. This will not do.

'You remember Maggie, don't you, Gwen?' Dilys smiles first at her, disingenuously, then at John in explanation. 'This is Gwen's old doll Maggie May. She nursed her, all those years, learning to be a mother. I think Rosie ought to have her now, don't you? A girl is never too young to learn her mothering duties.'

John eyes the doll with a frown, not sure what to make of it.

'I keep finding Gwen's old things round the place,' continues Dilys smoothly. 'They might as well be here as there. Come on, Harry. We'd better not be late.'

And they are gone, bustling up the lane to the grass verge where Harry has left his motor car, leaving John staring down at the rag doll.

Rosie gazes up hopefully at her father.

'Your mother's doll, eh?'

'Rosie will take care of it for me,' says Gwen quietly, her heart aflutter.

John nods. 'Mind she does though. She's got to learn to look after things.' And he goes off in pursuit of prey, dog circling round him, leaving the child clutching her trophy with speechless delight and Gwen nursing an agony of humiliation. The doll is not hers. The Maggie May she remembers was loved to death. It disintegrated long ago, buried decently up on Penbryn Common.

This is tact on Dilys' part, a gift to Rosie that John cannot be insulted by. Gwen knows full well how he would have reacted to an overt present, a new toy however modest, no matter how kindly and innocently meant. Even if he had kept his temper with Dilys and not thrown the insult back at her, the doll would have been confiscated as soon as she had gone, the child's pleadings ignored. It would have been ripped apart, consigned to the flames, eradicated from existence rather than sully the dignity of Cwmderwen with the taint of charity. No matter that Dilys is Rosie's loving aunt and happy to shower her niece with gifts, John's rejection would have been absolute.

And there is the terrible hurt. All of Gwen's pretence, her struggle at concealment, is futile. She supports her husband with dutiful determination and papers over their want with briskness and smiles, refusing to acknowledge any unreasonableness on his part, but her sister sees through it all and understands. Dilys has constructed a stratagem to work around John's sensitivity, and her tact is more painful to Gwen than a thousand direct insults, ridiculing and diminishing the pride that is the foundation of her husband's worthiness.

5

'They're all so pretty, aren't they?' Caroline spread the sketches on her polished mahogany table. 'Those rosebuds. And that Alice look. I love it. I know it's really difficult but you ought to try and make a choice soon. I'd love to have it all sorted before Marcus gets back. Wouldn't that be nice?'

I studied the array of bridesmaids' dresses in all their frou-frou glory yet again and tried to feel something. Would abject surrender get me out of this? 'They're all lovely. You choose. I really don't mind.'

'Oh but Sarah, of course it has to be your decision.'

Indulge her, I could hear Marcus saying. Remember she was dreaming, night and day, of her little boy's big day. It mattered to her. Well, I'd been dutiful and I'd indulged her, smiling all the while. I'd come to Essex, and talked veils and shoes and photographers. There was only so much I could take in one day. 'I tell you what. It's such a big decision. I'll take them with me back to Guildford, and I promise I'll make a decision in the next three days. Guide's honour.'

'Of course.' She kissed my cheek. 'Oh it's such a pity you live so far from Marcus and us.' She gave me a wistful little smile that wasn't quite accusation. 'If you were that little bit closer we could meet in the week and sort everything out in no time.'

I smiled fixedly. When Marcus and I first met, four years before, he had been with a firm of solicitors just down the road in Guildford, and his parents had lived two miles away. Then he had moved to a new career and flat in Docklands, and his parents had quickly decided on retirement to Epping Forest. 'I work in Guildford,' I reminded her.

'Not for much longer, I'm sure,' she beamed, giving me a scented hug.

Breathe, Sarah; stay calm. I bit my tongue until we'd gathered up the brochures, and she'd waved me away. Once I was safely out of sight and en route to the M25, I tried to see how many vowel sounds I could fit into one screaming snarl. Caroline was convinced that as soon as I married Marcus, I would give up everything to have babies and host dinners for my husband's colleagues. And I couldn't bring myself to argue with her, because that had been her role in life, and if I said I wanted more, I'd be undermining everything she was.

By the time I arrived home, I'd recovered enough to forgive her. I even took out the pictures of pink flounces and rosebud coronets and tried to care. I wasn't an unredeemed tomboy, I did like dresses, but... No. I couldn't do this. I just didn't want to.

When Marcus had first proposed to me – sheltering unsuccessfully under his jacket in the pouring rain outside Murphy's where I'd been singing – it had all been endearingly simple. 'Suppose we make a go of it,' he'd said, and I'd said, 'Why not?' Later that night, when I suggested a quick trip to a registry office, grabbing a couple of witnesses off the street, we'd agreed it was the perfect solution. Why hadn't we stuck to that? How come a moment's delay to sort out a few technicalities had burgeoned, before I knew what was happening, into a major showpiece, with lace and veil, the Trumpet Voluntary, 500 guests and Caroline debating whether she could get the bishop? That was when I'd fled.

But I'd come back, and here it all was again, and Marcus was still shrugging it off, telling me to indulge his mother.

Of course he was right. If it really mattered so much to her, why not let her have it? I could at least choose the bloody bridesmaids dresses. Trouble was, studying them without Caroline breathing down my neck merely reminded me of photographs I had of other weddings. Then, even knowing how intensely it would hurt, I had to fetch Jemma's. A snapshot outside a registry office five years ago. Not a single thing about it conventional or glamorous. Jemma and Josh in outrageous clothes they'd bought from a charity shop, everyone roaring with laughter, me included, Jemma happily letting the world see her expanding bump. It was the baby that had persuaded them to go through with something as conformist as a wedding. We'd all shared histories of broken homes, divorces, bitter family rows, thought ourselves free of all that, but along came the bump and they'd done it. Seven weeks it lasted, that marriage. Right till Jemma and her unborn child were crushed between an articulated lorry and a brick wall.

It shouldn't have happened. It should not have happened.

And I shouldn't have started thinking about it again. I could feel the bile rising, the shakes begin. I poured myself a large vodka, two seconds later topped it up again.

I shuffled the photo of Jemma and Josh out of sight, turned to the next one. Sophie and Robin. That had lasted less than two years. Toby and Rachel. Pouring rain. I'd lost touch but I knew Toby had moved abroad recently. No mention of Rachel, so I supposed they'd split.

And there was the photo of my parents' wedding, my mother looking like a slightly dazed Jane Austen heroine, my father apparently expecting his buttonhole to squirt him in the eye, three dear little Kate Greenaways in tow. All for what? Twenty-five years of sham domestic bliss, down the pan.

Indulgence be damned, I couldn't do this. If Marcus had been here, I could have shoved the bridesmaids dresses at him and let him choose. But he wasn't here, he was thousands of miles away, so I gathered up the dress designs and thrust them in an envelope. They could wait; I needed a quick plunge into something utterly different. Murder, injustice, vengeance denied. The ultimate escape from pastel taffeta. I fetched down my box of Owen papers and spread them on the table instead.

My phone started to ooze the Baker Street riff. I groped for it, trying to rearrange my thoughts quickly. I couldn't talk to Marcus in this state of tipsy anger and rebellion. But it wasn't Marcus. It was my brother Sam.

'Sai! Hiya Doll!'

I relaxed. No need for pretence with Sam. 'You don't look

anything like Indiana Jones, so stop trying to sound like him.' I clamped the phone against my shoulder as I shuffled my Owen papers. Was this really all I had? A few paltry photographs, a couple of certificates? No articles, no official reports. Pathetic.

'Hey, I got the hat, whip, everything,' insisted my brother, panting slightly.

'Sell them,' I advised. 'What on earth are you doing, if it isn't too indelicate to ask?'

He laughed, still panting, very rhythmically. 'Jogging round Golden Gate Park. How about you?'

'Me? I'm lying in a darkened room with smelling salts. I've just had a day with Caroline.'

'Still trying to get you to choose That Dress?'

'Oh no, that's done. I'll be wailing in whalebone. Now we're on to my attendants. I am going to have five bridesmaids and two page boys. How about that. Page boys!'

'Cute!'

'And Caroline knows how fond I am of music, so she's going to arrange something for the reception. I hate to think what. I offered to sing, and she said, "Oh no, we'll get some professionals."'

'Ouch.' Sam laughed in sympathy. 'So how close did you come to murdering her?'

I would have replied in kind if I hadn't just been dwelling on a real murder and all its repercussions. 'Don't even suggest it,' I said.

'And Marky wants you to be nice to her and take it on the chin, I suppose.'

'Marky's not here. He's still on your side of the pond.

Coming back Tuesday week, which means I still have ten days to amuse myself, and I'm not spending them all thinking about wedding arrangements. I'm the bride; get me out of here. Change the subject, quickly.'

'Okay. I was really phoning about Dilly. Her birthday.'

'It's in two weeks.'

'Yes. Sure. And I was wondering...'

'If I could buy your present for you. Don't I always?'

'Not always. Just mostly. You're so good at it and people never seem to appreciate the presents I buy.'

'You mean like the singing fish? Odd that. I'll think of something. A posy vase?'

'Sounds great. How's the old bird?'

'Much as ever. Cross with me. I've bought a house.'

'No kidding. A decision! I suppose it's Docklands?'

I rearranged my papers. 'It's not *our* house I've bought.'

'Whose is it then? A place for the butler!'

'Very funny. I mean, it's not the future Crawford residence. More of a weekend place. Sort of. Special. It's weird. It's so right, it's as if I were meant to find it. I couldn't not buy it, could I?'

'I don't know. Why couldn't you not buy it?'

'Because it's Cwmderwen.'

'Uh?'

'Cwmderwen!' I repeated impatiently. What was the point of Sam being able to trace the lineages of Aragorn son of Arathorn, Princess Leia and the entire cast of *The Matrix*, if he couldn't grasp our own family history. 'As in Nan Owen?'

'Oh, you mean like, the ancestral haunt?'

'Yes, *that* Cwmderwen.'

'No kidding? Good God.' I could hear a bird twittering half a world away in California. Sam had stopped jogging, in order to concentrate properly. 'Seriously?'

'By the end of next week I should have the key.'

'Wow. What's it like, investment-wise?'

'Investment-wise it must be fantastic, because I paid next to nothing for it.' I started talking fast, feeling my palms grow sticky with guilt. 'The asking price was ridiculously low enough to start with, but I offered half, just to show I wasn't a pushover. I thought they'd tell me to get lost, but the agent got back half an hour later and said the vendors accepted. It's owned by some corporation and it's been on the market for years. I was the first person who made any sort of offer. They couldn't wait to get it off their hands.'

'Nice one! Except, why hasn't anyone else ever put in an offer? You haven't bought a pup on a landslip or something, have you? Impulse buying will be the death of you, Sai.'

'You can talk! The Enterprise control panel?'

'That was worth every cent!'

'When you couldn't even get it through your door? Anyway, Cwmderwen is on solid rock, believe me. Just nothing else solid about it, that's all. No one wanted it because it's derelict.'

'Aha! And you bought it? Just like that?'

I gulped. 'I've got Granny Peterson's legacy.' Granny Peterson, who died when I was twenty-two, was convinced I'd go to the dogs fast if I weren't rescued, so she'd left me an impossible £50,000 in trust until I was twenty-five. When I'd turned twenty-five I had been in such a dark hole I hadn't wanted anything to do with it, or with anything else. So it sat there, accruing interest. Marcus had earmarked it for all manner of things for our joint future, including, of course, a down payment on the marital home when we finally chose it. Now I had managed to blow a sizeable chunk on a pile of rubble and I'd be blowing the rest and all my savings on doing it up. It was something I was still trying to excuse to myself, let alone anyone else. Let alone Marcus.

Sam roared with laughter. He didn't need me to explain.

'Look,' I insisted. 'It's got incredible potential and I paid next to nothing for it, so it's bound to, I don't know, quadruple in value. Anyway, I didn't buy it as an investment. It's personal. It's where we came from.'

'So how come my birth certificate says Croydon?'

'You know what I mean. It's where our grandparents raised kids, where our mother was born—'

'She grew up in Peterborough. Still has the accent.'

'No she doesn't. And don't be pedantic.' God, Sam could be annoying.

'No, okay, so this is *the* family seat, right? Our country estate and all that.'

'Not exactly an estate. There's a bit of woodland. I don't think it was ever a real farm. Just a Victorian cottage, two up, two down, a lean-to scullery and a few acres that have been sold off.'

'Oh.' Sam sounded genuinely disappointed.

'That's the weird thing. It's derelict because no one has been near the place for sixty years. It's exactly as it was the day Nan left.'

'She left but you're not going to let her escape, right?'

'Escape? Do you know why Nan left?'

56

'Because Granddad Owen snuffed it and she wanted out?'

'Because he was the tenant, and when he died she lost the tenancy and was forced out.' I'd been building up a furious resentment, picturing a family driven barefoot into a blinding gale, without any evidence. 'And do you know why he died?'

'He was old? No, wait. War, wasn't it? Didn't the bally Jerries get him, what what?'

'What?' For a moment I was flummoxed. 'Are you sure of that?'

'Er. Maybe not. I remember something about the Germans.'

'You're thinking of Harry's cousin, the one who died in an air raid.'

'Yeah, maybe. I don't know. It was Uncle Harry talking, I think. Something about him having no time for the Germans, what with them doing for Cousin Mildred and Granddad Owen.'

I'd had time to get my facts straight again. 'Granddad Owen died in 1948. The war was over. Germans weren't gunning for us any more.'

'Okay, maybe not. It must have been just Mildred then. I remember Harry saying something about Germans and then Dilys bustling in to hush us up. "Let's have no more of that sort of talk, if you don't mind! Curiosity killed the cat and it will do the same to boys, young man."' Sam did a very good impersonation. 'You know Dilly. The things she won't talk about would fill a book.'

Sam had as much reason to know this as anyone. Whenever she saw him, Dilys made a point of asking him when he was going to marry and settle down. 'Gay?' she'd say. 'What's he got to be gay about? Time he found himself a nice girl.'

'Yes, I know Dilys. Anyway, Grandfather Owen died years after the war, shot in the head, by person or persons unknown. In other words, murdered.'

'Yow! No kidding?' Now Sam really was impressed. 'How did you find out?'

'I ordered his death certificate. Dilys gave me the person or persons unknown bit.'

'Yow!' repeated Sam, with more breathless astonishment. 'You got Dilys to talk about it?'

'Well, sort of. I squeezed that much out of her and it was worse than drawing blood. Like mugging an old lady.'

'An old lady who's more than capable of mugging you back. She said he was murdered?'

'Yes and the family lost the farm. Where's the justice in that?'

There was silence on the phone.

'Well?'

'Sai...' Another silence. I knew what was coming. 'You want to get on another crusade, don't you. Because you couldn't do anything about Jemma—'

'No! Stop it! This has nothing to do with Jemma.'

'No?'

I bit my tongue. Jemma had died, horribly, and someone should have been held responsible. The lorry driver. He'd been exceeding the speed limit. I didn't care that it had only been by a fraction, and that he'd had to leave his job with a nervous breakdown, he should have been prosecuted. And the council; they should have had traffic lights round the road works. Someone should have been sacked. What about the garage? Why hadn't they noticed that the brakes would need tightening before her next service? And Josh. Why had he let her drive around when she was eight months pregnant? I'd spent six months accusing everyone and everything, demanding justice for my friend and being told again and again that there could be none. It had been a tragic accident. No one was going to have to pay.

Sam had worried about me back then. Everyone had worried about me and the cesspit I'd fallen into. All right, I had risen. I was out of the shit. It had been an accident. Okay.

I took a deep breath. 'Sam, this is not the same. This was not an accident, it was murder. Right? Someone really was guilty, and they got away with it. No one got punished, except our family. It was our mother, Sam, forced out of her home while she was still a baby.'

'Okay.' Sam was sounding as sober as he ever could. 'Maybe it was unfair, but if her husband had been murdered there, you reckon Nan would have wanted to stay on?'

I thought about it. 'I don't know. That's not the point.'

'It might have been, to her. Where was he shot?'

'In the head.'

'No, I mean, at home?'

'Er. I don't know. I suppose so.' That was how I had been imagining it; my poor grandfather mown down on his doorstep, defending his home and family from marauding thugs. 'Where else?'

'Could have been a brawl that got out of hand down at the Pig and Whistle?'

'Nonsense.' I wasn't having a cheap scenario like that. A drunken brawl? 'I think it was at Cwmderwen. I feel it was.'

'Ohoho.' Sam risked a chuckle. 'You could feel it, could you? Ghosties walking by moonlight?'

'Don't be ridiculous. I just felt, it was his. Something he would fight for. And it was taken away.'

'And you're getting it back.'

'Precisely.'

'You're buying the house where your grandfather was murdered. Any lingering mementos? His brains on the doorstep?'

'Please.' I shuddered, remembering that I had stood on that doorstep. 'If you want a memento, there's Nan's dresser. It's still there, just where she left it. It must have been her pride and joy. Can't you see why I had to get it back, Sam?'

He must have heard the desperation in my voice. I really needed someone to tell me I was doing the right thing. 'Oh sure. At least, I can see why you'd want to investigate. Of course you do. Wish I was there to help you dig and probe. A real murder. Wow. Does Mum know any more about it?'

'I don't know. I didn't like to ask her. I don't suppose Dilys ever talked about it.'

'Of course not. It's death, isn't it. Dilys won't even talk about...' Sam lowered his voice to a stage whisper, '...Uncle Harry passing over. If she thinks his snuffing it at the eighth hole in the ample fullness of years is too indecent to mention, she's certainly not going to talk about something as unsavoury as murder. When Gran Peterson died and I mentioned it, you'd have thought I'd just farted.'

'You probably had. But why hasn't anyone ever

mentioned something as significant as a murder? Did Uncle Jack ever talk about it?'

'What? In his Christmas cards. Season's Greetings one and all, and let's chat about Dad being shot? Mum wouldn't have remembered anything about it, so he wasn't going to go on about it in his letters, was he?'

'No. I suppose not. Oh but it makes you realise; a murder doesn't just destroy one life. Everything would have been entirely different if it hadn't happened.'

Sam was silent again for a moment. 'We wouldn't have happened,' he said. 'Mum would have grown up in Wales, our parents would never have met, we would never have been born.'

'Well yes, but—'

'Fact. Because the murder happened, we happened.'

'Not necessarily. Mum and Dad met at college. They could still have done that. She'd have gone to college wherever she lived. The point is, there was once a family living there, in Cwmderwen, snug and cosy and happy, and then some murderer destroyed it all. It makes my blood boil.'

'What makes you think they were snug and cosy and happy?'

'It's so small, they had to be snug and cosy. Nan must have been happy, mustn't she? I want her to have been happy. I can't even remember her properly. Can you?'

'Not very much. She was a bit sad, I suppose. A bit like a woman whose husband had been murdered. Of course I didn't know that. She was just the quiet one. You know Dilly, like a steamroller at warp five, barking her orders, sorting everyone out, and Nan was a little mouse, who

61

smiled but never quite properly. Not with her eyes. Yes, I remember that.'

I detected a changing note in my brother's voice, as he recalled the Nan he had known just that little bit better than me, being five years older. 'Doesn't seem fair, does it,' he added. 'She had a crap life, all round. Family on their uppers, and she lost a brother and kids and then there was Robert, and then Granddad Owen gets shot—'

'And they lost the farm.'

'And you've got it back. Well, good for you. Marcus understands about the murder, does he? Or is it just a cute cottage to him?'

'Um. He doesn't exactly know about it yet.'

Sam barked a laugh. 'A little surprise to welcome him home?'

'Something like that. He bought me a diamond solitaire; I bought him a cottage. Hell, he'll love it. We did talk about a weekend place. Vaguely. Anyway, when Marcus realises that Cwmderwen is actually my family home, he'll understand it all.'

'He'll have to.'

'Must you be so negative?'

'You're the one not telling him. Don't you trust him?'

'Of course I trust him. That's why I went ahead. We've had other things to talk about, that's all. He's loving it over there. And we've got the wedding to think about.' I groaned. 'Oh God, I was changing the subject. Get me off the bloody wedding.'

'Ask Mum to step in? Mother of the bride. Isn't she supposed to do the organising? I bet she could arrange something quick and quiet in Ireland.'

'I can't do that! Not when her own marriage was such a disaster.'

'Disaster? Come off it, Sai. It wasn't the sinking of the Titanic. It was just "one of those things", as Mum says.'

'Of course she says that! She doesn't want to burden us.' Maybe because I was younger, I'd been more attuned to the agony of our parents' divorce.

'Sai.' Sam sighed down the phone. 'There's only one burden in Mum's life. You. You're the one she worries about. Dad's the same—'

'I don't need anyone's worry, thank you very much. I'm on track. I'm happy, I'm settling down, I'm engaged to a lovely man. I'm well-adjusted, I've got a successful career, I'm going to be a partner.'

'Partner? Heh.'

'I've told Trevor he's making me one. I run the bloody place. He wouldn't last a fortnight without me.'

'Well, if it's what you want. It's just, I remember, when you first took the job with Frieman and Case, you saying it was just another stopgap while you got going. You could have made it as a singer, you know.'

'No I couldn't. That was fantasy. This is reality and I've got a perfectly worthwhile career.'

'Writing captions instead of songs. One day your name will be synonymous with erotic fudge bars.'

'I knew it was a mistake telling you about that. Yours will be synonymous with animated troll wars. Computer games! Call that a serious career for a grown man? If people want to worry, tell them to worry about you instead.'

'I do, but no one listens.'

'You make sure they don't. You turn everything into a joke.'

63

'Can't see any good reason not to.'

'Murder is not a joke.'

'Give me time.'

What was I expecting? Sam was an eternal jester, not a caped crusader. Marcus, I knew, would be more understanding, maybe as intrigued as I was by the murder and the silence surrounding it.

Once Sam had returned to his jog, I turned again to the papers. Some old photographs, most of them from Peterborough or Leicester. A letter from Uncle Jack, where he mentioned, in passing, going to school in Llanolwen. A copy of my mother's birth certificate. My grandparents' marriage certificate. My old school work, the family tree with all I had of my past, until now. Births and marriages. Dates of death. Meaningless names neatly printed into an exercise book. But now the names were coming alive and the mystery with them. A mystery, a mission, something to strive for. Of course Marcus would understand it.

It would be such a relief when I told him. I should have done, right from the start. There were some things it just wasn't healthy to bottle up.

6

A visitation from Castell Mawr of the greatest importance. William George's bull is doing its duty. Not too difficult, getting a bull to do what comes naturally with a handful of cows, but it keeps the menfolk busy out there. That's a relief, because Jack is being temperamental and Rosie is having one of her sluggardly spells. She is barely more than a toddler, but it is time she learned that life is not for daydreaming. No time for that when she should be concentrating on the simple tasks set for her. Lives in a world of her own, that one.

Gwen hates to be constantly cross and nagging, but John is determined that his children should be raised properly. They must grow up to be a credit to Cwmderwen, God-fearing, hard-working and honest, not given to play and idleness. They are not born to privilege like Master Philip and Miss Alicia up at the big house. They must equip themselves for an unending struggle through life, and John never ceases to remind them of it.

It is perfectly proper for a father to be strict. Children need discipline. Spare the rod and disgrace and ruin are sure to follow. But sometimes there is nothing Gwen would not give for some moments of respite from the battle to bend them to John's will.

'And what have you got to sing about, Miss?' Mrs George, stately in her unforgiving corset and high-buttoned blouse, looks down on the girl as she pushes the peas she is supposed to be shelling round the table in a secret celestial dance.

Rosie, who has been crooning to herself, stops singing and looks up.

'Well.' Mrs George purses her lips. 'There's a time and a place for singing, young lady, however fine. Ask your father. Singing won't get those peas in that pot.'

Rosie looks guilty, too young to appreciate what Gwen had come very quickly to understand, that Mrs George's comments are rarely to be taken at face value. She must be gruff and judgemental because that is what the Lord and tradition require of a virtuous matriarch, but there is a compliment in her words somewhere.

She turns back to Gwen with a twitching of facial muscles that Gwen has learned to recognise as a smile. 'Just like John for the singing, isn't she? Now that's a gift for Sunday School. All very fine in its place.' She eyes Gwen with sudden suspicion. Gwen is leaning heavily on the table with one hand as she stirs the tea in the pot. 'You all right, girl?'

'Fine. Well enough.' Gwen manages a flicker of a smile and begins to arrange cups.

Mrs George scrutinises her slight form as she turns. Her stentorian boom is lowered as befits indelicate matters. 'Not overdoing things in your condition?'

Gwen does not need to lower her voice. It is always low.

'I lost the baby,' she says simply, and reaches for the milk jug.

Mrs George frowned. 'When was this?'

'A week ago.'

'You saw a doctor?'

'No need,' says Gwen hastily. No need or no money, what difference did it make? 'It's all over now.'

'Hm.' Mrs George casts her eagle eye about at the immaculate threadbare kitchen. Not a luxury and not a speck of dust in sight. The dresser that has stood there, tended by Owen wives for three generations, might be too cumbersome for the room and lacking in becoming china, but it is polished to mirror brightness. The range is old and inefficient, and the pots around it black and battered, but there is not a stain or fleck of ash upon it. Mrs George approves and understands. Gwen is a woman who does her duty by her man, makes do, does not complain. A proper wife. And proper wives have trials that good neighbours must attend to.

She turns abruptly back to Rose who has, solemnly if slowly, resumed shelling peas. 'Well, if you want to help your Mam, best get out from under her feet.' She shoos the startled girl from the table and Rosie is more than happy to flee into the garden, away from duty and furtive adult mutterings.

Mrs George sits herself down and addresses the pea-shelling, as if she has come for no other purpose. She glances sidelong at little Jack. He is still too young to be sent packing, but then he is too young to understand either.

'So, you were bleeding.'

Mrs George begins to ply Gwen with no-nonsense

medical questions, which Gwen parries as best she can, hiding her discomfort. There are some things just too embarrassing to talk about and it is all over now. The physical symptoms were mild compared with the heartache, but that is not something she can discuss with Mrs George any more than she could discuss it at the time with John.

'Well,' he had said, when she told him, staring at the rain spilling down the window panes. Just that. Nothing more. He had shrugged on his coat and gone off to call in the cows. He had never been a man to voice emotion, she knew that. It was simply another blow from a God set on testing him like Job.

Mrs George continues cracking peapods. 'Probably for the best. One baby after another, a woman needs a break. You'll have another one on the way soon enough, no doubt.'

'Maybe.' Gwen cringes at the thought that Mrs George will begin to pry into even more unspeakable subjects. There is a side to marriage that Gwen can never do more than endure, though she does so without complaint. Men have their needs, she knows that. It is a pity that they cannot be gentle with it, but enough of that. However unpleasant, it has given her children, and though she is no sentimental and demonstrative mother, she can no longer imagine life without that blessing.

A blessing that can still burden and torment. Gwen stoops over Jack, wiping his nose. He is thumping the table leg loudly with a spoon and reciting garbled versions of nursery rhymes with repetitive intensity. Just such noise as John hates. She rescues the spoon and Jack pads across the room, then plumps down on the floor, rolling himself up gleefully in the rag rug. Hastily Gwen moves him, twitching the rug carefully back into place and he screams with laughter at her.

All for the best? Yes, Gwen can do with a break from the chaos babies create in a house where chaos is not permitted. What is a miscarriage but a blessed relief? It is not as if it has been the first, though the baby she'd lost after Rose was barely conceived when it gave up the fight. This one struggled longer. Grasped at Gwen's heart as well as her womb. Gave her time to dream of...

No place for dreams. No place for sentiment or weakness. She can feel Mrs George's approval, next best thing to sympathy. After four years at Cwmderwen she has earned an almost resentful respect from her magisterial neighbour. Her lack of emotion now is another point in her favour. There is reassurance in that.

Gwen needs to get the potatoes peeled and washed. No water. Mrs George intervenes before she can get to the pump. Not that Mrs George will do it for her. Mrs George has the world organised better than that.

'William!'

William George ambles in promptly, sunny, smiling, under his mother's thumb and happy to be there. Never one for quarrels or rebellion or upsetting the status quo.

'Mrs Owen needs water drawing. Well, what are you standing there for? Make yourself useful, man.'

William obediently goes off to fill the pail. The biggest catch in the neighbourhood is William, with one of the most prosperous farms on the estate, and the cautious sense to keep it that way despite the bad times in farming. The Georges hadn't rushed to buy their land like so many other impetuous souls, only to be burdened with crippling mortgages when things went bad. There'd been a few suicides because of that. But the Georges, William's father and then William, have stayed careful and cautious at the helm, getting by when others crumbled, getting on when others were getting by. All the time ruled by Mrs George, Queen Empress of Llanolwen parish. A good catch William might be, and he might have been sweet on Evelyn Lloyd these last four years, but Gwen cannot see him leaping into matrimony just yet. Two queens at Castell Mawr? The very notion is unthinkable.

But married or a bachelor, William is a good neighbour, obliging, easy-going and impossible not to like.

He returns with John, for the clock is striking, and John acts by the clock, to the second. They stamp their boots clean on the doorstep.

'Will you have tea?' asks Gwen promptly. It is brewed and ready for the exact moment when he will expect it.

John accepts his cup and glances at Mrs George, still sitting with the peas. He frowns, with what might be a twinkle in his eye. 'Have you been setting our neighbours to work then?'

You. *Ti* and *chi*. Their Welsh language defines their relationship in formal style. Gwen addresses him with respect, he speaks to her with masterly familiarity.

'What are neighbours for if they can't help each other?' asks Mrs George gruffly. She is familiar with everyone except the Colonel and the minister, as befits her dominant position in the district. She has licence over all. So much licence that for an awful moment, Gwen fears that she will make some comment about Gwen's condition, say something that will seem like a reproof to John. Her stomach turns cold.

But she need not have feared. Mrs George has too much respect for the traditional order of things. Though she expects to rule without question in Castell Mawr, she likes to see a man master in his own house. That is the way it should be. Not for one moment would she admonish him under his own roof.

John nods approvingly and drinks his tea, while the conversation moves on to Chapel talk and the Sunday School outing.

Dinner prepared, Gwen takes the peelings and peapods out to the garden. The sun, what there is of it, seems to be working in reverse. Instead of daylight, a shiver of dark weariness engulfs her. She is paralysed briefly by the sights and smells and sounds that greet her, all so familiar that most days she scarcely notices them. Lichen creeping up the scullery wall, the dark foetid dankness of the privy, the washing line and the cinder path running between rows of leeks and cabbages and potatoes, down to the apple tree. Sprays of Enchanter's nightshade have clustered round the tree, seed heads brush against the wall where a few bluebells have daringly ventured in, but there are no flower beds here. She planted primroses once, but they were gone the next day. This isn't a place for colour and perfume and all the foolishness of a dainty lady's flower garden. It is a place for hard labour and dour subsistence, a place of penitence, overshadowed by the surrounding trees, the heavy dark dusty suffocating wall of oak and ash and holly, the smell of damp leaf mould and rotting timber. Her tomb.

She cannot breathe. Is there fresh air out there somewhere? She cannot remember; she seldom leaves this little world of hers. No time for rambles or casual visits. Her trips to Penbryn market are rare these days. John prefers to go alone, so she seldom gets to see old friends or even her family. She has Chapel every Sunday, and sparing grudging visits to the butcher's and the little shop in Llanolwen where Miss Evans, tragic spinster because of the cruel war, keeps the Post Office. At best she can hope for an occasional visit to Castell Mawr or Penfeidr, farm business that brings her a little human contact, but otherwise this deep cwm is her horizon. The world stops where the surrounding trees meet the sky.

It is the memories that make it worse, memories of a time when she wasn't so constrained. As a young woman she had got about, trips to Aberystwyth and Tenby, Swansea even, and occasional visits to the Picture House to see a wide, impossibly exotic world out there. Now Penbryn is the furthest she can dream of going, and that so seldom that the notion throws her into a fluster.

Only once since her marriage has she ventured further, the trip to Llangrannog last year, helping with the Sunday School outing. A great success it was deemed and the Reverend Harries was loud in her praises, but she will not go again. That one holiday of festive respite, of sun and sea and open sky, laughter and hymn singing is a ghostly dream now. There is so much to do, her health is not so good... and John had not liked it. He had not complained at her doing her part for the Chapel community, but he had not liked her going either. Abandoning her post, her place at his side. Better not try his patience by doing it again.

Better stay here, where her real duty lies. So much to do, to keep her going, day after day until she is ground down forever into this dark damp earth.

It is the miscarriage, surely, weighing on her heart and mind, giving her these gloomy thoughts. She must pull herself together. No place for melancholia on this farm. No place for a sensitive wilting lady.

And no place for daydreaming children either. She must call Rosie, hurry her up to wash and make herself presentable. It is dinnertime and there is nothing John hates more than sloth. Rosie can be so tardy.

She looked around for the girl but cannot see her. A twinge of nervousness. How far has she gone, rambling into the woods? Please let it not be far. Rosie knows she mustn't be late for her father's inspection, for his catechism of her behaviour and tasks. John is so strict on such matters.

'Rosie!'

Her voice, though raised, is swallowed up in the smothering silence of the woods. 'Rosie! Where are you, girl?'

No response, no sound except scurrying in the undergrowth.

Gwen hoists her apron and her skirt up to scramble over the low place in the wall that is Rosie's fantasy gateway to some enchanted hideaway. The weeds beyond the wall are long, full of goosegrass, clawing at her stockings. She pushes through, panic at war with a sense of implacable guilt that she has crossed a forbidden threshold.

Threshold? She has not escaped. The dark woods embrace her, their brambles and boughs John's secret sentinels, ensuring that she goes nowhere.

It is an absurd fancy, yet it possesses her. Gwen finds herself running, trying to force her thin legs into unaccustomed urgency, fighting against the constraints of the trees. And sure enough, John's guards are at her heels. They clutch at her, roots tripping her and she falls headlong, ankle wrenched, skin torn, nettles spitefully thrashing her legs.

She lies prostrate on sharp slate stones. Between them the earth is dark and deep, musty with leaf mould that has drifted and dampened and rotted over the years, the centuries, the millennia. How many bones are down there, rotting in this sour soil? How long before her bones sink down to rot there, like the child she has lost? Why draw back? Why not sink now, into the dark and be at peace?

Something soft stirs beside her.

'Mam?'

A fairy voice, from a world of life and light.

A tug on her apron. 'Mam! Get up!' There is a forlorn fear in the voice now, reaching through the despair to Gwen's maternal instinct. Rosie. Her child. The child who has survived, who has not embraced the dark...

She raises her face, eyes meeting battered boots, scabby knees, limbs stretching thin out of infant chubbiness. A baby becoming a girl, needing her mother. She pulls herself to her knees, coming face to face with her daughter, dark eyes wide with incomprehension, grubby thumb in her mouth.

'What you doing, Mam?'

What indeed? Utter foolishness. How can she give way to this blackness with so much to do and her children to tend to. 'Just having a lie down, child. I'm up now.' Kneeling, but Rosie's elfin strength helps her to her feet.

The child gazes solemnly up at her mother, hair straggling, clothes awry, spattered with mud and leaves and twigs. Rosie brushes her apron down with a prim expression, a comical imitation of Mrs George.

Gwen forces a smile. 'What a mess I am. Now we must go home.'

In the dark gloom of the woods, Rosie's child eyes meet hers with an unspoken question they both instantly comprehend. Must they?

'Jack will be up to Lord knows what mischief.' Of course they will have to go back. 'Hurry now. Your father will be wanting tea on the table.'

It is a command that Rosie cannot struggle against. She bows her head in acquiescence and takes her mother's hand in quiet trust as they hurry back down to the stone wall of their home.

Jess' claws clattering on the cobbles. John's sedate tread. The door opens.

The table is laid, Rosie is at her place, hands behind her back, a solemn child in a solemn world. Jack has been coaxed and bundled into seemly subjection. The potatoes are hot, the bread is buttered, the tea is brewed. Gwen stands by, ready, her clothes brushed down, her hair pinned back, waiting on his word.

John looks round in approval, nods in benediction on his well-ordered, well- disciplined household. They bow their heads as he begins to say grace.

7

'There's the possibility that I'll be going out there regularly.'
Marcus loosened his tie as he followed me from the table.
'Perhaps even something more permanent.'

'Does that mean I'm going to lose you on and off every
year?' I didn't want to spoil Marcus' triumph, but it wasn't
quite how I had imagined our future.

Marcus was behind me, slipping his arms round my
waist. He whispered in my ear as I struggled with the
wrappings of an M&S cheesecake. 'It means that you and I
could find ourselves living in America.'

'Oh.'

He laughed at my shellshock. 'You'll love it, Sarah. I
know you. Trust me.'

Trust me. Marcus' favourite phrase, the words I loved
him for; my anchor as I floundered and drowned in the
muddle of life. Our whole relationship had been built on
me trusting him. We'd met after a disastrous night at the
club. I'd been singing, on Freddie's persuasion, though I
hadn't felt in the mood, so I'd added copious alcohol to the
antidepressants I'd been on. The result had been a build-
up of resentful aggro. When a scuffle between a couple of
customers erupted into an outright brawl, I hadn't exactly

calmed things. It'd finished up with twelve of us being bundled off to the police station in the early hours. I went from belligerent to terrified. I'd felt hopelessly abandoned – without any justification, because Freddy was seeing a client back to his hotel and had no idea I was in trouble – and I'd never in my life been so glad to see someone as I was then to see the local junior who'd drawn the short straw as duty solicitor that night. He was a little dishevelled, blinking as if he had only just woken up, but he gave a huge smile, sat me down, and ordered me to tell all while he straightened himself, combed his hair and turned himself into a figure of cool authority.

'All right, Sarah,' he said. 'Don't worry about a thing. Trust me. I'll sort this out.' Five minutes later he was seeing me into a taxi and sending me home. The next evening he was at my door with a bunch of roses.

Of course I trusted him. But America. This was big. Monumentally big. I needed to get my head round it. I needed time to get over my instant response that America was absolutely not what I wanted. 'It isn't definite, is it?'

'I wish it were! No.' I could feel him pulling back a little. 'Just a possibility at the moment. You're not keen?'

'I'm not sure I want to live in America. It wasn't what we'd planned.'

'Just broaden your horizons, sweetheart. Think about it.' He knew when to back off, give me space to reorientate myself. 'Anyway, there are plenty of other avenues I'm exploring.' Of course there were. Was it only four years ago that he was the bleary-eyed junior in Green, Colby & Partners? It would always be onwards and upwards with Marcus. I didn't want to spoil our long-awaited reunion with negative vibes. A celebration dinner: I'd cooked, personally opening every packet. Marcus brought the champagne.

I turned in his arms to face him, offering him fingers smeared with cheesecake to lick. 'I know you'll work wonders, whatever you do.'

'I could work wonders right now,' murmured Marcus, and it was physically obvious he could.

'I've never been bedded before on a cheesecake,' I said. 'I think I'm getting kiwi slices all over the back of my dress.'

He peered over my shoulder and giggled. 'So you are.' He pulled back and looked at me, eyes gleaming. 'How do you fancy a weekend in Paris?'

'Paris! Not this weekend?'

'Why not? I could take a couple of days off. I warn you, if it isn't Paris, it will be Sunday dinner with my mother and you're going to have to talk wedding.'

My stomach plummeted. 'Marky, how about letting my mother fix up a really simple wedding in Ireland. Quick and quiet and we could just get on with life?'

He gasped with mock outrage. 'You want to give my mother a heart attack? Anyway, I thought you said Ellen had no money.'

'Yes but do we need parents to pay for it? Isn't that a bit...' I was going to say 'vulgar,' but thought better of it. 'A bit of a nerve at our age?'

'Come on, let my mother have her fun. You know this is her mission in life. Compensation for when she discovers we're moving to the US.'

'Possibly moving.'

'Yes, possibly, but fingers crossed. So what's it to be? Paris or the Sunday roast? Your choice.'

'Look.' I adjusted one of his shirt buttons. I'd wanted to choose my own time for this, but I was being bulldozed. 'I really can't do either. I've fixed up something else.'

'What, for our first weekend together?'

'I didn't know it was going to be our first, did I? I thought we'd be having this celebration last weekend.'

'I know, I'm sorry, but I really had to go to Birmingham. They demanded a full report.'

'Yes, don't worry, it's fine. It's just that I miscalculated, and I've arranged to go to Wales on Saturday.'

'Wales. I offer her Paris and she chooses Wales!' Marcus laughed tolerantly. 'Don't tell me Frieman and Case are promoting sheep. What if they mistake you for one, indeed to goodness, look you? Or send you down a mine, boyo, or...'

'Do you mind? I am Welsh, you know.'

'Since when?'

'I'm as Welsh as you are Scottish. More so. My mother really is Welsh.'

Marcus kissed my neck in forgiveness. 'If we keep quiet about it, the neighbours need never know.'

'*Très drôle.*' His levity was not helpful. 'Actually it has nothing to do with—'

'She's not really Welsh, is she?'

'Yes, she was born there. And Dilys, of course.'

'They don't sound Welsh.'

'I think Dilys does still, very slightly. She's lived in England so long. Mum's lived here since before she could talk.'

'Well then! They escaped.'

'No!' My Owen grievance reawakened. 'They didn't

79

escape, they were pushed. That's the point. It should have been their heritage.'

'You're not planning on a law suit, are you? I warn you, my fees are high.'

'I can't afford you. No, the thing is, I've found the family farm. I discovered it on my way back from Ireland. I just looked by chance, and there it was, for sale, so... I've arranged to go this weekend.'

'You're serious? The family farm?'

'It's just a cottage. You have to understand. Did I tell you about my grandfather?'

'The amateur aviator?'

'No, the other one; Grandfather Owen. The farmer.'

'If you did, I don't remember. What about him?'

'I've discovered he was murdered.'

'Good God.'

'It was this dark secret, buried in the family chest.'

'Which is just screaming to be opened, of course. But I know you, remember, Sarah. I'm going to have to watch you like a hawk. I know what you're like.'

'What am I like?'

'Oh, beautiful, enchanting, bewitching, tantalising...'

'Yes, yes, that goes without saying.'

'And utterly hopeless with tragedy. You can't cope with it. You're too emotional.'

'I should be a cold hard bitch, should I?'

'No, baby. But you know it's true. Remember?' He could sense my quickening heartbeat and turned it into light-hearted banter. 'One gloomy comment and you're off. You get maudlin, start drinking, and the next thing I know, you're launching into *Strange Fruit*.'

'You don't like me singing *Strange Fruit*?'

'I love it,' he said, magnanimously. 'I just prefer it when you don't.'

'Philistine. Anyway, I think I'm entitled to get maudlin about a grandfather being murdered and his family dispossessed. They lived in this cottage, and there it was, for sale, waiting there, my family history, my roots, everything. I couldn't just walk away.'

'No, of course you couldn't. How incredible.' He nodded his understanding. 'I can see why you couldn't resist the lure. Of course you want to see it. Tell you what, Paris can wait. We'll go together and take a look.'

'You'll come too?'

'Why not? Who knows, if it's any good, we might even consider buying it.'

Had I really not explained that bit? 'Marky...'

His hands slid down the back of my dress, peeling away sticky slices of kiwi fruit. 'You know this dress is ruined. I'm going to have to take it off.'

Yes, please, change the subject. 'Does that mean you don't want the cheesecake I bought especially for you?'

'Later, woman, later.'

All I had to do, I decided, was sell the idea of Cwmderwen as a romantic weekend retreat and it did have a lot of selling points.

'It's idyllic. It really is,' I explained as we sped along the M4. 'Deepest countryside, no neighbours for miles around, and there are hills, woods, castles, you name it.'

Marcus' eyes narrowed. 'No mines?'

'Of course no mines. Your lot closed them all down, remember.' He was rude about my Welshness, so I could snipe at his true-blue Tory credentials. 'And it's close to the sea.' Give or take ten miles. Close enough. 'The coast is gorgeous. Fabulous beaches, cliffs, seals and dolphins and—'

'I'm sold on the weekend,' he assured me with a laugh. 'And it's a pretty easy journey.'

Which it was, as far as Carmarthen. I left him playing with his satnav, finding the optimum route to Llanolwen, while I called in at the estate agent to pick up the waiting key. Cwmderwen was mine now. All mine. Something I had yet to explain, but give me time.

Unfortunately, my cup of time began to run over. The speed of our journey to Carmarthen was offset by our snail's pace from then on. The weather was clear and bright and it had brought out every caravanner in the country, all heading for the by-roads of west Wales. We were trapped in a convoy of old dears that dropped to 28 mph at every hill, and there were plenty. The long summer evenings must have prompted them to put off their cocoa for another hour or so.

Now, I knew the effect a driving wheel had on my beloved. Marcus was normally all cool reason. I'd seen him dealing patiently with senile biddies, little children, rude policemen, irate shareholders, drunken yobs. He would step in, take charge and charm away all tension. But put him behind a steering wheel, and he became James Bond and Mad Max rolled into one. God help us if he achieved his ambition of buying a Porsche. The company BMW was bad enough. The mere glimmer of a Morris Minor somewhere in the middle distance and he was instantly obsessed with overtaking.

Boys! Did it matter if our average speed dropped below fifty? All I wanted was to pootle gently along to Llanolwen and see Cwmderwen before the sun went down. It wasn't a race. If only Marcus were not fixated on getting past everything else on the road. I felt his tension ping as we approached the market town of Penbryn and the satnav ordered him to turn left. Relief. The caravan ahead of us swayed on into the sunset and we lurched off into the freedom of the open road.

A convoy of silage wagons. Great. This was a new experience for both of us. Precious little silaging in the streets of London or Guildford. You could see it as fascinating if you wanted to, but Marcus had lost the will to be positive. It had been a long day and he decided to be negative.

'Who are these people? Do they think they own the bloody road? I should sue them for obstruction. Why didn't they clear off at 5 o'clock?'

They worked, it seemed, on the outskirts of Llanolwen, because we were stuck behind them the whole way.

'Ten miles!' said Marcus bitterly.

'It was never ten. Not even five, I bet. Anyway, you can stop now. Here.'

He screeched to a halt and a disgruntled truck behind us hooted and edged past. 'Here?'

Wide entrance, white gates, trimmed conifers. A very reassuring sight.

'Yes. Well, not exactly. This is Castell Mawr. See the sign? You have to look out for it in order to find Cwmderwen.

Now, just go on to the end of the lay-by. On a bit further. Go on, a bit of mud and gravel won't hurt your tyres.'

Frowning deeply, he complied, edging onto the rough ground as the silage wagons waddled out of sight.

'There's the milestone. Ha! Four miles to Penbryn. I told you.' I unbuckled and opened my door. 'It's down this lane.'

'What lane?'

'There. Through those trees.'

Without a word, Marcus got out and stared down the overgrown track.

The summer evening air was warm but fresh, sweet with the smell of cut grass, flowers and warm earth. Wonderful. But not wonderful enough to enchant Marcus after that journey.

'Are you sure you've got the instructions right?' he asked, frowning into the gloom.

'Yes, this is the place.'

'I'm hardly dressed for a hike into the undergrowth.'

'No.' I hesitated. He was in his suit, straight from work, but I was in jeans and trainers. 'Actually, would you mind if I went alone? We'll go down together tomorrow.'

He laughed impatiently. 'I'm not letting you go wandering off down there on your own. Don't be ridiculous.'

'What do you think is going to happen to me? I'll be fine. Seriously. Let me go alone. Just this first time. It's important to me; private, you know. The place where my grandfather died. I'd like a moment down there on my own.'

Marcus folded his arms and perched on the wing of the BMW, shaking his head at my feminine whimsy. 'I warn you, if you're not back in ten minutes, I'll send out a search party.'

'Ten minutes,' I promised.

I tramped down into the shadows of the lane, picking my way with care. The sky was still white overhead, but the evening gloom was deep under the trees. As the lane, fortunately bone dry, turned a bend, the road and the outside world vanished. No sign of the tractor that had cut a way through in March. The hedgerows had crept back, brambles clutching at me, long grass and nettles whipping my legs. Silence.

Or not quite silence. Rustlings and snufflings in the undergrowth. The distant shriek of a fox. The unearthly scream of an owl in the trees above me nearly took me out of my skin. And then, a crunching and grunting, and dark shapes trundling out of the undergrowth and across the lane barely twenty feet from me. I froze. Badgers. My own nature reserve. Guildford couldn't beat that.

I emerged into the secret dell where Cwmderwen cottage stood, a black shape as the night had already closed in down there. The complete dereliction of the place, which I had somehow glossed over in the last few weeks, faced me with uncompromising honesty. How on earth was I going to deal with this – not the rebuilding, but persuading Marcus that it was a great idea? Thank God I hadn't dragged him down here tonight, in his present mood. Tomorrow, maybe, under a new sun...

Oh hell. The point was, whatever Marcus thought about Cwmderwen on first sight, he would understand my need for it. That trust thing: I could always trust him not to let me down. He was never going to see this as a dream purchase – he wasn't insane – but I knew that after a few weary sighs, he would accept my project and let me see it through.

I just had to show it to him in the right light. This was the wrong light. It was no light at all. Why hadn't I brought a torch? The house loomed over me. Door and windows, pits of darkness, were watching me. *Is there anybody there, said the traveller?* Long shadows. Shapes that could be anything. Creaks, trailing vines and a deep chill. A place of murder.

Ghosties walking by moonlight, Sam had scoffed.

Last time I had no sense of death. Murder hadn't been on my mind. Now it stalked in the shadows, long cold fingers reaching for me...

Jesus!

Calm down, Sai. It was just the owl hooting again, that was all. Ghosts indeed! But wasn't there a well somewhere? Probably uncovered. And the structure wasn't safe. I'd come back in the daylight.

I was up the lane in record-breaking time.

Another day, bright sun, and a decadent breakfast in our hotel on the coast, where the sea was a dazzling ultramarine and the beaches were wide, pure and empty. The food was great, and the bed was greater. Tested and not found wanting. Marcus was all sunshine again, relaxed, admiring the view, devouring eggs Benedict and dreaming about America. He was perfectly happy to return to Cwmderwen and take a proper look at my mysterious Owen inheritance.

We stopped at Penbryn because he insisted he had to be properly dressed, so I waited, pretending not to know him, while he bought a pair of green Wellingtons. In the lay-by at the top of Cwmderwen's lane, he pulled them on and tried them out, pacing in the long grass.

'You're not going for full protective clothing then?'

'I'll take the risk this time.' Like me, he was now in jeans, ready for the call of the wild. 'All right then, let's see this family treasure.'

No sign of badgers or anything else in the daylight. We tramped down to examine the bald truth.

'Good God,' said Marcus. 'This is it? It's a bomb site.' He was remarkably upbeat, amused more than anything as he peered in through the shattered windows. 'A family home? How on earth did they cope?'

'The way people did. It was a working farm.'

'Not much of one, surely. And I thought Mumsy had risen from the depths, with her father being a factory foreman. You've certainly come up in the world.'

I stiffened. 'We haven't come up anywhere. We've just got more money. Don't be such an outrageous snob.'

'It's not snobbery. It's economics. If you're stuck in this sort of poverty, it must take some guts and a whole load of luck to climb out of it.' He grinned at me, challenging me. 'Money opens doors, that's the truth.'

'Open doors don't necessarily make you happy.'

'Oh sure, people can be poor and happy. But being rich and happy is a hell of a lot easier, admit it.'

'No! Anyway, it wasn't like this then. It's been standing empty for sixty years, remember. It was probably quite grand in its day.'

Unconvinced, Marcus stepped back into the middle of the yard, to gaze up at the sagging eaves and the adjoining rubble. 'I doubt that. So what exactly happened here, with this murder?'

'I don't know. Dilys is infuriating. She just said person or persons unknown.'

'That is what I call damned unsatisfactory. But you're not going to find any clues here. Just a bit of atmosphere. So, now you've seen it, is your curiosity satisfied?'

'Don't be in such a hurry.' I took his arm, turned him to face out over the rusted gate, into the sunlit meadow. 'Look at that view!'

We gazed out over a tangle of campion and meadowsweet, out across a glinting river, patchworks of tiny green fields and swathes of unspoiled woodlands, to the distant hills that were high, blue and mysterious.

'Mm.' Marcus breathed deep, taking it all in. 'It's fabulous. Spectacular situation. A pity the house is such a hopeless case.'

'I wouldn't call it hopeless.'

'Oh it is. Come on. Look at it.' He turned me back to face the cottage. 'If it had more going for it, it might be worth doing up. But as it is, they haven't got a chance of selling.'

'It isn't that bad. Think about it. My grandfather died here.'

Marcus burst out laughing. 'I'm not surprised!' He felt me flinch. 'Sorry, Sarah. Insensitive. I do understand the fascination, but seriously—'

'We were talking about a weekend place, a country cottage.'

'Sure. Eventually, when we're settled and we've got the cash to spare. Somewhere with four walls and a roof for starters. In Scotland, we'd decided, remember?'

'You said you liked Scotland. I don't remember us deciding on anything.'

'Well, wherever it is, it's not going to be—'

'I've already bought it.'

Marcus stopped in mid-argument, turning to face me to check that he'd heard right. 'Baby?'

'I bought it. I put in an offer as soon as I saw it, back in March.'

His jaw set. Hardly surprising. Under the circumstances, I wouldn't have blamed him if he'd erupted, although none of this confusion was my doing. Not deliberately. Events seemed to have run away from me.

'Sorry, Marky, I thought you understood.'

'No I didn't, and I still don't. How could you have bought it? With what?'

'Granny Peterson's legacy.'

'Sarah, that was for our home.'

'You're making a fortune, Marcus, and I'm earning too. We'll be fine.'

He wasn't listening, shaking his head. 'How could you have been so stupid?'

Time to play the wronged damsel card. 'This is my home! My grandfather was murdered here, my family was dispossessed and I want it back! Sorry if you think me stupid!'

He recovered his control. 'Yes, of course, the romantic impulse... you would have to follow it. I know what you're like, Sarah. Beautifully impulsive, but hardly ever practical.' He slipped his arm round my shoulder and turned me back towards the lane. 'All right, now let's see what we can do to sort out the mess. You haven't exchanged contracts yet, have you?'

'Marcus, I've bought it. The sale's complete. That's why I'm here; to pick up the key and take possession.'

His arm dropped, his eyes rolling. 'And you didn't ask me? You didn't think we might discuss it?'

'You were in America. I did discuss it with you, the first opportunity we had when you got back. I didn't want to talk about it on the phone. You were so preoccupied with America and I wanted to explain it without diversions.'

'My career is a diversion? Thank you! I thought it was our future.'

'I mean you were concentrating on that.' It was true. Marcus was not a multi-tasker. He gave himself, heart and soul, to one thing at a time, and when it was work, I and my concerns were firmly in the wings. I'd always accepted that. 'I wanted you to understand. This house means a lot to me, it's important. Really important. Okay, I'm stupid, or mad, or a silly little woman, whatever you like, but I had to buy it. I can't explain, but I had no choice.'

He sighed. 'How much?'

'Granny Peterson's legacy more than covered it. And plenty to spare for the building work.'

'I wouldn't be too sure.' He looked at the house again, shaking his head with despair. 'God knows how much it will cost to put right.'

'God and Sarah Peterson. I've had the estimates, and there's a local builder ready to start...'

That jaw was setting again. 'Were you actually planning on involving me in any of this?'

'Of course, as much as you want, if you want. And if you don't, it can be my little obsession. But I need to do it.'

He was still wounded, still angry, but I was not going

to repent. Not this time. We were having a grand wedding in St. Hugh's, because Marcus and his mother wanted it, and a honeymoon in Mauritius, because Marcus had found the perfect place. We were almost certain to find ourselves living in some designer apartment in Docklands, convenient for Marcus and inconvenient for me. And I was willing to bet that for all his talk of 'maybe' we were going to finish up in America, just as he was planning. It was the downside to loving a man so reassuringly decisive as Marcus. I was due, in return, this one little thing.

I could tell Marcus had reached the same conclusion. He was still shaking his head, but the anger was back in its box. 'Sarah Peterson, what am I going to do with you?'

'Marry me?' I suggested.

'I think I'd better, before you spend the rest of our money on any more mad schemes.'

My money, I thought, and you dream of buying a Porsche, which will probably cost more than my little cottage even after renovation. Quits? I fished out the key and confronted the house. It stood there, watching me. Waiting for me to unlock the door and release – what?

The answers, I was secretly hoping. Getting hold of my grandfather's death certificate was the only serious investigating I had done until now, but from Cwmderwen I could surely find more. Whatever Marcus said, I had to believe it would hold clues for me. I wanted explanations to come flooding out as I opened the door, but for my beloved's sake, I made turning the key a businesslike gesture, instead of the theatrical one I craved.

Leaves had clogged the entrance. I pushed tentatively

and the door freed itself, swinging open. Nothing came rushing out but a gust of chill musty air.

No answers, no ghosts, just darkness.

I still didn't dare go in. The ceiling had come down further since I first saw it. Had the clumsy wooden stairs been that riddled with woodworm before? Never mind; those details could be fixed. I stepped back into the dappled sunlight of the overgrown yard. It was mine, all of it, its past, its present and its future, and I was going to put it right.

Marcus was watching me, smiling, even if there was a wince of pain in the smile. You see what a dump you've bought, it was saying.

I laughed. Yes, I was mad, and all the other things he was thinking. But just wait. I set myself a target for the restoration. Christmas. Yes, come Christmas, Marcus would see things in a new light.

8

Gwen has been busy because it's second nature, she cannot be still. There are plates to carry, cups to wash and she must help, that is only right. But there are more than enough George daughters and George aunts and cousins to do all that is required, and Betty John has been firm with her. 'Go and sit down, Gwen. Rest your feet. You deserve it.'

So she is doing what she has almost forgotten how to do: nothing at all. She sits, out of the way, soaking up the warmth and the exotic experience of being still, watching the scene with a sense of faintly wicked contentment. The children of Ted Absalom, one of the Georges' hands, are huddled nearby over the unspeakable luxury of an orange. Gwen leans down to help them with the peel, the small business helping to assuage the sinfulness of being idle.

The smell of orange. When did she last savour that? Christmases of long ago, happy faces that have vanished forever, her mother, her brother before the TB, her father still hale... all recaptured by the sweet sharp spicy warm smell of Christmas at Castell Mawr. The frosts have set in with a vengeance, but inside the old farmhouse, all is cheerful flickering warmth. A monstrous fire flames in the huge hearth, roaring up the massive open chimney. The oak beams are festooned with greenery and paper chains made by the children. Candles twinkle on the Christmas tree and the sideboard is groaning under the spread of hams and mince pies, cakes and cheeses and preserved fruit.

Rosie and Jack are red-faced with pleasure and overeating, romping among the other children with squeals of delight. Tom, smallest and slowest of the Absaloms, triumphantly bolts down the last of his orange and struggles over to join them.

Light and warmth and laughter. The resinous smell of greenery, flickering flames, a feast for the entire parish. The Georges are as careful with their money as their neighbours, but maybe that is why they can afford this annual prodigality.

It is all a far cry from the spartan Christmas chill of Cwmderwen, though Gwen has done what she can, saving up spare coppers from her housekeeping, and attempting rashly to roast a scrawny old hen, past laying, that should have had two days slow boiling in the stock pot to render it edible. They ate it regardless and the children had presents.

Not toys. John would never tolerate that sort of thing. Their gifts from the Chapel tree on Christmas Eve, dispensed by a Father Christmas looking strangely like William George, disappeared within hours of their return home. Jack's tin trumpet was confiscated as he came through the door and Rosie's bead necklace was gone by bed time. Toys have no place in the house. Rosie's doll, Maggie May, survives only because she lives secretly in an old biscuit tin concealed just over the garden wall. But John permitted the mufflers, mittens and tam-o'-shanters that Gwen has knitted out of old wool and he accepted the new boots that Rosie must have for growing feet, with the old ones falling to pieces. He sniffed in disapproval at the sprigs of holly Gwen brought in from the woods to brighten the hearth. Christmas is a time for chapel and reverence, not for bawdy frolics and pagan merriment.

His disapproval, she notes, is reserved for the hallowed soil of Cwmderwen. No such censure for the celebrations here at Castell Mawr, but then who would dare criticise with Mrs George presiding over the revelry from her rocking chair? One glance at her solemn bulk strapped into her best black satin will dispel any idea that there is anything ungodly about this gathering.

After all, they have spent most of the day at prayer, up at six, chapel at Beulah, then at Caersalem over at Felindre, then back to Beulah for the children to recite the *pwnc* and be catechised. And now the minister is come, to prove that all this feasting and laughter in a God-fearing house is perfectly righteous.

Mrs George's eldest daughter, Annie Lloyd, and her sister-in-law, Evelyn, are organising the children into a choir. Hymns and carols around the Christmas tree, while Annie plays, thumping on the piano with joyously inaccurate goodwill. Rosie's little voice rings out clear and pure above the others. Mrs George looks across to Gwen, with a nod as if to say, 'I told you so.'

The gesture of approval is dear to Gwen, but she does not need to be told that Rosie has musical talent. Of course she would have, with a singer like John for her father. It is his turn now. He is standing solemnly in the background, hands clasped behind his back, aloof even here, but they are having none of that, summoning him forward.

The Reverend Harries claps his hands. 'Yes, come now, Owen. Let us have some sacred music worthy of the season.'

John demurs and then complies, standing dignified by the piano as Annie anxiously leafs through the music. Should Gwen offer to help? There is no need. John's repertoire, which she knows by heart, consists mostly of hymns that Annie mastered years ago, and a few pieces from the great religious oratorios.

Calon Lân to start with, because Annie can play it with her eyes shut. John begins and his audience joins in, a quiet accompaniment at first and then a rising crescendo of *hwyl*. Then *The Messiah. Every valley shall be exalted.* The roof timbers are ringing, threatening to exalt themselves into the night sky. John is in truly wonderful voice, his breast swelling, the liberated spirit within him finding its wings and soaring as only music allows. He finishes amidst a roar of applause. The Reverend Harries beams round proudly as if this prodigy of Beulah Chapel were his very own creation.

A pause. They are debating. Some Bach? Annie is not sure she can do it justice.

The Reverend looks up suddenly, in Gwen's direction. 'But of course, we mustn't forget Mrs Owen. Quite a reputation in her youth, so I've been told. Is that not so, Mrs Owen?'

Gwen smiles and shakes her head, eager to divert their attention. The smile is a mask concealing a sudden flutter of pain. *In her youth.* When was that? She is scarcely into her thirties and her youth is already something barely remembered, a dream of long ago from which she has woken with a vengeance. 'Oh no, don't think of me, I haven't played for years.' When was the last time she had been permitted time to play, on her fleeting visits to Penbryn? She cannot remember.

They are not listening to her objections. Evelyn and Annie and her sister Betty have gathered round, cooing and twittering and insisting that Gwen must perform too. She can accompany John. What could be more appropriate than that?

'I really don't think—'

'Play us one of your father's hymns,' suggests Mrs George, and no one dares to argue, least of all Gwen.

Tentatively she seats herself at the piano stool. Perhaps she can no longer play. Her fingers ache from scrubbing and boiling and mending and milking and the onset of rheumatism. They cannot possibly move smoothly enough.

But they do. They awake, at her command, as if they had been waiting. She plays, one of her father's best compositions, and it all comes back as if she were practising still at her old instrument in her room over the grocer's shop.

She is the focus of all attention. It is not right; she feels a guilty twinge. They should not be minding her. That had not been her intention when she had agreed to play. She had expected John to sing the words, but he has not understood her intent and is silent, so she plays while the others gather round in earnest admiration, humming along, the Reverend and Sidney Lloyd finally adding the words.

It is such a pleasure, to be playing again. She had forgotten how overwhelmingly pleasurable it was. Annie has her hands clasped in ridiculous admiration and William applauds loudly, though Gwen realises, with an inner smile, that he is not just complimenting her, but currying favour with Evelyn Lloyd, whose enthusiasm is gushing.

'Why, Gwen! I didn't know you could play. Play some more. Here, let me see.' While Evelyn is rustling through the papers, others crowd round in ungrudging admiration, but Gwen barely notices them. It is Rosie she sees, Rosie sitting still with the other children but suddenly apart in spirit, thumb dropped from her mouth, eyes wide with astonishment that her mother can do this thing. It is Rosie's poised expectant eagerness that persuades Gwen to go on, quickly, into a silly little song that instantly has the children jigging and dancing. Rosie laughs with delight.

'You are going to play the Bach accompaniment for John,' the minister reminds her.

Of course. The Bach. She looks at John.

He is standing, stony faced, waiting, and her innards freeze. Has she done something wrong? She senses his petrifying displeasure, but the audience is impatient, the minister is nodding and she must play and he must sing.

Gwen turns back to the keys with a shiver. Beautiful sacred music that must be treated with respect, and she plays with greater care, giving it its due, waiting for John to share with her.

But something is wrong. Is it her playing? He sings, but they cannot keep time together. He has to keep correcting, missing, slipping, and it all goes awry. He stops in mid-phrase, hand to his throat, coughing, and immediately they are all consternation. He should not have exerted himself, not after so much singing in the chapel. He must rest his voice.

Quietly, Gwen rises from the stool and accompanies Betty into the kitchen to fetch tea and a spoonful of honey for the cracking voice. It is enough. Nothing they say will persuade her to return to the piano. Besides, their idle hour is done, they must be going. No help on the farm tiding things over in their absence, and they have chores to do, the cows to see to. Everyone understands when John abruptly announces that they must leave.

Gwen gathers up the children, bundling them into coats and scarves and gloves against the biting winter chill. Jack is a sturdy little boy, thank God. He'll manage most of the walk back to Cwmderwen on his own now, although she'll have to carry him if he is too slow. She has just time to smile at the company, her arm patted in benediction by Mrs George as she follows John out into the frost. The little Absalom faces, glowing with food and excitement, peer round the matriarch's bulk at her, a picture of warmth in contrast to the needle-sharp bite of the night air. In contrast to the beds the Owens are returning to. No roaring fire awaiting them at Cwmderwen. Gwen will have to heat the stone bottles as soon as they get in, or the children will be all night shivering.

Too dark to cross the fields on a December night, the mired footpath too treacherous with ice. They must climb to the road. Their breath clouds in the cold air, their boots ring out on the cobbles of Castell Mawr yard. She hurries the children along because John is striding ahead, not waiting, and he will not have them dawdle. They must keep up. The track up to the road leaves them panting, and

Gwen has to carry Jack in the end. Rosie trots along, gripping her hand.

At the gate, John stops, turns, waiting for them impatiently. She can see the anger still simmering in him. Why? All she did was play the piano.

'Are you content, then, woman?'

'Content, John?'

'Putting yourself forward like that.'

'I did not mean to put myself forward, John.'

'Flaunting yourself!' He turns away. 'Showing me up in front of my neighbours.'

'I'm sorry that I played badly.'

He does not hear her apology. He has already gone on.

Resigned, she follows. What has she done that was wrong?

Out in the open on the road, out from under the trees and the shelter of the valley, the sky arches over them, ink black, and strewn with a billion diamonds. A lid lifts off her world and her understanding. The stars twinkle with piercing clarity in the frost, so bright they cast dim shadows. A different light. A new comprehension. Revelation.

John is jealous.

The ice-cold knowledge washes over her. John Owen, her John, walking tall, upright and proud along the road, is a small man. Small and mean.

Immediately she pushes the thought to one side. It is not permissible, she must block it out, too humiliating for words. She cannot allow for the futility of it all, if that terrible thought is true. But for a moment it has touched, settling, searing onto her brain, a black treacherous scar that will not fade. He is not worthy of her.

Put it out of your head, Gwen, before it destroys you.

9

My second visit since the building work started. The first very brief one, with Marcus watching like an eagle for flaws in contracts, was taken up with sorting out what was what and where and how, and being told firmly that I had better keep out until things had been made secure. This time I'd come on my own, and had a day in hand.

It was a shock to see how my plans for restoration involved so much ripping and stripping and laying bare. The cottage was now accessible, but the romance of the place had been blasted away. A hedge trimmer had neatened up the lane and a mountain of hardcore had made it passable, revealing the badger's sett in the banks. I heard his men cheerfully muttering about anticipated culls, but my builder, Matthew Harries from the next village, Felindre, swore that he would keep the badgers safe. It was easy to trust a man with such a round, guilelessly innocent face, who tacked 'honest to God' onto every sentence, but I was having trouble believing he was really going to make something out of the chaos. Vans, rubble, concrete mixers, scaffolding, timber, tarpaulins, a JCB and utter mess.

Marcus had taken a good long look at my detailed plans and decided there was investment potential in the place, so he was willing to tolerate my private project, my play house, keeping me out of mischief. In return, I'd thrown myself into the hunt for our future home proper. We'd spent the previous weekend viewing Dockland apartments.

He wasn't helping though with Caroline's current line of nagging: wedding presents. Apparently we had to draw up a formal wish list. I found the idea repugnant; I was twenty-nine, Marcus was thirty-two, we both had careers and had two flats full of furniture and all the toasters anyone could possibly want. I thought lists were for teenagers who needed help with the bare necessities, but Caroline was proposing a catalogue of serious items, and Marcus was wickedly playing the game. A longcase clock (walnut). Any pre-Victorian silverware (no reproductions). First editions, any title as long as they were signed.

Okay, it had been funny, watching Caroline solemnly noting it all down. But I was beginning to feel uncomfortable with the way Marcus sometimes toyed with his mother, even if I wanted to throttle her myself. He was very good at playing obedient Mumsy's boy in order to wind her round his finger, but there was a dark thread in his mockery. Something close to contempt. Half of me liked to believe she deserved it, but the other half knew she was just a hapless mother panicking at the thought of the umbilical cord being cut. She didn't know yet about his plans for America. I'd hinted to him to warn her, but he'd just laughed, promising to tell her as soon as it was a *fait accompli*. I knew what her reaction would be when she finally heard, and I wasn't looking forward to it.

But I wasn't looking forward to a weekend of Knightsbridge catalogues either, so I'd decided to immerse myself in the world of timber treatment, lagging and septic tanks instead.

The minutiae of restoration were actually fascinating me far more than I'd expected. Builder Matthew had an eye for curious details, probably because he was itching to rip them out and flog them to the next conversion down the road. But I was adamant that everything of interest was staying put, and that included the oak roof beams, which, Matthew told me, were surprisingly old. Maybe the place was a lot older than it looked on the outside.

'How old?'

'Hard to say. Could go way back, behind all that rendering.'

The rendering was coming off, and I thought about letting them dismantle the whole dressed facade, the Victorian sash windows, the slate slab flooring and see if they could unearth something really ancient. Something Tudor, or even mediaeval. Who could say how long ago someone had singled out this sheltered little nook for a home? Some ancient Owen in woad? According to the beautifully detailed Ordnance Survey map that I now kept in the car, there was an Iron Age fort nearby, as well as several standing stones, a burial chamber and hut circles, not to mention a Norman castle mound in the village.

I reminded myself firmly that my aim was to reclaim the family home of the 1940s, and even that simple reconstruction was going to be costly enough.

I was allowed in, to the ground floor at least, and I had my chance to poke around for clues. No words scrawled in blood on the parlour wall. No half-burned scraps in the grate. Nothing but an old kettle rusting away, a rotting plate rack by the stone sink in the clammy scullery and a green farthing, George V, 1934, that Matthew had prised from between floorboards. I held it, thinking, John Owen must have touched this.

There was the dresser. My first real link to John and Gwen, and it must be worth keeping. I had an idea how much genuine old dressers were worth.

'Better if I just carted it away for you,' Matthew assured me. 'Honest to God, it's not worth saving.'

I was obstinate. It had to be salvaged. Some discreet supports for the sagging shelves, the doors rehung, the rot and the mould and the worms treated, the disintegrating feet replaced.

With the help of Matthew and a chisel, I wrenched open the warped cupboard doors. Nothing but a bolt of chintz cloth, mildewed almost out of recognition. We prised the drawers open too. Empty except for some pins in one and a desiccated mouse in another.

I stepped back, disappointed, as four of Matthew's burly men set to work to budge it from its position by the stairs. It fought back, apparently welded into place. As it finally shifted, releasing a couple of spiders the size of small terriers, something shook loose at the back, flopping down into the cupboard space.

An old notebook, pages creased and torn. It must have slipped over the back of a drawer and been forgotten by all but the mouse, which had devoured most of the cover and several pages.

I pounced before Matthew could sling it into the rubble going to the skip. At last, something. A detailed diary would be too much to hope for, but anything was better than nothing.

It was a school exercise book. The mouse had left enough to show that. I leafed through it hopefully. An Owen school book. There was a picture of a man and his camel. I knew it was a camel because the careful childish writing, spelling out the story of Joseph and his coat of many colours, said so.

A page of sums. A page of Welsh. It couldn't be my mother's work, for sure. Uncle Jack's maybe. I took it to add to my box of evidence, while Matthew's men clattered around me, and the gagging stench of rotten plaster filled the air.

I wanted this place back. I wanted the silence again, when I could feel the breath of the past brushing my skin, when the house was waiting, almost ready to speak to me. But while the builders were busy wrecking and rebuilding, I'd just have to be patient, pay their bills and keep out of their way.

Which meant I could spend the rest of my visit indulging my other obsession; the question of the murder, the demand for justice.

I'd found a base nearby; a country house hotel, Plas Malgwyn, along the valley; a low-slung grey stone place, with a touch of Edwardian elegance about the front. At the back, in a shameful 1960s extension, was a restaurant with pretensions to international cuisine, and there was a stable block converted to a mini health spa. Only five minutes drive to Cwmderwen and the map showed a footpath between the two. Less than a mile to walk.

In my room after dinner, I studied the school book at my leisure. Thick yellowing pages like blotting paper, scratched with a metal nib in a handwriting immature but far more elegant than the boxy script I'd learned at school. I couldn't judge the Welsh, but the English was awkward, correct but artificial. Someone's second language. There was the story of Llywellyn's butchered dog, told with childish relish, then more pages of Welsh. It was weird to think that this family that I wanted to claim as an essential part of myself wouldn't even have thought in the same language as me.

The book was only partly filled. After a section of long division and a list of the countries of the Empire, there were a couple of empty pages, then a final story. A very Welsh story with characters called Culhwch and Olwen, although it began in English. Culhwch was a hero and Olwen was the princess he was after but she had a big bad giant of a father, whose name I couldn't even begin to attempt and he – whatever it was, Jack had given up on English and drifted into Welsh. The writing lost its copperplate crispness and became a blotchy cramped scribble.

Result: teacher was not pleased. The last used page made the penalty clear. One phrase, over and over again. *Fi'n casau ef, casau ef, casau ef, casau ef.* One hundred lines? I must write neatly? Just to prove the point, the writing became smaller and smaller and then ceased in one final blot. Oh dear.

It hit me. This was probably my uncle Jack's last work book here in Cwmderwen. His father had been murdered, of course his school work suffered. Didn't the teachers allow for that? My heart swelled with pity for the poor boy. This sad little book could be the one real memento I had of the black day with all its horror. It was all there, between the lines.

I carefully filed it in my box of Owen records, wishing there had been more like it in the dresser.

And I found more. Not at Cwmderwen, but there at Plas Malgwyn, of all places. As I left my room in the morning, I realised there were photographs everywhere, up the sweeping stairs and in the lounge and the reception hall.

I glanced at the printed labels and discovered that Plas Malgwyn had once been the centre of a large local estate, probably the very estate that had owned Cwmderwen. Grandfather Owen's squire and landlord must have lived there. Well, well. I hoped he'd have felt some satisfaction to see his granddaughter there now, calling the shots as a pampered guest.

I thought about making some loud and unreasonable demands, as a matter of principle, but I made do with asking about the history of the place as I went into breakfast. They gave me a leaflet, which I read as I studied more of the photos. A manor once held by a Malgwyn ap Hywel ap Griffith, who was second cousin to a Someone ap Someone Else, and some time in the seventeenth century it was granted to...

Unpronounceable genealogies and Jacobean land deals meant nothing to me. There was a quote from a George Owen, but nothing I could directly link to my family. In the early nineteenth century the place had been acquired by the younger branch of some aristocratic Glamorgan family who sold it, towards the end of the Victorian era, to an Arthur Parker, newly returned from the Cape with a fortune in diamonds. Most of the photographs on the walls were of the Rhys-Parker clan or their tenants.

A boating party; blazers and white organdie drifting on the meandering river; an election rally, men with stiff collars and large moustaches, outside Penbryn town hall; huge hats and driving goggles in a vintage Rolls Royce; an Edwardian hunting party gathering on the drive, in frosty winter fog and a couple of unsmiling, rather jowly daughters of the house, done up in strapping finery for some soirée. No, I wasn't going to find my Owens among the gentry.

Happy peasants in the hay fields, armed with scythes. There might have been an Owen among them, but the figures were too distant to identify. A household of dignified retainers, dapper gents in black, pert maids in white aprons, a waspish old lady armed with a saucepan and an elderly gardener. This was more promising. Some of the Cwmderwen children could have been sent to work as servants at the big house.

An estate celebration – harvest supper? 1920, it said. Perhaps my grandfather was one of the blurred faces.

A picture of the squire, Colonel Rhys-Parker, and his good lady in tweeds, with home guard volunteers, 1941. The colonel was a stout whiskery gent, more at ease with his position in the world than Captain Mainwaring. My grandfather could be one of the Corporal Joneses and Private Pikes. I didn't recognise him, but then I only knew him dimly from a couple of flaking photographs.

My first real find was with the other memorabilia plastering the walls of Plas Malgwyn. Among the unbelievably extravagant butcher's bills, the yellowing newspaper cuttings and patriotic jubilee banners, there was a poster advertising an evening of entertainment at Llanolwen Village Hall, to raise money for a mission to

China. Colonel and Mrs Rhys-Parker to be present as patrons, Mr Thomas Jenkins on the pianoforte, Mrs Florence Phillips on the harp, Miss Gwladys Jenkins, soprano and Mr John Owen, baritone.

My heart missed a beat. My John Owen? 1932. It was possible. More than possible. It had to be him. I had never thought of my grandfather as a singer, and a public performer at that; he had been just a farmer. But no, he sang. Of course he sang. We were linked. Of course. Suddenly he seemed more real.

Then I found a newspaper cutting. Colonel Rhys-Parker, his stockman, and a local farmer, William George of Castell Mawr, standing proudly by a prize bull. It was the bull, phenomenally masculine, that most guests would probably chuckle over, but it was the mention of Castell Mawr that struck me. This William George would have been my grandparents' nearest neighbour.

It was a fine warm day, so I took my coffee and croissant out onto the terrace at the side of the house. An early morning mist still clung to the valley, cloaking the trees and the green river. Some of the other guests were already down there, fishing. I could see up the winding vale, along lush meadows and copses. Then the valley side rose a little more steeply and there was a shadow in the enveloping woods, indicating a narrow side valley. Cwmderwen.

I could see it more clearly from Plas Malgwyn than from the road just above it, but only because I knew it was there. There was the meadow where it opened out, full of alders and reeds. That would once have been John Owen's land. That long strip of rough pasture rising up beyond, under the shady eaves of the woods, must be the field beyond the rusty gate. My grandparents had probably stood there, looking this way, towards their landlord's house. It seemed hopelessly unfair that little Cwmderwen should have had to pay rent to keep a mansion like this in its aristocratic glory. Just as well the house itself was hidden in the trees. Not quite spied upon by the squire.

He could have spied on Castell Mawr though. There it stood, this side of the dark gash of Cwmderwen. Our entrances up on the road shared the same lay-by, but our respective lanes wound off down the hillside in different directions, and Castell Mawr, on a broad sunny bluff, faced Plas Malgwyn with serene confidence; a primrose yellow house with a side order of Dutch barns and a vast expanse of corrugated roofing. All around it, spilling down the valley, was rich green pasture studded with Friesians, and a couple of newly harvested fields, pale and naked. Brooding over it were the grassy ramparts and concentric ditches of the Iron Age fort. Perhaps Castell Mawr had first been farmed by the fort's inhabitants. It dominated the landscape. Plas Malgwyn, the interloper, however elegant, couldn't compete.

I guessed that Castell Mawr had acquired my grandfather's land when he died. My land. There it stood, unrepentant, challenging all comers.

Right. I'd take the challenge. I'd mentioned the murder at the hotel, hoping some local might remember something, but the manager just panicked and assured me that no murder had ever occurred in this area, ever. But then he wasn't local and most of his staff seemed to be Polish or Asian. If I wanted local gossip, I'd have more luck at Castell Mawr. I decided to call at the farm and introduce myself. Just to see how they'd react.

10

Washing day. The kitchen is festooned with damp steaming linen that Gwen has dragged from the boiler to feed through the mangle. Her arms ache as she turns the handle, trying to avoid strains dangerous in her condition.

Barking outside. Not John so soon, surely? No, please God, with the kitchen in this state. She wipes the steamed window to peer through. Jess the dog has backed through the gate from the field, hackles up, defending her territory, and a big lolloping hound follows her in, daft-looking but interested. Gwen's hand closes on the broom handle to chase him off, but the reason for the dog's appearance becomes apparent. John is there, at the gate, pushing it open, and another man follows him through, into the yard.

There is a footpath running through their fields, up the valley towards Beulah Chapel. People use it of a Sunday, though their presence rankles with John even for Sabbath business. He will not like this, someone taking liberties on his land on a Monday, no matter what ancient rights of way they think they have.

But he cannot object to this one. He dare not. It is Colonel Rhys-Parker. Recognising him, Gwen steps back in alarm, instinctively trying to avoid detection. Why has he come? The presence of their landlord instantly raises fear of eviction and disgrace. This is foolish. She needn't fear. John has paid the rent.

She steps back to the window to look again. Unmistakably Colonel Rhys-Parker. The stocky figure in tweed cap and jacket, blurred by steam and condensation, could be one of any number of local farmers, but there is no mistaking that grating English accent. A voice being pleasant and jocular, she can hear that much though not the words. They are safe then.

Safe from instant eviction at least, though Gwen knows other potential dangers attend this visit. Their landlord, squire, magistrate, strolling up in person to speak to his tenant? At Cwmderwen such an honour is barbed. Tenant or no, John is lord of this place, very clear about that. He is absolute ruler of his own small plot of God's earth and brooks no rivalry or opposition. She watches him through the window, his gaunt angular frame stooping slightly to his shorter stouter guest. Can she gauge his mood? Not angry at least. Respectful of course, in a way that does not diminish but reinforces John's stiff-necked pride. The Colonel even seems to appreciate it. He is chatting to John if not as an equal, at least as if John were an equal to the Georges and the Lloyds.

'Mam?' Jack is slithering down the stairs. Gwen has put him up there out of the way of the hot, messy dangerous business of washing. His arrival in quest of new entertainment or food distracts her attention from the business in the yard. Washing everywhere, unfolded, unironed. The place looking like a Chinese laundry and they have a guest! What will John say if he brings the

Colonel in to see all this? The Colonel can go in the parlour, which is cold and immaculate as ever, but he must reach it through the kitchen, through this chaos.

In a panic, she shoos the little boy back up stairs. 'Off with you now, quickly. Can't you see I'm busy? Be good now.'

'Who's that in the yard?'

'Never you mind. Now be off with you!'

'I'm hungry.'

In desperation she finds a crust, smears it with butter and thrusts it at the child.

'Now up those stairs quickly!'

He obeys, mouth full, stomping on the bare boards and she turns to the business of creating order. Moving like a whirlwind, bundling linen into the basket. It is a hopeless task. There is more to be pulled from the boiler. It cannot be left. It will have to be wrung.

Loud laughter in the yard. The Colonel's laughter. Six years and close neighbours but she has seldom been in his presence. Coming from church on a Sabbath sometimes, as they come from Chapel, and once or twice at the village fête, but he has not called here before and she does not go visiting at the big house. John deals with business, not her place to interfere in money matters. Four times a year he strides off, shoulders hunched in silent resentment down that same footpath to Plas Malgwyn that has brought the Colonel here today.

She did go once, a year ago, on her husband's arm, one of the humble tenantry arranged on the immaculate lawns to pay their compulsory respects at Master Philip's coming of age. Not having daughters in service there, like many of the other farmers in the area, it was Gwen's only opportunity to see the big house at closer quarters. She did not see inside the house, but she was permitted to gaze humbly on that double row of sparkling windows and the porticoed front door.

Not a great mansion but quite impressive enough for this area, like the family living there. Mrs Rhys-Parker was loud and horsey, gracious and patronising to the tenants' wives. Miss Alicia was all thin elegance, with a pained disdainful smile, and Master Philip, playing the responsible son and heir for once, addressed them all with hearty paternal words about doing a good job and all pulling together and the estate would do well by them if they did their bit. There was a bevy of bright young things too, down from Oxford or London where Master Philip mostly did his bit. They looked supercilious, drawling in their loud English voices, mocking the peasants.

And the Colonel, playing the bluff squire for all he was worth, pumping hands and saying, 'Good man.' Not real gentry at all in Gwen's books, no real blood. His father was just Arthur Parker, a tradesman who made a fortune in South Africa and came home to buy a genteel wife and a country estate, adding his wife's name to sound more impressive. It took more than that to make real gentry, Gwen thought.

But then she had known real gentry a lot worse than the Colonel, and it is not him she worries about now, with the kitchen in turmoil.

What should she do? It is her duty to make herself respectable and go out to meet their guest. John will surely be expecting it, but if she does, what will John say if he comes and finds all this? Always before, she has contrived to have it out of the way when he comes in for his dinner. He hates untidiness and disorder. He demands discipline in everything. That is how he stops the universe slipping into chaos.

She sees John glance at the house with a flash of impatience. A command. It is no good, she must go. Hastily, she pulls down her sleeves, straightens her apron, pushes stray wisps of hair behind her ears and goes to the door.

The sound of the door, the steam suddenly billowing out, makes the Colonel turn. Instinctively she bobs a curtsey, then feels foolish.

But the Colonel is an affable man, who gives a kindly laugh at her confused gesture of respect, and proffers her his hand, shaking it vigorously.

'Mrs Owen. A fine day for a stroll, so you see I have come visiting.'

A fine day? Is it? Gwen has only noticed that the wind is not as strong as she would have liked for the washing.

The Colonel is eying her with amused condescension. 'And you are blooming, I see. You're reaping a bonny harvest there, eh Owen?'

Gwen blushes, shielding her swelling belly with her hands. His remark, in a tongue alien to Cwmderwen, is gross and indelicate, but he is the Colonel and has a landlord's liberties.

'The other children thriving? Let me see. Ruth, is it, and John?'

'Rose and John.'

'Ah yes of course. Little Rosebud. All well with them, I hope?'

'Yes thank you.' She feels she must explain why they have not been wheeled out to pay their respects. An explanation not for the Colonel but for John. 'I've put Jack down for an hour's nap and Rose is cleaning potatoes out the back.' She knows Jack is a mess, probably butter-stained and hair on end. Rosie certainly has been in the back garden, but for all Gwen knows, she might have rambled off by now, into the woods, to Maggie May and a secret land of fantastical mystery. Gwen was not expecting her husband at the house this early and she has let the child run.

'Of course. Bless 'em.' The Colonel beams. He comes surprisingly naturally to the topic of children, usually the preserve of women, but everyone knows he is inordinately proud of his own, young glamorous creatures determined to be a cut above their parents. They have their eyes fixed on the wide world of high society, but the Colonel is content to play the country squire in his Welsh backwater, this little kingdom of his own, where he can chivvy his subjects into health and happiness. 'I've just been trying to persuade your husband to help us out with another concert, Mrs Owen. What do you think? Can you spare him?'

'Oh.' How is she to answer that? Is he asking her for an opinion? What if she goes against John's wishes? 'John is such a good singer.'

'Shame to waste his talents, eh? Just what I thought. There you are, Owen, your wife thinks you should oblige and we wouldn't want to contradict the little woman, would we? And it's for a good cause, man. Refugees, eh?'

John is stiffly silent. Has she helped push him into this concert against his will? John does not like being pushed. And for refugees? What refugees? Whoever they are, she knows he thinks all his energy is required for the support of his home and family. Let others take care of their own, not come to him with a begging bowl.

'Wouldn't your children be proud to hear you, Owen? Best baritone in the county, I say, and I challenge anyone to disagree with me.'

Still John withholds his answer, resorting instead to the role of host, as if to remind the Colonel of his position on John's land. Guest, not master. 'You'll take tea, Colonel? Well, woman?'

Gwen panics. She had hoped they would be content to stand talking on the doorstep, but now she must step back to invite him in. The Colonel is not a fool though. He has glimpsed enough, the telltale steam, her damp hair and red knuckles and tradesman's son or not, he is gentleman enough not to embarrass her. 'Oh indeed no, I don't want to drag Mrs Owen from her household duties. Washing day! I know just how chaotic that can be. Whole house turned upside down.'

Gwen doubts this. She suspects that laundry causes no chaos at Plas Malgwyn. Not above stairs at least. Mrs Rhys-Parker has surely never been up to her raw elbows in suds, callusing her fingers on the washboard, sweating red-faced over the boiler.

The colonel has strategically pulled back from the doorstep, to assuage Gwen's distress and confusion. The sight of washing has probably reassured him that his tenant has a wife who pulls her weight. A meagre farm this, but the rent gets paid, just. He has been glancing around, while he talks, noting the tools, the milk urns, the signs of never-ending husbandry. All as it should be.

He turns away, drawing John with him, a familiar slap on his shoulder. 'So Owen, the Reverend can speak to you about the music? Good man. And let's not forget the meeting on Thursday. See if you can attend. We all need to do our bit, see what we can do to get this country onto a war footing.' There is a note of wistful enthusiasm in his voice. A brief career in the army and the Great War catapulted him up through the ranks to an ordered dignity he still secretly hankers after. He is never happier than when drilling the local yeomanry.

John gives a silent non-committal nod.

'Will there be war then?' ventures Gwen. Should she have dared to speak on subjects John will surely regard as a man's preserve? War? Can the outside world intrude enough to break through the isolation of this place?

'Ah, alas, yes, I believe it is inevitable. But no need to worry about your man, Mrs Owen. He's doing a valuable job just where he is.' The colonel smiles patronisingly, knowing better than to expect a woman to grasp politics.

She does not argue with that. A King has died, a King has abdicated, a King has been crowned and somewhere far away a man called Hitler is on the move doing desperate things in countries she has not even heard of. It is all meaningless down here in this timeless place where nothing changes, nothing matters except work, more work, the struggle to survive and make ends meet and satisfy John's exacting standards. She has heard Dilys' Harry speak of war, almost eagerly, like a boy keen to go and play soldiers, but that is all a game. She cannot equate it with real life. How can it impinge on her?

They shake hands again and John accompanies the

colonel back to the gate, across the field to the footpath. Making sure he leaves.

Gwen hurries back to her work, setting the iron back to heat, folding sheets away, anxiously eying a tear in a pair of Rosie's drawers. That will have to be mended. And Jack needs new socks. She has darned the toes too many times. She can unravel these and another old pair, get enough wool for new ones.

She has the kettle on before John returns. He stands silent in the doorway, looking around with a resentful determination to find fault, though she has managed to clear up most of the mess. Just a few damp things still hanging.

'A fine way to entertain our landlord.' There is a bitterness in his voice, but she cannot tell if its source is her slackness or the word 'landlord'. 'Not that it stopped you giving your opinion.'

'I'm sorry, John. I did not know what to say. Do you not want to sing?'

'Do you think I have time for that nonsense?'

'The colonel will not insist if you tell him.'

'Oh, so you know the way of it, do you? You know about these matters better than I? Well, it seems I must do this concert, since you have ordered it.'

'Oh John, I—'

He will not hear her apologies but stalks off into the scullery. She hears the back door open, pleads with God for Rosie to be there, in the garden where Gwen has said she would be, busy, obliging, not petulant or dreamy or resentful. When she is in a docile mood, she is a wonderfully soothing antidote to John's black moods, lulling him into a taciturn toleration of life. She listens, heart stopped, for the raised voice, the blow, the child's cry. Nothing. The door opens again and she hears low voices, a child meekly questioning, a man grunting acknowledgement. Thank God for that.

Speedily she clears away the last of the laundry, puts the mending in a basket ready for later. Why is he so reluctant to sing at this concert? She knows that his voice, this God-given gift, is his one means of liberation. She realised it in that first concert where they met. She had seen it in their own parlour, of an evening in the early days of their marriage, when he had sung for her, or for himself, the hymns her father had written. When he sings, his soul soars to the heavens. But perhaps it is that dangerous freedom that alarms him, urging him more and more to curb it as the years pass.

She does not compete with him. She has never played again at Castell Mawr, though the Georges have coaxed and pleaded. She knows better now. But however dutifully determined she is to let her husband shine alone, the golden glow has faded. He is smothering it. He still sings in the chapel choir, an enforced duty, and she believes he still finds some peace in it, but she seldom hears his voice raised in song at home any more.

It is as if negation has become a way of life for John, eating into him so deeply that he must reject everything as a gesture of denial. Needless expense, yes. Loans, debt, yes. The expenditure that other farms are risking in order to improve and modernise, yes she understands that he regards these unproven fertilisers, tractors and milking machines as beyond his means, fine for the Georges and the Lloyds but not for the likes of him. But why must he deny himself singing too? A hair shirt that he has vowed to wear.

Over the splash of water in the scullery, she hears Rosie's voice tentatively beginning a hymn. A sweet clear childish voice that might one day soar like her father's. But should it be soaring now, or will her impudent rivalry only rub salt into whatever wound it is he is nursing today? She waits nervously for John's sharp word to silence Rosie.

Instead, he humphs, hums and breaks into *Bread of Heaven*. Oh, bless Rosie. Feed me till I want no more.

11

Farming was in a desperate state. Wasn't it always? I'd never heard a farmer who wasn't teetering on the brink, hanging on by his teeth in the face of floods, drought, disease, world slumps and bureaucracy. But Castell Mawr's teeth must have been good strong gnashers, because the farm looked flourishing to me. The broad concrete road passed down through lush pastures to a small industrial estate. As I pulled up in the yard, between farm vehicles that could eat my Fiat for breakfast, a man emerged from one of the sheds, short, slight, fiftyish, dressed in overalls.

He looked me over with quiet curiosity, waiting for me to do the talking.

'Hi. Do you live here?'

'Oh yes. Over from the cottage, are you? The new owner? Saw you were down.' Of course he had. I should have guessed that everyone probably knew everything in a place like this. Which was all for the good.

'Yes, that's me. Sarah Peterson.'

He shook hands solemnly. 'So how's the old house? Bit of a wreck, isn't it?'

'A bit, yes. I've got a lot of work to do.'

'Matthew Harries doing it up for you then?'

'That's right. I'm hoping he won't take too long.'

He adjusted his cap with a hint of a knowing smile. Another schmuck in the neighbourhood. 'Holiday cottage, is it?'

'Well, sort of.'

'You know the story of that house? Nasty business. Murder and all.'

I'd thought I'd have to skirt round it, just as I had with Dilys. But no, he came out with it, just like that. Didn't even need prompting. Almost gloating over it, taking a ghoulish pleasure in shocking the English newbie. What he couldn't guess was that I could parry him brilliantly. 'Yes, I know. It was my grandfather who was murdered, actually. It used to be my grandparents' farm.'

He definitely wasn't expecting that. 'John Owen? Well. Good God.'

'Yes – Sorry, I don't know your name.'

'Gethin George.'

'Oh, of course. There was a Mr George at Castell Mawr when my grandparents were here. I expect he got the land when my Nan lost the tenancy after the murder.'

He looked momentarily nonplussed. 'My dad, that was. They didn't want a new tenant at the cottage. Not viable.' He stopped, squinting at me to convince himself I was real. 'So you're John Owen's granddaughter?'

'That's right. Do you remember him at all?'

He laughed, less formal now there was a link between us. 'No, that was a long time before I was born. You'd have to ask my dad about that. He's in the house. Come in and see him.'

'Your father?' I knew I sounded shocked, because I was.

123

Shocked to find that my grandparent's nearest neighbour was still alive, still living here. A man who would know the truth. Please let him not be as coy about it as Dilys.

'He'll want to meet you.' Gethin smiled. 'But not all there in the head sometimes. He's old, you know. And a bit deaf. You'll have to shout.'

'I've got a great-aunt just the same.' Oh I'd shout. I'd bellow if I had to.

Gethin accompanied me to the house, past white palings separating the industrial estate from a large neat garden. We strolled up across trim lawns to a farmhouse newly reglazed and guarded by concrete lions, Georgian-style. It could have been part of a modern executive development, although as Matthew's lessons had taught me, the building that lurked somewhere under the primrose rendering could be any age.

As honorary friend of the family I was ushered in through the kitchen door. Not the sort of farmhouse kitchen I'd imagine, with gingham cloth on an old pine table and antique dresser and rocking chair by the big black range. There was a shiny green Aga, but everything else was smart, modern, fitted and immaculately, depressingly clean. What really disturbed me was the smell. Not of disinfectant and air-freshener as the cleanliness suggested, but the warm comforting aroma of cake and bread and bacon and steak and kidney, doused in cabbage and chips. It lingered like a fine patina on the place. It wasn't fair: how could anyone actually cook there, with all the chaos cooking entailed, and still leave the place as spick and span as if it had been fitted yesterday?

Mrs George bustled in from another room, a laundry

where she had been ironing. She was stout and smart with immaculately trimmed short hair, dressed like a managing director, and I felt slovenly in my jeans and trainers.

'Sarah, our new neighbour up at the cottage,' explained Gethin, though it was obvious that Mrs George – Carys – already knew this.

'I saw you'd taken the place back in June. Came to see it a fortnight back, didn't you? Matthew Harries says you've got a big job on your hands there.' There was no stopping her. She had the kettle on and while it boiled she established that I was single but soon to be married and that my young man was a lawyer and that I came from Surrey and I'd studied music and I'd reached grade 8 in piano and I used to be in a band and I was now in advertising and I was to have five bridesmaids and my brother lived in California and my mother lived in Ireland, and that she was one of the Felindre Thomases and she and Gethin had three children and Mared was married and living in Cardiff and Rhonwen was a musician and performed at the Eisteddfod and Dewi was being persuaded to consider university and last year they'd all had a holiday in Turkey, but she was keen on Florida.

I found myself trying to catch breath for her.

Gethin, a perfect foil for his wife, said very little, but he silenced her at last with the one fact she didn't know. 'Sarah is John Owen's granddaughter.'

'Oh.' Carys' shock was almost comical. It told me my grandfather's murder was still a matter of notoriety round here, even sixty years on.

'I'm taking her to see Dad,' said Gethin. 'Have a talk.'

He ushered me on into the house, past a lounge with vast

padded sofas and glass tables, everything plush and new. We went through into a back parlour, and there, preserved like a museum exhibit, was a little corner of the house as it had once been. Cosy and cluttered, an old black fireplace with tiled surround, heavy polished sideboard, chenille tablecloth, a piano and dark framed prints of highland cattle. It was like stepping through a time warp into the past. A wizened old man sat buried in a faded sagging armchair. His chair. One modern touch, an enormous TV, filled one corner, its volume deafening. Gethin turned it down, which finally captured the old man's attention.

'Dad!'

'Eh?'

Gethin spoke in Welsh, explaining carefully. The old man looked at me in bleary wonder and asked something I couldn't understand. I should have realised. My grandparents must have been fluent Welsh speakers, but I don't think my mother picked up more that a couple of random phrases from Dilys, and I knew nothing at all. Welsh roots or no, I was a foreigner here.

'Sorry,' I said to Gethin. 'I don't understand.'

He leaned over the old man and said clearly, '*Saesneg*, Dad. English. This is Sarah. She's John Owen's granddaughter. You remember John Owen? From Cwmderwen?'

'Ah.' The old man struggled, peering up at me with eyes that saw little, not in the present at least. 'Is it Rosie?'

'No.' I tried to speak distinctly, without shouting. 'I'm Ellen's daughter. Siân Ellen Owen?'

'Siân?' His mind was groping into the past. 'Little Siân? *Y baban.*'

'Yes, the baby,' Gethin confirmed, to encourage him. 'Sarah is her daughter.'

'She went to England.'

'Yes! That's right.' A good sign if he could remember a detail like that.

'Sarah wants to know if you remember her *tad-cu*,' said Gethin, helping him along. 'John Owen.'

William munched. 'John Owen. Shot, he was.'

'Yes.' I sat down beside him on a chair Gethin had pulled forward for me. 'You were his neighbour, weren't you? You must have known him well. What was he like?'

He was having difficulty dredging up forgotten things, let alone explaining them in English. He struggled for the words. 'Tall. Tall man, John Owen.'

'Yes?'

'Hard working. Very hard.'

'I expect he had to be, yes.'

'And a singer. Grand singer. Both musical, they were.'

'What, my Nan too?'

'Mrs Owen. Gwen. Played here, she did. The piano. In our house. Used to play the harp when she was young.'

So she was musical too. How strange. It was like catching a ghost in a painting. I thought of her old frail fingers on the hospital blanket and tried to picture them plucking at harp strings. No, I couldn't. 'And the...' I hesitated, desperate. 'The murder, do you remember that?'

'Murder, there was.'

'Can you tell me what happened?'

'Oh. Yes.' Surprisingly definite. He stared into an invisible horizon as the memories sorted themselves out and suddenly it all dropped into place. 'German. It was the

German, that's who it was. Peter Faber. Yes it was Peter Faber. I saw him. I saw him running off, down the road. The boy Jack came to get me, trouble see, but when I got there, John Owen was dead. Nothing I could do. Or her. Mrs Owen. Terrible state she was in. Shock, yes. Nothing to be done. But it was him.' He looked at me, watery eyes searching earnestly. 'Peter Faber. That's who it was, shot him down.'

All this from a man who was having trouble with three-word sentences a moment before. I was overwhelmed, my spine tingling, even though I'd been praying for any sort of detail. A German? Just as Sam had said before I had proved to him conclusively that it couldn't possibly have been a German.

'A German? I didn't know that. Could you tell me...'

I had to stop as Mrs George bustled in with the tea and plates of fruit bread and Welsh cakes.

She wanted to know my plans, when the wedding was to be, if I hoped to have children, how many, if I planned to settle at Cwmderwen, and would I be interested in singing at the Chapel, fortnightly. I tried to chat politely in return, though I just wanted to get back to the old man and his shocking revelations. But when Mrs George finally retreated, William George had fallen asleep in his chair. His head drooped on his chest, a half-eaten Welsh cake in his hand.

Gethin shrugged, patting his father on the shoulder. 'On and off like a light switch. Best leave him be for now.'

I swallowed my raging frustration, and tiptoed from the room.

'I knew he'd remember it,' Gethin said. 'He'll be thinking about it now. Tell you more when you come next.'

'It's something for me to think about too. He did say a German, Peter Faber, didn't he?'

'In the war, was it? It would be the camp then.'

'Camp?'

'Up the river. Prisoners of war. Your Mam, she got over it all, did she?'

'Mum? Oh yes, I don't think she ever knew much about it.' Had she heard this story?

I thanked Gethin for the tea and promised to call again. He saw me out, watching me drive away with the faintest shake of his head.

My brain was whirring as I went back over William George's words. A name, Peter Faber. What about the person or persons unknown? Was that just the official verdict of the inquest because he hadn't been caught and charged yet? And never was, it seemed, or surely Dilys would have mentioned it.

A German, Peter Faber. If there had been a prisoner of war camp, what was he doing, roaming around the Welsh countryside? Surely prison camps were intended to keep prisoners in, not let them out to murder local farmers?

Anyway, this wasn't during the war. It was three years after. We'd got rid of them all by then, hadn't we? And if not, if some Nazi storm trooper had been on the rampage in the countryside, why the hell wasn't he caught? How hard could it have been to track him down?

Every time one door opened before me, another one appeared. There was so much still to learn. William George had seen the German prisoner running off and had found my grandfather dead and my Nan in shock. Dear God, had she witnessed it then? Watched as her man had his brains blown out?

I swallowed bile. I knew what it was like to be a witness. I knew what it meant to stand and watch someone you loved violently killed in front of your eyes.

I'd stood there on the kerb, waving Jemma away, watching her car edge round the traffic cones of roadworks, and I'd watched the vast crushing bulk of the lorry, like a tidal wave, plough into her wing, swinging the little Peugeot round, pushing it, crushing it into the brick wall as casually as swatting a fly. And, somehow divorced from sight, I'd heard the squeal of brakes, the crash, the sickening grinding that seemed to go on and on.

None of it real. Not for a few seconds. Just an incomprehensible jigsaw of meaningless sight and sound. Until my brain clicked into action, saying 'No, no, no, no, no.' I could remember going forward, trying to run, my legs not working because my shins had turned to jelly and my innards to lava. I could remember the smell hitting me. Diesel, metal, something worse. I fantasised afterwards that I saw what was left of Jemma's car, and Jemma in it, but I think that must have been my imagination. An imagination that began working overtime then, and would still slash at me, years later, when I least expected it. All I could genuinely remember was sitting on the kerb, someone's hand pushing my head down between my knees, while I waited for the hallucination to end and someone to tell me it wasn't true.

It must have been like that for Nan. Sam said she never smiled properly. Oh yes, I could relate to that.

I gripped the steering wheel, forcing the memories out of my head. I'd got over it. After Jemma's death they'd made me talk. Called it therapy, making me sane again. Did

Gwen get therapy? Had she been allowed to talk out her misery? Dilys would have listened to her; Dilys must surely have heard the whole story. Why did she have to be so infuriatingly secretive about it? Unless...

An unpleasant thought struck me. Perhaps the murder was such an embarrassment to prim and proper Dilys that Nan wasn't a welcomed refugee in Peterborough after all. She was an awkward problem, shunted off to Leicester at the earliest opportunity, to work in the junior branch of the family firm, provided for but out of sight. Maybe my mother was only kept because, being so young, she would have hindered Nan's removal?

Parking up back at Plas Malgwyn, I kicked myself, ashamed of my doubts. It was rubbish. I knew Dilys. Under that no-nonsense respectability, she was all warm blood. She'd kept my mother out of love. She and Nan would have talked, wept, commiserated together, sharing the secrets that no one else was allowed to hear. But Nan was dead now and no one else was left to grieve over the memories, so why couldn't she speak at last?

Back in my room, I went through my box of Owen trophies again, retrieved mostly from the detritus Dilys had left behind when she'd downsized and moved into her nursing home.

A black bible in Welsh. Not the family bible Jack remembered, which seemed to have vanished without trace. This one had a Sunday school certificate in the front. Gwenllian N. Lewis. There was a page of handwritten verses inside, also in Welsh, so I couldn't make head nor tail of them. A hymn sheet from some service, maybe.

There was a folded strip of newspaper in there too,

serving as a bookmark. I could date it because although one side was a long article in cramped Welsh, the other had part of an exhortation from the Ministry in 1943, 'the most critical year in our history'. It told me I was to be thorough and timely in my cultivations, and plan for winter calvings. I'd thought of framing it as a memento of the war years.

And there was my grandparent's marriage certificate, 1933. John Francis Owen, farmer, of Cwmderwen, to Gwenllian Nesta Lewis of 43 Pendre, Penbryn, at Beulah Chapel, Llanolwen, witnessed by Dilys Lewis and William George. William George. I hadn't even noticed that before.

My Nan's death certificate. Gwenllian Nesta Owen, 75, at Leicester Royal Infirmary. Cause of death, carcinoma of the breast.

A meagre handful of photographs: Gwen on holiday in Scarborough in her last years, already sickening perhaps. Slight and withered and barely smiling, in a flowered frock that hung upon her. My parent's wedding – there was Gwen, just as solemn, but this time in an unforgiving suit and a dour hat.

Gwen and the boys in a park. Early 1950s? Gwen was the same. Weary. Jack, hands in pockets and one sock down, looked like any teenager whose mother had just tried to make him look respectable for the camera.

I never knew Jack except as a name and, once, a jovial voice on a cassette, along with equally jovial wife and daughters. He'd emigrated to Canada twenty years before I was born and an annual Christmas card to my mother with a letter about cousins we'd never met, plus the one experimental recording, was the only contact we had. My mother wouldn't have dreamed of losing touch, but they'd grown up apart so they were never close. At least it meant she hadn't been too upset at his unexpected death last year.

Robert, in the photo, already had the faraway unfocused gaze of a boy who was not all there. Where was he, if not in the park? Lost in another world. Had he been there in the house at the time of the murder? Seeing, hearing everything? Another traumatised soul?

In theory, as he was still alive and in Britain, I could ask him. But questions, even 'How are you?' were a problem for Robert. Of course it made perfect sense that a boy would finish up with psychiatric issues if he'd seen his own father murdered. Not that I could say that in front of Dilys. His sad history was of the many things she never talked about, but I was fairly sure he'd spent some time in a mental hospital after Nan died. He'd probably be there now if care in the community hadn't put paid to it. He lived as a recluse somewhere in Yorkshire, in a battered old caravan. Or he did twenty years ago. We visited him once, when I was young; a smelly whiskery man who spoke in grunts and left my mother tearing her hair and trying not to cry. I knew she'd seen him regularly since, on her own, but Sam and I had been more than happy to forget him.

Yet he was the living evidence of the cruelty of the murder. The tragedy spread further than I had imagined. It was a sickening thought.

I turned back to my pictures. Photos from Cwmderwen. One was the wedding. Gwen was a frail pallid bride, her hair wispy and her wrists fragile. She had played the harp? It seemed far too strenuous for a woman who looked as if the slightest exertion would finish her off.

John. The singer. He stood stiff and formal. I couldn't

imagine him singing the blues at Murphy's, but something more dignified perhaps. I tried to picture his lungs swelling for a recital as I revised my image of home life at Cwmderwen. Musical evenings in the parlour. Maybe that was why the house called to me so clearly? The song goes on?

There were other people in the wedding photo. A grim Presbyterian community, done up in their sombre Sunday best. I recognised Dilys as a very young woman, something of the Queen Mother about her even then, the only one daring to smile at the camera. And the old man with her, shambling in ill-fitting clothes; was he my great-grandfather? Henry Lewis, a shopkeeper, that was all I knew about him.

William George? I searched the faces, trying to match them to the wrinkled old man in the back parlour at Castell Mawr and the blurred newspaper clipping at Plas Malgwyn. That one, possibly, by the groom. Not a film star's face, but comfortable and friendly, if on his dignity.

There was one other photograph, taken in those early years, still oddly posed but far less rigid. John was grasping a rake, like a warrior with a spear, and Gwen was holding a baby, with a young girl clinging to her leg, hiding her face in her mother's apron. They were standing among mint and cabbages, the open back door of Cwmderwen behind them. I had thought about having this photo restored and enlarged, to take pride of place in the new Cwmderwen, but it probably wouldn't be feasible. It was badly worn, flaking at the edges and at some time it had been folded, the crease slicing down through the faces of mother and daughter.

I studied the picture anew. The girl would be Rose. She'd died young, before my mother was born. Dilys had a photo of her in an album I'd been allowed to look through once, years ago. I remembered Rose because my mother had pointed out that I looked just like her, and Dilys had said, 'Stuff and nonsense,' as she would, and then they'd turned the page and were arguing over the length of my mother's skirt in a photo taken at college. No further mention of the long-dead Rose, though she'd made her way onto my family tree. Dilys had never spoken of her since, but William George remembered her. She'd died and I had an idea from things my mother had said, that there had been other lost children, or miscarriages at least. That must have been common enough in the bad old days, but how tragic for Gwen and John.

The crease in the photo had obliterated whatever there was to be seen of young Rosie's face, but John's was clear enough. My grandfather. A fleshless face, high cheekbones, deep-set intense eyes. Compelling rather than handsome. I could feel the strength in him, sense his possessive love for his family, his home and his land. Gethin George said Cwmderwen had been too small to be viable. It must have been a heart-rending struggle, year after year, to hold things together. The rigid iron control was palpable in the photo. He'd have done everything necessary to survive.

12

'It's a birthday present for Rosie.' Dilys places the cake on the kitchen table. 'I know it's late but you know how it's been.'

Gwen knows. Another seizure and their father is gone. Dilys had so much to do, washing, feeding him, nursing him day and night through the last painful month, then the funeral to arrange.

Or perhaps endure rather than arrange. The funeral was taken over by the black-clad elders who had been waiting so long to do Henry Lewis proud, his obsequies the mirror of theirs, still to come. Everything remembered from a past era, his hymns, his bardic crown, his fight for disestablishment, for the language, for the pacifist cause in the Great War. Councillor Beddoe had even written a long and fulsome obituary for the newspaper. Gwen has it carefully folded into her bible, the well-deserved tribute to a life of gentle commitment. Yes, the Penbryn elders had seen to it that Henry Lewis had his honour in death, even if he had received precious little in the last years of his life. A sonorous acclamation from the pulpit for one of their own.

And Gwen was still one of theirs, remembered first and foremost as Henry Lewis' daughter. 'Ah, you must be Gwen Lewis' husband,' the elders had said, shaking John's hand.

John had not liked that. Stiff and formal in his chapel best, he had said nothing, but Gwen could sense his resentment simmering. Waiting to boil over in the privacy of Cwmderwen.

Gwen must not think about that. Here is Dilys, the one who bore all, with a resolutely cheerful smile, and Gwen must smile too. The sisters can no more speak of their grief in private than they could at the funeral. How could they contemplate giving voice to the impermissible thoughts that their father's death have aroused? Could his loving daughter Dilys ever dare express her relief that she is now free to escape from Penbryn and marry? It can never be said, although Gwen understands it well enough.

And Gwen's thoughts, as ever, must be silenced. No outlet for the secret anguish that she was not there for him at the end, to hold his hand as the shadows closed in. Swallow the tears. Never dare repeat her helpless sobs when she had first heard the news. Sobs that John chose to take as a reprimand for not permitting her father to come to them.

John does not like to be reprimanded in his own house. Keep silent, woman.

Move on, look to the future – Dilys' future at least. She has come to say goodbye and of course she has brought a gift. What sister would not? The cake is tempting. Dare Gwen keep it? She glances at the clock. It will be nearly two hours before John returns from Penbryn. More than enough time for her hungry brats to devour every scrap of this unbelievable luxury that John, if he saw it, would hurl from the house. 'Rosie will love it,' she says.

'Now what better sight is there than a house full of greedy children?' says Dilys. She has laid out cups, filled the big black kettle in readiness. 'Mind you, it must be a relief for you to have two at school before the fourth arrives, what with Robert being so fretful.' She eyes her sister's thickening waist. Barely five months gone but Gwen is so thin it shows clearly enough. 'How is it going with you?'

'I'm doing well enough,' says Gwen, feeling the wistfulness in Dilys' words. Three children and a fourth on the way while Dilys has had to wait, single and barren, and quite bereft since Harry went to Peterborough. A damper on the relief Dilys felt when poor Harry, so eager to join up when war was declared, was rejected on medical grounds because of his eyes. He has found a way to make his contribution. His cousin's workshop in Peterborough is thriving. It has expanded with the years. Once tools and agricultural machinery, now it is something to do with the war, and business is booming. Harry has gone to do his bit against Hitler, running the Peterborough works while Alfred sets up a second factory in Leicester. Harry has been promised a partnership. His future is golden.

Now Dilys can join him. They can marry and she can have the children she so obviously longs for. Gwen could warn her that it is not all laughter, not when they are teething, or ailing, or sulking, or hungry and there is nothing to spare, and no money for shoes and she is scraping the butter ever thinner on the bread. But it will never be like that for Dilys. After her dutiful trials of the last years she is destined for a life of prosperous fulfilment.

'I'm glad you managed to visit before you leave for England. The children would have been so sorry to miss you.'

'As if I'd leave without seeing them!' says Dilys. 'The very idea!'

But she will leave without seeing John. They do not get on. John thinks Dilys is a silly flighty girl, Dilys who had taken Gwen's place nursing their father all these years. She lacks respect for him. There is a dangerous and impermissible gleam of criticism in her eye. John will not tolerate it.

Dilys thinks John is a bad-tempered miser. Not that she says it to Gwen's face, knowing that Gwen will do her duty and defend him. Gwen is a dutiful wife and Dilys is a dutiful sister, saying nothing to cause Gwen distress.

'Let's walk up to meet them,' says Dilys. She wants to be out of the gloomy house, up into the sunlight. Gwen buttons up her coat, fetches Robert from the back yard. He is a plaintive child, always ailing and whimpering. He does not want to go with her but she takes his fist firmly.

'A handful, that one,' says Dilys as the sisters begin to tramp up the muddy lane, Robert dragging and whining as they go.

'He's sickly again.' There is nothing she can do about it. She cannot call out Dr. Connell. They cannot afford such extravagance and John has no insurance, so she has dosed the child up with every remedy she and her neighbours know, but nothing seems to boost him into the sturdy good health of his brother Jack. The perpetual whining is a constant irritation to John, chaffing on raw nerves. It is hard for Robert at only three to learn to keep silent when his father is near by, but he is beginning to understand.

At the top of the lane they wait by the churn stand, opposite the milestone, for Rosie and Jack to come home from the village school. A mile's hike, nothing to young legs. Soon they will come skipping round the corner.

But not today. No sound of children hidden by the high banks, just the rumble of a truck chugging along the road. An open mud-spattered farm truck slowing to round the corner. The driver waves. Two men in the back help Rosie and Jack jump down, laughing and joking, their voices loud and alien – and evidently shocking to Dilys. She greets the children with protective fondness as they rush to meet her, but her eyes are fixed suspiciously on the truck as it rolls on towards the gates of Castell Mawr.

'Gwen, are those prisoners?'

'From the camp.' She has grown accustomed to the sight of Italian prisoners of war working on the farms around, replacing the local men who have gone into the forces. So many young men gone, even Master Philip from the big house, and there are farmers who'd struggle without the Italians. Where is the danger? Certainly none from the Castell Mawr contingent. Mrs George deals with them as effectively as any general.

'They are Giuseppe and Paolo,' explains Rosie, seizing her aunt's arm as they set off down the lane. 'Giuseppe comes from Milan and he has a wife and five children and three aunts and five uncles and thirty cousins!'

'Goodness,' says Dilys. Foreigners, breeding like rabbits.

'And Paolo comes from a little village in the south and he's homesick for the sun and he says it never stops raining here.'

'Nothing wrong with our weather!' says Dilys warmly. She looks at Gwen. 'Don't know that I'd feel safe in my bed with enemy prisoners roaming around.'

'They're not enemies any more,' says Jack. 'Giuseppe says they're on our side now.'

'Hm.' Dilys is not appeased by Italy's about-turn. She is

not disposed to forgive anyone responsible for the war that has taken her Harry away.

Gwen smiles. The politics mean nothing to her, countries invading others' lands. The only land that matters is Cwmderwen, that tiny kingdom ruled by John, and defended to the hilt against rebellion from within and invasion from without. 'They are safe enough. There's no harm in them.'

Dilys will not be easily convinced, but the children have her now, eager with news and jokes, chattering just as eager children talk with an affectionate aunt.

Gwen picks up Robert as he begins to complain, and carries him down in their footsteps. She realises with a pang how seldom she hears Rosie and Jack chattering eagerly. Perhaps they do at school, among friends, but here they have learned to keep the peace their father demands.

Jack can cope. A self-sufficient boy who accepts the rules and knows how to make things easiest for himself. He shrugs off any unpleasantness, turns away to sunnier subjects. Most days, home from school, he would be straight off, into the barns or the fields, occupying himself safely out of sight.

If only Rosie had the same ability to be happy at all costs. But some perversity in her resists the easy path. The magic she once wove over her father has faded with every inch added to her slight frame, smothered by that germ of impudence inside her, a dangerous hint of rebellion that goads her father's ire. It is difficult for a growing girl, Gwen knows, but the more the woman wells up within the child, the more John is determined to assert his authority and master her.

Sometimes the girl can bite back with the snarl of an incipient shrew and how can Gwen complain when John wields his belt? A man is expected to keep order in his own house and everyone approves of strong discipline.

So Rosie has learned to curb her tongue – growing sullen, deliberately uncommunicative, aggressive. No sweet singing any more.

Gwen knows the cause of the change, but there is nothing she can do except pray that Rosie will come to understand. A man who has struggled through such hard times must be forgiven for his impatience with his children's noise and his wife's clumsiness. He must be forgiven or life cannot go on.

But there are no sulks from Rosie today. She is chattering with Dilys nineteen to the dozen. A normal happy girl. And back in the house the children whoop and swoop on the cake like a cackle of starved chickens. A small modest cake, skilfully made with a thimbleful of sugar and the little extras Dilys has quietly gleaned from her farming friends, but it is a feast to them. The kitchen is strangely full of shrieks and laughter.

Gwen smiles to hear it as she reaches up to hang her coat on its hook. A thoughtless move. The long sleeves of her frock ride up, revealing her thin arms, bruised and scarred and scorched with hot iron. Hastily, she pulls the sleeves back over her wrists, but Dilys has seen.

White-faced, she has seen.

Anger stirs in Gwen. Dilys has no right to see or to judge. What can she know?

But Dilys does not judge, not openly. She meets Gwen's eyes, she looks away, chiding the children for spilling crumbs. They are wooing her, these children suddenly hungry for attention and praise. Jack has produced a catapult he made himself, and volunteers to demonstrate his skill with it. Rosie brings her schoolbook for her aunt to approve. Even Robert wants her to see his knee, a bruise mending scabbily.

'Oh, brave boy,' Dilys extols, and turns for relief to Rosie's exercise book. 'Good work, Rosie. Ten out of ten for your sums! And here's the story of Gelert. My favourite.'

Dilys entertains the company with her dramatic reading of Rosie's careful retelling, in studious English, of the tale of the prince's faithful hound, falsely condemned. Rosie had written with vigour, but the story ceases short of its customary ending. Gelert is slain, in unsparing detail, but there is no mention of Llewellyn's remorse. Perhaps Rosie had run out of time.

'Poor Gelert,' says Dilys, smiling at the girl. 'And he hadn't done anything wrong after all, had he?'

'No,' agrees Rosie.

'It's very sad that Llewellyn killed him.'

'Yes,' Rosie explains, 'but Llewellyn was allowed to kill him because he was the master in the house.'

Dilys' eyes flit to Gwen's, but they are both drawn back in an instant to Robert as the boy, so passive and expressionless a moment before, comes to life.

'Master here!' He thumps the table leg with a blow that must surely bruise his little hand. 'Master here!' Thump. 'Master here!' Thump.

'That's enough, Robert!' Gwen stoops hastily to pick him up, seizing his fist before he can thump again. 'Hush now, boy. Hush.'

'Master here!' he shouts, thumping her cheek with his other hand.

Again the sisters' eyes meet. Dilys confronts the beseeching blankness of abject panic in Gwen's, and she looks hastily away, for something, anything, to break the spell.

'Come on children, into the garden. I want photographs of you all to take with me to Peterborough. You don't want me to forget you, do you?'

The bustle and organisation is a diversion, allowing the sisters to recover their composure, bite back things that must not on any account be said. Dilys might not understand John's pride, but she understands Gwen's.

And Gwen, in the kitchen, hugs herself in silent grief.

The children are anxious for Dilys to stay, but wishes are not enough. She has to go. She has a bus to catch, back to Penbryn and her rooms over the shop, bags to pack, affairs to settle, before the journey east, to join her Harry. She babbles to fill the silence.

The bus is due soon and the children, not wanting to lose their aunt, insist on accompanying her up to the road. Gwen scoffs and chides, but the despair of loss has gripped her too. Peterborough, what is it, where is it? A big city far away. As impossibly distant and unreal as the prisoner Paolo's sunlit village in another land beyond the seas. And dangerous. Cities aren't safe in this war, everyone says so. Dilys could be killed! Even if she lives they will be separated just as completely.

Against her better judgement, knowing that time is pressing, Gwen goes with them up the lane.

'You'll come to Peterborough, won't you?' asks Dilys, as they wait by the milestone, the unofficial bus stop. 'Just for a visit.'

'We'll have to see,' says Gwen, as if making a note to arrange it in a month or two, but they both know she will never be allowed.

A desire to act takes hold of Dilys. 'Try, if you can,' she says, seizing her sister's arm. Then she sees Gwen wince and she lets go to talk to Rosie, the happy smiling girl.

The bus is late. Gwen cannot stay, but neither can she go. When will she see Dilys again? Five, ten minutes, quarter of an hour delayed. The children do not notice, oblivious to timetables. Dilys is irritated and yet thankful for the delayed parting. For Gwen the delay looms over her like a black cloud. Her flesh crawls with anxiety.

The bus comes at last, the children cry, Gwen and Dilys hug, stiffly, formally, an unnatural intimacy. As the bus pulls away, Gwen gives one last wave, takes a deep breath, then bustles the children back down the lane. John will be home at any moment and he will want his dinner on the table. No excuse for lateness.

Fumbling in her haste to get water on, bread cut, Gwen knows she is doomed. She will be late and he will be incensed by this petty violation of his authority. He is such a proud man, he has so little, life has been so hard, but at least he is master in his own house. Doesn't she owe him that?

What Gwen cannot understand is why life must still be so hard for John. She does not know their financial situation. John deals with the accounts and will not have her interfere. No matter that she kept the books for her

145

father, money is not a woman's business. Hasn't she enough to do, without prying into his affairs? He doles out her weekly mite for housekeeping and that must suffice.

Ration books are no burden here. They cannot notice the lack of what they have never had. Well, he works hard enough for every penny and she must not complain.

But she knows, even imprisoned in this gloomy dell, without wireless or newspapers, that the world has changed utterly. The war in its fourth interminable year has had its impact even here. Ships lost out there in the bay and Pembroke Dock hit, such a fire the sky glowed red above Cwmderwen's trees. Swansea had it bad, they say. She recalls Swansea from her youth, a monstrous city, dirty, noisy, busy, teeming with more life than she had thought possible. She tries to picture it now in ruins but she cannot. It defeats her imagination.

No bombs here, but still the outside world has stormed their forgotten little backwater. Not just the Paolos and Giuseppes shipped in from faraway battles to work the land. Evacuees from Liverpool have brought loud voices and strange ways into their quiet midst. Land has been taken over by the ministry, converted into an airfield, bringing more foreigners, Americans, Czechs, Poles.

Gwen may see little, but she hears about it on her brief excursions to Llanolwen. She gleans too how good the war has been for farmers, though they are cagey about saying it out loud. They are valued at last, encouraged to produce, to improve, to go from strength to strength. William George is thriving, full of energy, urging John to make the most of what is offered.

It's just proper business sense, says William. Why must

John resist as if his very soul were at stake, spurning every improvement, every fertiliser, every mechanisation as too costly, too risky, too untried, not fitting for the likes of him? All aid is charity that he must fling back in the faces of the givers. He will not have labour foisted upon him: Italian, English, Welsh, they are all foreigners to him, all aliens to be repelled. This is the war he fights, the war to keep Cwmderwen undefiled. All words of advice and encouragement, every dictate from the ministry is an insult, interfering with his own authority on his own land.

His independence has passed beyond the point of perversity. He is no longer proud despite being poor. It is as if it has become essential to his pride to be poor. To be better off, even by a little, is to diminish the honour of his struggle. He must be seen to suffer, and Gwen must scrimp and save and make do and mend and turn and improvise in order to preserve his dignity.

The worst of it is that his pride no longer earns respect. Others begin to shake their heads in contempt at his folly. That she could bear, but he is putting their tenancy at risk. Mr Allen, the estate manager, has no time for a tenant who so resolutely drags his feet. Even the Colonel, paternally tolerant of the little family in the cwm, has begun to grow impatient. He is full of energy these days, wanting to match his son in the army, all for helping with the war effort and he wants to see his tenants pulling their weight, and prospering into the bargain.

John's determination to labour on with poor land and underweight stock wins respect only from himself. And from Gwen, because she is duty bound to honour and obey, rising with him in the cold dark hours to milk, struggling

147

beside him with awkward calvings, turning the hay with him, tending the chickens, feeding the pig, and then ensuring that his home, poor though it is, is immaculately clean and tidy, clothes washed and ironed, his children disciplined and respectful and food prepared with clockwork precision.

She is guiltily aware that the respect of the community, which John once monopolised, is now directed at her. Her neighbours do not complain about her endless labour, which is, after all, no more than her duty, but her duty is fulfilled and they esteem her for it. William George calls often, occupying John in grudging talk, leaving Gwen the necessary peace to sort herself. Mrs George or one of her daughters visit now and again, seemingly to poke their noses in and comment, but in reality to lend a hand with the endless chores. The Colonel once even doffed his cap to Gwen at the chapel steps.

Perhaps, deep down, John is aware of this. It might account for his increasing resentment, his ready temper ever more frequently snapping. He must feel that she is goading him sometimes by her determination to cope and make good. It takes so little to rouse his anger.

Like a late tea. The water is not yet boiling.

Gwen hears his footsteps in the yard, as the children fall silent. Her heart freezes in a deadened despair. There is no escape.

He stands in the door, looking from the kettle, to her, to the table, bread not yet buttered. The bleakness in his eyes kindles into the so well-known glow of dissatisfaction. No greeting. 'Will you not learn, woman?'

She has learned. She has learned that there is nothing

she can do to avoid his wrath or break from the inevitable cycle: Robert's whimpering, Jack's retreat to the cowsheds, Rosie's silent watching eyes filling with an unnatural hatred for John, as her mother pleads wordlessly for her to be silent.

13

Marcus was off to Birmingham, to give a star turn at a conference. Not as bad as three months in New York but it still left me at a loose end for the greater part of a week. He had done his best to tie me up while he was away: I was to see Caroline and discuss the caterers. That, he promised, would leave us free for the following weekend in Paris. The hotel was booked.

I wanted Paris, I appreciated the plan, and I did fully intend to do my duty and trek into darkest Essex, but in the end I couldn't face it. Maya, my understudy at work, was desperate for more responsibility and kept reminding me that I had leave owing, so I packed for a long weekend at Cwmderwen. It was too good an opportunity to waste.

Marcus was quite enthused now with the prospect of a renovated cottage that we could sell at a vast profit when we moved to America, which was seeming more certain by the day. He was happy to leave the sweaty complications of restoration to the builders, waiting for the slightest slip on their part to open the way for a lawsuit so that he could recoup some of the money my impulsive silliness had frittered away, but I was still finding the building work fascinating. I wanted to be involved and I'd have offered myself as a hod carrier if anyone would have had me. Things were happening at last at Cwmderwen. A good roof of Caernarfon slate was back on, in readiness for the onslaught of serious autumn rain. The stripping of the hideous external rendering was going on piecemeal and work continued within.

Cwmderwen had never witnessed an electric light bulb before. Or even gas lamps. Or running water. It was 1948 when the place was abandoned but anyone would think it had been the Middle Ages. My restoration was going to bring it into the twenty-first century without it ever being touched by the twentieth.

I was itching to get in and start on the decorating and furnishing, to see the place not as a shell of stone and timber, but as a living, breathing home again. An Owen home. I had to bring back the music. Not a harp maybe, which was way beyond me, nor my electric guitar, which wasn't quite the right thing, but a piano undoubtedly.

What had happened to the piano that must have stood there once? I was almost sure there wasn't one in Leicester. Maybe Nan had left it with her sister and it was the one I'd thumped on happily as a two year old. Dilys had always been so keen for me to learn, always wanting me to sing. Because I, unlike my mother, had inherited their musical flair. That was why she'd sat me at that piano every time I'd walked through her door. Of course. Not that she'd ever explained it, not Dilys. Okay, I would have a piano here again, learn a few Welsh hymns and conjure up John and Gwen weaving blissful harmony here on a cosy winter's evening.

That was a long way off still. All I could really do for now was finalise the positioning of the lights and power points.

I couldn't even do anything useful with the yard while it was a builder's store. My hanging baskets and terracotta pots of herbs and scented shrubs would have to wait. There was the garden behind the house, of course, but that was altogether more daunting. Matthew had promised to remove the remains of a rickety privy, but for the moment I suspected his men were using it. The surrounding garden wall had crumbled and tumbled; within lay an expanse of nettles, hogweed and dog roses, overhung by the engulfing woods as they tumbled down the steep valley side.

There were traces of a cinder path between what must once have been vegetable beds, leading down to the old apple tree. Could I save that? Its crop was minimal as there was more moss than leaf, but the blossom had been very pretty in the spring.

As for the rest, I was not a gardener. I'd once tried some bedding plants in a window box and watched them die. Would it be unthinkable to install decking, a gazebo and a solar-powered water feature? The weekend visitor in me said fine. The guardian angel of the Owen legacy whispered no. My family farmed here, tilled the earth. My grandfather's blood had fed this soil. I could feel his ghost commanding me to take up my plough. Or at least a trowel. The land must bring forth again. I tried to imagine myself tending neat rows of beans, leeks and cabbages, and I winced.

But there was another sort of digging I could do while I was there, and it wouldn't involve straining any muscles.

It was a sunny evening when I arrived. The next morning it poured, but I'd packed a very uncool cagoule so I headed for Llanolwen, Cwmderwen's nearest village. If you could call it a village; one long street of grey stone terraces, touched up with an oddly depressing turquoise on the woodwork. No obvious centre or purpose, perched on a windswept plateau, straddling a neglected B road. I'd driven through it before and the only thing I noticed then was a one-pump petrol station on the far side. This time I was going to be more thorough.

Poor Llanolwen. Whenever its time had been, that time had gone. Half the houses looked abandoned, not even demoted to holiday cottages. Life was seeping away. There was no vital spark left, and the place was slowly, quietly dying.

What makes a village? It did have a church, St. Llawddog's, squat and towerless, surrounded by a graveyard, but the door was padlocked, and a notice in the porch explained that Holy Communion was held four times a year. There was a chapel too, on the edge of the village nearest Cwmderwen, dour and stolid, grey rendering and heavy chocolate woodwork. The gable was inscribed 'Beulah.' Services once a fortnight, Carys had said, though it looked about as dead as the locked church.

Llanolwen still had a pub, of course; the Mason's Arms, in unprepossessing pebbledash, but the windows were dark, and there was no offer of pub grub. There was a post office, a drab grey house with a post box and a picture window littered with fly-blown posters. I went in and found it served as the village shop – sweets and magazines and a few basic groceries. Very basic groceries. Tinned ham, toilet rolls, marmite and a tray of limp onions. Surely, if any rural post office were doomed to closure, this was it.

The bell that rang when I opened the door summoned the postmistress from her tea in the back room. She looked pleased to see a strange face.

'Hi, I've just moved into Cwmderwen.'

'Oh yes?' The name didn't mean anything to her.

'The old cottage down by Castell Mawr.' I decided to keep quiet about my relationship with John Owen for now.

'Ah. The place Matthew Harries is working, is it?'

'That's it. Do you know anything about it? I've been trying to find out something of its history.'

But the postmistress had only lived in Llanolwen for ten years. No wonder she hadn't heard of Cwmderwen. It wouldn't be back on the postal rounds for a few months yet. 'Been empty for longer than I remember, that place. You could try asking in the Mason's,' she suggested.

It took courage, but I was determined. Who could tell? The interior of the Mason's Arms might be more promising than its exterior.

It wasn't. It was cold and damp, with lino on the floor and clammy vinyl upholstery. It had a dartboard and a jar of pickled eggs on the counter. There was the stale smell of flat beer and, despite the obligatory legal notice, tobacco. It probably only survived because the ancient balding landlord was determined to die here. He and his two solitary customers, elderly peas in a pod, were not New Men. I felt like a tart in a monastery, walking in alone to be confronted by three beady pairs of disbelieving eyes.

The landlord watched with deep suspicion as I approached. He began to wipe the bar compulsively, waiting for the terrible moment when I'd ask for a Babycham or sweet sherry.

I was tempted to order a pint, but the smell of vinegar warned me off, so I just smiled and I could swear he flinched.

'Hi, I'm new in the area, and I'm trying to do a bit of research on someone who used to live in the house I've just bought. John Owen?'

'Ah,' said one of the customers, kicking the bar stool with a muddy Wellington. 'John Owen. He was shot.'

'Yes, that's right,' I said. 'Do you remember anything about it?'

They nodded at each other and began to argue over the case, in Welsh, the only bit of which I understood was 'John Owen'.

One of them paused to inform me, 'That was over at Y Garn, that was.'

'At Y Garn? Are you sure? Not at Cwmderwen? Near Castell Mawr?'

The second drinker's face lit up with triumph. I think they'd been having a bet and the Y Garn champion had just lost. He grunted his disgust and took his beer glass off to a table.

His companion chortled and thumped the bar. 'Cwmderwen, that was it. Didn't I say?'

'But you don't know anything else about it?'

'Oooh, that was a long time ago.' He could just say no, but that would be too easy.

'You should ask William George about that,' the bartender advised, brightening at this opportunity to direct me out of the door. 'Over at Castell Mawr. He'd know all about it.'

'Thanks. I'll try him. Do you know anything about an old prisoner of war camp?'

'Up the river, that was.' The one who'd lost his bet refused to return to the bar, but he was definite about this one. 'The caravans.'

'That's it,' confirmed the barman. 'Morris' place. Over at Felindre. Holiday caravans and all. Used to be a camp there once for the Italians.'

So much for the collective wisdom of Llanolwen. Couldn't tell Italians from Germans. 'Thanks,' I said, and sauntered out, to their tangible relief.

I drove on past a scattering of cottages and an old school, boarded up and awaiting conversion. Beyond that, there was nothing except high hedgerows and the occasional farm gateway until I came to Felindre.

A village that knew how to survive. One long street again but it wasn't just a place to pass through. People stopped to visit the sparse ruins of a modest castle and the riverside picnic meadow, so there was a gift shop as well as a Spar grocers, a pottery, a riding centre, two pubs (one of them definitely promising) and a functioning school, complete with Portacabin.

Beyond the village, in a bend of the tree-shaded river, there was a holiday site with camping pitches, a dozen static caravans and a shower block that might, just conceivably, be an old Nissan hut. I hovered by the entrance to Morris' holiday caravans, but there was no point in stopping. Unless there were secret swastikas carved in the shower cubicles, I could see at a glance that all traces of the past had been obliterated. But a camp had existed.

The one-time home of the man who had murdered my grandfather. Peter Faber.

A name that was still as mysterious as his escape from justice. How do you track down a prisoner of war from 1948? I'd tried Googling him with a predictable lack of success, but at least I'd seen now the place where he'd been held.

I joined an A road that took me back along the river valley to Penbryn, the local town. Town in comparison with Llanolwen, though barely a village by Surrey standards. There were banks and a couple of building societies, a small supermarket, two chemists, several pubs and a long defunct cattle market. But this was holiday country, so there were gift stalls too, a health food shop and an ambitious bistro.

I pulled on my raincoat and explored, trying to picture how this town would have looked when Gwen did her regular shopping here. Forget the Goth outfitter's, with the skull in the window, and the art gallery, two doors along, offering Costa coffee, but I bet the shop between had been here then, probably with exactly the same display: high-necked blouses in flowered maroon, sensible navy shoes and hand-knitted children's bonnets. A sign above the door, in faded copperplate gilding, read *Prynne's Haberdashery*. There was a notice on the door stating firmly that it shut at lunchtimes and on Wednesday afternoons.

There were others like it, the residue of a forgotten world, ironmongers and cobblers and chapels, lurking amongst the new. Everything in this area wore the past just a scratch below the surface. Which was good, because what I was after was an insight into that past. In record form.

I found the library, over the market hall. It opened three days a week, and fortunately this was one of them. Climbing the wide stairs, I was greeted by the smell of ancient bibliography: musty books, well-thumbed grubby

157

card indexes, mouldering leather, wood polish. The interior didn't match at all. Metal shelves, with a selection of crime thrillers, one bay of reference books, two computers with internet access and a shelf of local newspapers and agricultural magazines.

I approached the librarian. 'Do you keep old newspapers here?' I explained my quest for old crimes, family history, archives, anything that would help.

The librarian gazed round her limited collection, and suggested I try the National Library at Aberystwyth.

So Aberystwyth it would be then.

The National Library of Wales, high on a hill. Vaguely Third Reich architecture with a sweeping view of uniform grey. In the sunshine it would probably be quite a different thing, but today it poured. I looked down on the murky cubist patterns of a grey town, the swelling curves of grey hills and the fine gradations of grey where grey sea met grey sky, all gently blurred together by unrelenting grey rain.

Safely within, steaming gently in a vaulted galleried hall, I was reminded uncomfortably of school. Instead of my stern headmistress, Miss Winstanley, a white marble patriarch sat gazing down on me. He looked benign enough, but was keeping order. Everyone was very quiet, immersed in a hush of earnest study, apart from the occasional jingle of Microsoft Windows as someone opened up a laptop. There was a communal intake of disapproving breath.

I ordered the relevant volume of old *Penbryn Gazettes* and while I waited, I looked around to see what else the library has to offer. Old parish registers, indexes of births, marriages and deaths, census records. Everything was here, so maybe I could trace the Owens of Cwmderwen back to Tudor times. What if they had been gentry after all? Celtic princes?

My volume of the *Penbryn Gazette* arrived. Good God. The volume, I swear, was bigger than me and weighed a ton. At least I knew the date I wanted. 27th April, 1948. The volume began with January 1947.

The idea, of course, was to turn quickly to the correct edition, but that was easier said than done with three years of brittle broadsheet, stuffed with bizarre reading. I found myself hooked, every few pages, deciphering the cramped microscopic print.

The countryside around Penbryn was a dizzying mêlée of village fêtes and W.I. lectures. Village eisteddfods were frequent. One prize was won by a German prisoner of war. I'd have thought that would warrant an editorial, but no. The county took it in its stride and moved on to more important matters. The local council was seething with plans for the arrival of electricity and water supplies, and the news-hounds were kept busy reporting on stampeding bulls, drowned sheep and truly gruesome accidents involving crushing mills. The accounts of funerals were an eye-opener, listing every mourner, and printing out pompous obituaries. The arrival of a new minister required a whole page of gushing testimonials. There was evidence of organised crime; the Penbryn district was suffering from an epidemic of rabbit-snare thefts.

An hour of searching and I was still only at January 1948. Alert! A grey squirrel had been sighted in the county! Five otters had been killed by a visiting hunt, with much rejoicing and festivities. Barbarians.

MURDERED BY SHOTGUN
Tragedy at Llanolwen

The headline jolted me. It was hard to miss when I did stumble across it, after all the parochial cosiness, even though it was exactly what I'd been looking for. Front page, ousting the council's debate on a new playing field.

Police, summoned by Major Philip Rhys-Parker of Plas Malgwyn, arrived at Cwmderwen, Llanolwen shortly after 8 o'clock on Tuesday and found Mr John Owen dead on the doorstep of his house, with a gunshot wound to the head. It is understood that Mr Owen had been involved in an altercation with a German prisoner, Peter Faber, interned at Felindre camp. The victim's son had run for help to a neighbour, Mr William George, of Castell Mawr, Llanolwen, who hastened to Cwmderwen to find Mr Owen already dead. His own shotgun was found in the yard where he died and it is believed that it was wrested from him during a violent struggle and used against him. His long-standing concerns about Faber, who had been seconded to work on an adjoining farm, are well attested in the district. Police investigation continues and it is understood that Faber failed to report to the camp, which has since been closed. He is being sought as a matter of urgency for questioning about the murder and the War Office has been informed. Colonel Rhys-Parker of Plas Malgwyn, who was summoned to the scene by Mr George, has offered a £50 reward for information leading to Faber's detention.

Mr Owen was a respected member of the community and a greatly valued baritone in the choir of Beulah Chapel, Llanolwen. Sincere sympathy is extended to his widow and children in their hour of sorrow.

That was it. Two columns. No 'continued on pages 2,3,4 and 7'. I couldn't understand how they'd let it pass without comment. Where was a full statement from the police? Interviews with the neighbours? I was hoping for a full account from William George. Surely they would have talked to him. How could there be so little detail?

In fact, reading through it a second time, I realised there was no detail at all. I searched further, expecting to find follow-up reports, but the *Penbryn Gazette* was a weekly and the murder was soon stale news. In the next edition, the playing field saga was back in pride of place, and there was just a brief note to say that police were still hunting Peter Faber in connection with the Llanolwen murder and it was believed he might have left the country.

I eventually found the report of the coroner's court. More detail this time, with some quotes.

Deceased's widow, Mrs G. N. Owen, confirmed that her husband had recently quarrelled violently with Faber, a German prisoner from Felindre camp. Her husband objected to Faber trespassing on his property. In response to the coroner's inquiry as to whether she had witnessed the murder, Mrs Owen became distressed and was excused from the courtroom. Dr. P. H. Connell, who certified the death of Mr Owen, explained that the widow was still suffering mentally following the incident.

Giving evidence, Mr W. George of Castell Mawr, neighbour of deceased, confirmed that Mrs Owen had been absent at the time of the murder, fetching the cows for milking and had reached the scene only a few moments before witness, who found her in deep shock and unable to speak. Witness confirmed that deceased had earlier been involved in a dispute with Faber, concerning access. On Tuesday 27th April, witness had been summoned by deceased's son, John, fearful of trouble at Cwmderwen. Witness hastened to the scene and saw Peter Faber running away down the road. On arrival at Cwmderwen, witness realised that John Owen was dead and he immediately informed Colonel Rhys-Parker whose son, Major Philip Rhys-Parker, contacted the police.

Giving evidence, Colonel Rhys-Parker stated that deceased was a man of good standing in the community. He also confirmed that the German prisoner, Faber, had caused problems and antagonism in the area, and had been banned from the local farm where he had formerly worked.

Detective Sergeant J. G. Price confirmed that the police were still seeking Faber in connection with the murder of Mr John Owen, and with his abscondment from Felindre camp, but there had been no further sighting of him, despite a reward being offered for information.

The coroner returned a verdict of unlawful killing by person or persons unknown, and exhorted the police to renew their efforts to find Faber.

That was it. I was relieved that poor Gwen's emotional collapse had been acknowledged, but surely there must be more on the murder and the pursuit of the murderer. Not a word more. I searched forward all the way into 1949, convinced that the local rag would be as obsessed with the case as I was, but the silence was thunderous. Looking again at other crime reports, I began to grasp why. The reporters were there to attend court hearings and take notes. Nothing more. My grandfather's murder was unique in being reported before any court had sat but because no later arrest was ever made, the coroner's verdict was as far as they went. I think they would probably not be employed on one of today's tabloids.

Deeply disillusioned, I arranged for the two articles to be copied, and decided to concentrate on other sources while I was there.

More disappointment. I searched through Llanolwen's parish register, but not a trace of Jacobean yeoman Owens or sturdy Georgian Owen farmers. There wasn't even a Victorian or Edwardian Owen on the list. Obviously not church people.

The census returns were a bit more rewarding, once my eyes were accustomed to illegible scrawl on microfilm and microfiche. It was there, the Owen family saga of a generation or two, and it was all a bit discouraging. The Owens weren't yeomen of the parish from time immemorial after all. John's grandfather, Thomas, was the first one to settle at Cwmderwen. He was there by 1881, occupation farmer. He was born apparently in Whitechurch, in 1836. And there was the family at Carregwen cottage in Whitechurch in the 1841 census, little Thomas and brother John and sisters Phoebe and Frances and their parents Mary and Owen Thomas. Owen *Thomas*? Even the family name had got lost. Owen Thomas' occupation was agricultural labourer. That was it. No link to princes or even gentry, just ditch diggers and muck spreaders. Only the parents were still at Whitechurch in 1851, so I guessed Thomas began his adult life like his father as a farm labourer, moving from parish to parish.

I really had wanted to find that Cwmderwen was an intrinsic part of my ancestral history, not a transient tenancy, but I wasn't going to find any ancient Owen ghosts lurking in the rafters. Disappointing, but then I decided to look at it differently. Just because my ancestors were not fossilised in ancient property records, that didn't stop them having a deep claim on the land. This land of ancient hills and woods and meadows. Peasant blood that had endured, nameless, down the centuries. Determined survival without the prop of social dignity. More admirable really than titles and silver spoons.

However humble the smallholding, it was some achievement for the family to hold on to Cwmderwen from 1880 to 1948. Tenacity, that was what it was. I was going to show it: I would dig and delve and nag until the full story was laid bare.

14

'Kurt doesn't want to go back to Germany,' Jack is explaining. 'He wants to go back to Canada but they may not let him.'

'If he's a prisoner, why doesn't he run away?' asks Rosie. There is a sullen note in her voice, as if she is searching for a quarrel.

'That would just make trouble,' says Jack reasonably, refusing to respond to his sister's mood.

'If I were a prisoner, I'd run away.'

'You'd get caught and they'd shoot you.'

'I don't care!'

'That's stupid.'

'No it isn't! Staying in prison is stupid.'

'That's enough!' Gwen intervenes. Foreign prisoners of war loose in rural Wales might be a worthy subject for debate, but their father will be in at any moment and God help them if he hears raised voices and finds them quarrelling.

'I'd run away,' mutters Rosie under her breath.

'Hush, girl, and lay the table. Jack, you get Robert's hands washed now.'

They obey. She can hear Jack in the scullery telling

Robert about Kurt and Canada and tractors. At least there will not be an argument from Robert. He is probably not listening to a word of it.

Rosie glowers as she lays the table. When she is done, she stands and stares out of the window.

Quarrels, mutterings, chat, all are hushed as John comes in. The dinner is ready, what there is of it. Potatoes lifted from the garden, scraps of bacon from the pig, weak tea. Rationing may be tightening its post-war grip on the rest of the country, but here there is nothing to tighten. John won't have his wife spending a penny that is not essential and accounted for.

He is silent today. She tries to gauge his mood without provoking him with questions. Is he just thoughtful? If the children are willing to appease him, all might be quiet.

The boys dutifully appease. Jack eats, bolting his food and holds his breath until he can escape to Castell Mawr, to the tractors and engines, and the men that laugh and joke and slap him on the shoulder. He knows better than to do or say anything that will cause trouble. Robert, crouched over his plate like a nervous animal, has his eyes fixed on his father as if he draws from him the will to live.

Robert is a problem child. Sometimes Gwen suspects he hardly registers her existence. His brother and sister scarcely enter his consciousness and his teacher sees him as an imbecile. But of his father he is always aware. Always watchful, fearful and fascinated in equal measure. Robert shows the abject obedience that should surely appease John's wrathful spirit. But it does not. It irks John as if it mocks him, egging him on to greater demands.

'Sit up, boy!'

Robert promptly sits up straighter.

John cannot complain. Yet the tension grows. Gwen, hopelessly, knows what it is. Rosie. Always a needle to scratch his resentment into life. The silly girl! Why does she have to do it? Why must she provoke him?

Gwen, with an inward sigh, acknowledges that Rosie is doing nothing. Nothing that can be reprimanded. She sits silent, eats without fuss, and yet... There is something in her, some flame of resistance, some hostility in her lowered eyes that is a perpetual challenge to him. Gwen feels the tension rising in him, groping for a reason to rebuke and chastise. He can find none.

'More tea.'

The pot needs more water. Gwen makes to rise, but John's hand pushes her back down. 'Let the girl do it.'

Without a word, Rosie rises, takes the pot, fills it from the big black kettle, stirs the leaves, tops up her father's cup, sets the pot back on the table, returns to her chair. Nothing to criticise. No slovenliness, no sullenness, no irritating clatter or slopping or jostling.

John glowers. 'Sit up, boy, I say!'

Already erect, Robert instantly thrusts his shoulders back. The potato on his spoon slips off, misses the plate, splatters on the floor.

It is enough. John rises, seizes the quivering boy's plate and, with tight-lipped deliberation, tips its contents onto the floor. He plucks Robert by the collar and drops him next to the mess. 'You behave like a beast, you can feed like a beast. Eat it!'

Robert meekly crouches and begins to eat.

It is too much. 'No John.' Gwen must speak. 'You cannot...'

The blow comes out of nowhere, although she knows it is inevitable. 'Am I master here?'

'You are,' she says, feeling her lips swell, hot and cold flushing through her bruised cheek.

He is rigid. The more his anger is fed, the more it grows, till the house cannot contain him.

'Clean it up, woman. I'll not stay in this pigsty.'

He is gone. The moment the door closes behind him, Gwen is up, lifting Robert from the floor, though the boy resists, whimpering. Jack has leapt up, as if fetters have sprung from his wrists. Rosie quietly fetches a cloth, wets it from the kettle, dabs at the blood on her mother's lip.

Gwen brushes it away. Better use the cloth to clear up the mess on the floor. There must be no trace of it when John returned. 'I'm all right, girl.'

'I hate him!' Rosie spoke softly but her voice trembles.

'Don't you speak ill of your father!' Gwen avoids their eyes. 'He has troubles. You must not provoke him.'

There is silence.

'Can I go?' asks Jack at last, inching towards the door.

'Yes, yes. Run along. Robert, be still. I'll give you some bread and butter. Rosie, help me with the dishes.'

The peace of abject surrender descends.

The blow has left its mark. A cut lip and Gwen's half-shut eye, as she sees in the cracked mirror on the chest of drawers next day, is darkening, purple and angry. Not uncommon these days. Once John made sure not to leave visible marks, but long sleeves and high necks are no longer enough. Now he does not care, lashing out at her and the world without restraint. It is how she lost the last baby, though Gwen took care to pass it off as another unfortunate act of God and Mrs George, pursed lips, chose to accept it as such. There will be no more babies, Gwen knows. Thank God.

She can bear the bruises. No one need see, she is almost always out of sight, hidden down here. More than enough to do here on the farm without wandering off to seek company and making a spectacle of herself.

But something is wrong. It is late. School is long ended and where are the children? Robert is by the range, quietly rocking on his stool. She hadn't sent him today, with his sniffle and watering eyes. Bad enough the teacher calling him slow, without accusing him of harbouring disease and God knows what. But the others went; she packed them off up the lane as usual in the morning.

No surprise that Jack is absent and no prize for guessing where he is. Castell Mawr. He goes there most days, returning home only when he must. But Rosie always comes straight back. Where is the girl?

Only half an hour late. Nothing to worry about. Gone to a friend, perhaps. Does Rosie have friends? Not close ones any more. She has become a loner.

Mocking her own foolishness, Gwen urges Robert out and heads up the lane. She dare not leave him in the house alone, fire burning, knives around; he is so accident-prone. They will meet the girl halfway down.

But there is no sign of Rosie. Up at the road, nothing stirs. No traffic, no sound of distant footsteps.

Her stomach clenched, Gwen ventures on, round the corner whose high banks conceal the road to Llanolwen.

Nothing. The road is empty as far as the next bend. Then

169

a motor car appears. She does not recognise it and it does not slow down, but the two men inside glance at her with prurient interest as they drive past. She feels her bruised eye shining like a beacon.

A panic begins to grip her. Be still, woman, and think. 'Hush, Robert, don't whine.' Perhaps Rosie came by the footpath across the fields. It has been dry, the stream is low, the little ford easily passable. No reason not to use the footpath, down from the chapel, except that the children avoid it because it leads across their fields, and taking it might bring them into contact with their father. Still, Rosie is feeling so perverse, she might have chosen to tempt fate.

Gwen tugs the reluctant Robert back down their lane. Rosie will be waiting, in the house no doubt, wondering what the panic is about.

No Rosie.

'I want a drink.'

'Peace, Robert. You can have a drink when Rosie comes home.'

'I want a drink.' Does he hear? Does he care? She leads him out, through the gate, into the empty pasture, over the stile, another corner of a small pasture, the cows regarding her with hopeful interest, awaiting orders, but she ignores them. No Rosie.

The path leads on, up, into the woods. Woods busy with birds, but no child. No footsteps on the deep damp leaf mould. Robert is letting out a non-stop whine like a kettle by the time they reach the road again, by the graveyard, the doors of the Chapel facing them. The first houses of the village are in sight, but no dawdling child. Should she go on? Her eye is throbbing, she must look a sight. All she wants to do is hide in her kitchen for a couple of days, but she cannot rest, not until the girl is found.

'I want a drink,' says Robert, mucus ballooning from his nose.

'Be quiet!'

Castell Mawr. It has to be. Rosie must have gone there with Jack. Gwen leads Robert down through the woods, back to their yard in case. But still no Rosie. She gives the boy a cup of water to silence him and takes the path again, down over the pasture this time, through the next little field, and clambering over the fence that has filled a gap in the hedge separating their land from Castell Mawr. No footpath from here, but the Georges will not mind. It is quicker than the road in dry weather – and no curious eyes to see her.

Please God, let the girl be at Castell Mawr with Jack.

It makes no sense, she knows. Rosie has no desire to talk engines with the men, like her brother, and she does not care for Mrs George's sharp tongue and prying demands. Rosie is not adult enough to see through the facade of Mrs George's scolding, so she avoids her.

Where else could she be? Gwen chides herself. The girl is an hour or so late back from school. What of it? Children roam, they dawdle and explore. If only Rosie had not spoken with such fiery feeling yesterday of running away. She cannot run away. It is unthinkable.

Nearly there. A hedgerow separates them from the last field and the barns of Castell Mawr yard. A man is sitting by the gate, or rather, crouching in the shadows of the blackthorn, unseen from the yard. For a moment, Gwen takes him for an animal, till she sees his hands gripping his knees, the knuckles white. A small dark wasted man. Twenty? Fifty? Impossible to say. A wave of fear clutches her, though reason tells her there is no need. It is he who is afraid. He trembles like a man in a fever, sweat gleaming on his grey brow, his eyes blank and staring. What is it he sees? Not her, as she draws close, shielding Robert behind her. Only when the gate squeaks on its hinges does he start into life and look at her, the horror on his haggard face fading as he wakes to reality. He clambers to his feet.

She does not know him. One of the Germans, still lodged at the camp, waiting for repatriation. The Italians are long gone. Giuseppe returned to his wife and children and thirty cousins in Milano, and Paolo, so homesick for the sun, married Rachel Williams and has settled over at rain-swept Trefach. The Germans have taken their places on the land, while the local lads are still away. Two of them at Castell Mawr, and she has met one, just a farm lad, nothing of the fearsome Hun about him. But this one is different. Troubling.

'I am going to Castell Mawr,' she declares.

He focuses, his eyes glazing over, but he does not reply. Perhaps he speaks no Welsh. No matter, he makes no attempt to hinder her. As she walks on, prodding Robert before her, the man's trembling hands are groping for a cigarette.

A tractor stands in the field, a big blond man peering into its mechanical depths, an oily rag in his hand. This is the one she knows. Kurt. Kurt is a mechanic from Dusseldorf. Kurt worked with tanks. Kurt spent years as a prisoner in Canada before being shipped back here. Kurt is terrified of the U-boats. Kurt has a soft spot for a

Canadian farmer's daughter. Kurt can do anything with engines. Kurt says, Kurt thinks, Kurt does... Jack seldom talks of anything else, these days. Gwen should be grateful that he has found a... She must not say father-figure. Jack has a father. He has found a big brother maybe.

But it is not Jack who concerns her now. 'Is Rosie here?' she asks, as Kurt sees her and turned round.

'Your little girl? I have not seen her.' His broad smile turns to concern but it is misplaced. 'Your eye is bad. You are hurt?'

'It is nothing,' she mumbles. 'Milking. I was kicked by a cow.'

'But that is bad! You must...'

'Never mind!' Foreigners will pry. 'I must find Rosie.'

'Rosie disbident slut!' says Robert, suddenly beginning to gesticulate wildly. 'Disbident slut, disbident slut.'

'Robert, stop it!' Gwen reaches for him but she cannot stop his wild thrashing. Kurt shakes his head, standing by helplessly. He does not understand the boy's gestures, but Gwen recognises them all too well; the violent flexing and snapping of a strap.

'Disbident slut, disbident slut!'

'Stop it!' In desperation, Gwen has him by the shoulders, shaking him into silence, then hugging him in guilt. 'Hush now, boy.' She looks up at Kurt, determined to sound calm though she longs to cry. 'I am looking for my girl.'

'Jack will know, perhaps. He is fetching tools.' Kurt wipes his greasy fingers. 'Come, little man.' He takes Robert's hand and the boy trots by him, instantly obedient.

Gratefully, Gwen follows him to the yard. Ted Absalom is there, William's head man, a good honest Welshman, thank God. She is beginning to feel the land is not theirs any more, so many foreign faces and strange tongues.

'Afternoon, Mrs Owen.' Ted looks, then politely averts his eye. 'You looking for that boy of yours? Jack!'

Jack emerges from a shed, runs towards them with a skip. Because Kurt is here? She does not see such eagerness at home.

'Do you know where...' She hesitates to speak the name for fear of setting Robert off again. 'Where your sister is?' she asks desperately.

'Uh?' Jack is surprised. 'No.'

'Didn't you walk with her from school?'

'She went on ahead.' The boy is defensive. 'She's been in a funny mood.'

Mrs George has appeared at the kitchen door and bustled forward to intervene. 'What's the matter? Gwen, is it?' She sees Gwen's black eye and then pretends she has not. 'What's wrong?'

'My daughter hasn't come home. I thought she might be here.'

'No, no, I haven't seen her.' Mrs George instantly sums up the situation. 'But mind you, I'll give her a piece of my mind when I do, worrying her mother sick like that.'

'She's just a little late,' says Gwen.

'Hm. No sense of time, that girl. So what are you great lumps all doing, standing around gawping? Do you think that will solve anything? Stir yourselves and go and find the girl.'

Ted is ready to organise. 'Where have you looked, Mrs Owen? Along the road? Kurt, you know the girl. Take the bicycle and try along to the village.' His eye settles on the strange dark prisoner who has shambled into the yard, still nursing his cigarette. 'Lazy bloody Krauts,' swears Ted, under his breath. 'You, Fritz, shift yourself for once.' He spits into the dust. 'I'd get more response from a deaf dog.'

Gwen does not like the idea of the stranger looking for her girl. 'Is he safe?' she asks.

Ted snorts. 'Safe from breaking his back with hard work, sure enough.'

'He had a bad war,' says Kurt, who had a very good war, farm work and cards and concerts in Canada.

'Leave him be,' says Mrs George. She eyes the stranger with impatient disapproval, as duty requires, but there is an unexpected note of sympathy in her voice. 'No need to turn the whole farm upside down for that little madam.'

'Oh no, please,' interrupts Gwen. 'I am sorry—'

'Nonsense,' says Mrs George, and lets out a snort, close to a laugh, as the bear-like Kurt mounts the old bicycle Ted has produced. They watch as he wobbles out into the lane, but he does not have to face the steep climb up to the road. William's motor car has turned in at the gate and is trundling down the lane. He meets Kurt, stops to talk to him, then rolls on and Kurt wheels round to follow.

In the yard, William, usually slow and deliberate, has his window down and is calling out, before he even has the brake on.

'Looking for this young lady?'

And from the car emerges sullen Rosie, dragging her feet.

'Found her halfway to Penbryn,' says William, cheerfully. 'Couldn't have her walking with those clouds brewing.'

'Walking to Penbryn indeed!' snorts Mrs George, swelling in magisterial dignity. 'And what sort of trick is that to be playing on your poor mother?'

Rosie says nothing, looks away, letting their neighbour's scolding and her brother's jeers wash over her.

'It's no matter, she's back now,' says Gwen, quelling her own urge to snap at the girl. The tight knot of frantic anxiety in her stomach unravels with relief and then clenches again as she faces new worries. 'We must get home.'

'All right, you lot. Back to work,' growls Ted, shooing the men away.

'Wait!' Mrs George stops Gwen in her tracks. 'I suppose you'll not have had time to prepare John's supper, thanks to madam here.' She will not permit them to stir until she has fetched a basket from the kitchen, a pot of stew from the Castell Mawr cauldron of plenty. Gwen's attempts to refuse are brushed aside. 'Enough of that. You won't want to keep your man waiting, just because of Missy. Here, you.' She imperiously summons the dark little German prisoner, who is fumbling for another cigarette. 'Put that poison away and carry this over to Cwmderwen for Mrs Owen. Look sharp about it.'

He might not understand Welsh, but he understands her gestures, and comes forward to take the basket.

'There's no need,' says Gwen. This stranger is the last person she wants accompanying her, but Mrs George waves her off, with irresistible command. Jack has already raced on, out across the fields, and Rosie, jaw set, is marching after him. With a sigh Gwen tugs Robert along, thankfully silent now, and the German falls in beside her.

Safely away from the yard, Gwen turns to him. 'There is no need to come further, Mr Fritz.'

'Please, I am Peter,' he says in clumsy Welsh.

'Oh. Well, I can take it from here.'

'I am carrying it.'

To the fence, maybe. She does not want him coming onto Cwmderwen land. That will be tempting a thunderbolt. Does she not have enough troubles to cope with? Her anxiety and anger demand an outlet. 'Rosie! Come here.'

The girl's shoulders tense, then she flings herself round to face her mother. 'What?'

'Don't you speak to me like that. What were you thinking of, halfway to Penbryn?'

Rosie shrugs.

'You realise Mr Absalom was sending men out to look for you?'

'I didn't ask them to.'

'Mind your tongue, child. I'll not have you going off like that, without telling me. Do you want people to think you are running away?'

'I was!'

'Don't be silly, girl! I've never heard such nonsense.'

A response bursts out of her. 'Why don't *you* run away?'

'What are you talking about, child? Why should I run away? This is my home.'

Rosie's face distorts as if she cannot decide whether to laugh or cry.

Peter meets Gwen's eyes and she senses a confused empathy. Why? What does he know about it all? A Hun, a foreign soldier, he had a bad war, Kurt says. God knows what evil things he has done, she has heard such things. God knows what horrors he has witnessed. Let him tend to his own miseries instead of standing there, judging her daughter, looking at her black eye. It is insulting.

'My daughter is at a difficult age,' she finds herself saying. 'Wilful. She doesn't understand that life cannot always be the way we want it. We have to bend.'

'We bend, we break. She hurts.'

He has no right to pass comments on her daughter. What does he know about hurting? She turns away so that she does not have to meet the hell reflected in his eyes as they reach the fence separating them from Cwmderwen land.

'Please go back now.'

'Frau George—'

'My husband will not want you on our land. Thank you.' She takes the basket firmly from him. 'Robert, get over now.' She has to let Peter help the boy over, but she refuses his assistance. He remains watching, as she walks on, the basket swinging, its savoury contents sloshing wildly. Well, no matter, John will never allow them to eat it. John will have her throw it on the midden, no charity here. And God help them all if he learns what Rosie did today.

Furious, she watches the girl running on ahead. *Why don't you run away?* What a question to ask her mother! She is not a prisoner, like the haunted Peter. She is a respectable woman. What would people say? And where would she run to?

15

There was something symbolic about the way the sky cleared as I drove back from Aberystwyth. Clouds of obscurity were lifting from the mystery of my grandfather's death.

Back in my room at Plas Malgwyn, I stowed away my notes and photocopies from the National Library, and read through the newspaper articles again. How would it have been covered today? *Judge Raps Bill in Fiend Hunt Fiasco.* How would they have dealt with poor Nan? Even the *Sun* couldn't have painted her as a nubile Blonde Bombshell, but there would have been plenty of shock-horror to work on. Give them half an hour and no one in a thirty mile radius would have been able to sleep peacefully in their beds.

The gentlemanly restraint of the *Gazette* had allowed Penbryn to linger in sedate inactivity. No way could I imagine urban riots and mass hysteria here on a late Saturday afternoon, as the shops cleared and I headed for the police station.

Vintage George V, ponderous weight without grace, Penbryn Police Station hadn't changed since its opening, apart from the posters advising me to watch for car thieves, and the faded picture of a teenager, gone missing sometime in the late 1990s.

The reception area was about six feet square, with a heavy sliding hatch opening onto an inner sanctum in which buzzed furious police activity: the soft chink of a cup.

My breathing was enough to get attention. A police woman – I couldn't believe how young she was – came to the hatch, and looked out at me with a bright strategic smile. I couldn't believe how short she was. I suspected she needed a box to stand on.

'Can I help you?'

'Please. I'm interested in an old case. A murder. Any chance you could let me see any details?'

She licked her lips, not sure how to handle this one, being outside her usual lost dogs and Saturday drunks. 'We're not dealing with any murders.'

'Oh no.' I smiled, feeling quite motherly. 'This is an old case. From 1948.'

'Here?' There was a look of panic. At the thought of murder or of 1948? 'I wouldn't know anything about that.'

'Probably not, but do the police keep records of old cases? All I've got so far are the details in the *Penbryn Gazette*.'

'Oh.' She was lost, but sensed salvation at hand, because her attention was now divided between me and a rattling door behind her.

'The *Gazette's* got half the story,' I continued, convinced I could wear her down. 'But I need more and I'm sure the police must keep records, especially on old murders. John Owen in Llanolwen. 1948. April 27th.' I was being very helpful. 'Anything at all would be useful.'

'*Gazette*, you say?' asked the other half of the Penbryn constabulary, emerging from the back, a burly middle-aged man, almost avuncular except for the shaven head. 'Old cases, is it? 1948, you say?'

'Yes, a murder. Never solved, apparently.'

He guffawed. I think that was the right word for it. Or snorted. 'And you think you could do better now?'

'I doubt it.' I was politely humble. 'But you know how these old mysteries grow as time passes. I really want to get at the real facts.'

'Well it will make a good story, I suppose. No luck with old files here, love.' He was won over by my humility, leaning on the counter with a cheery smile. 'But I'll tell you where you could try.' He paused, wagged a finger for patience, and pushed himself back out of my sight. 'Just check, now.'

The girl smiled nervously, still sublimely lost. I heard a phone dialling, the hm-dm-di-dum of the policeman as he waited for a response, then, 'Bob boy! How are things with you? You don't say...'

It wasn't polite to listen in on other people's phone calls. I could picture Dilys smacking my ear and tutting, so I tried to engage the WPC in pleasant conversation.

'Nice day.'

'Yes.' She seemed cautious about committing herself. Maybe she arrived in the pouring rain and she hadn't looked out since. It was hard to see anything out of the dimpled glass of the station's high windows.

'So you don't keep old files here?'

'No.'

For all my efforts, I caught fleeting snatches of the phone

conversation. '*Gazette*. Wants a story. Old cases. Well, I thought of you. Wouldn't hurt now, would it? Every little helps. Just what I was thinking.'

His head came back into view, craned at a wild angle, receiver clutched to his breast. 'What was your name again?'

'Sarah Peterson.'

'Sarah Peterson' he repeated, disappearing once more. There was some manly chuckling and vague rugby talk before I heard the receiver replaced and he wheeled back to the hatch. 'Bob Roberts, he's your man.'

'He is?'

'Chief Inspector Roberts from Hampshire Constabulary as was. Retired back here, after his wife died. Writing up his memoirs. Some big cases, he's been on. Nice juicy stories there.'

'Yes, but it was a case round here, in Llanolwen, I want to know about, not really Hampshire.'

'But he started in the force here at Penbryn, see. 1947. Just a constable then of course, but he'll remember the case. Always remember your first murder.'

'Yes, I suppose you would.'

'You want to talk with him? Tomorrow afternoon? He's free then.'

'Yes!' This had to be good news. A policeman who had been on the case was sure to have more concrete memories than the old codgers in the Mason's Arms. And if he was writing his memoirs, he'd be more on the ball than William George. 'That's great. Just what I wanted. Have you got his address?'

The officer did, having already written it on a post-it note that I stuck on my purse, trying to look businesslike and vaguely official. I thought, if he'd picked up the idea that I was a reporter from the *Penbryn Gazette*, I didn't have to correct him.

Chief Inspector Bob Robert lived in a nice modern bungalow perched on a heather-clad bank above a main road, with a lofty view of distant glistening caravans.

'Charming,' I said brightly.

'Functional,' corrected Bob, as he had invited me to call him. 'I keep pretty fit, but I can't be doing with quaint at my age.'

He was definitely not another William George. He was spry and natty, still in his seventies, with the slightly desperate activity of a widower determined to prove he could manage after fifty years of marriage.

'Vera didn't fancy Wales. Too many hills for her legs. That's why we settled in Peacehaven. Couldn't stand the place myself. Like living in a morgue, but there you are. When she passed on, I thought, why not come home? The hills don't worry her now.' He patted the urn that sat, neatly dusted, on the mantelpiece, with a touch of macabre humour.

Now that I was there, I wasn't sure how to play this. I'd half-expected either senile deafness or grudging superciliousness, but Bob was at least as eager as me to get down to the nitty-gritty. His desk in the corner of the spacious and brightly lit, if unimaginative, living room, was piled high with neatly stacked notes and files.

'Now then, it's old cases you want to hear about. That's what Rees said. Is that right? As it happens, I've been working on one only this morning. 1962. Sorting out my notes. Something to do in my retirement. How about a cup of tea?'

'Thanks, I've just had – tea. With lunch.' A mainly liquid lunch, but I shouldn't tell a policeman, even a retired one, that I'd driven there from a pub. I took out the digital recorder I'd found at an electronics shop in Penbryn's back streets. It looked vaguely professional and I wanted a precise record this time of everything that was said. I didn't want to risk any details slipping by unnoticed. 'Actually, it's one case in particular that I'm interested in. They said you started as a police constable in Penbryn?'

'Ah, now that really is going back to pre-history. But of course, you're after local interest, aren't you, rather than my Sherlock Holmes triumphs.'

'Do you mind?' I asked meekly.

'Not at all.' He was working on the assumption that any publicity was good publicity for when his magnum opus was published. 'So, when was it? April '47 to June '53. That was when I moved on to Cardiff. Cardiff not local enough, I suppose?'

I decided it was best to come straight to the point. 'April 1948. John Owen, murdered at Cwmderwen, in Llanolwen.'

'Ah.' He was sitting, legs splayed apart on his exceptionally ugly sofa, hands clasped between his knees and shoulders ready for the scrum, but this prompted a shrug of disappointment and he shifted back. 'Not one of our great triumphs, that.'

'The murderer was never caught, is that right?'

'Never apprehended. Yes, you could say that. Planning to crucify us, are you?'

'No, no. I'm just trying to fit the pieces together. Provincial journalism wasn't exactly in-depth in those days.'

'Not like now, you mean?' His eyes twinkled. 'Yes, things were rather more gentlemanly then, in these parts at least.'

'To me, you know, it seems unbelievable that a murder could happen round here.'

'They can happen anywhere,' said Bob dryly. 'It's in all of us if you look hard enough. All you need is the right switch. The impulse and the wrong moment. The last straw.'

'All right. But still, how can there be a murder and everyone seems to know exactly who did it—'

'Oh yes!' said Bob firmly. 'We knew who did it all right.'

'Well of course, there were practically eye-witnesses.'

'Yes, that was a real eye-opener for me. Lesson number one in detection. Don't try pitting yourself against the eye-witnesses of a village community. Amazing what the eye can remember if it wants to.' He was sitting back now, arms folded, enjoying the chance to play with me.

'You think maybe William George wasn't really sure about seeing the German running off?'

'William George.' He ran the name over in his mind. He could remember the case well enough perhaps, but not all the names. 'That was the neighbour, wasn't it? Ho ho, yes, never a moment of doubt there. Absolute as the Bible, that one. Most of them were. Neighbours, the village Bobby, the squire. Never a doubt among the lot of them. Like interviewing a brick wall.'

'They didn't like the police?'

'Oh, couldn't fault them. Polite as they come. And absolutely certain. Word perfect.' He smiled. 'We weren't stupid, even then, we could see what had happened but there's only so much you can do.'

'Do you think they knew where the German prisoner was?'

'I'm pretty sure a lot of them had a shrewd idea, but none of them were going to enlighten us.' His capacious memory consulted his mental file and as the images slotted into place, he prepared to expand. 'Didn't take much snooping around, however cagey they all were, for us to realise that this was a very nasty piece of work we were dealing with. And I mean a really vicious brute. Yes, I can't say I'm surprised it happened. I don't think anyone was surprised.' He shook his head, lost in suddenly vivid recall. 'The surprise really was that it hadn't happened before.'

'I can't believe this.' I'd sat up, too horrified to remember I was supposed to be a detached journalist. 'I'm sorry, but are you telling me everyone knew what he was like and no one did anything?'

He shrugged. 'They should have done, shouldn't they? It was just the way these communities work. They didn't want to acknowledge what he was.'

'But for God's sake, he was a Nazi POW, he was a sadist, he murdered my grandfather and everyone knew it was coming and no one lifted a finger to stop it!' I hadn't meant to play it this way, but I found I was more upset and indignant than I could contain.

I expected agreement. Or disagreement, if Bob chose to be perverse. What I was not expecting was the sudden stillness. No response whatsoever. He sat motionless for a moment, watching me without stirring a muscle, only his eyes alive, boring into me. Shit. I realised that I'd given the game away.

'You are a reporter from the *Gazette*?' he asked quietly.

'No. I found the story in the *Gazette*, that's all. I never said a word about being a reporter.' It was true, I'd never claimed anything. Buying a recorder didn't count.

He closed his eyes for a moment, then raised them to the ceiling. 'So John Owen was your grandfather?'

'Yes. And I just want to know who killed him.'

'Are you sure that's what you want to know?'

'Well, no, all right, I already know it was the German, but why and how could it happen? That's what I really want to know. How did an innocent man come to be slaughtered and my Nan come to be widowed and my mother lose her father and the family lose their farm, all because some P.O.W. was left to roam loose around the countryside killing people? Why did nobody try to stop him and turn him in? He was never caught and no one seems to care!'

He was rubbing his chin thoughtfully. 'How about that tea?'

I wanted to shout that I wasn't interested in bloody tea, but I realised I was parched. Anyway, Bob had come alive, determined to be active. He sprang up and padded off into the kitchen, to concentrate on the brew. I paced round the lounge, surreptitiously glancing at the papers on his desk, just in case some snippet from the Owen murder was lying around. But there was nothing earlier than 1959.

In the kitchen I could see Bob carefully, methodically washing and wiping two mugs, setting them on a tray, taking the lid off the teapot to stir the brew. And all the while he was gazing out of the window, deep in thought. Then he tapped the pot decisively with the spoon, nodded his head and came back to the living room with the laden tray.

'Shall I be mother?' He busied himself with the milk and the teapot, watching me all the while, presumably to check that I wasn't about to collapse in hysterics. But I was calm now and waiting.

'You have to understand,' he explained carefully, 'that it was a very difficult situation. You mustn't suppose we were all completely callous and indifferent just because the murderer was never caught. We did try. But we had to take local feelings into account. There were a lot of local lads, recently back from service overseas, and the camp at Felindre was still full of Germans, most of them working on the farms. Some captured in the war, some of them rounded up after, politically suspect, you know. We couldn't pack them off home until we were sure they weren't set on founding the Fourth Reich. And not all of them were keen on going home in the end. Some settled hereabouts, into the community. With the murder, well, we could have made a big thing about it being a POW, raised the hue and cry, ransacked the camp and stripped out every billet in search of him, but I'm pretty sure we still wouldn't have caught him and we would only have succeeded in inflaming local feeling. We didn't want anti-German riots on our hands.'

'Why are you so sure you wouldn't have caught him?'

'Because we were fairly certain he'd skipped the country the same day. Maybe some of his fellow prisoners helped, wanted to get rid of him, stop him fouling the nest. They were waiting to be repatriated, remember, expecting to go home to their families any moment, just wanting to keep their noses clean. They didn't want a murderer on their hands. Whatever their motives – and for all I know, they didn't help, maybe he just hitched a lift – we had a pretty reliable sighting of him boarding a ship down at Milford Haven on the day of the murder. But by then, he was God knows where. Couldn't go searching the whole of Germany for him. You have to appreciate what it was like in the years after the war. Complete chaos out there. He probably escaped to the East. I seem to recall that's where he came from.'

'I see.'

'So you see, we went through the motions of searching, but really we knew it would be useless and we needed to keep community relations sweet. People had suffered enough.'

'Of course.'

He smiled, full of understanding.

'Why did he do it?'

'Like I said, he was a vicious sort. No longer wanted at Castell Mawr, probably held your grandfather responsible. The children were...' His jaw set. 'A man who can terrorise children...Well, he might have done anything, mightn't he? Can't blame your grandfather for complaining about him. So he got a bad reputation, probably blamed your grandfather for that too. And then—'

'Yes, I see. But I don't get it. If everyone knew he was so vile, why were the locals stonewalling you? They were, weren't they?'

'I, er, wouldn't say that.' He slowly stirred his tea, once, twice, three times, round and round, controlled and calculating. He tapped the drips off the spoon and laid it carefully on the tray. Then he looked up, focussing on my right earring. 'Lynch-mobs, that's what we were worried about. I'm not saying anything for certain, you understand, but I reckon they were planning on something, finding this chap and hanging him from a lamp post. And as we were convinced they wouldn't find him, we were afraid they might pick on some other poor sod instead – pardon my French.'

'But they didn't.'

'No. Fortunately. It just died down, and people moved on.'

'I see.'

He sighed deeply. 'Must have been very traumatic for your family. Your mother, you said? I don't remember a girl. Apart from the one who died of course.'

'Rose. You remember her?'

'No, no. We were just told that there was a daughter who'd died. There was talk, you know...' Stirring again. 'So many tragedies in one family. Very ... distressing.'

'It must have been ghastly for all of them. Just as well my mother was only a baby.'

He frowned. 'Baby?' There was something ominous in his tone, but he was just struggling to remember. 'I don't recall a baby. Two boys. Terrible thing for children, to have their... to lose their father that way.' He looked me full in the face, honest and guileless. 'You have to understand, of course, this was my first big case. I was just a snotty nosed young constable, doing the leg work for the adults. Made a big impression on me, of course, and naturally I was pretty upset that it didn't all come to a nice neat conclusion, but I was never really in on the heart of the investigation.'

'No, of course not.'

'Sorry I'm not able to bury any ghosts for you. I'd love to know what became of the man, after all these years, but I don't suppose we ever will. Who knows, maybe he finished up in some Soviet Gulag. Some sort of justice after all, eh?'

It was a sombre note on which to end, but there really wasn't any more to say. We finished our tea and shook hands and he waved me away as I edged my Fiat out of his drive. He was very good-humoured, fatherly almost, which was generous, I thought, considering he'd realised I wasn't going to give him the publicity he was expecting for his memoirs.

His story was frustratingly incomplete, but totally convincing. The German prisoner terrorised the neighbourhood, frightened and maybe hurt the children, which would go a long way to explaining poor Uncle Robert. So my grandfather complained about him, demanded his dismissal and Faber was sent packing, only to escape from the camp and take his revenge.

It just made me sadder than ever to think of my grandfather being gunned down, just for being a good parent.

Back in my room I listened to my recording again.

'This was a very nasty piece of work we were dealing with... we were pretty certain he had skipped the country the same day... maybe he finished up in some Soviet Gulag.'

It all made such convincing sense. A gifted storyteller was Chief Inspector Roberts.

I would have loved to know, though, what the story would have been if he'd remained convinced I was just a reporter for the *Penbryn Gazette*.

16

Pallid streaks bar the sky above the mounting trees to the east and up there on the road there will already be enough light to tint the world with grey highlights, but even now in summer it will be hours before any light creeps down into this dell. The yard is pitch dark.

Hanging the oil lamp in its place on a rusty nail, Gwen starts on the milking, forcing her cold aching fingers to work. The cows low gently, softly, as if unwilling to disturb the silence that she brings to the task. Perhaps they are thankful she is alone.

She is alone.

Gwen takes a deep breath and shakes her head to clear away thoughts of despair. It is probably just the gloom of another damp dawn and she has neither time nor energy for such nonsense. Daylight will sweep it all away.

But such thoughts have been growing and the day will come, she feels with a shudder, when even the brightest sun will not dispel them. For weeks now she has been conscious that doom, indistinct and unspecified but somehow long awaited, has arrived, unfolding its black wings on the narrow valley. John has always been a driven man, but now he is driving himself to destruction.

Something is terribly wrong, and he can no longer cope, some failure within has unhinged him. Every morning he rises at four, as he has always done, to work and slave and struggle until darkness descends. But now he does not work. He moves to do a job and his will seeps away. He stands inert in the fields, staring, at the clouds, the rain, the soil, the dripping woods, or maybe at none of them. Just staring. Sometimes he takes a billhook, but the hedges remain untended, roses, elder, honeysuckle daring to assert themselves. Sometimes he takes his shotgun, but the crows caw in mockery and the vermin slink by unmolested. The cows stop their lethargic grazing to watch, waiting warily for commands that don't come. Jess runs with him, or round him, puzzled, a dog growing deranged for lack of employment, waiting for his word, but John barely seems to notice her.

In former times he would have been beside her here in the milking shed, directing her with a grunt and a gesture. Today, she is not even sure where he is. He has gone, striding off into the dark, shoulders hunched, as if to put space between himself and his family before the sun comes up.

Four cows to milk. Gwen straightens as she moves to the next, rubbing her aching joints. There were days when she had to drag the heavy-laden churns up to the top of the lane, stumbling along with Jack's aid, for John will not have the cart used. Maybe Jack has been talking too much at Castell Mawr, but things have mercifully changed, at least on that front. Not a word said about it, but William sends Peter down every morning to collect the churns for her. Time was when no one would have presumed to trespass onto John's land, doing John's work, but now the German comes with impunity. John is not around to notice.

It is something understood, not mentioned. Gwen is grateful, not so much that William is a kind neighbour, but that he is discreet, holding his tongue, keeping the disgrace of Cwmderwen quiet.

She feels a stirring of resolution as she finishes the last milking. Time to turn the cows out. Time to face the world. The cold air of early dawn washes over her, rinsing through her, forcing her lungs to breathe, her body and spirit to strive instinctively for life, smothering the dark depression of night. Another day, work to do, no time for gloom.

A shadow shuffles across the yard. Peter. He looks at her and smiles.

She smiles back. Two sad smiles, she knows. Two wistful attempts to keep the shadows at bay. 'You are early.'

He shrugs.

'They are ready. Here, I will help you.' A year of Mrs George's home cooking has added a pound or two to his insubstantial frame but he still looks as if a whisper of wind could blow him away.

He is stronger than he looks. He can manage the churns, but still, as usual, she walks with him, the farmer's wife and the last of the German prisoners. They have gone from the neighbouring farms now, working closer to the camp or repatriated or, in Kurt's case, settled in Canada, to Jack's abiding regret. Peter seems in no hurry to go. Why should he, with a warm bed and easy work, and Mrs George clucking over him like a mother hen?

The dark shadows of the overhung lane enclose them, hiding their faces.

'I don't know what is happening to us, Peter,' she says softly. She can talk with him, saying words she would not dream of uttering to anyone else, almost as if talking to herself. There is no knowing how much Welsh he understands, even now. He seldom replies except by lighting up another cigarette with trembling fingers.

'Something bad is happening. John ... No, it is the children. Rose. It's Rose. Everything is wrong. I think we are falling into a deep pit and there is no way out. Do you believe in Hell?'

Is he listening? Are his eyes on her? In the shadows under the trees there is no telling.

'What did the girl do to upset him so? What has broken him? He is no longer a man. He was a man, a good man, once. People will tell you. It was never easy for him, but he was ... a good man. It's Rose. I am afraid, Peter. It is easy for Jack, he can run off to the men. Escape. He's more at Castell Mawr than here. Not that I complain. William takes care that he comes to no harm.'

No reply, just a yawning silence, inviting her to immerse herself and reveal all.

'And I know there is no helping Robert. It's right, what they say about him. Something wrong in his head. A punishment to us. To me. I should have...' She will not say what. Perhaps she does not know. Their feet tramp on the thick mould of the dark lane, as feet have tramped from time immemorial. And she has done as every woman has been expected to do from time immemorial. What *should* she have done?

Does Peter understand any of what she is saying? He might. Isn't he as warped as Robert? Warped by the horrors

195

he has seen? The horrors he has done? She really knows no more about him than she had learned on the first day. That bad war, somewhere in the East, out in Poland. Peter never speaks of it. Not with his tongue. His eyes, his tremors, his sweats of terror speak volumes, but he says not a word. And she can talk on, confiding.

'Rose. My first. They always say ... I know she's only a girl, but there was such hope. She was such a happy child. Clever, they said. Full of song. Now she never sings. She is twisting, like a tree gone wrong. Poisoned. Why can she not just humour him? Sometimes I think there is no hope for any of us. Nothing left but...'

Something rustles in the undergrowth. A grunt and snuffle. For a second, terror seizes Gwen. It will never do for John to find her here, with this German, on his land. But it is only a badger. Nothing alarming. Peter does not recover so easily. She feels his trembling convulsions in the dark. Are the nightmares so easily awakened? She puts a hand on his arm, contact like an electric current, her horrors rushing into him, his into hers. Without realising what she is doing, she lets out a sob.

He sets the churns down, puts his arms around her. For a moment there is comfort, a deep dark comfort, blotting all else out, as they hug each another. Then propriety gets the better of her. What is this? She pushes him away, not in anger but in panic. What if someone saw? She is a respectable married woman. What does it matter if there were no more sin in their brief embrace than in the curling together of orphaned kittens? She'd be branded a harlot if anyone so much as glimpsed...

A flicker of flame, as he lights a cigarette, unable to resist the need. His black eyes gleam in the sudden brief glow. 'I am sorry.'

'No,' she says quickly. Forget it. Best not talk about it, or anything else. She is a foolish woman who should learn to hold her tongue. 'Get on now.' She helps him hoist the churns again and they trudge on in silence, up to the top of the lane and the slate bench where the milk waits for collection and up into near daylight out of the trees, a watery wash in the sky, colour creeping into the surrounding fields.

Out here he is just a wizened little foreigner, with grey skin and a cough and baggy clothes, not recognisable as the secret confidante of the dark lane. It can all be forgotten in daylight. She nods her thanks and turns away.

'Rose.' His voice grates on the name.

She turns, shocked to hear him speak.

'You must send her away.'

'My daughter? Send her away? What nonsense.' Daylight makes her indignant.

Peter only shakes his head over his cigarette. 'If she stays, she will hurt. He will not do good to her.' His eyes beseech, full of the knowledge of Hell. What does he know? There is nothing to know.

'She'll do well enough,' says Gwen, moving away.

'I see him—'

'You see nothing!'

He is silent.

'There is nothing,' says Gwen, hurrying down the lane, into the shadows, blotting him out. Utter nonsense. How dare he? It is her fault, of course, encouraging him by talking that nonsense in the dark, just because the chill blackness had filled her with despair. Time she snapped out of it. Another day to get through, and no more of this nonsense. What is she thinking of? Her silly forebodings. Perhaps she will come down to the yard and find everything as normal, the children stirring, John at his work, breakfast to be made...

No. The yard is silent. No sign of John, the work waiting. But perhaps this is normality now, her doing everything while the man goes to ruin. And if that is to be normal, how long do they have? A few more months before their landlord turns them out. The Colonel's tolerance means nothing now, for things have changed at Plas Malgwyn.

If Gwen were not so caught up in her own desperation she could pity the poor Colonel, the once proud father. Master Philip, the golden boy, the swanky young man up at Oxford, went into the army in the war. Better, some people say, if he had been killed, then the Colonel could have grieved properly. But fate was not that kind. The first Great War gave the Colonel rank and medals. The second brought Philip back from the North African desert, alive but with an artificial leg, a mutilated face, a foul temper and a filthy tongue. He rules now at Plas Malgwyn, while his father appeases and mollifies and tries to preserve a shattered peace.

Master Philip has no tolerance for John's manic independence. Even less will he tolerate John's ruin. He wants troublesome or unproductive tenants out, farms amalgamated, new ways brought in. Gwen's quieter more resolute pride can only hold things together for a little while longer. There is nothing more she can do. John has no heart now for anything unless it is the determination to whip his family into submission.

Most especially Rosie. Such an absurdity, this struggle between man and child. And Rosie is a child still, barely on the threshold of womanhood, a slight elfin creature, powerless and insignificant. What is it in her that John cannot endure, that he must be so desperate to crush?

Or has he already succeeded? What is it that Peter has seen? Gwen has to admit it, she has noticed a listlessness about the girl in recent weeks, moments when a silent helpless terror seems to break through the sulks and snarls. How should Gwen deal with her? Send her away? Where?

Gwen hauls a pail to the pump, working the handle, seeking the satisfaction of seeing the cobbles run clean. If only everything could so easily be washed away...

There is something not right, something different in the way her shins press against the wooden well cover. She stops, steps back, raising the lamp. Someone has worked the cover loose, prising out the nails that have secured it and pushing it askew. She lifts it, gazing down with foreboding. As if anything could be seen in that darkness. She raises the lamp, till its glow summons a reflection from the dark water below, and her heart misses a beat. A head, limbs, bobbing.

A strangled gasp escapes her. Her nightmare from former years, the deep well, black water, her babies unguarded for one careless moment...

Stop. She must get a grip. Her babies have grown beyond that. The well is not so very deep and the form she thought she saw was tiny. A rabbit? A kitten? What malice could have inspired anyone to pollute their well?

She finds a rope, attaches the pail, lowers it down into the water. Malice. Amidst Rosie's anger and petulance,

Gwen has begun to suspect a viciousness that makes her shudder. It is not fully fledged, not yet, but there are small cruelties, to Jess, to baby mice, to Robert. Pinching fingers, spitting, stones flung, spiteful words. Is this the devil that disturbs John so much? The mirror image of his own cruelty in his child? What creature has she tormented here?

The pail tilts, rocks, comes up empty. Determined, Gwen lowers it again. This time it snags on the pallid corpse in the black water, and drags it up, scraping the green stones.

Gwen stares at it, limp, sodden, naked on the cobbles. Maggie May, the rag doll. She does not know whether to be relieved or appalled. Rosie has always loved the doll, no matter what her moods. Why?

The question seems too much. Too much on top of so much else. Gwen sets the well cover safely back in place, wrings the doll out remorselessly and carries it back to the house. Sets it to dry by the range. The kitchen is dark, lit only by the low burning oil lamp that she has brought in with her and the red glow of the embers that flicker with gold as she attends to the fire, stoking it, filling the kettle for tea.

A rustle of paper makes her turn. Rosie is sitting at the table, clothes pulled on anyhow, hair uncombed, face dirty and pale, as she bends close over her school exercise book, nose almost to the paper, scribbling in the near darkness.

'Rosie? You up so early?'

'Couldn't sleep.'

Gwen glances at the limp doll, steaming gently now. She doubts if it can be saved. 'Rosie, I found Maggie May in the well. How is that?'

'She needed to wash.'

'In the well? What nonsense is that?' Gwen holds the doll up. 'Look, her seams are coming apart.'

Rosie looks up for the first time. 'Put her back!'

'In the well! I will not, and that is no way to speak to me, Miss.'

'She's got to be washed! She's not clean! She must be clean!'

'She will rot in the water, Rosie!'

'Good!' Rosie snatches the doll, thrusts it under her school book. The pages begin to soak up the dampness but it does not deter her. She is writing again, busy, nose back to the paper, shutting her mother out.

'What are you doing, girl?'

'I must do this for school.' Scribble, scribble.

'What is it then?'

'Story. It's for a prize.'

One more quirk of Rosie's nature that jars with her inevitable fate. Rosie's brightness. She had passed the scholarship exam, giving Gwen a thrill of pride, though it came to nothing, of course. John would have no child of his gallivanting off to Penbryn for fancy education. Let her stay in Llanolwen, if she must be schooled. There is no place for cleverness and learning in a girl, so John says.

'Culhwch and Olwen.' Scribble, scribble.

'That's nice,' says Gwen lamely. She can no longer communicate with her daughter these days. 'The old tales are the best.'

'I like it.'

'Do you?' Gwen knows the tale well enough, the hero who must win his bride from her giant father, through many adventures with the aid of Arthur and his men. Just such romantic nonsense as would be sure to rouse John's scornful wrath. No place for foolish fantasy in his world, but if it suits the child, can it really hurt? Gwen carries the lamp to the table so that at least the girl can see.

But Rosie won't lift her nose from the page. She is scribbling compulsively, the words gushing from her pen.

With a sense that she must do something, assert some control, Gwen lays a hand on the girl's to stop its frantic work, and takes the book from her. The story begins well, she can see, a school exercise in English, but then in the darkness, in a darkness somewhere deeper than night, Rosie has slipped into her native tongue, the writing shrinking, but the meaning expanding into cold and terrible territory.

Then Ysbaddaden roared and said she is my daughter and she shall never be yours because she is mine and I will never let her go and I will tie her up and chain her and hurt her and smother her and eat her and crunch her bones because she is mine and Olwen said it is time to kill him kill him for me and she took a sword and struck him and she cut off his head and she stabbed her father and she stabbed his eyes and she stabbed his heart and she stabbed his guts...

'Rosie!' Gwen is shocked, rigid with fear. 'This is wrong.'

The girl snatches it back. 'I haven't finished.' She bends again over the page.

'Rosie, you must not write like this for school. What will they think?'

'I don't care.' Her pen is scratching. Gwen can see the words gushing out. *And she stabbed him and killed him and she said I hate him, I hate him, I hate him, I hate him...*

'Stop it, girl, now!'

I hate him, I hate him, I hate him, I hate him, I hate him, I hate him...

'Rosie!' Gwen tries to stifle her fear in anger. She raises her hand, an unbelievable gesture, for she never strikes, and the girl responds, raising her eyes, pushing the book away, trembling, a look of anguish on her peaked grimy face.

But it is not fear of her mother's wrath that has stopped her. For a moment her dark eyes, wells of unfathomable unhappiness, meet her mother's, then she bolts, rushing for the door, for the clear clean air of morning in the yard.

Gwen hears the retching, goes to the door and sees the girl stooping, bent double by the barn, vomiting into the dirt.

'Rosie?' Gwen can barely hear her own voice.

Rosie straightens, wiping her mouth and looking at her mother. A look of such desolation.

Gwen's hand is at her throat, her stomach tightening, a coldness like ice pouring through her veins, and she knows. Please God, no.

There is no anger in the slight form now, just helplessness. The girl's lip quivers. To cry or to speak? To declare, to denounce...

'Now what have you been eating, girl?' asks Gwen gruffly. She grips the girl's shoulder, resisting the urge to slip her arm round her, to hug her into an embrace from which she will never ever be able to release her. Hold back. Be calm. Be practical. She wipes the damp hair from Rosie's face. 'Haven't I told you not to pick things in the wood?'

'Mam.' Plaintive. The girl clings to her arm, frock

streaked with vomit, desperate for reassurance. For absolution. For salvation.

'Come in, let's clean you up,' says Gwen briskly, firmly, quickly. 'What a sight you are. Back to bed with you, bach, and hurry now.'

Meekly, the girl allows herself to be led back into the house. A cool drink, a clean nightgown, back between the sheets to sleep, to hide, to shut out the nightmare. But no shutting it out for Gwen, although her mind works harder than her fingers ever have, to deny this thing. See to the boys, she must do that, and get them off to school. Clear the table for their breakfast of bread and tea. Take away the book, Rosie's testimonial, put it away, quickly, out of sight, behind the needles, the scissors and the pins and the wool, to the back of the drawer, where no one will ever read it.

Then maybe it will not be true.

17

'Baby, you were going to phone me.' Marcus sounded buoyant. Suspiciously buoyant. The conference was obviously going precisely as he wished.

'Sorry,' I said, with a kiss into my phone. 'I was just having a shower then I was going to lie back and phone you in bed. Next best thing, you know.'

'Mhm,' he agreed, laughing.

In reality I was perched on my queen-size bed in Plas Malgwyn, with papers scattered round me. I'd been listening to the Bob Roberts recording again, but I switched it off reluctantly when my phone rang.

'So,' I said, trying desperately to switch to erotic thoughts. 'How's it been going, oh my beloved? Are they all worshipping at your feet?'

'Totally. Offering me fine wines, rubies and concubines.'

'And apes and peacocks?' I purred, shuffling photocopies as quietly as possible.

'I told them to hold the apes. Seriously though, it's going great. I'm their golden boy. And another star turn tomorrow.'

'You're having the time of your life, and here I was thinking you'd be pining away for me.'

'I am, I am, but trying to ease the pain with all the compensations. Great food here. It's given me an idea about the catering. Has my mother kept all those leaflets or have you brought them home?'

'Leaflets?' I was scanning over the newspaper reports. *It is understood that Faber failed to report to the camp, which has since been closed.*

'The caterers, silly. You've looked through them with Caro?'

'Oh. No, I couldn't go.' *Mrs Owen became distressed and was excused from the courtroom.* I put the papers down. 'Sorry, something came up. Look, I'll try and get over to see her in the week. I'll be back on Tuesday.'

'Back? Where are you?'

'Wales. Cwmderwen. I thought, as you were going to be away for a bit...'

'Oh I see. While the cat's away—'

'Squeak. Look, I know the building work bores you rigid.' I picked up the recorder again, held it, thinking of that phrase, *He was a vicious brute.* 'And you were going away, leaving me all on my lonesome, no rubies and concubines as compensation, so I thought, why not? I have to find something to do while you're not there to cosset me.'

'All right,' he said indulgently. 'I'll forgive you. How's it looking?'

'Wet, mostly. Welsh rain. But the cottage is beginning to look like a cottage now. Intact. They're wiring.'

'Shall I be mother?' Chief Inspector Bob Robert's voice broke in. I'd accidentally pushed the play button. Hurriedly, I switched it off again.

'Who's that?' demanded Marcus. 'Have you got another

man in your life?' He didn't sound worried. The whole world couldn't compete with Marcus Crawford, especially when he was high on alcohol, coke and approval.

'My date,' I explained. 'I have to find my own concubines. Don't worry, he wasn't in the shower with me. It's a recording.'

'You record your dates?'

'You wanted to film some of ours, remember. His name's Bob, and he's about 104. The best I could find round here. All the sexy lawyers are taken.'

'Wild wicked woman. Have you been raiding old peoples' homes?'

'He's a retired policeman. I was asking him about my grandfather's murder.'

There was a moment's silence. When Marcus spoke again, his voice had dropped. I could tell he'd been lounging and now he was sitting up. 'Sarah, not that murder again. You've got to stop this. It's turning into an obsession.'

'What, because I want to know what happened?' I sat up too. Maybe I had harped on about it too often after a few drinks, but I wasn't going to be accused of obsession, just because I thought the truth mattered. 'I've discovered that one of my grandparents was murdered. You don't seriously expect me to nod and move on, do you?'

'Yes. Move on. You've done it before, Sarah. You've got to do it now. Put it behind you. It's for your own good. I don't want you having another breakdown.'

'I never had a breakdown.'

'You were having one when we first met. Off the rails, wouldn't you say?'

I bit my lip. Up to a point he was right. I'd been reeling with grief, guilt and inadequacy after Jemma's death. Because there was nothing I could do. This time there was. I could find the truth. 'I am very much on the rails now. I'm just trying to find out what happened. That doesn't make me a basket case.'

'But it will only upset you, and it's not as if you're going to resolve anything—'

'How do you know?' Solving it would resolve it and hadn't Bob given me all the facts I needed? A prisoner of war who'd escaped on a ship... What might a trip to Germany turn up? I wrenched my mind away from the prospect and tuned back into my phone.

'It's all ancient history.' Marcus was saying. 'Just drop it, Sarah. You'll do much better to try and forget the whole thing.'

'Hell no, I want to stop people forgetting it. Can't you understand that?'

'No!' Marcus was tanked up and not open to reason – usually a cue for me to play the cute and coy appeasement card. But this time I was tanked up too, on excitement and righteousness.

'Well that's how it is. Maybe if you had a murdered grandfather, you'd understand.'

'It's not as if you ever knew him.'

'That's precisely the point. I should have known him. Even my mother never had the chance to know him. I'm sorry, Marcus, but this is important to me, and if you can't understand—'

'All right. All right, calm down.' Marcus hadn't got where he was without being able to calculate when exactly to change tack. 'Of course it's important to you. Just as long as I am still important to you too.'

'Of course you bloody are. You know perfectly well you are.'

'And you to me, baby. I shouldn't be jealous of a man who died half a century ago, should I?'

'No, you shouldn't.' Obediently, I subsided. 'Because you know I love you, so so much.' Why was I doing this? I didn't want to be playing this game; I wanted to be listening to my tape, searching for clues within clues.

'It just proves how much I care about you,' said Marcus. 'I worry about you.'

'I'll be all right, I promise.'

'And you'll see my mother in the week?'

'Promise. Tuesday. I'll leave early. I've just got to tidy a few things up tomorrow, but then I promise I'll concentrate on the catering leaflets.'

'Angel girl.' His most amorous whisper, guaranteed to turn me to jelly. 'You can tell Caro I've been thinking: oysters. Mm? What do you reckon to oysters? Aphrodisiac. Perfect for a wedding?'

'Oo. Oysters. Great idea!'

Oysters.

As I kissed into the phone and rang off, I realised how totally, utterly, absolutely, I couldn't give a damn about oysters.

I couldn't give a damn about anything to do with the catering, or the wedding, or Marcus.

I jumped up, horrified at the thought that had tacked itself so casually onto my irritation. Of course I cared about Marcus. I was going to marry him. Spend my life with him.

I was going to move to America with him, make cookies, carry a gun, fly a flag on my lawn, retire to an all-white gated community in Arizona.

Stop it! Maybe Marcus had it right; I was obsessed. Sliding off-balance again. Well, there was only one thing to do. Sort it all out, solve the great mystery, so that I could move on.

It was my guilty conscience. I dreamed. I never dreamed when I was snuggled up next to Marcus, but there on my own, I dreamed. I had to get into Cwmderwen while the builders were away. Get in, ignore the creaking and the groaning and the long shadows. I had to fight the door, but when I was safely inside I was in the library at Aberystwyth, searching frantically. Somewhere in the rows upon rows of ancient tomes were oysters. I had to find them or Marcus would be furious and the wedding would be off.

I found one. At last I found it. I carried it carefully towards Marcus, where he stood waiting, and I realised it wasn't the library after all, it was a courtroom, and I couldn't go any further because I was in the dock. Trapped. I held out my hand, with the oyster. 'I found it,' I pleaded.

Marcus sat in the magistrate's seat, and dismissed it with a contemptuous wave. 'It's not an oyster,' he said. 'It's a dead thing. Admit it. You are wrong. You are holding dead things.'

I looked and he was right. The oyster was a dead thing. 'I didn't realise,' I said.

'Not good enough. You must confess. Confess your crime, Sarah Peterson.'

I looked up at him, weeping, and when the blur of tears

cleared, I realised that it wasn't Marcus, after all. It was Jemma.

'Confess!' she repeated.

'I confess!' I shrieked. 'I tried to confess, truly I did. I told Josh how I killed you.'

'Oh that,' said Jemma, shrugging as she used to do. 'That was nothing. This is the crime, this mess. I accuse you of letting go. Admit, you gave up. You're guilty of this.' She pointed at the dead thing in my hand and I realised it was Marcus.

'Guilty,' she repeated. 'Guilty, guilty, guilty!' She was screaming it, the sound ringing in my ears.

It was my alarm, ringing me into icy sweating wakefulness in a country house hotel in west Wales. Swamping me in dawn light, and guilt.

After Jemma's death I'd tried to blame everyone, all the while convinced that it had been my fault. She'd sat in my flat, nursing her enormous bulge, joking that it was just impossible to play bass guitar when you're eight months pregnant. Letting me realise that this was the end of the band for her. She'd embraced motherhood instead. 'But you've got to go on,' she insisted. 'You're a great singer. You can make it on your own. Go for it, Sai.'

'Easy for you to say,' I'd laughed. 'Dumping all the hard grind on me while you sail off into domestic bliss without a wave or a backward glance.'

'I'll look back and wave,' she'd promised. A joke. But she'd been doing just that, waving out of the window, looking back at me in the mirror when the lorry hit her.

Not watching the road.

My fault. Guilty, guilty, guilty.

I'd tried to launch the singing career that Jemma had commanded. Tried without heart or hope. Then there had been Marcus, and he'd seemed like such easy salvation, all calm certainty, taking charge of me and my misery. No need for me to get a grip. He would do my gripping for me.

By the time the wedding preparations were in full swing first time round, I'd known it was all wrong. I'd tried to escape. Josh, still recovering from the loss of his wife and unborn child, went out to India to do some volunteering and at the last moment, I'd fled with him. To wipe the slate clean. I'd tried to confess to Josh, to tell him how I'd killed Jemma. I needed the absolution of his wrath, his hatred turning on me, so I could escape from my own.

I'd forgotten that Josh had found God. I confessed, and he forgave me. 'It was no one's fault, Sai.' Just as they all kept telling me.

So I'd given up and come back, to Marcus and the wedding preparations and the promise of promotion in brand management. Back into the unabsolved guilt and the pretence that this was how it was meant to be.

Except that on this miserable dawn in my bedroom in Plas Malgwyn, I knew that what had been a mistake before was still a mistake. Only now, there seemed to be no way out of it. It was too late. Not a good way to start a day.

I got up, feeling grim, wanting resolution in the one small part of my life where I was in control. Cwmderwen and its mysteries might be an obsession, but it was one that mattered. My lifeline. Just for once, I was going to achieve something.

I needed to see William George again. He might be deaf and senile, but somewhere in his breast was the whole gory story, and it should be possible, with a little patience, to winkle more out of him.

I ate breakfast slowly and deliberately in order to calm myself down, then I headed for Castell Mawr. There was no point in being impatient if I wanted to get anywhere. I would chat with Carys, talk weddings, admire her house, have a little word with old William, and if he fell asleep again, I'd chat on and wait for him to wake, then tackle him again. However long it took.

My resolution was knocked out of me with one blow. The Georges weren't at home. I tried the front door, several back doors, the nearest barn, but the family seemed to have vanished.

One of Gwyn's men, working on a tractor engine in a nearby shed, strolled across to see what I was up to. 'You looking for Carys then?'

'Ah. Yes. Hi. I'm their neighbour. Just called for a word with William.'

'They're in Carmarthen,' he explained. 'Taking the old man to the hospital.'

'Oh God. Is it serious?'

He laughed. 'No, just his monthly check-up. He enjoys it, all those nurses.'

'Oh, that's a relief.' Very much a relief. 'I'll call again later.'

How old was William? I'd guess he wasn't far off receiving his telegram from the Queen. He couldn't last much longer, and when he finally went, that would be it. Hell.

What was happening to me? I was embarrassed by my own callousness, but I couldn't help it.

Frustrated beyond measure, I hesitated at the top of the lane and wondered what to do next. I couldn't sit there, waiting for the Georges to return. I could go down to Cwmderwen, discuss plumbing with Matthew. From the lay-by I watched a lorry, heaped high with sand and gravel, begin its descent gingerly down the Cwmderwen lane, so I decided to stay clear and headed on into Llanolwen.

I pulled up on the verge by the first building in the village, the hideous Beulah Chapel. This dour, unforgiving place, just right for funerals and divine retribution, was where my grandparents had married. The chapel door was padlocked. No matter; it was the plot across the road, separated by black railings from the surrounding fields, that I wanted. A cemetery, slate and black marble, an obelisk and one plaintive angel.

John Owen was a chapel man; the newspapers had made a point of that. His grave had to be here, among the grim nonconformists of the parish.

A strimmer had thrashed the long grass into submission, making a path for visitors, and people did come. There were flowers still fresh on one grave, polished black marble with gold lettering. Evelyn George, died 1992. I'd met hardly anyone in this area, but George was the one name that meant something and I shuddered. Not in fright, but with the feeling that I was standing where past and present meet. There was a space under Evelyn's name. Waiting for William? I guessed she was his wife. Next to it, a large grey stone read, 'David George, of Castell Mawr, died 1929, aged 59, and Elizabeth, wife of the above, died 1955, aged 81.' This was the Castell Mawr plot.

What must that be like, to have your grave booked, your place reserved, in the bosom of your family? Folded into their dead embrace.

I remembered standing by Josh as he cast Jemma's ashes into the wind on Grangers Hill, into the embrace of the whole world. This cemetery filled me with claustrophobic horror.

But I wasn't going to give way. I was here to seek. Where was the Owen plot? I searched further along the sad memorials in the pale light. Many were in Welsh, but the names stood clear, whatever the language, records of aged grandparents and beloved wives, of sons lost at sea, an uncle carted home for burial from Newport Pagnell. Newport Pagnell?

I found him at last, as the watery sun slithered behind another bank of rain clouds. It didn't matter, the letters stood out bold and clear on the uncompromising black slate slab.

John Owen 1901-1948.

That was it? That was all? Not a word about the murder? Maybe it was a matter of disgrace, something that shouldn't be mentioned in the polite society of a graveyard. Dilys certainly wouldn't have wanted the ghastly story set in stone, and she was probably representative of her generation.

I glanced at the graves encircling his. In the row behind, to one side, was an older grey slab. Mary, wife of Thomas Owen of Cwmderwen, died 1900, aged 60. Also the above Thomas Owen, died 1912, aged 76. Also Thos. their son, died 1882, aged 16, also Leah Owen, their daughter, died 1919, aged 45. A positive encyclopaedia compared with John's gravestone. Yes, I'd seen Thomas Junior and Leah on the census, along with two other daughters who must have upped and married.

Another stone stood beside it, blurred with lichen, but I could make out the names of John's mother Ann, died aged 28, and two of his infant siblings. What about his father, Francis? I couldn't be sure but there was a small stone further along inscribed F.O.1922. At least John's was an improvement on that.

This was the area then, the Owen plot. I searched further. Enoch Jenkins, 1978, aged 79, with a Welsh inscription, and next to him, Marian Jenkins, beloved daughter, aged 21. William Rees 1969 aged 73 and Florence Rees 1974, aged 74, also their son Morris Rees, 1926-1945.

John Owen lay alone, no children with him. So what about Rose, the girl who died? I searched the gravestones one by one, but there was no sign of Rose Owen.

The explanation was probably something banal and predictable. She died in hospital perhaps, far away from Llanolwen. What might have carried off children back then? TB? Pneumonia? Diphtheria? There would have been isolation hospitals and a resigned acceptance that God was going to take a few children each year.

Then there were farm accidents. I'd come across a few of those in my trawl through the papers, children falling under tractor wheels, or dragged into machinery. Weary pleas from coroners for farmers to take greater care. No health and safety officers demanding proper safeguards. Such accidents must have been depressingly common. Now that really was a nasty thought, my infant aunt mauled by a threshing machine. Rushed to the nearest hospital, but alas, too late... My stomach churned at the thought.

Still, I wanted to know. I could ask William that evening,

of course, but I was in a mood to know now. I paused for a lull in the rain to take photographs of my family graves and of Beulah Chapel, then I headed back for Aberystwyth. My reader's ticket was still valid and Rose was in there somewhere.

I realised that I could probably have done this in an instant online, but once I started trawling through the index of the Deaths register, I decided I might as well continue until I found her. Another loose family end to tie up. Bob had heard about a dead daughter during the murder investigation. Maybe it was something that still preyed on my grandfather's mind, the grief he carried through the years, to the bitter end. It made me weep to think of it.

I had no specific date. Not even a vague one, come to that. How long before the murder, was it? Five years? Ten? I could narrow it down. The photo of the family at the back door of Cwmderwen showed a little toddler of two or three. Difficult to be sure when all I could see was a pinafore, a pair of boots and dark hair, but she was very small. I knew my grandparents were married in 1933. She was born, say, 1934? Or 35? Still alive in 1937. There had been that photograph in Dilys' album but I couldn't remember it well enough to judge her age then. All I could do was assume that she had still been alive in 1937 and search forward from that date.

Which meant microfiche, one sheet at a time please. I was getting dizzy trotting backwards and forwards as I worked through the quarters. Had I missed it? I was ploughing through the 40s and still there was no Rose Owen of the right age. Had I overestimated the age of the child in the photograph? Of course, when I did finally find it, I realised I should have worked backwards, not forwards. Rose Elizabeth Owen, first quarter 1948, age 13.

I was stunned. She died in the same quarter as my grandfather. Was it disease or accident as I had imagined, or was it linked to his death? My scalp prickled. A delayed double murder? Could the beast that killed my grandfather have killed her too? This was awful. I had to find out and I didn't want to wait for a copy of the certificate. If nothing else, the *Penbryn Gazette* would contain a coroner's report.

I asked for the old volume of the *Gazette* again and waited, my mind seething with lurid scenarios, until the ungainly volume was wheeled to my table. This time I refused to be diverted by fêtes and poaching scandals. I went straight to the beginning of 1948 and worked forward methodically, looking for the story I had overlooked yesterday.

March 18th.

18

It is nothing, Gwen tells herself, with fierce insistence. It is nothing, a childish malady, it will pass. Surely it will pass, even though Rosie's dawn sickness repeats itself day after day. One monthly show, never repeated? What is so odd in that? The girl is young, far too young. These things are sure to be irregular at her age, especially if she's ailing.

Gwen will not, cannot acknowledge what she instinctively knows. Even to herself she cannot say it, slapping the very thought down, because to say it would make it true. But all the while she acts, instinctively and perversely, to conceal what must not be said. Perhaps there will be another child in the family. Gwen has had three, she is not too old, why not a fourth? Where is the harm in her feeling broody?

The deception begins, subconscious actions, barely deliberate. When she ventures abroad to Chapel, to the shop in Llanolwen or so rarely to market in Penbryn, she envelops herself in cardigans and thick coat, no matter the weather. Thin blood, she is always so cold, she tells herself. But she does not tell that to others. She smiles gently at sympathetic enquiries about her health.

'You keeping well, Mrs Owen?'

'Oh yes, very well. Trying not to overdo it though.'

'Well you sit there, bach. Rest your feet.'

Who can tell, under all that padding, what condition she is really in? Even at home she wraps up, vests, blouses, two or three of everything, even a towel tucked in. Must keep warm.

The hints she drops contain no direct lie, some religious or superstitious scruple prevents that, but the passing comments are there to deceive. Aching back, swelling ankles, taking it easy, best get on while she still can. It is Mrs George's eagle eyes that she must deceive above all others, but she can rely on her neighbour to pick up any hint or innuendo.

Mrs George promptly swallows the bait. Gwen cannot tell if she is genuinely deceived or if she merely chooses to play the game for decency's sake. It doesn't matter which. Somehow the ruse succeeds and the gossip spreads like floodwater, seeping through the district. Gwen Owen is in the family way again.

And Rosie? All this while she remains a pathetic waif, the wild cat in her tamed into compliance by her mother's quiet decisiveness. The lie is accepted, Rosie falls in with it, relying implicitly on the maternal protection that must not fail.

The summer passes, blessed relief from school, but when the new term starts she seldom attends. Gwen, heart in mouth, packs her off some days, but doubts that the girl ever makes it to the school gates. There is nothing new in that, no need to fend off sudden suspicions. Gwen was warned months ago of the girl's increasing truancy, but it was never viewed as the sign of unspoken desperation that it surely was. Everyone in the area knows John's views on the subject and the inspector calls at his peril. What use is education to girls? Filling their heads with useless knowledge, giving them foolish ideas. How will geography and science help them when they are wives and mothers, as nature intends? They need to learn to cook and sew and mind their tongues, that is all. Better for Rosie to give up this nonsense now and get to work over at Plas Malgwyn, where they are short-staffed, desperate for maids. That is proper woman's work. Let her earn her keep and not fancy he can afford to support an idle brat.

He is not the only one with such opinions. The law is the law, and it says that Rosie and her like must go to school still, but no one expects legal reasoning to penetrate the timeless walls of Cwmderwen. A mind of his own, that John Owen.

Gwen tries to avert trouble, writing notes of excuse. Rosie is sick. No doctor of course. How can the likes of them ever afford a doctor? Even if this new notion of free doctors and medicine came to pass, it will be of no use here. Free? Tell that to John and see how he reacts. It is a notion he will never tolerate. Are people suggesting he cannot pay his way? He'll not have charity in his family. If they cannot afford to pay, they go without. So of course they will go without.

For once, Gwen is thankful for the illogical obsession of John's meanness. No one would seriously expect old Doctor Connell to be called to Cwmderwen, even if an Owen were dying. A sick child must stay in bed and be nursed with coltsfoot or beef tea. So Rosie stays at home, hiding, from friends and foes and from herself.

Only the twilight brings her out. Out of the gloom of the cold house, into the older more forgiving shadows of the woods. What does she do there? Seek out some memory of an innocent childhood, playing games of fantasy in the kingdom of the trees, she and Maggie May? The doll has gone. Rosie has retrieved it from her mother's care and now it lies God knows where, buried in the leaf mould probably.

Rosie thinks no one sees, but her mother glimpses her sometimes, flitting like a little white ghost among the trees, while Gwen is milking or helping Peter with the churns. Once they see her in the lane, crossing, hesitating, looking upwards, to the road, to that image of freedom that she can never quite attain. Or can she? The hesitation becomes decision. She sets off up the track, shoulders set.

Far behind her in the darkness, Gwen draws breath to call, but Peter breaks in, pleading, 'Let her go.'

'Let her go? What are you talking about? You know nothing about it. Rose!' But the summons that ends Gwen's confused indignation is wasted. Rose has already heard their voices, frozen in mid-flight and turned aside, back into the undergrowth.

'Why can you not let her go?' asks Peter.

Gwen turns on him, hating him, his ugly accent, his ugly face, his warped little body. His ability to comprehend. 'What do you want me to do? Let my child run off like some tinker's brat? You think that will help anything?'

'She hurts. He will hurt her more.'

'How dare you! Who are you talking about? Don't you dare talk about my man! You have no right!'

She catches the gleam of dampness in his dark eyes. He has no right to weep for Rosie or for her or for anyone. He is no one, an outsider, he understands nothing of their lives or this community.

'So you'd have her run away, live in a gutter? Become a slut in some big city? You don't know what people would say, the disgrace would...' The words dry in her throat. Disgrace is what they are facing now, whichever way they turn. How much longer can the deception last? Is Peter right? Would Rosie really be better off, wandering free out there, starving, begging, a prey to every villain, every man who chose to abuse her? Whereas if she stayed...

In the silence, Peter plods on, hauling the churns. There is nothing more to say. The child has gone, the thought of escape stifled. Folly even to think about it.

At home Rose says nothing of flight. She says nothing on any subject. She is meek and sullen in turn, avoiding her father with the cunning of a cat burglar, obedient to her mother, complicit in the deception Gwen is weaving, but resentful and hurting, as if the silence she must endure were an acid eating into her. One word of truth and cleansing, that is all that is required, but it is forbidden, it will unleash too much for this community to survive. Silence is the price to be paid for life.

There can be things said without words. Gwen longs to put her arms around the child and comfort her. Sometimes, while Rosie sleeps, she does, a furtive stifled hug that for a dark moment blocks out the miserable world. But in the waking hours they must both play the game, pretend, say nothing, shut the truth away behind bolted doors.

Deceiving themselves. As the months pass, Gwen cannot bring herself to admit this disintegration of all she has, even while she obsessively confuses and obscures. She sets her daughter proper woman's work to do. Shirts, sheets to be hemmed, socks to be darned or knitted. Not baby things. Gwen works on those, mending and repairing the smocks and bonnets put away when Robert had outgrown them. What has Rosie to do with baby clothes? Time for that when she is a grown woman and wife. But it is quite proper for her to be out of sight, doing household repairs. A wise move, for John's black hopeless guilt has moved on, gathering like a thunderstorm into a towering anger that lashes out at everyone. As well it is a towel Gwen is carrying round her waist. She'd have lost a real baby by now.

Rosie is never there to face his wrath and feel his fists. Does he know what condition she is in? Has he taken in the rumours about his wife's state? Has he understood the Hell to which sin has led? It is impossible to tell. Gwen has certainly not said a word of the matter in front of him and she can no longer guess what her husband is thinking. He swears at Rosie's name, calls her slut, but he rounds his anger equally on the boys. Jack helps his mother, working with her like a true man before retreating to Castell Mawr for the comfortable companionship of men who don't glower and rage and smite. Robert, like a sad puppy, trails round after his father as if he feeds on his own terror, an addict to misery.

The farm trembles still on the brink of catastrophe. Heavy rains, the hay harvest is a disaster and the barley threatens to go the same way. John blasphemes and rages against a world intent on heaping punishment on him, but it is Gwen and Jack and William George and Ted Absalom who struggle to salvage what they can.

The business of harvest, such as it is, rolls past into autumnal gales and the glowering clouds of winter. Christmas. No angels, no wise men or peace on earth here. Not even the balm of myrrh. Only the bitterness of thorns and nails. But it cannot be much longer now. No more thoughts of Rosie returning to school. The pretence would be futile; the girl has begun to swell unmistakeably. Eating too much, Gwen tells herself, as if the sound of the lie in her brain can make it come true. She pours out pathetic little notes to the school, pleading sickness. And still the truth engulfs the house, facing them at every turn but not a word is spoken.

Disaster has to strike. Does she think she can stand staring forever at the cracks ripping through the dam, the seeping, the trickle, without sooner or later facing the roaring deluge? Gwen, toiling over the hot steaming washing, has stripped off her wrappings and does not hear the footsteps in the yard. The door opens and there is Mrs George, large and bustling, beady eyes taking in the steam, the chaos, Gwen's skeletal frame.

With a start Gwen gathers up wet linen, hiding behind it. What business has this woman to come calling on a Monday morning? But she has come and she has seen, and as if on devilish cue, there are Rosie's dragging footsteps on the stairs. Before Gwen can stop her, the girl emerges, blinking like an owl, swollen and heavy-footed, staring startled at their visitor.

Startled, then fearful, then defiant and angry and desperate in one.

Mrs George looks. Gwen sees the sturdy frame quiver.

'Well!' says Mrs George. 'So you've been no better than you should have been. There's disgrace on your parents!'

The words are so utterly predictable, signifying nothing. Gwen knows, after fourteen years, that meaningless phrases spill out of Mrs George, the proper cliché for every occasion, trotted out with automatic righteous indignation, while within that matriarchal bulk her mind is working on a quite different plane.

But Rosie cannot understand this. To her, vulnerable and desperate, this brick wall of condemnation is too much. Her simmering resentment boils over into a scream of anguish. 'Go away!' She lashes out at the woman. 'I hate you, I hate you! I hate everyone!'

'Hush, girl!' says Gwen, frantic.

'What a way to speak to your elders and betters!' Mrs George must open her mouth and out it comes. 'If you were a child of mine, I'd have your father take a strap to you. Such wickedness.'

'Wicked!' Rosie is almost choking. She cannot hold back. 'You are all wicked! He is wicked! Do you want to know who did this? Shall I tell you who did this? Shall I tell you what he—'

'Hold your tongue, girl. I don't want to know!' Gwen snaps the shrill words in frantic haste, sharp and commanding, anything to cut short this flood of unspeakable revelation.

The girl is silent, instantly, as if a slap has taken the breath from her body.

Mrs George must go on as her decades have taught her, the meaningless babble. 'A bad lot, that one. She'll come to a nasty end, mark my words.'

Gwen says nothing. She cannot. She can only see, etched forever on her brain, that look of utter betrayal in the girl's eyes, before Rosie flees the room. *Hold your tongue, girl. I don't want to know. Hold your tongue, girl. I don't want to know.*

Silence descends on the room. Mrs George's huffing and puffing has ceased, dried up at last as she digests the truth.

And the door opens and John stalks in. He stops, seeing Mrs George, an old respect there that still curbs his anger and his manners.

'Good morning, John,' says Mrs George, looking at him with the eyes of a hanging judge. What has she concluded? The truth? So instant and so obvious? So predictable if anyone had thought to predict?

But John does not know that as he grunts an acknowledgement. He sees her standing, empty-handed, somehow expectant, and turns on Gwen. 'Is this the way to entertain our neighbours. You don't even offer her a chair?' He glowers at the chaos of the kitchen.

'Thank you, I'll not be stopping.' Regally, Mrs George sails past him, dismissing him, and John stands there, diminished, injured even though a swelling anger gives him a semblance of vital energy.

'Clear this mess, woman, or must I clear it for you? Clear my house of the lot of you, nest of vipers!'

Gwen scarcely feels the blows. *Hold your tongue, girl. I don't want to know.*

Well, people will know now. Mrs George will see to that.

The walls of deception must surely fall and yet, somehow, they hold. Gwen waits in dread for Mrs George to speak, to denounce the wickedness of Cwmderwen to the world, but Mrs George stays silent. She has been drawn into the web of lies and no one in the district has learned the truth through her. Or if they have, they have been placed under a vow of silence.

Instead of condemnation, Gwen finds unsentimental support. The Georges rally round, not a word spoken. Peter comes to Cwmderwen every day now, helping out through the critical days. Castell Mawr is overmanned, explains William, what with the machinery he'd bought and the boys coming back from the war. Might as well find some work for the German still awaiting repatriation. Make him earn his crust like a proper Welshman. If there is no need for him at Castell Mawr, let him go and do odd jobs for neighbours. One neighbour, to be precise.

It is a mark of John's decline that he suffers this transparent subterfuge with no more than a scowl and savage mutterings. No one else is fooled. Peter is there to do more than the odd job. He takes all the heavy work that Gwen has struggled with alone these past months. He keeps to himself, gets on with the work, avoids John with the soft-footed nimbleness of a well-trained servant.

Gwen avoids him, resenting and desperate in turn, hating him, wishing and dreading he might speak. But Peter does not. He watches, yes, her and Rosie, the pain and the anguish. Why will he not go away? Why must he stay, when most of his compatriots have gone? Why is he not begging for a return passage home? Because his crimes were too terrible? Or because he has no home, no escape from the prison he carries with him. The pain that allows him to understand.

She does not want his understanding. She wants nothing from him. Her pride would revolt, send him packing but she knows she cannot afford to reject this help. Without it the farm will be lost and she must keep the farm going for the sake of the children. Cwmderwen is little enough but what else do they have?

The world sometimes intrudes. Mrs George is delivered regularly by pony trap or by William's motor car, invading the kitchen of Cwmderwen, bullying the boys with sharp words, keeping them busy, out of their mother's way, bustling in with brusque nosiness masking any surreptitious help that her swollen joints can still allow. With Gwen she is the same as ever, as if she has seen and heard nothing.

With John she is not the same. She is polite, but her stiff unspoken condemnation hits home as nothing else has done. It curdles the resistance in him that once found its outlet in ceaseless blustering anger. He grows furtive, convinced that he can sense accusation in every glance and he rails against them all, against his family, his neighbours, his landlord, his God. It is as if he has waited all his life for this predestined nemesis to snare him and all his former pride, his restraint, his self-control is wasted, a futile struggle that it is pointless to continue.

He misses Chapel. Is it shame or drunkenness? After a life of iron abstinence, he is drinking, furtively, but Gwen knows it all too well. He avoids company in his torment – no rolling home drunk from the Mason's Arms like his father – but he has whisky bottles, secreted in the kitchen, in the bedroom, in the barn. God knows where he finds the money when they can barely afford a crust to eat. John's demons, held at bay for so long, have finally broken their bonds and have caught him, dragging him down to hellfire and damnation.

Let them, she thinks, racked with bitterness, lying beside him, sleepless, in the dark, listening to his drunken snores and watching moonlight throw flickering shadows through the trees. Hell is too good for him. And too good for her. She is bound to him, is she not, by her marriage vows? For better or for worse. His damnation is hers, just as this Hell on Earth is hers too.

The bitterness must be buried with the sunrise. By day, she must pretend that all is normal, no beast is gnawing at the roots of their world, its fangs deep in her entrails. Every day, when she looks at Rosie, it bites deeper. Rosie never stirs from her room now. She never speaks. When her mother brings her food she turns her face to the wall, shutting her out. Hold your tongue, girl. I don't want to know. The words echo between them.

The terrible day comes. Inevitably Mrs George is there, in the kitchen, boiling water, making tea, buttering bread, scolding the boys and ignoring the sounds from upstairs, where Gwen is tending her daughter. Not that there is much sound. Rosie moans but she does not scream or cry out or struggle and still she will not speak. Still she will not look at her mother. Without Gwen to take charge, she would just lie there, sodden, tormented, willing death.

She is so small and thin, this child. It is a cruel business, not an easy birth. Gwen longs for help but she dare not summon a doctor. Mrs George? She is tempted. The old lady would manage the business with a no-nonsense competence, Gwen is sure of that, if she could cope with the stairs, but no, she cannot admit her, not to this most private of moments between mother and daughter. Not when Mrs George has witnessed, even prompted, the terrible betrayal that still crucifies Gwen with guilt. So she struggles on alone, praying fervently.

She talks, soothingly, as if Rosie were a little child again, no matter that the child will not listen. 'Don't fret, my love, don't worry, Mam's here, it will be all right.' Will it ever be right again?

At last, scarcely believing that it could ever end, it is all over. The baby, wrinkled and red, wails and gasps triumphantly for air.

A fine baby. How odd that out of this twisted affair should come a normal healthy girl. Not a fanged monster, not deformed, not a mewling waif barely clinging to life, but a bright-eyed elf, demanding her due, eager for food.

Gwen looks upon it with a surge of unexpected feeling. Surely this sight, at last, must strike some spark in Rosie, drag some response from her.

She shows the mite to the girl, offering her, but the girl lies back on the soiled linen, blank-eyed, refusing to look. Wearily, Gwen cradles the small bundle, sits on the bed, rocking it back and forth, crooning softly. Was there a time, secretly within her scarred soul, when she wanted this creature dead? An end to all their troubles if only it would disappear, be stillborn? If there were such thoughts they have evaporated now, swept away by the miracle of this eager lust for life.

Life that needs to be nourished. Not by Rosie, that is for sure. Gwen doubts that her daughter could do it, even if she were willing. She must see to it herself. After all, isn't that what people will be expecting? She tiptoes downstairs.

Mrs George pours tea, looks up with a twitch of her nose, tuts as her eyes meet Gwen's in mutual understanding.

'Well now Jack, I told you you'd have a new brother or sister soon.'

'Sister,' says Gwen. Her voice is hoarse. She is overcome with fatigue as if it had indeed been her giving birth.

Mrs George stoops to peer at the wrinkled face, as she would at any new infant, to bestow her contrary blessing, to find fault or predict sickness. But for once she says nothing, merely nods.

'Is that your baby then, Mam?' asks Jack. Too young, too masculine to understand that there is something odd in all this. He is eager to question, like a child, but he has a child's willingness to accept the answers given.

Gwen smiles in reply, sufficient confirmation for him, and shows him the pink face, the gem-like glint of blue eyes.

He is briefly fascinated, but his upbringing rescues him from any unmanly enthusiasm. 'Another girl,' he says, with knowledgeable scorn, although he has always got on more easily with Rosie than with Robert, until the last few months. Boys of his age are obliged to despise girls. How else are they to become proper men?

'Now if you've finished peering and prying, out from under your mother's feet,' says Mrs George. 'Hasn't a growing boy anything better to do than hang around in the kitchen? Off with you. And you too, Robert, or do you mean to roast yourself alive by that fire?'

Jack grabs bread and butter and dashes off, curiosity about his new sister fully satisfied. Robert has no curiosity. The baby does not impinge on his self-absorbed consciousness in any way. Nose running, he trails off after Jack, with a half-hearted whine. He has not looked at his mother or at the burden that she holds, and Gwen knows now not to expect it of him.

'They're good boys,' says Mrs George. An utterly meaningless remark in the circumstances, but she must say it. Gwen nods agreement. Neither of them mention the other one, upstairs in the darkened bedroom, but Mrs George takes charge of the baby, preparing its feed with the bottle and well worn teat that has stood ready on the dresser for days. Gwen has always been spare of milk. A matter of distress in the past, but at least it has left her prepared for this.

An unexpected pang of jealousy. She does not want to relinquish the mite, even to one as competent in the matter of babies and calves and lambs as Mrs George. But she must be sensible, and there is another child she must attend to.

Pulling herself together, Gwen carries fresh water and towels and linen upstairs. Rosie has not stirred and she will not stir now, not even in response to her mother's caresses. Gwen softly, tenderly, washes her down, pulls away the bloody sheets, combs her long lank hair. She goes down again and returns with a bowl of gruel. Good invalid nourishment, better than any this house has seen for many years. There is proper beef in it that Mrs George left a few days ago, along with sugar, like a neighbour absent-mindedly leaving a hat or gloves.

Rosie says nothing. Gwen spoons the warm liquid between her lips, with soothing words. The lips are slightly parted, there is no resistance but she does not see Rosie swallow. The gruel dribbles from the side of Rosie's mouth. Gently Gwen wipes the girl's chin and briefly, for one short moment, their eyes meet.

No love, no anger. There is nothing in those eyes but the hopelessness of betrayal. Gwen squeezes the girl's hand. 'I know,' she whispers. Understand, please, Rosie, I know it all, I am denying nothing.

'I know.'

But her penitence is too late. The girl no longer hears.

Forcing herself to be brisk, Gwen patters downstairs to prepare the old crib, tucking in the worn bedding that has been airing by the fire. Mrs George is rocking the baby with grandmotherly dignity, as it sleeps, replete. Together the women lay the infant to rest, gazing down on the cradle as if they have, between them, concocted this unexpected miracle. Perhaps they have.

Heavy irregular footsteps. A dog whines as it is kicked. The door is flung open and John stands there, frozen in his tracks, the scowl suddenly slack. He stares at the cradle and the baby, colour flushing then flooding from his face. He cannot ignore it now.

'Well, John, so God has seen fit to bless you with another daughter,' says Mrs George, and the cracked window panes reverberate with the whiplash of her scorn.

A baby to tend, a family to feed, work to do. Nothing stops as day follows day. Gwen fetches water and sees Peter in the dark gloom of early morning, limping feet slapping on the cobbles, as he arrives from Castell Mawr. Very well. He will get on with his work, she will get on with hers. No need to speak.

Words hang on the air between them, but she will have none of it. He looks at her, sly foreign eyes so insolently observant, but she will not respond. She nods, to set him about his work and turns her back, making for the house. With relief she hears his feet dragging towards the barn, to fetch the lantern, the tools he needs. Two currents pulling them implacably apart. As she opens the door of the house, the barn door creaks in response. She will not look back.

'Gwen.' It is not a shout he gives but it is a voice full of force. How dare he use her name? How dare he summon her back and demand words? This is Owen land. She is mistress here.

Aching with a desire to talk, to let the words come tumbling out, she steps into the house and slams the door behind her. The kitchen is dark and cold. Too cold for the little mite nestling in the dark shadow of the crib. She must bring the fire to life. Work to do.

Is he calling again? A word muffled by door and distance. Gwen? The nerve of the man. She is going to have to speak to William about him. Have him taken away. She can manage. Has she not always managed? She does not need him to mind the farm and mind her pain. She will ignore him.

She cannot. She flings the door open again, ready to snap at him, give him a piece of her mind across the dark cold gulf of the yard.

'Gwen!' His voice is breathless, burdened. Has he fallen, hurt himself? He might be an interfering little German tramp but she has her Christian duty. She stomps back across the yard. If there were a grain of former spirit and grace left in her she would flounce, but she stomps, ready to round on him, berate him for his clumsiness.

The barn door is open, the interior a musty darkness, black shapes in grey shadows.

But one shape is a softer grey. The grey of mist on the moors on a dark winter's day. A shroud of grey. She beholds it, the bewildering image, the grey mist shroud of a nightgown dangling.

A nightgown enfolding her daughter.

Her daughter dangling. Rose, dangling, dank dark hair spilling down the soiled white cotton.

19

'Look. Er. We'll cope, no problem.' Trevor, my boss, sounded as if coping was a serious problem, but then he always sounded like that. 'You take your time, right? Take off as long as you need.'

'Trev, I really don't...' My head drummed. Don't fight it. 'Is Maya there?'

'Maya? Yeah. Sure. Maya!'

He handed over the phone and I was greeted by Maya's enthusiasm. 'Sarah! Oh you poor thing. I heard. So sad. But don't you worry, I'm dealing with the PCA account, so you just, like, sort yourself out, okay?'

I opened my mouth to explain, then stopped. I needed a clear head to deal with the situation Marcus had created, and a clear head was exactly what I didn't have. Marcus had phoned my office while I was still in bed, to tell them that I was distraught over the death of an aunt and incapable of working today. Trevor naturally assumed I'd had a bereavement, and I decided it wasn't entirely a lie. I did feel bereaved. 'Thanks, Maya. Maybe I'll take today off.'

'Oh, more than that,' insisted Maya. 'Wait till after the funeral.'

'We'll see,' I said. I slipped the phone back into my bag,

curled up on the sofa and shut my aching eyes. The death of an aunt. Rose. My child aunt Rose. My stomach was curdling again.

'Have this.' Marcus was standing over me with a cup of tea. 'How are you feeling now?'

'All right, really.' As all right as a hangover would permit. I gazed up at him guiltily. I'd allowed atrocious treacherous thoughts to creep in, and here he was, at my side, the man for whom ambition was everything, quitting a conference his career depended on, all because I'd summoned him at midnight in incoherent distress. No hesitation. He'd come straight to me.

'Thank you. Thanks for everything.' I sipped my tea... and nearly spat it out. 'Sugar!'

'Hot sweet tea is good for shock.'

'I'm not in shock. I can't drink this.'

'Yes you can. Do as you're told.'

'Hattie Jacques had nothing on you, you know that, Matron?'

Marcus laughed and firmly held the cup for me to drink. 'Good,' he said, as I obediently sipped again and tried to swallow without retching. He smoothed my forehead, then plumped the cushions around me. 'I've sent for Sam,' he said.

'Good God!' I sat up, nearly sending the tea flying. 'You haven't!'

'You were in such a state.' Marcus removed the cup to safety. 'He's on his way.'

'Sam is coming here?'

There was the sound of a car outside and Marcus backed to the window to look down. 'That's him now. I'll just have a word.' He went, probably to warn Sam that I was teetering on the brink and needed sensitive handling.

This was ridiculous. All right, I'd given the wrong impression the night before. When I'd read the article about Rose, my day, my life seemed to have hit rock bottom. I'd wanted out. I hadn't waited for William George to return from hospital. I'd shoved my gear in my car and headed for home, feeling darker and emptier that I'd done for years. And then I'd got drunk. Drunk and inevitably darker and emptier than ever.

That was when I'd phoned Marcus. I was no longer sure, in the light of day, what I'd planned to say to him. By that stage, I was babbling about Rose and Jemma and death, about wasted lives and wrong decisions and desperation. I couldn't even recall what Marcus said in return. The next thing I knew, he was by my side, cradling me, wiping me down, getting me into bed, with a wet flannel and a bucket, holding my hand while I puked.

That was what love was about, wasn't it? So I owed him. But I hadn't been in the grip of grief the previous night, I'd been blind drunk, and I was not distraught this morning, I was hung-over. It was no reason to summon Sam all the way from California.

And surely it couldn't be Sam so soon? It wasn't physically possible, unless... I winced. God, I hadn't been out for twenty-four hours, had I?

It was him; I could hear his voice. I stood up hastily so he wouldn't misinterpret my sprawl on the sofa as complete mental collapse. Sam followed Marcus in, and I was relieved to see that he was smiling, puzzled rather than frantic.

He was looking good, tanned, brimming with health, which he should be; he worked on it hard enough.

'What have you been up to then? Marcus says you were having a regular screaming fit.'

Both Marcus and I jumped in with indignant denials.

'I said she was upset,' corrected Marcus. 'She's got caught up in this ghastly murder business, and she's unearthed something that distressed her.' He squeezed my hand.

I squeezed back. 'You make me sound like a maiden aunt with a touch of the vapours.'

'What have you found?' asked Sam, instantly curious. 'Anything involving sheep?'

'No!' I thought back to the newspaper story and wanted to cry again.

'I knew it was a mistake getting obsessed with all this,' chided Marcus.

'If I hadn't investigated, I'd never have known.'

'And that would have been a very good thing. Ask yourself, why has your family been keeping it under wraps all these years? Because it's distressing, and digging it all up isn't going to do any good. All it's done is make you miserable, and I can't have that.' He kissed me. 'Someone has to look after you, you know.'

'I'm a big girl, really.'

'Not always. Just remember last night and tell me you don't need looking after. Wasn't that why you phoned me?'

'I'm so sorry I messed up your conference.'

'Never mind that. You know I'll always be there for you, but we've got to get you off all this gory murder business. It isn't healthy.' He sat me down, handed me the sweet tea again. 'I should have put my foot down about that cottage right at the start.'

Behind him, I saw Sam's eyes widen.

'Listen, darling,' I said, meekly taking another sip. 'I know I've been a prat, and you've been wonderful. But would you be hugely understanding and leave me with Sam for a bit?'

Marcus smiled, perfectly willing to oblige. 'I know he'll take good care of you – and I really need to call in at the office. But don't worry, I'll be back this evening.' He kissed my fevered brow and stepped aside to make way for Sam. 'Keep an eye on her.'

'Oh I will.' Sam grinned. He waited until Marcus had gone, then rubbed his hands. 'Anything to drink round here?'

'Hot sweet tea? It's vile. Do you want it, or can I feed it to the poinsettia? There's gin in the cupboard, or vodka. Let me—'

'No, you stay there. I'm taking care of you, remember. Or Marky might put his foot down on me.' He laughed as he filled a glass.

'He didn't mean it to sound like that. It's his job, taking charge of situations. Even so... It's lovely to see you, Sam, it really is, but I can't believe he summoned you.'

'He had to, didn't he? One man alone can't possibly cope with my baby sister, when she's having a nervous breakdown.' Despite his light-hearted tone, he was watching me over his glass, assessing me.

'I'm not having a breakdown. I was very very drunk and now I'm very very hung-over. I phoned him when I was well and truly plastered, to say... I don't know, to say stuff.

241

And now he thinks I'm going to pieces. Again. He's given Trevor the idea I have. That's going to look great at work, isn't it?'

'No, but then I always got the impression Marky wasn't too fussed about your career.'

'Don't,' I warned him. Then I groaned. 'Oh hell. Well, if we finish up in America, I'm not going to have a career, am I?'

He raised an eyebrow, said nothing. The comfort of having a brother who understood could sometimes be anything but comforting.

'Look, never mind that. I'm fine... or will be when this headache goes.'

'So what sparked off the vodka session? Something about the murder. Come on, tell me the juicy details.'

I winced, partly because of the pounding of my head, partly the memory. A great many things had sparked off the vodka, but the ancient family tragedy seemed the safest place to start. 'It's horrible. You know Mum had a sister, Rose, a lot older than her.'

Sam, who'd never cared about family history, thought deeply and pretended he could remember a Rose. 'A girl? I know there were stillbirths or something. You know I'm squeamish about girlie stuff.'

'Rose wasn't a stillbirth. She was their first child. Dilys has a photo of her somewhere. Anyway, I thought she'd died really young, but she was thirteen, and it's horrible. She committed suicide.'

'Yow!' Sam was taken aback.

'Can you imagine it? Just thirteen and she killed herself. Isn't that a good enough excuse for the vodka?'

Sam sighed. He couldn't quite connect, but he tried to see my point of view. 'Okay, it's bad.'

'Bad? A girl, Mum's sister, and she was driven to *that*, and we barely even knew she existed. All that agony, hushed up. We never knew. Of course I was upset.'

'Okay,' repeated Sam. He could laugh most things away, but there weren't many good jokes about teenage suicides. Now he biffed me compassionately on the shoulder and blew out his cheeks, raising his eyebrows with a grimace. 'Hell, I suppose it is a bit of a shock, considering that I'd forgotten there was an aunt.'

'Isn't that awful? I knew that there was a girl who died, but I thought she was a five year old dying of scarlet fever or something.'

'That would have been better?'

'Yes. Killing herself at thirteen! That's so horrible. Just think what she must have gone through.'

'But we don't know what she went through. Anyone telling you what was going on way back then? Don't tell me Dilly's been spilling the family beans at long last.'

'No of course not. Not that I've asked her about it yet.'

'Don't envy you trying.'

'I will though. But I've been researching things over at Cwmderwen, the library in Aberystwyth, newspaper reports and that sort of thing. I've even driven around interviewing retired policemen.'

'Jeez, you are serious about this stuff. Newspapers eh? So our family made the headlines at last!'

'Sam! Don't joke. It's too horrible for that.'

'Yes.' He was being as sympathetic as he could, but he couldn't see the faces, sense the ghosts strongly enough to feel the pain. On the other hand, he had cared enough to come thundering across a continent and an ocean. In record time; I remembered that puzzle.

'I'm sorry about Marcus bringing you over here. There was no need, really, but how did you get here so quickly?'

He shrugged. 'Traffic wasn't too bad.'

'From Heathrow?'

'From Wimbledon, Sai. My meeting with Greg Taylor? I got in on Saturday. I did email you.'

'Sorry, I haven't checked. Too busy in Wales.' But Marcus must have checked my mail for me. I laughed. 'He let me think he'd summoned you from California.'

Sam found this most amusing. As if he'd rush anywhere for me. 'He probably would have done. From the way he was talking, I thought I'd find you in a straightjacket.'

'He thinks I'm obsessed, I should drop it. But you do see why I have to know more, don't you? Don't you feel horrified at what happened to Rose?'

'The girl, oh yes.'

'Rose Elizabeth Owen. Mum's sister. She must have suffered so much and now nobody even speaks about her. We've never bothered to find out about her. I feel as if we've let her down.'

Sam squealed a mocking laugh. 'Hang on. A girl tops herself fifty years ago—'

'Sixty. 1948.'

'Whatever. She snuffed it a long long time before we were born. You can't seriously want us to feel guilty about it now, Sai.'

'No, we don't have to feel guilty for her death, of course

not. But we can feel guilty about the way she's been forgotten, can't we? It's like our grandfather. The same story, really. Of course we couldn't have stopped it, but shouldn't we at least have asked questions? She was thirteen. How could it have happened?'

'Well you know, they figure depression is mostly down to a chemical imbalance in the brain. We're probably talking a serious serotonin deficiency here.'

'Serotonin deficiency! Do you have to be so clinical?'

'Okay, why do you think she did it?'

'I don't know. I really don't. It said "while the balance of her mind was disturbed". What is that supposed to mean? The inquest was reported in the newspaper. It said she'd been ill, so maybe that left her depressed. There could have been all sorts of problems. Her father was murdered not long after. Who knows what was going on? And maybe her mother didn't have time for her. It was just after the baby.'

'Ah! Now I can see why that would drive anyone to suicide. Another bawling kid in the family.'

'Shut up. I'm not suggesting it was sibling jealousy. Don't joke. You don't hang yourself because you suddenly acquire a baby sister.'

'I don't know...' Sam was going to quip, then he turned thoughtful. 'Just after a baby?'

'February 23rd. And she killed herself on March 10th.' Our eyes met and I realised, as if there were a giant light bulb flashing between us, that Sam and I had just come up with the same scenario. 'Oh no. No, surely. But then, it could make sense. I mean, Robert was born in 1939.' I had the dates of the family fixed clearly in my head by now. 'That's a long gap, isn't it, to 1948—'

'Unless,' said Sam gleefully, 'the baby wasn't Nan's at all, but Rose's.'

'Of course! She had a baby and the disgrace killed her. That would make sense!' I stopped short, understanding one implication that Sam hadn't yet thought through. 'You realise it's our mother we're talking about.'

'Uh?' I was right. Involved in the riddle, he hadn't made the connection. 'Jeez!'

'February 23rd, 1948. Mother Gwenllian Owen, née Lewis, according to her birth certificate, but if we're right, she's really the illegitimate daughter of a suicidal thirteen year old.'

There was a pause. Sam was as stunned as I was. 'This is incredible. Do you think she knows? No. She wouldn't have thought to ask, would she?'

'Of course not. She never asks. That's her trouble. All those years, behaving as if everything was normal, while Dad was carrying on with his secretary.'

'Crap.' Sam burst out laughing. 'No he wasn't. Mum and Dad got divorced because they were bored with a dead end relationship. So long and thanks for the fish, you know? They did the marriage thing, they had children and raised them, and they even quite liked each other, but they just wanted to move on. At least Mum did.'

'Don't blame Mum! He was the one who went off to his bimbo!' Bimbo wasn't really the right word for my stepmother Mandy, forever ironing and lusting after heated hostess trolleys, but it was the principle of the thing. 'Mum's got nothing.'

'She's got everything. She used to be a suburban housewife, going nowhere. Now she's an independent woman, having the bohemian time of her life. It's poor Dad you should feel sorry for – couldn't cope with freedom. He only knows about being a suburban husband, with a lawn to mow, so he went straight to the first woman who'd give him the same again.'

'At least he's got someone. Mum's got no one.'

'Come on, Mum's had at least a dozen guys hanging round her since the divorce, and she loves them all.'

'Don't be disgusting!'

'I'm not. She's one happy bunny.'

'This is bullshit, you know that?'

'Why are you so determined to be so uptight about it? I know you were never exactly happy about it, but you didn't make a fuss at the time. Why is their divorce such an unforgiveable thing now?'

I didn't reply.

'Because you're scared of the thought of a marriage not working? Think about it this way. It proves there's life after it.'

'I have to wait that long?' Even as I said it, I hoped Sam wouldn't understand, but I knew he would. Straight off.

He looked at me, hard. 'When did you last sing?'

'I sing all the time. Hear me in the bath.'

'I mean professionally.'

'Look, I did a few gigs at a few clubs, just for fun. The band was a kids' idea. I was never going to make it professionally. Marriage to Marcus is not copping out.'

'*I* didn't say it was.'

'Neither did I.' I couldn't afford to let that turmoil get a grip on me again. 'Anyway, what has any of this got to do with Rose's suicide? It's Rose that matters, not... other stuff.'

Sam folded his arms, shaking his head. 'Have you ever paused to wonder exactly why it's so important to you? Why you have this urge to go rooting around so passionately?'

'You know why. I found Cwmderwen, and it made me realise that we'd never questioned, never looked, never even thought about them.'

'The Owen family.'

'Yes. You'd have to see it to understand. It pulls. It wants me to dig. It won't let go.'

Sam smiled. 'And how are the wedding plans?'

'It's all in hand. We've settled on a date. Did I tell you? March 24th.'

'Your birthday? Nice idea, makes sure he can't afford to forget the anniversary.'

'That's what I thought. Do you want the gift list? We have one.'

'I was thinking of giving you the singing fish, since Dilly didn't want it.'

'Do! I want it in pride of place on display at the reception.' I imagined it and groaned despite myself. 'I'm not going to think about the wedding just now,' I said brusquely. 'At the moment, I'm far more concerned with Rose's tragedy.'

'Yes. QED, that's the point.' Sam held up his glass. 'You want a hair of the dog?'

'Best not, the way I feel. Make some coffee.'

'Okay.' He headed for the kitchen.

'What is "the point" supposed to be?' I shouted, at his disappearing back.

'The point is Rose has nothing to do with the wedding.' Sam gave me a quaint look through the open door, then returned his attention to the cafetière. I waited in silence until he brought two mugs of hot strong coffee and pulled up a chair to sit and face me squarely.

'What are you going to do next?' he asked.

'I have to find out more, obviously. I can't leave it here.'

He laughed. 'All right, never mind what you're going to do next about the wedding. Let's play Agatha Christie, if that's really what you have to do.'

'Of course I have to. Look at it. 1948. It's like a great gash through our family. Rose gave birth, she committed suicide, a German prisoner shot her father...'

'German prisoner? German! Really? Didn't I say?'

'Yes, all right, you said it was a German. There was a prisoner of war camp just down the road. Still some prisoners there, waiting to be repatriated or whatever. Apparently everyone knew it was this Nazi who shot him. The police say he escaped back to Germany, which is why he was never caught.'

'No kidding. Gerda's dad was a German prisoner of war in Canada.'

'Gerda?'

'Uncle Jack's wife? I got talking to one of our cousins, Lucy, at the funeral—'

'Of course, you took Mum. Did Lucy say anything useful?'

'Just that her grandfather had been a prisoner of war out there in Canada, and uncle Jack was his friend and came out to live with him and married his daughter.'

We both puzzled over this for a moment. 'How did Jack come to be the friend of a German living in Canada?'

'Good question. I didn't think of asking. Lucy was more fascinated by Jack's British past. Wanted to know all about

Wales and Leicester. Fat lot I could tell her. She said she'd always been intrigued because Jack never spoke about his childhood.'

'Aargh!' Another knot of frustrating secrecy. 'Why is everyone so determined not to talk?'

'Beats me. A bit late to ask Jack now.'

I sighed in exasperation. 'Why did I leave it too late?' Another avenue closed. But there must be others still to be opened. Cwmderwen told me there were. Why else would it have summoned me, if not to unearth the truth? God, if only there were more clues to be squeezed from its stonework, like the old notebook, hidden in the dresser.

I put my mug down and grabbed Sam's arm. 'Since you're here, will you come and see Cwmderwen?'

'Sorry, I've got to be in L.A. on Friday.'

'I wish someone would be interested.'

'Ah, poor little orphan. Listen, I am interested. I'm going to be back in Britain in a few weeks' time. I promise, you can take me there and we'll both go and pay our respects at Rose's grave. How about that?'

'She hasn't got a grave. She committed suicide.'

'Oh Christ. Look, you keep digging, girl. Keep me posted on every development.' He looked at me, askance. 'You're not thinking of telling Mum all this, are you?'

'No,' I lied with a tone of exasperation. I was thinking about it, dismissing the notion, but I couldn't help wondering what she would say.

'Not that she'd sink under the strain, but there are ways and ways of suggesting that her mother was probably...' He paused, eyes narrowing, intrigued again. 'Just thinking. If

John and Gwen weren't Mum's parents, who was her real father?'

'I don't know,' I replied. But I had a horrible suspicion that I did.

20

Rose hangs.

This cannot be.

Peter's arms are round the girl, holding, supporting, his thin legs braced to take the weight, his voice stifled by the effort. 'Gwen.'

But his one word is drowned out. Drowned by a whirlwind, a whistling gale that descends out of nowhere, out the dark shadows, down from the trees and the windswept moors to shriek and howl around the creaking timbers of the barn.

And it is her, Gwen, shrieking, not knowing that the sound is her own. It bursts from her like a beast in agony, a long thin steady shriek of pain.

The spell breaks and she stumbles forward, groping, grasping at the white cotton, pushing his supporting arms away, taking the weight, her child, Rose, who is quite frozen, suspended like some Satan's clockwork from the hook in the cobwebbed rafters.

Freed, Peter staggers back, gropes on the wall, returns with a billhook, reaching, slashing at the greasy, blackened rope. Hack. Hack. His breath is heavy, desperate.

Why is he desperate? Why does he strive so hard?

Doesn't he know she is dead? Rosie is dead, Gwen is dead, all is dead. Dead, dead, dead. And still the shriek tears from Gwen's lungs and she is unaware, except of a distant meaningless sound.

The stiff cold body is free and Gwen crumples on the floor with her, in the straw and mud and filth. A sob axes its way from her breast. So cold and stiff, not a sigh, not so much as a spark of the poor raped soul remaining.

When was it? At dusk? At midnight? Was Gwen so occupied with tending the baby, little Siân Ellen, the imp so greedy for life, that she could not hear the child who had no greed left for anything but death?

Silence is the natural state at Cwmderwen, but it has nuances. This new silence is not that of iron discipline. It is deep, shocked, guilty. It seems to infect all who cross the threshold and it weighs upon Gwen, crushing out of her the ability to think or act.

People come and go, ghosts whose eyes will not meet Gwen's. Mrs George, from a vast distance, says, 'Well!' and then she is at a loss for words, a balloon deflated. The small part of Gwen that still functions pleads inwardly that Mrs George's speechlessness will continue. For if she speaks, if she begins to trot out the inevitable scripted nonsense of meaningless opinion, Gwen might well transform into a savage rabid dog.

But Mrs George remains subdued, her jowls slack, beady eyes misted, though she has not lost the instinct to take charge. She bustles the boys away to her daughter's care – Jack quietly frightened, too scared to ask questions, Robert thankfully uncomprehending – and she presides as others arrive, all at once, a crowd it seems in the small kitchen.

Constable Bowen, stout and bristly, good at calling small boys to order, being the father of six. He wallows, out of his depth, struggling to look professional in the face of a child's suicide. He has not had to deal with anything this bad since Albert Evans shot himself over at Y Garn in '32.

'Now then, yes, so, er, who is it found her? Faber, is it? Ah, the German prisoner. How was that then?'

Dr. Connell, elderly, short-sighted and not quite sober, still unshaven in the early hour. 'Bad business, bad business.' He looms, wielding his big black bag like a badge of office. What use is a black bag now?

William George and Ted Absalom. The stunned silence of strong men who suddenly have no strength. But they have enough to do what is needed: bring her in, lay her out on the kitchen table, so that Gwen can stare at her, touch her cold hand, see in the cruel daylight the cutting blue rope marks round her neck. Constable Bowen coughs and hesitates. There are correct procedures, but they are having none of that. Let him keep his peace. They know how things should be done decently. They tiptoe around, speaking in whispers, not interfering, as if something primal must be played out and not interrupted.

Dr. Connell and Constable Bowen are asking questions. Is Gwen supposed to answer, when she cannot hear them? She can hear nothing but a roaring in her brain. It does not matter. Mrs George has found her voice.

'She was ill,' she says thickly, her commanding voice breaking through to Gwen's consciousness. 'For a long time. Ask anyone. Off school with it. It affected her mind.

That's what it was. The balance of her mind was disturbed.'

'That's for the coroner to decide, Mrs George.' Dr. Connell has opened his bag. What is he going to do, take the girl's pulse? Stupid, stupid man!

'No call to go mauling her around,' says Mrs George indignantly. 'Any fool can see how she died. Leave the poor girl be. Sign the papers man, and leave her family in peace.'

They are putting their efforts into pacifying the old woman. Gwen stands over the forgotten child, willing the eyes to flicker open, willing the scarcely budding chest to stir with breath, willing the ghastly flush of strangled death to fade into fretful living pallor. But her will is not enough. The child will never stir. She has escaped them all.

And John? He is not there. This bustle, the gathering, the consultation, the taking away of the body, it all happens without him. Someone else picked Gwen up in the barn, sat her up, thrust a jacket around her for warmth. Peter? She does not recall. He has vanished. Had he gone to fetch the others? He has not returned.

It was William who carried her back to the house, white with shock. William who restrained her, stopping her from beating her own brains out against the wall. William who cradled her in tweedy comforting arms when John appeared at the door, on unsteady feet, staring blearily at the scene, the muscles of his face twitching uncontrollably. William who soothed her tears as John, twisted with an unfocussed rage, shouldered his gun and snarled Jess to heel and strode back out into the darkness.

Gwen has not seen John since. He is somewhere out

there in the fields, refusing to hear and see, turning his back on it all.

Other visitors come through the day, neighbours bringing uneasy solicitations, some tears, some words of devout wisdom. The Reverend Harries preaches Christian resignation, uneasily, as if for the first time he is aware of the triteness of his words. The communal compassion weighs down on Gwen like prison chains. She longs to brush it off, to be free to... to what, she does not know. Weep? Grieve? She cannot name this great black gaping hole that has opened up under her feet.

All these people flocking round her, they are all her people, her neighbours, speaking a common tongue, but now there is no comprehension between them.

'Mrs Owen, my sincere condolences.' The Colonel? Yes of course, landlord, magistrate, he must interfere. 'I know how terrible it must be to lose a child.'

No he does not. He knows nothing. His children are alive and... She meets his eyes, and there is the same embarrassment she sees in the others, but in his dull eyes perhaps a grain of understanding. Master Philip, warped and twisted by war, is the colonel's lost child. But Master Philip still lives and breathes, however viciously. He is not cold and stiff and blue. He is not a raped and tortured little corpse.

She cannot respond and he is gone, organising, ordering, directing. 'This Jerry chap, William. Faber, is it? Thorough black Nazi I expect, if he still hasn't been sent back. Are we sure he has nothing to do with this? You should question him, Bowen. I'll have a word with the camp commander. Can't go foisting Hitler's psychopaths on us...' His voice shakes with a stifled rage for the Germans in a faraway desert who destroyed his boy.

Gwen listens to their responses. Half-hearted denials longing for the comfort of being able to blame the foreigner, longing to tie the red cord round Peter's neck and send him off into the wilderness with their sins.

She should speak, but she cannot. Too late now. Far, far too late. She must salvage what she can, get on with life. Why? For the boys, for little Siân Ellen.

Night. Day, night, day. Dress, cook, clean, eat, milk, toil, scrub, dig, drink, sew, polish, undress, sleep. Numbing fathomless grief converts itself into repetitive action. She ignores well-meaning advice and gets on with her work, keeps busy, feeds the baby, chides the boys, scarcely aware of what she is doing, only that she must not be still for one moment. Other people are in control, Colonel, police, doctor. She registers little of it, not even the passage of time. Nothing makes her pause until the door opens and Dilys is there.

Dilys, white-faced, eyes brimming with tears.

Dilys looking plump and blooming and well dressed, a creature from another world, with Harry, tall, broad, reliable, compassionate Harry behind her.

'Gwen.' A kiss on her cheek, hands on her shoulders, an urge to embrace and hug each other that is, of course, resisted.

Dilys is no longer local, not part of this community. She commits the ultimate social solecism; she asks questions. 'Gwen, what happened? Why?'

Gwen answers vaguely, giving nothing away, telling no tales. No need. There is still sufficient telepathy between the sisters for Dilys to understand more than she will ever say.

Finally Gwen speaks, asserts herself. 'I don't want her buried here.' A bitterness that is unformed, undirected. She wants Rosie taken away, safe from Cwmderwen, safe from him. Or does she mean safe from herself, a self-flagellation to exorcise her sins?

Dilys does not delve, she merely accepts and Harry takes charge. Seion Chapel in Penbryn; that is the sisters' spiritual home, where their father's funeral was held. Best let her lie in Penbryn. Harry arranges it, as soon as the perfunctory coroner's hearing, satisfied with Dr. Connell's unexacting testimony, is over and the body is released. A quiet affair, only the family in attendance, Gwen, Harry, Dilys. Not John. John will not bury his daughter.

Where has he gone to? How long was it before he turned up again at the house. Gwen cannot remember, she scarcely saw him. But there is a stiff righteous dignity about John now. Is he stunned into sobriety or has this been his cue for one more sally against inevitable fate? One last attempt to hold together and be the pillar of respectability he once was. He has gathered himself, stands upright, unyielding. Rosie is no daughter of his, a sinner, a slut and a suicide against God's ordinance. He washes his hands. Let them do what they like with her.

It is a stalwart performance, but it does not quite convince. The murmur of agreement doesn't come. John is left standing aloof, while his neighbours nod their sympathy to Gwen and ignore his taciturn dignity.

It is going to break, she knows, this parade of restored propriety. Very soon the dam will burst and Hell will break its bounds. For herself, she does not care, but there are the children to fear for. That is the one thought nagging at

Gwen now. One child destroyed. What can she do to protect the others? She is powerless, clawing at the walls of the pit she is in.

Back at the house after the funeral, Mrs George hands over the infant Siân. She is keeping the boys tonight. She has laid out a funeral spread as well, tea and ham and cake, a bizarre but apparently necessary ritual. She says nothing when they return, bustles away, leaving the sisters to comfort each other.

Dilys, childless for all her dreams, cradles the baby, crooning over her. Gwen's child, Rosie's child. Nothing has been said and Dilys does not ask. The light fades and the fire in the range is the only glow. No one moves to light the oil lamps. Dilys reaches out to hold Gwen's hand and the darkness conceals the tears.

Dilys and Harry are staying at the Temperance Hotel in Penbryn. No room at this inn. They would not think of seeking hospitality from John, not that he has stayed around to be asked. He has recovered, briefly, the will to work, hard crippling work, mending gates and fences, imagining perhaps that he can re-erect the barriers around his life with nails and wire. The futile labour keeps him out into the late hours. Just as well. Best for Dilys and Harry to be gone before he confronts them.

The next morning there is an emptiness. The funeral is over, should life not stop here? The book closes. But no, the sunless daylight must creep back, the world must roll on, ready to forget.

Dilys and Harry return to say farewell. Gwen is busy in the yard, sweeping, swilling, washing it all away.

'Gwen, can't you rest? No need for that now.'

'Oh? And will the yard sweep itself? We keep no servants here.' She can hear the sourness in her voice but cannot help herself. 'Chickens to feed.'

'I'm sure Harry will...' Dilys has stopped, with a short gasp of shock and Gwen looks round.

Peter is standing at the entrance of the yard. She starts. She has not seen him since... He is gaunt. Was he not always gaunt? A withered wisp of a man.

'That's the German they are talking about,' says Dilys in a loud stage whisper. 'Get rid of him, Harry.' She looks round for a broom as if to sweep him away and she might easily do it by the look of him.

'Now then,' says Harry, swelling. Dilys and Harry hate the Germans because his cousin's wife died in a bombing raid. Heart attack. It is only proper to take these things personally. 'I don't know what you want, but...'

Gwen must interrupt. They do not understand. No one understands, except Peter. She must not have him swept away. But neither can she succumb.

'How are you, Peter? I hope the police weren't too rough with you.' She has heard that he was questioned. Suspected of being a foreigner and therefore the source of all woe. Mrs George's gruff protectiveness has dissolved. He no longer sleeps at Castell Mawr. He has been returned to the prison camp up the river.

'I am going away.' He waves aside her concern, just as he had waved aside Harry's ineffective aggression, and the west Wales constabulary in its wrath. He has known the worst that men can do, in and out of uniform.

'Going? Where?' She contrives to sound calm, though his words throw her into panic. Why should she care if he goes?

'They are closing the camp. We are being moved on.'

'You are going home?'

He looks at her, not so much pathetic as sardonic. His home is Dresden, someone has said.

'You'll be glad to go,' she says inanely. Anything to keep the dark passions down.

'You must leave,' says Peter. 'This is an evil place.'

'What? What's he saying?' blusters Harry.

'Good gracious,' says Dilys. 'Well I—'

'Come,' says Peter, reaching out his gnarled, claw-like hand.

'I—' Gwen teeters.

'You must come. Come with me, or you die. He kills you too.'

'You!'

It is all so quick, she cannot think, only observe as in a dream the stooping menace of John as he lunges into the yard, a fence stave thrust towards the little German.

Peter backs away, she sees the sweat on his grey face. Her reprimands, Harry's flatulent protests, Dilys' indignation mean nothing to him, but John is an all too real embodiment of the fears that haunt him. A real demon from a real hell.

John wields the stave with a roar as Peter retreats. The wood misses his shoulder but catches in his loose baggy clothes, ripping the jacket. John raises his arms to strike again.

'Now look here,' says Harry. Hating the damned Krauts is one thing, only reasonable. Braining them with a fence post is another. 'I don't think you should... Now see, man.'

John has not heeded, prepared to strike again. It is Gwen

who steps in his way. He glares at her, a mad dog, almost foaming at the mouth, then thrusts the stave to push her aside. She feels the splintered wood bruise, ripping through the thin cotton of her blouse, the wool of her vest, the flesh of her breast.

'Good God man!' Harry moves from words to action at last, wrestling the post from John's grasp.

Dilys thrusts her brother-in-law aside to throw her arms protectively round Gwen. 'Oh my God, Gwen, has he killed you? Oh good God.'

'It's nothing.' Gwen pushes free, her blouse clasped protectively round her. 'A scratch. It hasn't even broken the skin.' It has. She can feel the blood trickling, matting the fibres of the vest, but it will heal. She turns to peer over her shoulder at Peter, where he stands, grey and trembling. 'Go! Peter, go. Now! Just go.'

He does not move.

'Go!' she repeats, hand raised against him, her body stiffened with resolve until she sees him crumble. He stares one last time then turns away, one step, two. He lopes away, still staring at her.

She can turn back. Dilys is nearly hysterical. 'Hush now. It's nothing.'

Harry and John face each other. The post has been flung to one side. They glower, waiting for the other to break. Harry, it will be, surely. Kind happy Harry does not have the backbone to stand up to a man like John. But it is John who backs down, John who looks around, almost forlornly, trying to recover his dignity in self-righteous anger.

'Is a man not master on his own land? I will not have that beast here. Filthy brute. I know what he's been up to while he's been here. And that slut of a girl, that harlot. Animal. I'll whip him off my land if he shows his face here again.'

There is silence. He is nonplussed, waiting for a response, agreement or argument, but none comes. They only look.

'Be off, the lot of you. Wastrels, gossips, ungodly wretches, go on, get off my land, before I—'

'Now listen,' says Harry. 'You can say what you like to me but I'll not have you talk that way—'

'Be still,' orders Gwen.

John points an accusing finger at Gwen. 'I know your tricks, bringing that animal here, defying me. Deceiving me. Devil's spawn. I find him here again, you'll answer for it, and that brat with you! Drown it like the vermin it is!' The vileness spews out but its poison has been drawn, his authority countered. Abruptly, he strides away, out of this quagmire of his own making.

Dilys gives a sob of relief and Harry swells up in indignation, but Gwen hushes them. 'You are leaving.'

'I can't go, Gwen. We can't leave you—'

'Yes, yes.' Gwen brushes their concern aside. 'You must go back to Peterborough now.' She pushes them to emphasise her words, then holds up a hand to stop them on the starting block. She hurries back into the house.

Siân is asleep in the crib, eyes tightly shut, lips a rosebud, peaceful and unaware. Gwen lifts her, wrapping the old shawl round her. The baby does not stir. Gwen carries her out into the yard, shielding her from the damp chill of the autumnal air.

Gwen does not say a word. She simply places the baby in

Dilys' anxious arms. The bottle, the old shawl, all that Siân Ellen can carry out of here into the wide world.

'Now go.'

The sisters stare at each other, Dilys reading all that there is to be known in the void between them. She looks down at the child, the innocent unconscious fruit of so much torment. Of course it cannot stay here, to be poisoned and sullied and destroyed as its mother had been. Dilys bends down to kiss the peaceful forehead in acceptance.

Harry is frowning at the baby, not sure what to do, but Dilys, with the first shock over, is decisive enough for both of them, and she snaps into life, startlingly normal.

'Goodbye then, Gwen, if you're sure. We'll see you soon, I hope. No we will, I insist. You must come to Peterborough. Soon. Bring the boys, stay as long as you like. Harry, come on, we've got a long drive.'

He falls into step as she sets off up the lane. He is not sure, glancing back. Should they go, leave her here so vulnerable? What is the meaning of Dilys' seemingly heartless resolution? Surely she would want to stay with her sister.

Stony-faced, Gwen watches them go, understanding as he cannot that Dilys has responded to Gwen's unspoken urging as promptly as she ever did as a child. The words repeating in Gwen's brain transmit themselves to Dilys as effectively as a hand on her shoulder pushing her into action. 'Take the child, take her to safety, never mind the rest, never mind me, just keep her safe, take her now before it is too late. It's all I want. If you love me, go.'

Gwen does not move until they are out of sight. Then

she can breathe again. She does not know how they will resolve it, but they will find a way. They will cope, a loving couple, fine home, glowing future, money in the bank. All far far away from this dark abyss.

They have gone and she is left alone to face the storm.

21

I didn't tell my mother what I'd guessed, even though I was itching to do so, in my weekly phone call to her. Nor did I mention my recent flight from Wales or my drunken ramblings. Mothers should be left in ignorance of some things, and the stroke of luck that put Sam on hand in London had stopped Marcus from summoning her instead. Her ignorance could be my bliss.

So when I phoned her, we talked about Dilys and Sam's visit and of course the wedding plans and she joked about having to wear a hat, and I was thinking of her, as Sam described her, surrounded by a swarm of Irish lovers. I couldn't cope with the image. Not my mother.

'Everything fine at work?' she asked.

'Oh you know, exciting as ever.' More frustrating than ever, thanks to Trevor's chaotic laziness. I'd taken to working from home more to avoid the temptation to throw things at him. But the change was in me, not in him.

'Well, be good. Speak to you next week, darling.'

'Bye.' I put the phone down, thinking about the one piece of information I had managed, quite innocently, to get from her. Sheffield.

I'd go to the ends of the earth if I had to, and Sheffield was a lot closer than that.

Marcus sauntered in from the bedroom, where he'd retreated considerately to let me talk to Mum. 'How is Ellen?'

'Fine.' I glanced at the laptop and legal documents he'd spread on my coffee table. I'd switched mine off when he arrived, but he never stopped, sorting out the world, his career, my future. I'd heard, from one of his colleagues, that abandoning the conference for me had done his prospects no harm at all. He'd demonstrated sterling family commitment, and besides, he'd already given his presentation and made his useful contacts. Okay, so now he could concentrate on work for a few days, instead of mollycoddling me. 'Look, Marky. I'm taking a trip this weekend.'

To my surprise, he dropped down beside me on the sofa and gave me a kiss on the forehead. 'Good idea. A break will help you get over all this.'

'I don't need—'

'And I know Ellen will look after you. Do you want me to fix your flight?'

'I'm not going to Ireland.'

'She's coming here? Good. Where's she taking you?'

'No, I'm not going anywhere with my mother. I've got to go up to Sheffield. Nothing more exotic than that.'

'No.' He was firm and absolute. 'I'm not having Frieman and Case sending you off round the country while you're still so fragile.'

'Marcus, I'm not fragile. Look at me. And this isn't work. I want to see my uncle.'

267

'Charles? What's he doing in Sheffield?'

'It's my mother's brother, Robert. He's in a sort of nursing home in Sheffield, apparently.'

'That sounds bad. Is he very ill? You're in no state to go looking after sick relatives, you know.'

'Look, stop trying to turn me into an Elizabeth Barrett, will you? I'm in rude good health, as I've been demonstrating in all manner of naughty ways. Anyway, Uncle Robert isn't sick. At least, not what you mean by sick. I just need to speak to him. He was there, you see, at Cwmderwen. He was Rose's bro—'

'No.' He spoke calmly, but firmly. 'We've had enough of that. No more murder. Right?'

'What? Sorry, but—'

'You're dropping this family saga thing and moving on. No argument.'

'Don't be ridiculous. How can I leave it now? I have to know.'

'No, you don't. I'm sorry, but you're not going. That's final, Sarah.'

I laughed. 'You're a solicitor, not a high court judge.'

'No, I'm your partner. We're getting married.'

'You're my partner, not my boss and I'm not going to be promising to obey, so don't tell me what I can or can't do.'

The magisterial control was giving way to temper now. 'I'm supposed to stand by while you shut me out? While you mess around with this stupid business? If you're as fit and well as you claim, there are more important things for you to deal with. You're supposed to be seeing the dressmaker, remember, and we're going to finalise the guest list with Caro.'

'Marcus, the wedding is months away. It can wait. This can't.'

'You mean it takes priority over our wedding.'

'Right now, yes!'

'Well then.' He stared at me, slammed his laptop shut, scooped up his documents and dropped them pointedly into his briefcase. 'That tells me everything I need to know, doesn't it?'

I knew what I was supposed to do when things reached this stage. I was supposed to play illogical and emotional Sarah, the wayward child, reassure him that I'd put it badly, that of course he was my top priority, but, pretty please, I really really wanted to go. It was a role he'd created for me and I'd embraced it because it made life so very simple. But not this weekend.

'I'm going to Sheffield,' I said, sounding calmer and cooler than I felt.

There was a moment's silence while my response registered. I didn't know what sort of reaction to expect. This wasn't a scenario we'd played out before.

For a brief second, quite irrationally, I was afraid.

His jaw clenched, his nostrils flared, the alpha male on his dignity. 'Perhaps you'll find time to let me know when you get back,' he retorted stiffly, and walked out.

I actually found myself shaking. Marcus had flared up at me before, but always I'd used proven tactics to calm things down. I was probably going to spend the rest of my life using them. But I had to make one small stand now, for my sanity's sake.

I poured myself a drink. Well, I'd done it, and now I could concentrate on Uncle Robert instead. I checked the route to Sheffield.

He looked cleaner than I remembered him. I recalled a grimy, hairy man, smelling of urine and old sweat in an unravelling cardigan so filthy I couldn't tell its colour. Now he emitted a faint odour of institutional sickness, but he looked thoroughly scrubbed. Hardly any stubble on his chin and his grey hair was trimmed short and neatly combed.

Of course, when I'd seen him as a child, he was fending for himself in a battered old caravan as smelly and filthy as himself. Now he was in a care home, a modern Lego block, shielded by trees and carefully tended shrubs from the main road. He had his own room, a shared lounge and a sunny conservatory, with meals three times a day, a doctor on call and carers watching over him, all of which meant that my uncle Robert looked like a human being, not a wild animal.

And yet I was infinitely more shocked than I had been before. As a child, I'd accepted that he was odd, but then adults could be odd. Later I guessed that he was a little disturbed. Now, seeing him for the first time in twenty years, I realised how utterly cut off from the rest of the human race he must be. How had he ever coped on his own? And how had I imagined that I would be able to sit down and have a quiet chat with him?

Connie, the round-faced, smiling West Indian carer had shown me along to his room, delighted to have conjured up a visitor for him. 'Robert, here's your niece, come all the way from London to see you,' she said.

Robert didn't respond in any way – until I put my foot across his threshold. Then he reacted with instant alarm, without looking at me once.

'No, no, no, no, no, no, go away, no, no, go away.'

'He doesn't like people in his room,' Connie explained. 'You come along to the conservatory and have a nice chat in there.'

So I retreated to the conservatory and waited, uneasily admiring the lawns and beech hedging until Connie brought him along. No complaints from him now. He was clean and well enough fed, but pasty and flabby. He didn't exercise or get enough sun. His trousers were hoisted high up over his waist, too short, exposing the ankles. As he sat, his feet were placed exactly parallel; he leaned forward to inspect them and make sure they were set right.

My mother's brother. Or, if we'd guessed right, her uncle. There was nothing, no similarity, no family trait that I could recognise, no affinity at all. He was a flesh and blood link to Cwmderwen, to Rose and Nan and John Owen; he saw, heard, lived it all, and there was nothing there. He was the last battered piece of the shipwreck, the drifting flotsam shattered by the events of that terrible year. I looked at him, wanting to weep with pity.

He still didn't look at me though. Sure his feet were in position, he rocked quietly in his high-backed chair and stared at the carpet as if I weren't there.

'I am Sarah,' I said. 'I'm your sister Ellen's daughter. We met once, many years ago. Do you remember?'

No response.

'Do you remember Ellen? Siân Ellen, your baby sister?'

He rocked.

'When you all lived at Cwmderwen. Do you remember Cwmderwen?'

A response at last. Robert's eyes moved around the carpet. 'Teatime.' His voice was totally expressionless.

271

'Yes, that would be nice—'

'Teatime,' repeated Robert. Then more urgently, 'Teatime!'

'Yes, that's right, teatime,' said Connie, to my relief, appearing with a clattering trolley. 'Robert always knows when it's teatime, don't you, Robert. Here we are. There's a tea for you, Bertie.' She was dealing with the only other occupant of the long narrow conservatory, an old man nodding quietly under a blanket at the far end. 'And your ginger biscuit.'

'Teatime,' repeated Robert with satisfaction.

'Tea for Robert,' said Connie, coming to us. 'Two sugars.' She offered the cup to me. 'You give it to him,' she suggested.

Robert received the cup from me, watching my fingers warily as if they might do something unexpected.

'And a ginger biscuit,' said Connie happily. 'How about you, Sarah? Cup of tea?'

'Please.' My throat was parched and I sipped the scalding tea gratefully, as Connie bustled away.

'Cwmderwen,' said Robert.

'Yes?' I froze, the cup half way to my lips. Had the spell broken?

'Robert Owen, Cwmderwen, Llanolwen,' he intoned.

'Yes! That's right.'

'Robert Owen, Cwmderwen, Llanolwen.'

I swallowed. He was speaking as he had been taught long ago. His name and address, in case he wandered and got lost. 'Do you remember it?'

'Robert Owen, Cwmderwen, Llanolwen.'

'You lived there, in the cottage? With your mother and your father and your—'

'John Owen, Cwmderwen, Llanolwen.'

'Yes, that's right!' Something I was saying was getting through. I laid my recorder on the table, just in case. Who knew what might emerge from that confused mind? 'John Owen.' I hesitated over mention of the murder, but I couldn't do it. Not yet. 'And your brother Jack, and your sister Rose.'

'Rose a Jack a Robert. Rose a Jack a Robert. Robert Owen, Cwmderwen, Llanolwen. Teatime.'

It was teatime and his schedule was not going to be disrupted. He applied himself to his teacup and his ginger biscuit as if nothing else in the universe existed. Slurp. Nibble. Slurp. Nibble.

I waited, trying to compose a meaningful question. My original intention of chatting merrily about Mum, Dilys and family affairs was clearly pointless. I'd only have any hope of getting anything out of him if I went straight at it. It wouldn't upset him. He probably wouldn't even realise we were speaking of tragedy.

'Cwmderwen,' I said, to refocus him when he put the cup down. He was rocking again. 'Rose. Do you remember Rose? Your sister Rose?'

'Rose a Jack a Robert.'

'Yes, that's right.'

And suddenly he was speaking, a few disjointed phrases, and there was a sort of expression. Not in his eyes or in the drone of his voice, but there was something in the words that suggested anger or distress. For Rose, or against her? I don't know. It was all in Welsh. A stream of mono-tonal Welsh.

Of course it was. Take Robert back to his childhood in Cwmderwen, and what else would he have spoken? His first language. How long had it been, I wondered, since anyone had talked to him in the language he still knew best after all those years? One extra layer of isolation on all the rest.

Apart from one, two, three, there was only one word of Welsh I knew, not too taxing even for me. I tried it. 'Mam.'

'Mam,' he repeated. 'Gwenllian Owen, mam. Gwenllian Owen mam. John Owen nhad.'

'Uh, right.' I nodded encouragingly. I didn't have any other Welsh, but I had names. 'Dilys,' I tried.

'Dilys,' he repeated.

'Do you remember Dilys?'

'Dilys. Dilys *cacen*. Dilys *cacen*.' He gripped his knee and, to my alarm, rolled up his trouser leg. His knee was white and fleshy but he nursed it, mumbling in Welsh again.

'Good,' I said helplessly. 'Dilys looked after your sister, Siân Ellen. The baby.'

'The baby.' Robert puts his hands over his ears and rocked more violently, his trouser leg falling into place.

'What about William?' I suggested. 'William George. Do you remember William George, Robert?'

'William George! William George!' Triggering memories like this was probably not a wise move. Robert's voice was still expressionless, but it was rising, as if I had opened shutters on the past and let light flood in. He blurted a few phrases more in Welsh.

'Jack. Your brother Jack?'

'Jack, Jack, naughty Jack...' Welsh again. Why hadn't I used the last few months to learn a little of it? I let him talk, hoping against hope that somewhere in this babble I would be able to interpret words, gestures, a tear in the eye, that would tell me something.

274

It was telling me something. It was telling me that my uncle was damaged beyond repair. I'd have hugged him if he hadn't flinched when I leaned closer. Should I try one more? What was the point?

But I did it anyway, because it hung there before me, like Macbeth's dagger. 'Peter Faber,' I said. 'Do you remember the German, Peter Faber, Robert?'

'Peter Faber, Peter Faber.' He took up the refrain so readily that I was sure I'd hit gold. He sat back and his hands came up. They rose, fell and waved, thrashing, cringing, and he began to speak. There was no stopping him. He talked, the Welsh slurred but unending. My heart was pounding, wondering what I could do with this, how I could make something of it.

'Oh, Robert's off again.' Connie returned, chuckling at the sight of him. 'Does this, you know, every so often. Something sets him off.' She plumped herself down beside me. 'It's his language, Welsh,' she explained. 'Do you speak it?'

'No, sorry.' I listened to Robert with one ear and Connie with the other. 'It must be horribly lonely for him here.'

'Oh bless you, Robert has lots of friends here,' Connie assured me, laughing merrily. Not that Robert would know what a friend was. 'He's quite happy. We let him talk. We had an old gent a couple of years ago, from Wales, he spoke Welsh. From Caernarfon, with the castle, you know? Prince Charles. He had photographs of the investiture. What do you think of Camilla, then? Will she be queen?'

'I don't know.' I didn't give a toss about Camilla or Charles, and Robert was still talking on. 'Was the old gent from Caernarfon able to chat with my uncle?'

'Ah, we thought he might. It would have been nice for

275

Robert. But Rhodri was very deaf. Said he didn't understand a word Robert was saying. Grumpy old so-and-so. Still we tried. Bless him, doesn't he sing away when he gets going?'

I wouldn't call it singing, but Robert was still talking. Rocking and talking. Getting repetitive. Or maybe I was tuning in, beginning to hear repeat phrases. In time, surely I could understand.

Connie patted my arm as she heaved to her feet. 'You say your name a few times. Then he'll remember you.'

She left me with Robert who was beginning to falter. There were silences, a few more repetitions. I glanced at my recorder on the table. Would it ever be of any use? I'd assumed that Robert was talking Welsh, but now I couldn't swear to it. If grumpy Rhodri couldn't understand it, maybe it wasn't Welsh at all. Maybe Robert babbled away in a language all of his own. Utter isolation.

And utter desolation for me. I could guess what I'd been listening to. My grandfather's murder, played and replayed by Robert. There it was and not a single word of it comprehensible.

He stopped and was rocking gently again, still looking at the carpet.

'Do you know me?' I asked gently. 'I am Sarah, Ellen's daughter. Ellen is your sister. Siân Ellen. She is your sister and I am her daughter Sarah. I am Sarah and you are my uncle Robert.'

He was not listening, not looking. What was I doing here? I felt like someone at a freak show. I gathered up the recorder. 'Thank you for having tea with me, Robert. I haven't seen you in such a long time.'

'Sarah, Ellen's daughter.'

'Yes! Goodbye Robert. I'll come again soon.'

I would. Not to question or to probe. Just to see him and make sure he wasn't quite forgotten.

Back in my car, overwhelmed with sadness, I listened again to the end of the recording. Pure gibberish. A name or two, here and there, I thought. John. Owen. And Rose and William George. And there was a Dan. I could definitely hear him saying Dan. Dan and Gwen? No, Danny and... another name, Gweyden? Gweyden Valley. Perhaps it was the name of Cwmderwen's dell. I couldn't make it out but it sounded like Danny Gweyden Valley. Several times he said it. So who was this Danny?

22

John is approaching across the rainswept fields. Gwen can see him, stalking, stiff gaited, shoulders drooping, head bent against an invisible gale. A gale of opprobrium, a storm that he can weather if he only holds out steadily enough. The community wants to survive, and it knows what it must do. An open probing at this vicious cancer in its belly will only lead to fatal haemorrhaging and decay. It must cover up the wound and move on, let life overwhelm the stench of death and corruption.

That means that though John will never again be the respected pillar of the chapel, he'll be left in peace. The book of judgement must be closed. Rosie, strange child, is dead. Very tragic but there you are. She must have been sick, not right in the head, and the things you heard... A nasty little piece she could be. Pinched the Phillips girl and spat at little Gareth Absalom. She'd have gone bad in the end, one way or another. Perhaps it is a blessing...

And Mrs Owen had another baby, but now it has gone. Given it away, they say. Odd that, but it is her business. No good can come of dwelling on these things.

Not in public at least. In private, of course, in every village house and scattered farm there is gossiping and scandalised shaking of heads over the kitchen table, and eyes narrowing and lips pursing. 'I've heard... Well, good God...'

What tales are they telling? Why make up wicked slander about John Owen, one of their own, when a more satisfying culprit is to hand? That German, of course. It will be he who did whatever it was that was done. Let's not put a name to it. Unspeakable, the lot of them. Just as well they're being moved out, before they bayonet us all in our beds. Send them all back. Hanging's too good for them. Small wonder John Owen is tried beyond endurance.

Gwen sourly accepts the inevitability of all this tidying up. The prison camp is closing. An easy solution. The community needs to forget and the stillborn truth that Rosie took to the grave is a necessary sacrifice for their own survival. They do not want to hear it spoken any more than Gwen had wanted to. John has only to endure the sidelong glances, the lowered voices, the sudden hush for so much longer, before it is all buried.

But can he endure, or is he the link that will destroy the community's anchor chain? Tragedy has shaken him into one last obstinate attempt to recover, restoring to him a temporary security by driving him back to work, back about his business. Working, working, never pause, never breathe, never think.

The Georges approve, wanting to believe it is the old John back in control, but Gwen knows it cannot last. Guilt shadows his every move, and reflects back at him from every face. If he keeps his peace when he is abroad in agonised pride, at home he roars, challenging any word, any look that dares to question.

The words and looks do not come. For the sake of the

boys, Gwen takes care not to aggravate him. She serves in silence, her penance. She has chosen this, she must endure.

Her submission appeases him a little. He is master in his own house again, no thirteen-year-old eyes of hate fixed on him, no child in its crib to speak to him of sin and damnation. This is a righteous house and if there has been wrongdoing, it is Gwen's. Her moral laxness, her inability to discipline her children, her failure to be a good wife.

It is her own failures that haunt her, as she feeds the chickens with spartan scraps. Failure to be a good wife? No, that is not one of them. The world has got it all wrong. She has been too good a wife. That is her failing.

She carries the swill to the pigsty. She has left the children at the table with tea and bread and a smear of butter, gulping down their supper to be out of the way before John comes in. She does not have to tell them to hurry.

'Gwen.'

He is standing there in the shadow of the barn, baggy clothes crumpled and stained as if he has slept under a hedge. But he had always looked a tramp.

'Peter, you cannot be here. Go, quickly, before John returns.'

The fear in him is palpable, but he does not stir. 'No, this time I do not run away. Unless you run too.'

'What on earth do you mean?' She realises she is flapping her apron at him, as if to shoo him away with the hens. It hides the trembling at the thought of John's return.

'Come away,' says Peter, stepping forward, reaching out his hands. 'Come away before he kills you.'

'Don't be absurd. I don't know what you are talking about.'

'He kills you. As he killed her.'

'How dare you! No one killed Rosie. She died by her own hand. She died because I—'

'He killed her soul and he kills yours.' His shuffling steps have brought him to her. His hand touches hers and she flinches. 'If you stay, you want to die. Or are you already dead, Gwen? Dead, like me.'

She cannot take in what he is saying. What is he offering?

'Run away. Before it is too late.'

'Don't talk nonsense. Even if... How do you imagine I would live?'

'I will look after you.'

'Ha!' She barks a short sharp laugh, the nearest she can come to humour. Peter, who could be blown away by a puff of wind. Peter the foreigner, forever haunted by old horrors she cannot bear to imagine. Peter, too crippled within to cope with the slightest silliest alarm. Peter, who even now stands there with the sweat breaking on his grey creased brow. He will look after her?

In his urgency he has grasped her hand. She looks down, her fingers entwined in his, the grasp returned, fixed, as if neither of them can bear to let go. Each one the other's lifeline.

She looks at him afresh. How old is he? She has grown accustomed to thinking him old, crippled by time, withered by experience too painful to be spoken of. But he is young, she realises. A boy? A youth? How would it be for Jack if he were torn away and sent to war? Would he too have become this haunted ghost?

'Peter, what can you do for us, for me and the boys? How would we live?'

'I can work.'

'Yes. You can work, I don't doubt it, but who will give you work round here? You know...' Does he know what is being said? She shrinks from asking.

'We can go away. Far away. It does not matter. As long as it is away.'

'We would need...' Her hand is on her breast, wondering how she came to be here, thinking of how... not of how Peter would take care of her, but of how she would take care of him. Can she really be so foolish? And yet...

'I know how to find food. I have...'

She does not hear the footstep, but she feels it. John's shadow falls across her. The dream crashes into the pit of her stomach, and she sees the blank black fear in Peter's eye.

She does not turn to confront John. She knows he is there. 'Go, Peter, now.'

But Peter must stand. He fled before. This time he must be a man, whatever the terror that sucks the blood from his gaunt features.

'Didn't I warn you off my land?' John's voice, behind her, is soft, so much more menacing than if he raged and roared. 'Did I not say what I would do if I found you here again?'

'Please go, Peter.' Gwen hopes the sobs in her voice will convince him that this is not a time for manly boldness. He does not move. In desperation she lunges forward, pushing him away with both hands. 'Run, Peter, please!'

'No I will not let him...'

The blow catches Gwen on the ear, sweeping her to one side like corn scythed. She lands heavily on the damp cobbles, but somehow she finds the strength to turn, in falling, and to beat, with stupid ineffectual childish blows, on John's boots.

She looks up, seeing the blood flood to his face, his lips draw back into the snarl of an animal. For a moment Gwen fears, hopes, that a seizure will carry him off. But John twists out of its grip, the monster of rage bursting out of him as he kicks Gwen away and turns to confront the forlorn boy who thinks he must protect her, fists raised. She does not see, she only hears the thud, the expelled breath. Peter is lying winded halfway across the yard.

'Come here, will you, you filthy beast, to find yourself another whore?' John has loped, like a werewolf, to the barn, emerging armed, a heavy chain in one hand, pitchfork in the other.

Gwen staggers up. She pulls Peter to his knees, no time for gentle compassion. 'Go, Peter, now, get out of here now!' Her voice is raised to a shriek of urgency.

'Bitch!' She expects to feel the chain across her own back, but instead John's fingers claw her hair, pulling her away. 'You've played in the muck with him, have you, spreading lies about me? Evil foul-mouthed slut!'

She is fighting back, defending herself, but he has dragged her across the yard, hurling her against the door frame, fists flailing, chain coiling round her as the handle of the pitchfork smashes into her slight body. He is possessed. Like a rag doll she is thrown into the house, her head crashes against the wall and the door is slammed behind her. Slammed and locked.

Barely conscious of the two boys staring at her, white faced, she drags herself to the window. Please God, let Peter be gone.

But the fool has not gone. He is hobbling forward to meet his demon, and John is striding towards him and in a red black flood of pain and dizziness, Gwen passes out.

She is propped up against the wall, a cushion behind her head, lukewarm water trickling down her face as her forehead is clumsily bathed. She opens her eyes, fighting back nausea, and Jack stares at her in shock and terror. So unlike happy Jack. That is bad. Very bad. She moves and every bone seems to scream.

Robert is standing by the cracked window, mouth open, eyes wide, breath coming in short frantic pants. She must see to him. She must – She is confused. What has happened?

For a moment she stills her hammering heart, listening. Deathly quiet, but for the voice, low, muttering, sometimes fearful, sometimes angry. The voice of a demon talking.

'I will smite the unrighteous. Out Satan. Not in my yard. I am master here.'

The voice, enveloped in the darkness, grips at her vitals.

She hears the sound of something dragging. Something being dragged, across the yard. It is almost dark outside. Evening shadows have swallowed up the valley.

Tears have washed white grooves down Jack's grubby face, but he is sufficiently in control to tend her. He must help her now.

'What has happened?' The words seem to come from somewhere else, not from her.

Jack cannot talk. When he tries to do so, sobs rack him. She reaches out a swollen hand to pull her to him. For a moment the pain threatens to make her swoon again, then her head clears. She remembers.

The dragging has ceased but she dare not go out into the yard. Leaning on Jack, she gets to her feet, pulls herself across the kitchen into the scullery, leaning heavily on the stone sink. She fumbles with the door latch and jerks the door open.

John stands there. John as she has never seen him before. A terrible sobriety about him. A demonic sobriety, Hell in his eyes. 'Get back in, woman.' There is not even rage in his voice now, only the coldness of absolute command. She is pushed back, the door slammed and locked.

Insanely, she rattles it, but it will not open. She moves to the scullery window, peering out into the gloom as her husband merges with the shadows and the dragging resumes. A heavy shapeless mass. A sack of potatoes it could be. John drags it into the darkness at the end of the garden, under the apple tree.

She stands, breathing slowly, trying not to be sick, as she hears the sharp ring and thud of spade biting into earth and stone. She returns to the kitchen, tries the front door again. No good.

Jack is clinging to her, eyes dilated. Not Jack. He must not fear. Instinctively, not realising what she is doing, she tuts, scuffing his hair into place. 'Upstairs, now.'

She is surprised by the normality of her own voice. The boys obey, propelled by her, up the steep wooden steps, into the pitch dark chill of the first bedroom. As if it is the most natural thing in the world, they climb together into the big iron bed, mother and sons, cradled together, listening to the thud, thud, thud outside, waiting for the night to end.

23

Dilys was well. She was still complaining about the rates, which she didn't pay, public transport, which she never used, and the manners of young people whom she never met. She abused the staff, poured scorn on her fellow residents and berated me for not being a married woman yet. All of which meant that she was fine, her usual self, rejoicing in the triumphant immunity of old age.

I visited her at least once a month, partly to keep my mother updated, and today I could safely report that there was no cause for concern. So, complaints dealt with, walk taken, tea brewed, I could start on my own business. Uncannily, Dilys seemed to know I was about to raise awkward subjects, because as soon as I opened my mouth, she whipped out a new blouse that she had bought a week before and began to fuss over it. Did it fit, was the colour right, should she take it back?

'I've been to see Robert,' I said.

She frowned over the buttons. 'Robert? What business did you have, up in Sheffield?'

'None. I was visiting Robert. He is my uncle, after all.'

She was annoyed with the collar, looking as if she had half a mind to wrench it off. 'How is he? No better I suppose.'

'He's well cared for.'

'Of course he is. Your mother sees to that. You think we'd leave him in a gutter?'

'No, of course not. The home is very nice.' A wholly different affair from the Edwardian grandeur of Dilys' nursing home, but I doubted Robert would even notice, still less appreciate, the extra refinements of this place. 'He seems quite... happy.'

Dilys put the blouse away, rummaging through the drawer for something else to fuss about. 'I don't expect he has much to say for himself.'

'He talked a great deal.' I could feel her tensing. 'But I didn't understand any of it of course, except a few names – his father and mother and so on. He was talking in Welsh.'

She snorted, turned, busied herself with the wardrobe. 'Stuff and nonsense. Where is that coat?'

'You mean the one behind the door? What happened with my grandfather, Dilly?'

'You know very well,' she snapped. 'He was shot. Now then...'

'Nan told you what happened, didn't she? She was there. She must have talked about it.'

'No.' Dilys was angry. 'She was in shock, girl. Traumatised, isn't that what they call it these days? You know what that's like, don't you?'

'Yes. Yes, I do. It's horrible. But it helps to talk. Didn't she get to talk? To you?'

'No! After that terrible time, with the police questioning her, no need for me to keep dragging it up again. She wanted to forget. It's best forgotten. Now.'

So much for counselling therapy in the 1940s. Poor Nan.

'I've been speaking to people.'

'No good listening to Robert. You know he's not right in the head. Never was. There's no good you pestering him.'

'I've been talking to other people too. Around Cwmderwen. William George.'

'William!' Dilys sat down, hand to her chest. 'William George? At Castell Mawr? He's still alive?'

'Very old.' I smiled. 'Not like you, Dilly. But yes, he's still there at Castell Mawr. His son Gethin farms there now.'

'Son! So he finally got round to it with that Evelyn Lloyd, did he? Well well.'

'Evelyn? Yes, I think that was the name on the gravestone...'

I caught Dilys' sniff and realised what I'd said. William being still alive only emphasised how many others of her generation had gone. One by one, all the companions of her long life. The inevitability of death clawed at me. 'But William's looking good,' I added hastily. 'Very deaf though.'

I caught her black eyes watching me. 'What were you doing, pestering an old man? Leave him be.'

'I went to call because I'm their neighbour now. You'd want me to be polite, wouldn't you? He remembers John and Gwen. Especially their music. Isn't that's nice?'

'Music. Hmph.'

'And he remembers the murder.'

'No call to go talking about that.' Her lips worked together. 'What did he say?' she asked at last.

'He told me the same as I've read in the newspapers. That my grandfather was shot by a German prisoner, Peter Faber. Is that right, Dilly?'

'No business to go poking around in all that.'

'Peter Faber argued with my grandfather. Jack went rushing off to Castell Mawr to fetch help and when William arrived he found Grandfather dead and the German running off.'

Dilys' face screwed up with an emotion I hadn't expected. Her eyes began to gleam. There was a moment's silence while she fought off this disgraceful surrender to sentimentality. She cleared her throat. 'Yes it was the German. Peter Faber. But he was never caught.'

'Oh.' Just like that. She'd known and never breathed a word. 'What was he doing there? That's what I don't understand.'

'They worked in the fields, the prisoners, Italians then the Germans.' She was angry with me and she slammed down decisive judgements. 'Shouldn't have been allowed, having them out on the farms, sleeping there, some of them. I wonder we weren't all murdered in our beds.'

'Did prisoners work at Cwmderwen?'

'No! No, your grandfather would have none of them.'

'So what was this Faber doing at Cwmderwen?'

Dilys humphed. 'Came from Castell Mawr. One of William George's men, he was.' She tutted.

'And people knew Faber was dangerous?'

'Faber was... People said...' Dilys' eyes were deeply troubled. 'Just like the rest! Your grandfather couldn't be doing with him. Ordered him off Cwmderwen more than once. But Peter wouldn't listen. He wouldn't go.' Her voice trailed away into private memories that wild horses were never going to drag from her. 'Now that's enough!'

'Tell me about Rose,' I said.

The subject caught her unawares. She started, rubbing

her arthritic knuckles. 'You leave that well alone, my girl. It's none of your business.'

'Not my business? How can you say that? Whose business is it then? You never mention her. Why does she have to be forgotten?'

'Because it's for the best.'

Dilys' simmering anger only fuelled mine. The cruelty of it all was so shocking, I couldn't help myself. 'I know she killed herself and that's a terrible thing, Dilly. It's so sad, so awful I can't bear it. I think it's wicked that no one will even talk about her.'

Dilys stared at me, a look of intense, white-hot – hatred? 'Wicked, is it? I'll tell you what's wicked!' But she didn't tell me. The words dried up on her lips, now firmly pressed together as if she had vowed never to speak again.

'She was just a child, Dilly. And she must have been so miserable. Don't call her wicked. That's what they did, didn't they? All those virtuous chapel folk? That's why she's not buried on hallowed ground.'

'Stuff and nonsense. What would you know?'

'She's not at Beulah, Dilly. Not with her father.'

'Of course not!' she snapped. Lips pinched together again.

'I think that is awful.'

Dilys was messing with a tissue, ripping it to shreds. 'Leave it, girl!'

'I can't. I've got to know. She had a child—'

'Who says so?' Dilys looked like a tigress roused.

'Are you going to tell me it's not true?' I'd only been guessing until now, but her all too instant response, the defensive way she twitched her skirt and jutted her chin, convinced me I was right.

Behind the bravado, Dilys swallowed, trying to work her way around a direct lie.

'Isn't it obvious?' I asked, pleading for her surrender. 'All those years after Robert was born and there's my mother suddenly, out of nowhere, and a couple of weeks later Rose kills herself. It all fits.'

She tried to snort and failed.

'Sorry Dilly, but I have to know. Who was Mum's real mother?'

She stared away stiffly at the window, as if about to reprimand the sun for shining too brightly. Obediently, it slipped behind a cloud. I felt a chill. 'Ask her,' she snapped.

Why was I doing this? I knew I was tormenting her, but it seemed such a betrayal if I didn't get at the truth. 'Dilly, I know Grandfather had a fight with Faber. He frightened the children, that's what I was told. Frightened them or worse. Was the argument about Rose, Dilly? Was the German prisoner the father of her baby? She was only thirteen. Did he rape her? Is that what no one will talk about?'

Dilys said nothing. Her hand was shaking on the arm of her chair, so I went to the window to give her space. I realised that my questions have been little short of an assault, but I didn't appreciate how violent until I turned back. I had never, in twenty-nine years, seen Dilys cry. She did it with dignity, sitting bolt upright in imperial silence, tears streaming down her cheeks.

I was aghast.

She recovered, reached for a fresh tissue and blew her nose noisily. Then she coughed to clear her throat. Her voice was gruff but chill. 'Leave it, girl.' It was an order. 'Let the dead sleep in peace. You have no right to disturb them after all these years. No right, you hear? They are with God. He knows the truth. That is enough.'

God knows.

How could I go on? As far as I knew, Dilys had always attended chapel, regular as clockwork but with an ironic twinkle, as if to demonstrate that it was mere lip service to social convention. Like supporting the Liberal Party. I'd never heard her mention God in any personal way. If there were a secret part of her that genuinely prayed, then it was so private that I felt I'd committed some obscene desecration in dragging it to the surface. I'd intruded far too deep.

'I'm sorry, Dilly.'

She looked at me, stern as a guardian angel expelling me from Paradise. 'Let them be,' she commanded.

But I couldn't. I had to ask one more question. 'What about Danny? Robert kept mentioning another name. Danny. Who was Danny? He kept saying Danny Gweyden Valley. What was he trying to tell me?'

Dilys stared at me with grey horror.

'Sarah?' My mother was speaking horribly clearly on a phone I'd answered while still half-asleep. I pushed the duvet off and struggled up in bed.

'Are you awake?' she demanded.

'Just about.'

'Good.' She was sounding alarmingly brisk. 'I want you to go to Hove. I've had a call from the home. Dilly's had a stroke. I'm coming on the next flight, but you can get there sooner than me. Will you do that?'

Oh God! What had I done? 'Yes. Yes of course.' I scrabbled for my clothes. 'Oh no. Is she bad? Did they say how bad she is?' Please, please don't let Dilys die. If she died, I would have killed her. Not again. How would I live with it?

'I don't know,' my mother was saying. 'It can't be good at her age, but you know what a tough old bird she is. Will you be all right to drive? Sorry, I didn't mean to upset you, but I would like someone to be there as soon as possible.'

'Don't worry, I'm fine.' I was dragging on my jeans. 'I'll be on my way in a couple of minutes. I'll see you there.'

Dilys' room at the nursing home wasn't as chaotic as it must have been in the early hours with the bustle of getting her into an ambulance. Someone had been in, cleaned up, made the bed and left her scattered possessions in a neat pile by the pillow.

I'd sat with her, by her hospital bed, riddled with guilt and shame at the sight of her, suddenly small, helpless, a frail old doll, whom I had tormented to breaking point. When at last my mother arrived and took over the vigil, the nurse told me Dilys had seemed anxious for her things, so I'd rushed to the home, desperate to do some small thing to make amends. I'd pack up everything she might need.

Her handbag, capacious as ever. I had her slippers and her night jacket, her dressing gown. I'd take her some day clothes too. She'd want to be reassured that she'd be on her feet again soon.

I was so sick with remorse I sat on the bed, burying my head in my arms. Why couldn't I have left well alone?

Pulling myself together, I looked again at the debris of

the night. The posy vase I'd bought her from Sam must have fallen from her bedside table. The flowers had been swept away, but the pieces of china had been picked up and placed with the library book which it had soaked in falling. I would take her some books. And her reading glasses, there on the table. Her brush.

A photograph album, old and battered, the dull green cover bound with a silken tassel. It was on her bed under the other things. It was the one I remembered being shown as a child. Had she had it out, in the middle of the night, to look through it?

Gingerly, I opened it.

It was all there: her youth. An ancient family group, in best dress, with potted palm and a harp; my shopkeeper great-grandfather with his wife and three children, Dilys the baby. Pictures of Dilys as a young woman, smiling and almost coquettish. Dilys and her father, crippled old man now, with a sad lopsided smile. Dilys on a bicycle. Harry, out of focus, standing grandly by a dumpy little black car. The Owen family – the same photo I had, but not creased. I could see Gwen's face now, vaguely anxious. And Rose. Her face was still half hidden in her mother's apron, but I could see her mischievous eye, and half a smile.

My fingers were trembling as I turned the pages. More photographs of Dilys and Harry and faces I didn't know. Then three children in a vegetable garden. I recognised the door behind them. The backdoor of Cwmderwen.

Robert was there. And not there. A toddler, fascinated by his scabby knee, apparently unaware of the camera.

Jack. A scrawny boy, one sock down, but standing to attention, a big beam and crumbs on his face.

And there was the picture of Rose. A girl of nine or ten. Hair in plaits, cotton frock, tight cardigan, pretty in an undernourished sort of way, dark hair, big eyes. Big direct eyes looking straight into mine. As if she recognised me. Of course she would. 'Doesn't Sarah look just like her,' my mother had said.

The child who killed herself. Who looked like me. An ice-cold hand kneaded in my stomach. I dragged my eyes away, turning the pages, searching for more. Dilys, Harry, my mother as a happy baby, my mother as a toddler, school girl, my mother on family holidays. There it was, the photo they had argued over: my student mother, outrageous in miniskirt and gorgeous boots. That was all. I shut the album and realised there was something under it. A framed photograph. It was the photo of Rose. Larger, clearer, haunting. Where had Dilys concealed it all these years, hidden away from my sight? On the back, in fading ink, was written: 'Rose Elizabeth Owen. Rest in peace.'

'I'm glad you could get here so quickly,' said my mother, as we took a walk in a park. We both needed the fresh air. 'I feel terribly guilty being so far away from her.'

My mother felt guilty! I winced. 'You're always coming over to see her.'

'Yes, I know, and I have you to check up on her regularly, but even so... What's the matter, Sarah?'

'I think I did it. I caused the stroke.'

'Don't be ridiculous.' Maternal impatience. My mother was tired, of course, after coping with her hastily arranged journey and the nursing home and, at Dilys' obvious wish, the bustle of BUPA, but still rational. 'You weren't even there.'

'But I was there, yesterday. I was asking her questions, awful stuff I should never have raised.'

My mother looked at me, thoughtful. 'Is this something to do with Cwmderwen?'

'Sort of.'

'Dilly's told me very firmly what she thinks. I must say, I'm delighted that you can still be impetuous occasionally, but wasn't buying the house where my father died rather ghoulish?'

I sighed. It was beginning to seem that way. 'I don't know. It felt... I had to know what happened.'

'And you asked Dilys. She doesn't like talking about death, you know that. But I really don't think that would have caused this stroke.'

'There was more.'

'What?'

How could I not tell her? I had to be shriven. 'I asked her about things. Your father. He was shot.'

'Yes, I know. Oh dear, you didn't, I suppose. I should have told you, but it never seemed to need explaining.'

'You know about the German POW?'

'I heard about it. Harry let it slip but Dilys got so terribly upset I didn't like to ask too many questions.'

'How come I didn't inherit your discretion?'

'Because you are a force of anarchy, darling. I suppose you asked Dilys and she didn't want to talk about it?'

'Yes. And then I asked about Rose. Your sister. Did you know about her, too?'

'I knew of her. She died long before I was born. I used to ask, of course, but I realised that it was something else Dilys didn't want to talk about, so I let it rest. Why are you so fascinated?'

'Because she didn't die before your birth. It was after. Just after. I think... I thought... Maybe... It could have been her giving birth.'

My mother stopped, astonished. 'Good heavens. Good Lord.' Amazement gave way to pain. 'Are you saying she died in childbirth?'

'No! Even worse. She committed suicide.'

'Oh no! How terrible.' My mother's face instantly contorted with pity. Real heartfelt pity for a child so miserable, but I realised at once that it was the pity she'd feel for any such child. There was no connection. There had never been any connection. My mother had been removed from it all, beyond the reach of hurt.

Until I started digging. 'I kept going on at Dilys, you see. I just wanted her to tell me who your real mother was, and...'

'Sarah.' My mother pursed her lips, shut her eyes, then flashed quiet anger. 'I know the answer to that one. Dilly is my real mother.'

'Dilly!' I couldn't get my brain round this impossible conundrum.

'Of course she is! Dilly took me almost as soon as I was born. I know she never adopted me officially, but she raised me, nursed me, protected me, loved me, and that's what a mother is. How could you go asking her who my real mother is! Didn't you stop to think how cruel that question would be?'

'Oh God.'

'Oh Sarah, come on now.' My mother took my arm, comfortingly. 'Why have you never talked to me about all this?' She looked around for the nearest route to a likely pub. 'I don't know about you, but I need a drink.'

'Several,' I agreed fervently.

We found a place with comfortable armchairs and dark cosy corners, and sat nursing our glasses. My mother eyed me over her beer glass. Shepherd Neame. She'd said she was desperate for a change from Guinness. It could be the beer that had added inches to her waist line. Not so long ago I would have seen it as a sign of her sad decline, letting herself go. Now, I realised it was proof of her stubbornly, happily not giving a damn.

I had to admit she was looking good. Full of life and satisfaction, despite the worry of Dilys' sudden collapse. I couldn't recall her ever being unhappy in my childhood, but there had always been a quiet restraint, a faint frown of stifled frustration. Now she looked fulfilled, free as a bird. She had an exhibition coming up in Cork. One way or another, I was going to have to come to terms with the notion of her entertaining a troupe of middle-aged lovers.

I could tell from the look in her critical eye that I wasn't looking remotely as fulfilled. 'You know what Sam thinks,' she said, putting her glass down. 'He thinks buying this house is all Freudian displacement.'

'Oh, that is typical Californian psychobabble.'

'Well, maybe. But aren't you using Cwmderwen as an escape?'

'No! All right, yes I suppose it has been a blessed escape from Caroline and this bloody wedding stuff.'

'Be truthful. Is it really Caroline you want to escape from? Or her son?'

'How can you even ask?'

'Everything is really fine between you and Marcus?'

'Fine... enough. We've had a bit of a row, but I'll sort it out.'

'What sort of a row?'

'Marcus didn't want me to go and visit Uncle Robert and I went anyway.'

My mother was taken aback. 'You went to see Robert?' She folded her arms. 'I'd love to think you went out of the kindness of your heart, but I suppose it was just to do with this obsession.'

'You sound like Marcus. This obsession.'

She laughed grimly. 'How was Robert?'

I shook my head. 'I think he's as well as he'll ever be. I didn't realise how bad he was. I'd only met him once before. In that caravan.'

'Oh yes, that.' My mother scowled at the memory. 'They let him out of hospital without telling us. That was a bit of an emergency visit or I wouldn't have dragged you along. Did he know who you were? He never recognises me.'

'It's awful.'

'I wish there was something I could do to make things any better for him, but I don't know what. He has the trust fund to keep him safe, and his routine, and the staff are kind. But it's not a happy story, no.'

'So sad.'

'Yes, well, right now, I'm more concerned about your sad story.'

'You mean Rose and—'

'No, let's stop these evasion tactics. You know very well, I mean you and Marcus. You really are determined to go through with it?'

'For God's sake, it's all arranged. The date's set.'

'Getting married on your birthday.'

'My thirtieth birthday. A symbolic farewell to my youth.'

'Oh Sarah!'

'Well, what else can I do?' I had determined to lock up my treacherous terrors and throw away the key, but as I began to speak, it all erupted. 'Everything's booked, the church, the flowers, the caterers, the chamber orchestra, the... I don't know, she's probably booked the chimney sweep. The invitations have all gone out, people are buying presents. How can I back out now? Again. When everyone knows I walked out on him once before.'

'No they don't. You weren't away long enough, love. Two weeks. Really, you should have stayed away two months at least for people to have got the message. Instead you hurried back in time for Marcus to pass it off as a quickie vacation. Why couldn't you have stayed out there longer?'

'Because... because Josh couldn't give me what I needed.'

'Love?'

'No. Hatred. I wanted him to hate me. To blame me. Oh, don't ask. It was all, you know, Jemma. Grief. Guilt.'

'And it still is, isn't it? This horrible tragedy of Rose. You're still looking for closure.'

I swilled my drink in my glass and took a deep breath. 'I wanted to blame someone for Jemma. Myself if no one else. And there was really no point in blaming anyone, even me. Blind fate is so impossible to cope with. But Rose is different. Call it displacement, if you like, or obsession, but I feel I can't walk away from something so bloody unjust, and not try to fight for the truth.'

'Well.' My mother shook her head. 'I'm glad you're reaching for something once more. Maybe it is something you need to do to find yourself again. But Sarah, what are you going to do about Marcus?'

I tried a joke. 'Nobody dumps Marcus Crawford.' Then I realised it wasn't a joke. He'd swept me back into his suffocating embrace when I'd returned from India, precisely because no one dumped Marcus Crawford.

'Do you honestly love him?'

'Sometimes. I don't know. I did. I really did. At first...'

My mother groaned.

'I know where I am with him,' I argued.

'Well of course! You always know where you are with a bully. But that's not a reason to marry him.' She looked at me straight. 'Sarah, don't just slide into the wrong match.'

'Is that what happened with you and Dad? Slid into a loveless marriage—'

'It wasn't loveless!' My mother was shocked at the suggestion. 'Don't say that. But maybe, yes, we did slide. It was just the thing to do. I'd read *The Female Eunuch* and smoked a bit of pot and gone on a couple of marches – great fun – but I wasn't nearly as radical as I liked to imagine. Just a middle-class girl pretending to be liberated, but assuming that sooner or later I would settle down, get married, have a mortgage and babies. I am not complaining, especially about the babies. Your father and I rubbed along just fine. Until I came to realise that was all we were doing.'

'Isn't that how most marriages go? Marcus and I can rub along. We've rubbed along so far. We can keep going. I'll probably be as happy as most people get to be.'

My mother leaned forward to look into my eyes. 'You were a singer once, remember?' No further explanation; she just looked at me.

'I have to let you make your own mistakes, don't I?' she said. 'That's the rule. Just as long as you know you're making one.'

24

Dawn dispels the shadows in the house, but not the shadows in Gwen's aching head. Shadows that rise, hallucinations of... Of what? She is no longer sure what she saw.

John's steadiness mesmerises her. He behaves and speaks with a monstrous calmness as if nothing needs to be explained. He does not drink, he does not swear or even raise his hand. His will simply sweeps over them. Gwen is submissive and the boys take their cue from her. Even the dog, grown wild with confusion over the last months, has come to heel, grateful for this miraculous restoration of certainties.

Wise dog. Certainties. That is what Gwen must cling to. The certainty of work, obedience, duty. Shut out the dark shadow: it is a dream, a mad bad dream, and if it is not, she does not want to know. Please God. Hold your tongue, girl, I don't want to know. I don't want to know.

Dawn to dusk, a day creeps by in unreality, panic locked up deep down inside.

Another night. Silent. No one stirs. No one speaks. She lies still, John beside her, every muscle paralysed by his presence.

A second day. John is still quiet, calm, mastering them. Once more, he is the unquestioned patriarch and it is so easy, so comforting to surrender. Easier than to think. The boys say nothing, creeping about the house. Should they be at school? She cannot remember. What day is it? It does not matter because John chooses to have them at home, uncorrupted. Who should have command of his children but himself? They must stay where he can keep an eye on them, where he can protect and govern them. A good man, her John, master in his own house.

Until William George calls.

John solemnly greets him in the yard and William raises a hand in salutation, a twitch of a smile, a casual pushing back of his cap. A normal neighbourly performance to disguise the wariness in his eyes.

Gwen sees the wariness. It stirs a fear within her, beginning the dissolution of the spell. William is wary of her John?

Knows how to keep quiet, does William, how to keep things comfortable and easy. One of life's peacemakers, no matter the provocation. Now that John is working again, no call for charity here, but a friend and neighbour can always visit. For the sake of the community and of Gwen and of the boys, William and his mother will continue to visit, braving the unpredictable reception of this house.

The two men stroll amicably in through the door, William already stating his purpose. 'Truth to tell, had a visit from the police and my Mam says she'll never live down the indignity of it.' A pause; the joke falls flat. 'They're looking for that Faber boy, worked for us, till...'

He stops. It would almost be comical, if Gwen could remember what laughter was, seeing William's easy-going face freeze, the blue eyes blink once, the mouth propped open in mid-word. What is he seeing that so startles him? Is it them, her and the boys, three pairs of eyes instantly fixed on him as he enters the kitchen? Eyes expressing what? Dumb terror?

He only falters for a moment. 'Good afternoon, Mrs Owen. Fine day. I was saying to John here, they seemed to have mislaid one of the Germans up at the camp. They're moving them out in a day or two and there's one gone missing. Peter Faber...' His eyes are roaming round the kitchen, taking in whatever clues there might be, looking for anything to explain this wall of glazed blankness that greets him.

'Thought he might have come looking for work. You haven't seen him around here, have you?'

Gwen's hand is at her throat. She is unaware of having raised it. Jack's face is white; Robert whimpers. William sees and hears, but John's answer is instant, off pat, as if he has waited for this moment.

'Oh, I won't have that Hun round here, frightening the children, making trouble. I ordered him off my land, last time he was here. He wouldn't dare show his face again. Down to the docks, that's where you should look. He'll have found a ship, skipped the country. You'll not see sight nor sound of him again.'

William's eyes flicker to Gwen's, hearing the shuddering intake of breath that she cannot help. The nightmare is coming back to life. John's words are resurrecting it. No dream. A nightmare maybe. A nightmare from which she cannot wake.

'Ah yes,' says William. 'Could be. The docks, yes, maybe.'

'It will be the docks,' says John with a certainty that defies questioning. 'Sneaking off to his fatherland.'

'Yes, that's...' William nods as if in agreement. 'I'm sure you're right. I'll try over with the Devonalds at Rhyd Eynon. They had him there a couple of times.'

'The docks, I tell you,' insists John, gruff impatience creeping in. Does he think a prisoner would sneak away and take ship back to Germany when the whole camp is being repatriated anyway?

William nods again. He is watching Robert. And now they are all watching Robert.

The boy is cowering, hands over his head, face contorted into a silent grimace, his shoulders flinching, writhing, bent double, and he babbles, blank words, hellish counterpoint to his actions. 'Why will you not die, devil? I'll finish you off for good. Take that, Satan. Take that. Smite the devil. I am the master here.'

Gwen watches him, acting out Peter's last moments, and she feels the panic rise up in her like a dark shape, blocking out the light. His meaningless movements and blurred words are a scream of accusation and she feels John snap, the strange unnatural control of the last two days crumbling as his anger surges.

'Woman, will you take that brat out of here, if you cannot control him, or I'll take a strap to the two of you!'

Gwen hastily gathers up Robert. He is a grown boy now, too heavy for her, but somehow she finds the superhuman strength to clutch him to her.

'He's not here! The German isn't here!' thunders John. 'Go look for him elsewhere. We'll not have that animal on this land!'

'Indeed. No. I see I'd best try my luck elsewhere.' William, grey-faced, is talking gently to pacify the man. 'Not to worry. I'm sure they'll track him down. So, you are well, Mrs Owen? My mother means to call with some of that jam she spoke of. I expect...'

'My wife can tend her own table,' says John, seething in his impotence. 'Do I need you to provide for us, William George? I'll not have your charity here.'

William merely nods, not taking umbrage at the words because he is not really listening. He is thinking, working it out. Not the truth; he has already grasped that. She can see the shock in his eyes. He is working out what to do. Nothing hasty, William George, but he will decide what is right, do something, speak to someone. His mother, or perhaps the Reverend, or he will go to the Colonel, or Constable Bowen. The matter has gone too far for turning a blind eye, but how to put things right when nothing can be right again? William will think it through, but the end is coming.

'Well I'll be on my way then. You'll be over to see the tractor, Jack?'

'My son will stay here!' orders John. 'I'll not have him running to Castell Mawr as if he doesn't know where he belongs.'

William nods, patting Jack on the head, leaning forward to whisper. Gwen reads the words on his lips. 'You know where I am.' Then aloud. 'Now then, Jack, you be a good boy, eh?'

'Oh you will direct my own son now?' demands John, throwing the door wide, picking up the shotgun as if to chase his neighbour from his property.

Gwen watches William give a wave as he sets off up the lane, his broad shoulders set, squaring up to the problem, his brows drawn in a frown of deep thought.

John stands there, still holding the door and the gun and staring out. Gwen stands, still holding Robert. Only Jack moves, edging out into the scullery. He, poor lamb, is not ready for apocalypse. Gwen waits for John to turn, but he does not and she senses the shame within him that will not let him face her.

Instead, he throws the gun down, thrusts the door wide and steps out, striding across the yard, through icy drizzle, heading for the first field, hurling the gate aside. Jess runs after him, padding in his footsteps, her allotted place in life. He turns, kicks the dog savagely, and Gwen hears it whine. It creeps away into the hedgerow. John stoops for a stone to hurl after it. Then he stalks on into the grey murk of the pitiless rain.

There is silence in the house. The spell is shattered. Gwen feels the blood stir in her, the instinct to cling to life, to fight for it. She looks at Robert, quiet now, his eyes dull. How damaged is he, this child of terror? And how great a threat to them all?

Jack peeps round the scullery door. Robert's mind broken, Rosie betrayed and dead, is Jack to be struck down too? What has Gwen done, to destroy her own children? John's sick perverted pride, what had that been compared with her own? Her stupid, pointless pride that concealed and stifled and said nothing while her children were crushed.

What must she do? *Go,* said Peter. Why did she not listen? Why did she argue and resist? Why did she not gather up the boys and flee with him?

She must listen now. Too late for Peter but she must go. Robert will speak, and John will not allow that. He dare not. What will he do, now that he has already done the worst a man can do?

Cold certainty grips her. She has no money, they have no home except this, but somehow, whatever the cost, they must cast themselves adrift.

Robert begins to squirm. How long has she stood there holding him, rocking backwards and forwards on her heels? She needs to move. Putting the boy down, she systematically begins to prepare the tea. It is the action of an automaton that even now cannot break from habit. Her mind is desperate, but her body knows John must have his tea. All must be seemly and punctual. While she works, her brain revolves. They must go. Somehow and somewhere.

Dilys. She would take them in, no doubt of that. But where is Peterborough? Somewhere far away is all Gwen knows. How will they get there, when she has one shilling and sixpence in her purse?

Castell Mawr. Could they seek refuge there? Would Mrs George understand, or would she be shocked, denouncing Gwen for her treachery to her man? A wife should stay dutifully in her place.

Maybe they should just walk. Take to the road and walk away. Keep walking until they drop.

Where is Jack now? The scullery door stands open. He is in the back garden, hands in pockets, forlornly scuffing at the earth.

The earth in the backyard. Gwen's heart freezes.

'Come in!' Her voice is shrill. 'I don't want you out there! Stay away from the garden! Stay away from the apple tree.

There is nothing there.' She feels the nausea rising, her head spinning, the monstrous image rising up before her. 'Come away from the apple tree!'

Jack stares at the tree, realisation dawning, then he hurries in, the fear that is threatening to become a part of him rising to the surface again.

'Wash your face,' she orders. They are filthy, her children. Can she not even keep them clean? They look like savages. 'Outside.' She has them both out in the yard, working the pump, ignoring the wails of protest at the sting of icy water. She is scrubbing away the dirt and the pain and the grief and the terrible images.

And John is there, come home to face her, fortified somehow, eyes wary and suspicious.

Let him suspect. Fifteen years of hurt boil over in her. She has had enough.

He knows it. He sees the revolt in her eyes and he must act now, or be doomed. 'Well, woman, what are you looking at me like that for? Do you think I'll put up with insolence like that in my own house?'

'Murderer.'

His face flushes crimson. 'What did you say, woman?'

'Murderer.' She cannot stop herself. 'You killed Peter and you killed my Rosie. Killed her, you filthy beast. Do you think I don't know what you did?'

'Hold your tongue, you foul-mouthed slut, you whore! Like mother, like daughter, is that it? The two of you in it together, concocting lies about me, filthy lies—'

'Not lies! I know the truth, beast! Silence was the lie. I should have cried out to the heavens what you did to Rosie, to your daughter. You called Peter an animal, but I know—

He lashes out but she moves out of the way. He is quicker, stronger, catching her by the wrists, slapping her face.

'I'll teach you, whore! Like her, like that whore you brought up on my hearth, teaching her to flaunt herself, to throw herself at men. Filthy whore of Babylon! Jezebel!'

Robert squats on the cobbles, repeating compulsively his cowering cringing act. 'Why-will-you-not-die-devil-I-will-finish-you-for-good...'

John stops, staring at the boy. 'Stop that! Stop that! You've done this, woman, feeding him lies! Well I'll teach him to—'

'He is no liar! He is the voice of God! He knows what lies under the apple tree, and I shall—'

'You lie!' John is roaring, swelling, a monster cornered. 'There is nothing under the apple tree! I will cut his tongue out!'

'You will not touch Robert, you'll not lay one finger on him, ever again!'

'Am I not master in my own house? Can I not discipline my own children, when their mother is a filthy lying whore?' His face is dark, spittle on his lips.

For a moment, free from his grip, Gwen picks up the pail and swings it at him, catching his legs as he unbuckles his belt. He totters off balance and she picks up Robert and runs. Into the house – where else is safe?

Jack is nowhere in sight. Please God he escaped. Heart thudding, she manages to draw the bolt before John reaches the door. He pounds on it. She is glued to the spot, eyes fixed on the solid planks. A pause. Has he gone? No he is back, hammering now, huge heavy blows. She can see the flimsy bolt begin to give.

Outside John is swearing. 'Bitch! Liar! There is nothing under the apple tree. Harlot! I will have that devil's whelp! I'll teach you who is master here!'

What can she do? Where can she go?

Pushing Robert behind her, she stares at the door, reaching out for support, and her fingers close upon salvation.

25

I was just the right age to embark on a mid-life crisis. My problem, though, was that I had been having one for the last five years, so maybe it was the right time to end mine.

No more displacement – and I didn't mean my quest for Cwmderwen's tragic truths. I'd come to realise, without any blinding moment of revelation, that my anguished guilt over Jemma's death, and all that had stemmed from it, had become a self-indulgent substitute for fighting. 'That was nothing,' she had said, in my dream. My real fault had been in giving up. She, or my deeply buried self speaking through her, was right, of course. Rosie's tragedy had destroyed all her might-have-beens for ever, but mine were still out there, if I could only find the nerve to grab them back. If, just for once, I could charge straight at life, instead of running for the hills.

My first target would have to be Marcus. Get the worst over first.

There was a sort of peace, the moment I faced the truth: I didn't want to marry him. It swept away all the desperate self-delusion of the last two years. But peace quickly gave way to panic. Was self-delusion so very bad?

Yes. And it had to stop.

I dreamed up ways of managing it. I could engineer another furious quarrel. Cwmderwen would easily do it. Or I could flee to India again. Or I could make him think there was another man...

Cheating. There was no other man, and there wouldn't be, until I had done what I should have done long ago, and saved myself. Sorted out who I was without help from anyone else.

He came with his briefcase, the guest list and a slightly impatient willingness to forgive my wilfulness, in the face of family crisis. 'So sorry to hear about Dilys, baby. Is she any better? No need for you to go rushing around. Just say the word and I'll drive you down...'

'Sit down, Marcus. I've got something to say.'

He sat, indulging me. That was what I was, a child who needed indulging. Needed to be tamed and trained and brought to heel.

'Marcus, I can't marry you.'

For the briefest of seconds he stood rigid with incomprehension. Marcus' life was planned, I was part of that plan, and there was no room for negotiation. Then his powers of calculation and control clicked into gear. A weary sigh. 'Let's not have another of these panic attacks. I know you—'

'No you don't, though.'

'Yes, I do. Now sit down. I love you, you know that, and I'm here to deal with whatever it is that's worrying you, so—'

'You don't love my music.' Inane as the issue was, in that moment it embodied everything.

'What? Nonsense. You know I think you have a lovely

voice, baby. When we're married you should join a choir. I'm sure—'

'No. Sorry. I don't want to join a choir. I don't want to have a grand church wedding. I don't want to live in America. I am not the woman you want me to be. I want to sing in clubs and get drunk and chase old murders and sit on Brighton seafront eating fish and chips. I want to be Sai Peterson, and I can't be if I marry you. Sorry. I really am. This whole marriage thing was all a terrible mistake.'

I'd started to turn away, subconsciously stressing my point. His hand closed round my arm, just to turn me back, but I felt its strength, fed by his resentment. My heart jumped. All he'd done was turn me back but my instincts babbled at me to calm things down, to back down, to dispel that anger.

Not this time.

I confronted his black eyes. 'You can't bully me, Marcus. You can tell people I'm a slag, a stupid bitch, whatever you like. Tell them you dumped me. But I am not marrying you.'

'At least he wasn't heartbroken,' I told Sam, who was back in Britain again, visiting Dilys and coming to commiserate with me. 'Although he refused to believe me for about an hour. I thought I was going to be worn into submission, but I stuck with it.' I was still sweating at the memory.

'I suppose he got angry.'

'Well, what would you expect? I have messed him around unforgivably. I couldn't make him understand that I'm just not who he thinks I am. Or who he thinks he can make me. Still, I'm glad he was angry. Better than crying.

314

That would have meant he really was heartbroken and then I'd have felt even more guilty.'

'Don't feel even slightly guilty, girl. Marcus will land on his feet. He has the killer instinct. Just be glad you discovered enough of a survival instinct.'

'Recovered my focus, you mean, instead of letting him do my focussing for me. Marcus is an extremely focussed person.'

'That he is. Focussed as a cruise missile.'

'But I did behave atrociously.'

'Come on, he can take it.'

'Can everyone else though? Poor Caroline, Mum, Dilys. It isn't just Marcus I've messed with.'

'I suppose you told Mum our little theory about Rose.'

'Most of it, yes. It doesn't seem to worry her too much who her real... her birth mother was, although she was upset about Rose's suicide.'

'She would be.'

'I didn't tell her all of it. Not my final suspicion.'

'Which is?' Sam sat back comfortably.

'I think it was the German prisoner, Peter Faber. The policeman I spoke to, Bob Roberts, admitted he was a monster, and children were terrified of him. I think he more than terrified Rose. I think he raped her, and she was too afraid, or too ashamed to tell anyone, so she had the baby and then she hanged herself.'

Sam winced. 'Christ. Poor kid.'

'Then you can realise how awful it must have been for her parents. Grandfather must have been beside himself with grief. If Rose refused to speak, there wouldn't have been proof, so no punishment for Faber unless Grandfather

315

meted it out. I bet that was what it was about, the murder. Grandfather tried to shoot Faber, but Faber got the gun off him, shot him and then ran. Maybe all the silence about it is just because no one wanted Rose's memory sullied.' I recalled the photo I found in Dilys' room. Those eyes looking into mine. Waiting for me to be her voice, after all these years.

'Yes,' said Sam cautiously, thinking it over. 'Maybe. This means our real grandfather was a soldier of the Third Reich who went around raping little girls. An interesting genetic twist, don't you think?'

'Christ! I hadn't even thought of it that way.'

'Fancy tracing our German ancestors? See if he was a one-off monster or do we come from a long line of psychopaths?'

'Shut up. Don't.' But behind Sam's black humour lurked a genuine appalling query. It wasn't one I felt up to pursuing. Peter Faber might be the man who raped my grandmother. That didn't mean I was ready to accept him as my grandfather. It was a conundrum I needed to put aside for now.

'There's something else. Someone else. You know I went to see Uncle Robert. He talked. I think he was describing Grandfather's murder. When I mentioned Faber, it set him off.' I fetched the recorder and played back the long drone of Robert's monologue.

Sam grimaced. 'That's Robert? Sounds like a parrot reading a shopping list.'

'That's the way he talks. But he keeps mentioning someone at the end. Danny something.' I heard it. 'There. Danny Gweyden Valley?'

'Okay.' Sam frowned, ran the recording back, listened again. 'Mm.'

I looked at him guiltily. 'Whoever he is, I know he's important because I said the name to Dilys, and I think that's what caused the stroke.'

'Yow! Did she say who he was?'

'No. And I have no idea.'

'Are we going to find out?'

'I want to. I don't know how.'

'Get it translated?'

'Yes, but how do I do that without making things worse? I think he's describing a murder, word for word. Probably very graphic. Maybe things are said, about Rose, about our family, about... I don't know. I can't just hand it over to some translation agency. It would be like handing in a film for developing, knowing it's crammed full of porn shots. Anyone who hears it and understands any of it will probably pass it over to the police.'

'You could explain it all happened sixty years ago.'

'I know, but it was never officially closed and how would Dilys react to it being reopened? Or even made public? I've already had one stab at killing her. I don't want to finish the job.'

'Okay, so we try another tack. A trip to Cwmderwen. You said next time I was in Britain you'd show me the place. What are we waiting for? That's where the answer's going to be, isn't it?'

So we went to Cwmderwen. I'd just worked twelve days on the trot to secure a deal for Frieman and Case, and Trevor was not going to complain if I took a couple of days off. The visit was perfect timing in practical terms, because

Matthew Harries had rung me a week before to say that it was all mine, if I wanted to move in and start playing with my Wendy house. Decorate it and dress it in time for Christmas.

He'd done a neat job. A few details I might have argued with, but on the whole, the old cottage had been transformed into a perfectly acceptable weekend retreat. The former parlour was now a kitchen, tiled, cool and clean, one door hanging not quite straight on the limed oak fitted cupboards. The lean-to scullery was now a bathroom. Plumbing was functioning – Sam rapidly christened the toilet.

Next to it I'd added a brand new sparkling conservatory. At least it would sparkle when it was filled with cane furniture and potted plants instead of cardboard packaging and black plastic bags of rubbish. In the living room, the huge oak beam of the inglenook had been oiled and polished, the old range, too rusty to be salvaged, replaced by a wood-burning stove. No furniture, except for the dresser, which still sat, large, dark, sagging, awaiting renovation. Up the new but quaint winding stair, the two connecting bedrooms were clean and fresh, with all the charm that low beams and tiny windows could bestow.

It was impressive. Anyone would be impressed. Sam said he was impressed, although he was instinctively stooping at every doorway.

And how pointless it had been. What had I been doing, trying to impose twenty-first century comfort and picture book appeal onto this place? Somewhere in this house, a suicidal girl gave birth, a grieving father was shot down – and I had built a conservatory.

318

'So this is it,' said Sam. We had retreated to the courtyard to survey the exterior again. The rendering had gone, exposing the stone beneath. Black slate. Under leaden December skies, it was as dreary as the grave. The deep dell closed in around us. 'Yeah, I can see why it haunted you. Certainly feels like a murder was committed here, doesn't it?'

It did. When I had first seen it, back in March, a tumbled ruin, abandoned for sixty years, I had been convinced that only echoes of forgotten happiness remained. Now that everything was neatened, clean, wrestled into ridiculous smartness, the house seemed indelibly contaminated, as if the words Rape and Murder and Suicide, in big brass letters, had been exposed and burnished for all to see.

'I think getting rid of the rendering might have been a mistake,' I said, my heart sinking. 'Do you think whitewash would help?'

'Wouldn't hurt. It is kind of funereal, isn't it?'

'Plants. When I first saw it, it was just a ruin and there were brambles everywhere, and grass and nettles. I think they may have been an improvement. If I grow something over it, maybe?'

Sam laughed. 'Food and wine, that will do wonders.'

We were staying there. Now that the cottage was properly mine, I was not spending another night at Plas Malgwyn, so Sam and I had brought camp beds and sleeping bags and a hamper of goodies. We cooked an indulgent dinner in the brand new kitchen, stark under fluorescent tubes. The last time this room was inhabited, there had been oil lamps and candles and it had been the parlour. Was this where John sang and Gwen played? If we were very still, would we hear the hum of harp strings?

'It is kind of spooky, being here,' admitted Sam, as we perched on one of the camp beds, plates of pasta on our knees, a bottle of wine between us. 'Like stepping back in time. Have you seen anything, you know, odd?'

'Ghosts, you mean?' We were still, listening for supernatural creaks. Silence. 'I think maybe the house itself is the ghost.'

'So what's it telling us to do?' Sam prodded my pile of notes and photographs with an outstretched toe. He'd had the opportunity to look, read, listen to all of it, and was impressed with my research so far. 'How do we go about finding the mysterious Danny?'

I'd already decided on my next move. 'I'm going to see William George again, first thing tomorrow. And you can go shopping. A couple of chairs at least.'

Barely December but Castell Mawr was ready for Christmas. I had thought I might get a tree and perhaps some candles for Cwmderwen, but this wasn't enough for Castell Mawr. The house was festooned with lights, coloured lights flashing in sequence, round every window, along the eaves and over the porch and round the chimneys. Three conifers in the garden were sparkling with white lights as if a passing radioactive angel had sneezed on them and there was a glowing reindeer on one of the sheds.

Carys George saw me coming and threw open the door as I approached.

'Hello then, you down to sort out the cottage? Matthew Harries done a good job with that pointing.'

No entertaining in the kitchen this time. I was ushered

into the family lounge, transformed to a Christmas grotto. Were they really going to live with this for the next month? Glittering Christmas decorations draped the walls and ceiling. A large Santa in the window periodically threw back his head and bellowed with evil laughter and an enormous tree stood in one corner, flashing in red and purple.

Gethin George rose to greet me, politely turning off the TV. 'You down for Christmas then?' I assumed they knew, to the minute, when I had arrived.

'Just for a few days this time. Making a start on getting Cwmderwen habitable.'

'Ah.' As laconic as I remembered. The Yuletide extravaganza, I was fairly certain, was Carys' work. I couldn't see Gethin pining for neon reindeer. Nor his youngest daughter, Rhonwen, a stunning Celtic beauty, who was sprawled on a sofa and greeted my arrival with teenage indifference.

Carys bustled in with trays. Tea, chocolate cake, mince pies, bara brith. All home-made, prepared in readiness for casual visitors. Sam, still muffled in his sleeping bag when I left, would have relished this.

'Where's that boy then?' asked Carys.

'Computer,' said Gethin.

'He should be down here to say hello to our guest. Dewi!'

'Oh no!' I protested. 'Please don't drag him down just for me. I was only calling to say hello and... I was hoping I might have another word with old Mr George?'

Gethin nodded, but Carys was already at the stairs, bellowing to her son, who loped reluctantly down, shook my hand sheepishly, swiped a large piece of chocolate cake and retreated, without an actual word being spoken, to Tomb Raiders XXXII.

Rhonwen remained defending her sofa, picking at a mince pie and looking bored, while Carys told me what colour kitchen tiles I had chosen, and where to buy carpets and what day to put the rubbish out and why I should avoid the butcher's in Penbryn High Street because he kept dirty videos under the counter.

Finally, my tea finished, Gethin halted the flow. 'You'll go in to see Dad then?'

'Oh yes, the old boy loves visitors,' said Carys. 'I'll just go wake him up.'

I worried William's cosy den had been transformed with neon, but the back parlour was untouched, except for a couple of paper chains. William was still sitting, comfortable and drowsy, in his ancient chair, the TV still booming and ignored.

He didn't recognise me at first. Then he did. He struggled for the name.

'I'm Sarah. Ellen's daughter. Siân Ellen Owen?'

'Ah, Siân. Rose.'

'Yes, that's right!' No worries here about speaking the name, maybe because he was not entirely aware of what he was saying. He could answer my questions, I was certain. But just how did I go about bellowing indelicate questions about my mother's birth to an elderly deaf gentleman, with his curious son and daughter-in-law in the room?'

'Bad business,' said William, helpfully. 'Murder there was, over at Cwmderwen.'

'Yes, my grandfather. John Owen.'

'John Owen, yes. Grand singer he was. He was shot.'

'That's right. Just after Rose died.'

'Rose.' His eyes drifted away, down a lane of memory so convoluted I couldn't follow. I didn't know how to bring him back.

'Can you tell me about her?'

'Pretty girl. Sang, she did. Sweet voice. Sad. She died. Very sad.'

'Yes.' I couldn't do it, not with Carys hanging on every word. It was a private grief, not for public entertainment. Maybe I was beginning to understand why Dilly kept such determined silence.

But there were some questions I had to ask. 'I wanted to talk about the murder. Do you mind?'

'Eh?' He focused on me again. 'John Owen. Murdered, he was.'

'Yes, by a German prisoner. Do you remember, you told me about him last time? He worked here, on this farm. Peter Faber.'

'Peter Faber.' William stirred in his chair.

'Do you remember him?'

'Not right. Not right.'

'What was he like?' I prompted. Keep talking, please!

William sank back again. 'Bad war, they said. Bad business. It wasn't right.' He was staring into nowhere, his head slowly shaking.

'Did he—?' How should I put this? 'Did he go to Cwmderwen very often?'

'Oh yes. Always there, he was. For her. He was there for her.'

'And was Rose afraid of him?'

'Rose? She was a sweet one. When she was little, sang like a bird. But not then.'

'Why not then? Was she afraid?'

'Afraid, yes. They were all afraid. I should have said something.'

'And the murder? Was that because of what he did? You know what happened, don't you?'

'What happened?' William's wandering took flight. He raised his watery half-blind eyes to mine, or to eyes like mine that had faced him sixty years ago. 'It was Peter Faber. The German. That's who it was. I saw him running down the road. That's what I saw. Jack fetched me, see. I saw Faber running down the road and there was John Owen lying dead. Nothing I could do. Nothing. God forgive me, it wasn't right.'

There was a moment of silence as his eyes closed. Was he falling asleep again? Or hiding in drowsiness. The story was so pat. Suspicion crawled along my flesh. Too pat after all these years. What was he still trying to conceal? I was desperate to get more out of him. 'Danny,' I said. 'Was there a Danny?'

His eyes opened again, peering at me, bewildered.

'Danny?' I repeated.

I remembered the expression on Dilys' face when I mentioned Danny Gweyden Valley. I couldn't do it. I'd done too much damage that way already.

'Never mind. Thank you,' I said quietly. Carys beamed. We tiptoed out, leaving William to his TV.

There were two chairs in the living room. Nice turned legs and well worn polished seats, plus a little gate-leg table. Sam must have found a useful junk shop in Llanolwen. That was quick work. The conservatory door was wide open, and I found him in the back garden, with the fork and spade I'd bought on my last visit. The place was still a barren wasteland, but the weeds had died back for the winter, leaving withered stalks and folds of rotting vegetation.

Sam, down at the far end, looked up from prodding the hard soil with the fork. 'How did you get on?'

'I'm well-fed, at least. I talked to William George, but he's very confused. Except about the murder. He's still certain about that. Too certain. You know, he's got a story and he's sticking to it. I couldn't bring myself to ask about Danny Gweyden Valley. Maybe next time.'

'No need, little Sai. I've done my own investigating.'

'You have?' I looked down on the leaf mould Sam was raking back. 'What on earth are you doing?'

Sam grinned, triumphantly. 'Took a stroll along to the village. You see the chairs and table? I saw an advert in the post office. The guy selling them gave me a lift back.'

'Very nice, but—'

'He's a local, so I asked him about your Danny. You see, I don't think you're hearing it right. You're struggling to make it sound like something that makes sense to you. But I listened to it again and it was more like this.' Always a better mimic than me, Sam repeated Robert's droning phrase with its original intonation.

'Yes, all right, maybe,' I agreed, grudgingly. 'And?'

'I·tried it on the guy with the chairs. He reckons it's, wait...' He fished out a piece of paper from his pocket. 'I got him to write it down. Here. He reckons it should be, "*O dan y goeden afalau.*"'

'Oh.' I took the paper, read the words. 'So what does it mean?'

'Aha! "Under the apple tree." So, I'm wondering, are those apples?' Sam peered at some withered fruit that still clung to the mossy grey tree. A few slug-ravaged remnants were rotting in the wet grass.

'Yes.' I had a sinking feeling. 'What are you doing?'

'Under the apple tree, says Uncle Robert. So let's look under the apple tree.'

I stood transfixed, as my brother started to rake the weeds in an ever widening semicircle round the tree. 'I don't think this is a good idea.'

'Come on. We can't just leave it. If there's something here, I want to find it.'

'Sam.' An icy shiver prickled down my spine. 'We're not looking for buried treasure. We're investigating a rape and a murder. I really don't think—'

'Hey! There's been a cover-up, hasn't there? That's obvious. Suppose there were clues. Suppose Rose left a true account of what happened and it had to be hushed up, so they buried it. A diary or something.'

Was he being hopelessly obtuse? 'That's unbelievably far-fetched.'

'Okay. But there must be something here. The murder weapon! Under the apple tree; Robert keeps saying it. Listen to the tape.'

'It may be nothing. He repeats anything endlessly if he gets going.'

Sam looked at me, oozing scorn. 'You don't seriously think we should ignore it?'

'No, I suppose not, I seriously did not think this was a good idea.

Sam's raking produced results in one place. The dead

vegetation and loose soil yielded up an old kitchen knife with chipped bone handle, a cracked cup, shreds of brittle wire fencing, blackened burnt wood, a few charred buttons.

'This is where they dumped stuff,' said Sam confidently. 'Look.' He prized free the remains of a spade, its handle rotted to soggy splinters. 'It's as good a place to start as any.' He was missing his much loved gym and what better way to hone his muscles than by digging a hole. The spade had left a convenient starting point for serious digging: a patch of bare purple impacted soil, etched with wormholes.

'Right!' Sam plunged the spade.

Suddenly, I didn't want to be there. Leave him to it, I thought. I could do something more useful. Measure for carpets, check his chairs for woodworm, make a pot of coffee. When I came out again, with the mugs, Sam had made some progress. He'd expanded the hole he was digging, so he could get down into it and dig more easily.

'Great,' he said, swigging back the coffee.

'How about taking a break?' I said. 'Have a bath, check out the local restaurants?'

'Might as well do a bit more while we've got the light.' He was back into the hole with the spade, showering me with the earth he'd loosened.

'Thank you! Have you found anything new?'

'Not yet. Just earth so far. But I'm getting into the swing of it now.'

'Heading for Australia? How far down are you planning to go?'

'Hell, a bit further.' Another spadeful sailed past me. 'I'm barely a couple of feet down. But it's not bad going. A bit of shattered slatey stuff but no rocks. Except for this... I'll just... Jesus!'

Sam leaped from the hole. He almost levitated, dropped the spade, peered into the pit again. 'Christ!'

Reluctantly I stepped up to join him. And looked down. At a skull.

26

The rain is cold, ice-cold, but she is colder still. It has soaked through her clothes, her hair is bedraggled rat's tails across her brow, and the ice has entered into her, freezing her from within. She hears a howling, or does she feel it? Her senses blur. The howling is the sound of the cold that will entomb her now forever.

'It's all right, Gwen. Let go now. Let me have it.'

William George? What is he doing here? She watches him, dispassionately, as he gently prises her fingers from the shotgun.

'It's all right, Gwen,' he repeats. 'It's all over now.'

Strange light this: his face looks white, though she knows it is really sun and wind-tanned. He has the gun from her, laying it down on the cobbles, to be swilled by rain and mud and blood. He moves away, shouting to someone in the lane. 'Go fetch the Colonel now, Ted! There's been an accident. Run, man!'

Such urgency in him. How odd. She has no wish or power to move. She can only stare down at John. Not at his face. He has no face any more. No eyes to fix on her ever again.

Something rough and warm around her. A blanket. The smell of dog. What is the dog blanket doing round her?

'Come inside, Gwen. Come away. Leave him now. It's all over.'

William is guiding her away, into the house. She resists, snatches of earlier panic surfacing. 'Jack.'

'Jack's with my mother. Don't you fret about him. Where's Robert?'

The boy is in the house, staring wide-eyed, rigid. William hustles him upstairs to the bedroom, then comes thumping down again. A good neighbour, William, but he is a man, he does not know what to do. He stands, big black kettle in one hand as if he is not sure how to use it. He puts it down; he's seen a better option on the dresser. A whisky bottle.

A lifetime of pledged abstinence goes out of the window. William takes a quick swig, swallows, eyes shut, and shudders. She should warn him, don't go down that road, good will never come of it. But her tongue does not respond, the words will not come, and William is gone, outside, busy, busy.

Time to move and get on with work, she must get the tea on the table, sweep the floor, before John comes in. But her power has gone. Someone has cut her strings. She sits in the hard-railed chair and stares at the fire. Though she is still cold, it must be heating something. The blanket has soaked through and is beginning to steam. She can see clouds rising around her, but nothing melts her ice. She has begun to tremble and the trembling will not stop. It is all that she is conscious of.

She is aware, at intervals, of shadows coming and going. There is noise, so much noise. Footsteps, walking, running, doors slamming, someone vomiting, and voices, urgent voices.

330

'Oh good God.'

'Someone shut that dog up!'

'Are we going to leave him like that? It's not decent.'

So many questioning voices. Gwen hopes they are not questioning her, because she cannot answer. Her mouth cannot manage the words.

Distant cars and squealing brakes. Goodness, they must be loud to carry down here. People will drive so recklessly, it is a disgrace. There will be an accident one of these days.

Plump maternal arms encircle Gwen. A shadow solidifies into a recognised face. William's sister, Betty John. Betty come over from Penfeidr on a night like this? 'Come along, love. The state of you. A nice cup of tea, poor dab.'

Gwen is being led into the parlour. Quiet and cold, the parlour, kept in formal splendour, poised in polished readiness for visits by the minister and such. The family seldom ventures in here. Only John. This is the master's room, where he does his accounts and scowlingly fills in forms and reads his big black bible. But he cannot read now, because he has no face. So he will not be coming in to work at the little gate-leg table, to fetch his locked strongbox from the big dark cupboard, to swig at the whisky she knows is secreted in the bottom drawer. He will not come but still Gwen feels as if she is trespassing here on the horsehair sofa where Betty has gently placed her.

No fire in the parlour. Never a fire here unless they know the minister or the Colonel will call. A chill washes over her as Betty pulls away the dog blanket. She's found a thin wool blanket from upstairs instead, and a quilt. Gwen recognises her handiwork. That is the quilt off the boys' bed. Would never do to get it wet. John will thrash her if she gets it wet.

'Be still, love,' says Betty, firmly resisting her attempts to push it off, tucking it round her.

'Robert?'

'Hush now, Annie's taken him to Castell Mawr. Better he be with Jack, isn't it? Mam will look after them, get them into nice warm beds with bread and milk. Now you stay still and drink this.'

Tea. Hot strong tea. Betty must have been generous with the tea leaves. More generous than Gwen dares to be. John will not like that. But it is good, the scalding water burning down her gullet, searing into her.

The parlour door stands open, framing the strange inexplicable performance going on in the kitchen.

Men. Dark wet coats. The Colonel. He has come too. That is an honour but John will not like it. Gwen should let him have the sofa. She should get up... but her limbs will not move. He looks in on her, the Colonel, troubled by the sight, his attention elsewhere, mind too busy for courtesy, listening to the low murmur of voices. William's voice. Not so shocked now. Just insistent. Very quiet, but it carries to Gwen, a whisper on the air.

'There's no way of telling, is there? And the dead are beyond help.'

'And if the man turns up?'

'He won't. God help me, he won't.'

'Dear God. Not that I have any time for Jerries. But if what you think is true—'

'If it's true, he's gone, but no call to go poking around for the truth, is there?'

'No. And this Faber was vicious, wasn't he? All the damned Germans are.'

'Yes,' says William. It is a strangled agreement. It wins him the prize he wants but costs him his soul. Gwen recognises the sound of souls being lost. Be quiet, I don't want to know.

'Still, the truth should out, I can't help thinking.'

'Wouldn't help him anyway, would it, the truth?' adds William, convincing himself. 'Who'd suffer? Not John, just Gwen. Is that justice?'

'Well, as to justice, there's no telling what evil deeds Faber did. Damned Germans. Beasts, the lot of them. One reads such things in the papers. Who's to say justice wasn't done to him?'

A pause. 'Indeed.'

'If a body were found, it would be proof that Owen was a violent man. A woman would have rightful cause to fear for her life. Self-defence. Any sane jury would see it so. They couldn't hang her for that.'

'But it would be a trial. Judge and lawyers, strangers who don't understand, don't know the way of it, no accounting for the way a jury will decide. Hasn't she taken enough?'

'Yes, of course,' agrees the Colonel, the magistrate in him slowly backing down.

'No need, if you don't want her punished more. It's not as if there's any proof.'

'No? The boy, Jack, when he came to you. Wasn't he saying—'

'He was upset. Maybe I misheard. He'll not say anything now. Not with his mam like this.'

'Very well, but what about the gun?'

'Oh that got picked up, pushed around while we covered him up. No saying who's handled it now.'

The Colonel is looking at her again, brow furrowed, then his mind is made up. Like a spring snapping him upright. 'Very well, but you'll have to get it right. You found her. You'll have to speak to the police. I'll speak to Bowen, he'll understand what's required, but my son called the station in Penbryn. Of course I can pull strings with the Chief Constable but they won't be so...' They have moved away. She cannot hear any more of their strange pantomime, the gibberish that they have been speaking. Sounds without meaning.

And here is old Dr. Connell, far too spruce for this farm. Looks as if he's come from a grand dinner. He must not come here! Gwen cannot pay. John will not have it. But maybe he is here with the Colonel, been dining with him, that must be it. She will not tell him about her bad head.

Constable Bowen is talking to him. So many visitors. She ought to make them tea. Constable Bowen has a notebook. She sees his hand shaking as he pretends to write. Poor Bowen, always one for an easy life. Does not like coming out on a night like this. He should be at home with his family.

'I'll certify death,' says Doctor Connell. 'But you don't need me to tell you he's dead or how.' He? Doesn't he mean she? He's come to tell them she is dead. That would explain everything.

The Colonel is talking to him now. They both stand in the parlour doorway looking at her. She should not be in here, they will tell John.

'Clearly in shock,' the Colonel is saying. 'You'll have to

give her something, man, put her out before they start interrogating her. Poor woman couldn't cope with that yet. In her state she might say anything. Good man.'

There is a pulsing light, torches flashing around the yard. Strangers, policemen from Penbryn. The Colonel is dealing with them. Perhaps Betty can make them tea.

Dr. Connell is looming over her. She recognises the smell of spirits on his breath.

'Well now, Mrs Owen, what you need is a good long sleep. That's the ticket, isn't it?'

He has a needle, Betty is holding her arm. What are they doing?

Something clicks. Something has washed away the clouds in her brain, bringing memory flooding back. Just briefly. She knows why they are all here. Come to arrest her. Because she has shot John. Because she has picked up the shotgun and fired it at him. Fired it in his evil, murdering, twisted, mean, pathetic face. She has killed her husband and they have come to hang her. Like Rosie, hanging. That is only fair. It is justice.

'Be still, Mrs Owen, just let this take effect.'

'Don't you worry about them out there,' soothes Betty. 'William will take care of it.'

Beyond them, out in the kitchen, William is holding court by the range, like the master of the house. That is good. William knows it all. He can tell them what she did. Policemen stand around him waiting on his account, and briefly his eyes flicker left towards her.

Drifting, fading, bewildered, Gwen listens as he stoically tells his story.

'It was that German, Peter Faber. I saw him making off

down the road, looking as guilty as sin before I ever got to Cwmderwen. Jack came to fetch me in a panic because there was trouble. When I got here, John Owen was lying dead. The shotgun was lying there in the yard. Mrs Owen was in a state, in shock. There was nothing I could do. It was that Peter Faber, I'll stake my life...'

27

'What are we going to do?' My heart was thumping with panic. I looked at Sam who was staring down at the half-exposed skull, his initial shock turning to revulsion.

'I don't know.' He wiped his face. 'Dig the rest of it up, I suppose.'

'Must we? I suppose ... we can't just bury it again?'

'Don't be daft. You can't leave it there.' He stepped back into the hole. There was a faint crunch and he came up again, quickly. Sam had wrestled with grizzlies, tackled gun runners in the Amazonian forest, fought off orcs, but only on a computer screen. There was nothing virtual about this skull. It was indisputably real.

'It could be old butcher's bones,' I suggested. 'If it's just the family rubbish heap. We don't know it's human.' Wishful thinking, but I'd known, the moment Sam had explained the meaning of *O dan y goeden afalau* that we were about to uncover something bad.

Sam thought about this. The exposed dome was pale against the dark soil. Could it be anything else? There was only one way to find out. He gingerly stepped back into the hole, placing his feet with care, and crouched over the skull, working the soil loose with his fingers.

An eye socket.

Sam swallowed, worked on. A jaw bone, teeth. We could see enough. It was a human skull.

I was going to be sick.

Sam was looking pretty green too. 'It's getting too dark,' he decided, hauling himself up. He was breathing heavily as he brushed his jeans down. 'Take another look in the morning.'

'What if it rains? The hole will flood.' I pictured the crumbling earth washed back over that white Thing.

Sam found some blue plastic sheeting, left by the builders, with a small heap of sand and half a bag of rock hard cement, in the remains of one of the barns. Using stones from the garden wall, we pinned it out over the pit, with mutual relief as the skull disappeared from our gaze. While it was visible, it seemed impossible not to look at it. Even now that it was safely under the blue plastic, I had an almost irresistible urge to lift a flap and look.

We went out for dinner. The idea of food didn't really appeal to either of us, but neither did the thought of staying at Cwmderwen. Even when I turned all the lights on as a gesture of encouragement, the stark bright light only emphasised the pitch black that had settled on the back garden. So we drove out to the pub in Felindre where we skipped the Thai-style crab cakes and red mullet couscous, and settled on sausage and chips and sticky toffee pudding. There was nothing quite like nursery food by a log fire to convince us that all was well, and that somewhere out there were adults who would deal with this problem.

But when the sticky toffee pudding was devoured and

we sat and faced each other over the pub table, we had to acknowledge that we were the responsible adults. Coping with Marcus was nothing to this.

'So who is it?' asked Sam, his voice low, although the few other customers, mostly gathered round the dart board, weren't bothered with us. 'It can't be our grandfather, can it?'

'No, I've seen his grave. He's buried at the chapel in Llanolwen.'

'Okay, so ... You know it could be nothing to do with us.'

'Nothing to do with us!' I squeaked. 'It's buried in my back garden!'

Sam patted my hand to hush me. 'I meant, nothing to do with the Owens. It might be really ancient.'

'Robert said "under the apple tree," remember? This has to be what he meant. He wasn't talking about a pile of buttons.'

'No, okay, so who is it?'

I felt the tears welling, couldn't stop myself. 'Rose isn't buried at the chapel.'

'Rose? Oh hell. Surely not.'

'She was a suicide, remember. What did they do with suicides?'

'Dump them in a shallow grave in the back garden? Oh Jesus.'

'It makes sense. I felt it as soon as I saw Cwmderwen; I felt there was something it wanted me to do. This is it. It was Rose calling me. My grandmother. The child who was raped, abandoned, as good as murdered. She wanted me to find her and...'

Sam looked at me, to see just how serious I was. At that moment, more than a little drunk, I was deadly serious.

'Shit,' he said.

Our return to Cwmderwen was no fun. Why hadn't I thought of having a security light fitted? Why hadn't we at least left a light on?

I didn't sleep at all that night, and I knew, from the persistent creaking of the camp bed in the adjoining bedroom, that Sam was doing no better. But daylight helped, even the half-hearted light of a December morning. We sat at the gate-leg table, with mugs of coffee and bowls of cereal, and reconsidered the problem.

'You realise we ought to call the police,' said Sam, having another helping of muesli, since it was all I had.

'No. Not yet at least. If it's Rose, can't we, I don't know, take her out gently? With a bit of dignity? I don't want policemen stomping all over her. When she's out, maybe.'

'We get her out?'

'We have to.'

So, fortified with coffee, we ventured back out. The blue plastic was still there, and when we rolled it back, so was the skull. We hadn't dreamed it then.

There was nothing to stop us, no one to see. The garden was enclosed by a wall of trees. Even in their winter nakedness, they were too tangled and crowded to let anyone spy on us. Unexpected visitors or hikers on the footpath through the field would only glimpse the front of the house. We could quietly dig up or bury half a dozen bodies round the back and no one would see a thing.

Sam set to work with the spade again. Yesterday, he was digging with wild abandon. Today, knowing what to expect, he was more circumspect.

He dug a coffin-shaped pit down to the level of the half-exposed skull, and more fragments of bone began to appear.

What do you do with exhumed bones? It was all very well declaring that I wanted Rose treated with dignity, but how exactly? On a previous visit, having ideas about a quaint brass bed, I'd bought some equally quaint bed linen. It was still in its cellophane wrapping in the dresser. I unpacked one of the floral sheets. We both eyed the whisky bottle, decided it was not a good idea. Not yet, anyway.

'Right,' said Sam. 'Let's get on with it.'

The larger bones were easily exposed. Shoulder blade, pelvis, arm and leg bones. She lay on her side, crumpled up as if forced into a tiny space. How could they have done this to her, dumping her with such callous contempt? My Nan had allowed this?

Sam started working with an old paintbrush left by the builders, sweeping delicately round each bone.

'We're not going to be able to get it up in one go, you know,' he said. 'Can I pass you her arm? It's in the way.'

I steeled myself. 'Wait.' I spread out the sheet, pinning down the corners against the sharp gusts of wind that whipped round unexpectedly. 'All right. I'm ready.'

One by one, the bones of an arm. In one scoop the bones of a hand. Rose's hand. I looked at it, pathetic on the flowered cotton. I would not cry. The humerus had been broken once. I could see the break, snapped and mended. How had she broken her arm, I wondered?

Sam was working to free the ribs now. I could see breaks there too. Unhealed, this time. Jagged edges. 'If I can just loosen here,' he said, sitting back on his haunches, to get better purchase on the rib cage. 'It's got...' He stood up suddenly.

'What is it?' I asked, straining to see what it was he could feel.

'I'm not sure.' He crouched down again, leaning over the ribs, working, brushing, loosening, tugging, then he stood up again. 'Yow!'

In his hand was the corroded head of a pitchfork.

I had to run to the wall, to throw up.

'Are you okay?' asked Sam, following me.

'Wonderful.'

He sat beside me on the wet grass, as I buried my face in my hands. I couldn't believe they could have done this. Thrust her into her grave with a pitchfork? What sort of animals were they?

'Come on,' said Sam, his arm round me. 'Let's leave it for a bit.'

'No! No, I want to finish it, get her out, now.'

It took Sam all day and the light was fading again, but all the bones were exposed now. He made other finds: heavy rusting chain, metal shards and there was what appeared to be a sledge hammer, at her feet. Sam was no longer shocked. He merely held the hammer up and looked at me.

I took it from him, my jaw clenched shut.

We looked down again at the huddled skeleton, the curve of the spine. That was intact, right up to the skull. A pang seized me. It meant that when she'd hanged herself, her neck hadn't broken. Had she slowly throttled on the rope?

Licking his lips nervously, Sam got a firm grip on the skull and pulled it free from its cradle of stagnant earth, a nightmare parody of Yorick in his hands. I saw, full on for the first time, the face of my poor aunt, grandmother, tormented child... and the gaping jagged shattered hole in the left temple.

Sam's hands were trembling. I took the skull from him, staring at it with pity and revulsion. Sam picked up the heavy weight of the hammer and tentatively held it to the gaping wound. A perfect match.

'Sai,' he said, keeping his voice steady with difficulty. 'I don't think this is Rose.'

'It stands to reason.' Sam had had three whiskies to relieve the strain and was getting loud. 'I mean, 1948. It wasn't the Middle Ages. I don't know what the law was then about disposing of bodies, but they couldn't have just tipped a dead girl in a hole in the ground, could they? And if it isn't Rose, so who is it? More to the point, what are we going to do about it? It's no good. We're going to have to call the police.'

'No!'

'Sai, it's a murder. We can't just cover it up and pretend we haven't noticed it. They'll have to have it, see if they can find out who it is. Probably a bit late to investigate, but—'

'It's obvious who it is.' I buried my head in my arms on the table. Why hadn't I guessed long ago? Everything made sense now, including the resolute silence.

'Who?'

I looked up with a sigh. 'It's got to be Peter Faber.'

'The German? The German! Of course. That explains the

old breaks in the bones. And all that metal round the legs, maybe that was shrapnel.'

'Probably. I expect he was wounded in the war. Plenty of time to heal up.'

'Yes, but hang on. I thought he was seen boarding a ship?'

'They would say that, wouldn't they? And don't you see, if it is him, we can't possibly go to the police.'

'I don't see why not?' Sam gave a macabre laugh. 'Means they can finally stop looking for him.'

'I don't think they ever were looking for him. Not really. They probably guessed. Bob Roberts was dropping heavy hints about lynch mobs. They just chose not to pursue it. But if we tell them now, they'll want to dig up the whole story, and we can't let them do that.'

'Why not?'

Did I have to explain the obvious? 'Faber killed our grandfather. So who killed Faber?'

'Good question.'

'Who had just seen her husband shot dead? Who had just lost her raped daughter? Whose garden was he buried in?'

'Nan?' Sam slammed his glass down and stared at me. 'Nan Owen took a pitchfork to a German soldier, bashed his brains in and buried him in the back yard? Jeez.'

'Who else could it have been?'

'Well, I take my hat off to her. Sounds like she did the world a favour.'

'Maybe that's what everyone thought. William George was protecting her, pretending he'd seen Faber running off. Everyone else in the village probably played the same game, so the police never had any proof, even if they suspected. We can't just hand them the evidence now, can we? Or do you want to be the one to tell Dilly that the police are about to label her dead sister as a murderess?'

Dawn was late. It was nearly eight o'clock and I could hear, distantly, the hum of cars ferrying people to their work. Sam and I would have started earlier, but it was so dark we would not have been able to see a thing. Torches would have been asking for trouble, even with the protection of the trees.

It was frosty. I was wrapped up in all my spare clothes, but Sam braved the cold in bare arms. He was putting so much energy into digging that the sweat was pouring off him. Neither of us wanted to waste time on this.

The grave where the bones were found was shallow. Barely three feet down. Probably as much as Nan could manage. If we were putting him back, I wanted him a lot deeper. Deeper than anyone would ever dig. Deep, but it didn't have to be large; the bones were bundled up ludicrously in my floral sheet. Any idea of treating them with respect had evaporated when I'd realised they were the bones of a rapist and a murderer.

My true grandfather. I didn't want this. Could I disown my forebears? Him, maybe, but I was not disowning his victim, Rose. I was claiming her with all my heart and soul.

When Sam was finally done, we dropped the package in, and I helped him shovel the earth on top. There was no escaping it; even when I'd raked the soil as level as I could get it, it still looked ominously like a grave, one patch of fresh bare earth in an expanse of dead weeds and sodden grass. Midwinter. It would take months for the weeds to grow back and cover the deed.

'So.' Job done, we'd retreated to the house for showers, and a second breakfast. Sam poured himself coffee. 'What are your plans now?'

'I don't know.' I glanced round the virtually empty room. It was no longer possible to see Cwmderwen as a place of lost laughter and happiness. I sensed only the misery, and the bones buried in the backyard. Had I avenged Rose by unearthing them, or had I just been sucked into the conspiracy of silence by reburying them?

Here I was, the keeper of the family tomb. I'd become a character in one of Sam's computer games. 'I'll do the place up, I suppose.' I tried to concentrate on thoughts of Laura Ashley and scrubbed pine.

'Invite Mum here for Christmas?' suggested Sam.

I grimaced at the thought. 'We'll be spending Christmas in Hove, with Dilys.'

'You're not going to tell either of them about the, you know.' Sam nodded towards the back garden.

'No of course not! I'm not going to tell anyone. I'm sure Mum knows nothing about it, and Dilly will take the secret to her grave.'

'And Robert?'

'Robert!' I'd forgotten him. We both thought of that recording. Under the apple tree. How many more secrets were hidden in his long rambling? How many times, I wondered, had he sat reciting an account of my grandfather's death and Nan's revenge, to uncomprehending ears?

'We still don't know exactly what he was saying,' said Sam, picking up the recorder from my pile of evidence and turning it over in his hand.

'We can guess, can't we?'

'Yes, but come on. We've got to know.'

'How? There's no way I'm going to hand it over to some complete stranger. Whatever happens, I'm going to make sure the police are kept out of this.'

'Let me make a copy, take it back with me. I know people. I'll think up some story.' Sam grinned. 'I'm good at that. And it's all far, far away; no one is going to ask too many questions.'

The temptation was overwhelming. 'Go on then. Take it.'

It was three days before Christmas when I got Sam's call. 'Sai. Season's greetings and all that.'

'You don't sound in festive mood.'

'Too much on. Listen.'

'Go on.'

'That recording. I know a guy here at the gym. About as Welsh as Nelson Mandela if you ask me, but he belongs to one of these expat *I Love Wales* groups. You know, flying red dragons on St.David's Day.'

'And?'

'So I asked him if there were any proficient Welsh speakers in the group and I came up with this story—'

'Knowing you, it was a complicated one. Did it involve orcs?'

'No, a therapist in Wisconsin, who – Just take my word for it, it was convincing. And Sai, I got the translation. My friend knows a guy, an academic and he agreed to do the deed.'

Was I ready for this? 'Good. I think.'

'It was the best he could do. Sai.'

'Yes?'

'It's not what we were expecting. You won't like it.'

'No? Somehow I didn't think I would.'

'I'm telling you I've got it done, but are you still sure you want to read it?'

'I don't want to, but of course I have to. I haven't come this far just to let this last bit rest.'

'All right then, but don't say I didn't warn you. Okay, there. I've sent it. Check your emails. Merry Christmas.'

Merry Christmas. I downloaded my mail, opened the attachment, prepared for Robert's revelation of murder and violent revenge.

Sam, I've had a go, as requested. Some major problems. It's very colloquial Welsh, not my dialect, Pembrokeshire I think, and it's pretty indistinct. Think in terms of a spoken equivalent of an old letter whose ink has run and smudged. And there's the lack of expression. I am guessing there are several voices, but they all blend together, so it took me a while to make any sense of it. I haven't attempted to guess where one voice leaves off and another starts. I suppose it's what you get with hypnosis. Don't know if the result will be any help to your therapist friend. Not surprised the old man was traumatised, if he's been burying this for 75 years. Here it is.

Translation for Sam Peterson.

Rose and Jack and Robert. Disobedient slut. She was a harlot child of the devil, she was no daughter of mine. I curse her. Dilys. Cake. God, there is a brave boy. Now then, Jack, be a good boy. William George, I do not need you to keep us. No charity here. *** *Sorry, can't make this out, but it could be Biblical.*

Did I not tell you to keep off my land? Please, Peter, go. I beg you, Peter run. Filthy beast, have you come here to find another whore? Go now, Peter. Run Peter now, or he will kill you too. *** *expletives?* You will not hurt her. You will not speak to me, dog. *Bits here I can't understand at all. Sounds like a cat mewing.* Why will you not die, devil? I will finish you for ever. Take that, Satan. I am master here. Get away, devil, I will take care of this. Not on my land. I am master...

...There is nothing under the apple tree...

...murderer, you have killed Peter and you have killed my Rose. You are an animal. You have told lies about me. Silence is the lie. I should shout out what you did to Rose, evil animal...

...He is the voice of God – he knows what is under the apple tree. Liar. There is nothing under the apple tree. I will cut his tongue out. You will not touch Robert. You will not lift your hand against him again.

...You are the devil John Owen. Murderer, you will not kill another child of mine.

It was raining in Guildford. My room was dark, lit only by the computer screen, as I endlessly reread the translation of Robert's regurgitation of uncomprehended memories, making piecemeal sense of the confusion. What was there left to say? For nine months I'd been seeking answers, but I never thought to ask the right question. Not, why did my grandfather die, but why didn't she kill him sooner?

'Merry Christmas, Dilly,' I said, softly, invalid talk. I was amazed to see her so well. But it would take more than a stroke to defeat my great-aunt Dilys.

Her eyes were bright black buttons, as observant as ever. 'Merry Christmas, Sarah.' I could distinguish the words although they were slurred. Dilys shook her head in frustration at the refusal of her lips to obey her precise commands.

'Sorry,' I whispered.

She glanced at me sideways. Body language: stuff and nonsense. She didn't have to say the words.

'I know,' I said. 'What happened. I know. Peter Faber, Nan, everything. And I will never tell.'

Her eyes met mine, her hand over my fingers.

'What are you two whispering about?' asked my mother, coming into the room with a plate of mince pies and a bottle of sherry.

'I'm explaining about Marcus.'

'Nothing to explain,' said my mother complacently. 'Don't you go nagging her, Dilly. I know you were looking forward to a wedding, but she did the right thing.'

Dilys scowled, and muttered, and then she smiled. 'Stuff and nonsense.'

'So let's open the presents,' said my mother. 'Let's see.' She sifted through the pile of glittering packages we had heaped around the tiny tree we'd insisted on installing in her room, much to Dilys' indignation. 'Here's one for you from Sam, Dilly.' She shook it. 'He wouldn't dare send you a pipe again, I'm sure.' She handed it over. A silk scarf. I knew; I'd bought it for him. 'And here's yours to Sarah.'

'Thank you, Dilly.' I took the neat little package, ready to untie the ribbon, but Dilys' hand was on mine again.

'No. Something else.' She was struggling to get up.

'Let me,' said my mother, but Dilys slapped her away, stubborn as ever. 'I can do it.' She hobbled to the wardrobe, and rummaged in a box. 'This is for Sarah.'

The old photograph album.

'Goodness,' said my mother. 'Well that will keep her occupied. Look.' She talked lightly, leaning over my shoulder as I turned the pages. 'The Lewis family, isn't it? How lovely. That must be the garden of the cottage you've bought, Sarah. There's Jack! He looked just the same, the last time I saw him. And there's Rose.' My mother said the name without hesitation. I knew that the suspicion I'd sown at our last meeting had stuck. It had aroused curiosity, sympathy, even pain, but it hadn't wounded her. Not enough to make her forget that Dilys' feelings were her sole concern. She was speaking, I knew, because someone had to speak. A silence would be too awkward. 'Yes, Sarah does look like her.'

This time, Dilys didn't say, 'Stuff and nonsense.' She nodded.

While my mother left the room to find an extra glass, I kissed Dilys' cheek. 'Thank you,' I said, hugging the album. 'I promise I will never say another word, except this. Rose. I have to know. Where is she?'

351

28

Not a bad day for a journey, considering. The clouds are gathering, but they have not broken yet. The harvest heat has hardened the muddy ruts in the lane. Emrys Roberts, owner of the Garn roadstone quarry, has been able to bring his lorry right down to the cobbled yard.

William George, Ted Absalom and Sidney Lloyd are manhandling Gwen's furniture onto the lorry's boards. Iron bedsteads, rolled mattresses, chest of drawers, cupboard, chairs. The kitchen table is not worth taking, scrubbed to the bone and splintered, one leg sawn short to allow for the uneven floor. After consultation, the men dump it in the yard. It will come for firewood.

The dresser is a matter of greater debate. A heavy thing and ungainly, even if they detach the racks. Difficult to get through the door, let alone transport safely across the country.

'Leave it,' says Gwen. It has never been truly hers, his grandmother's dresser, the bulky domestic altar requiring ceaseless elbow-cracking tribute. Great ugly old-fashioned thing, far too big for any place she is going to find, when she can move the boys out from under Dilys' feet. Which she must. However welcoming Dilys is, Gwen will not impose a moment longer than she has to. No cluttering Dilys' house with her and her boys and their foolish ways. Their foolish words. Off they'll be to a place of their own. Somewhere among the English, where no one will heed.

While the men sweat over the heavy stuff, she packs a box of bits and pieces. Her sewing box. The flat iron. The boys' school books. A cracked teapot? It will do still. A cracked cup? No, add that to the heap.

John's big black bible? She opens it with hands that tremble with a sense of illicit trespass. Only John opened this book, to catechise his children as they stood solemnly by him in Sabbath neatness, waiting for the rapped knuckles and the stinging blow.

He had written on the frontispiece, adding to the spidery details of past Owens; his marriage, the births – where Rosie's name should be – there is a black blur of ink, the letters carefully obliterated.

Gwen's trembling ceases, replaced by a gush of hatred. She will not take the book. Burn it? No. Rip out the page of his spite … No, she cannot even bring herself to perform that small sacrilege. He has a sister, older than he, went into service when she was twelve and never came near Cwmderwen again. Married a Phillips down south, went to America, Pittsburgh or some such place, but the husband's people are still here, over Haverfordwest way. William will see that it is passed on. Let them do what they like with it.

Only one last thing to pack. A tattered mouldering rag doll. Gwen found it, buried under leaves in the wood. Retrieved, to go with her into her coffin, a reminder to the bitter end of her ever-haunting guilt. I don't want to hear.

A moment of anguish. She busies herself with the rubbish – taking it out the back, she tells the men as they glance after her. The back garden lies neglected, for what purpose was there in sowing seeds this season? How could anything grow here? Except the wild rose. Of all living things, a rose has planted itself here, arching over the wall, where John would once have thrashed it down. Well, Gwen will not touch it. She has no right. Let the rose flourish if it will.

Gwen carries the rubbish down the cinder path and stares down at the dark earth, the bare earth half concealed now by the trash, the half-burned broken stools and bowls and tools that she had deposited here with some vague idea of concealing the spot. No need to do more, now William has taken over the land. Master Philip wants no new tenants, so the house will be abandoned, swallowed up by all-concealing weeds and shadows.

The wrong screams at her. It will scream at her forever. She kneels, her knees scored by cinders, to deposit her burden among the rest of the debris. 'Peter,' she whispers. 'Forgive me, child.' Then she rises, empty-handed, and walks back to the house.

They are done at last. Her box is tucked in between two chairs, everything strapped in place. The men watch critically as Emrys Roberts gets the lorry into gear and starts negotiating the steep ruts up to the road. He is taking her furniture all the way to Peterborough. She wanted to pay him. She can. She has found the key and opened the strongbox hidden in the parlour cupboard. £263. A fortune. How long had he had it stored away there, while they went without?

Emrys Roberts will not hear of payment. Good neighbours help each other out. Keep the money for the boys. They will need it in Peterborough. Big city like that, sure to be costly.

The lorry only needs one push to make it up the lane. Shoulders braced, boots seeking purchase between the hardened ruts, the men strain in chorus. Then it is away, with a hoot of its horn.

Nothing left to sort out. The horse and the cows have already gone to market, fetching a bit more for her purse. William would have bought them, but Gwen would not have it. What would he want with her sorry beasts in the fine sleek Castell Mawr herd, or another old nag when he has tractors? She has let him have the hay, what little there is of it. Ted Absalom has taken Jess, poor creature, broken leg and ribs. He is good with dogs, healing the wounds if not the madness; maybe in time he will bring her round. Shoot her, more likely.

Ted Absalom and Sidney Lloyd brush aside her thanks and amble off, touching their caps in farewell. William George stays a little longer. There must, of course, be a more considered parting between such close friends and neighbours.

But what can he and Gwen say? No confusion about her now, no shocked paralysis or numbed delirium. She knows what he has done. Not with her consent. She wanted to stop him, to tell the truth and take the punishment. There were dues to be paid, to Rosie, to Peter. But it was no good, she had been skilfully, firmly outmanoeuvred. She had to think of the boys, the living, not the dead, they told her, whenever she opened her mouth to speak. And her brain told her they were right. Lies have been told, silence has been established and there is no going back, not unless she drags down yet more innocent lives with hers.

So now she stands by, with a ghost of a smile, while William chats with Jack about engines. At least Jack has come through it all alive and kicking, thank God, even if there are scars on his sunny nature, moments of unusual silence and withdrawal. Jack will always have the ability to up and walk away.

She looks at Robert where he crouches, rocking, in the dirt, locked forever in the prison of his own mind. He does not know her, he never did. What business has she to desire a child's love when she can only destroy? But she knows, William knows, Robert has the power to destroy. She sees William regarding the boy with half an eye, ever watchful lest some unconsidered word or gesture spark him into life. Sooner he goes, thinks William. No one will understand him over there.

Except Gwen. She will be there, keeping Robert safe, while she has the strength. What can she do now but care for him and not mind his blind disregard of her existence?

They are waiting for Harry. He's been over at the big house, sorting things out for her. Now he returns, accompanied by the Colonel. Gwen had not expected that. The estate manager maybe, but not the Colonel. She wonders if she should make him tea. The kettle still stands on the range, but the furniture has gone, there is nowhere to sit.

The Colonel hushes her concern, joining Harry in a compassionate pat of her hand. 'A sad day, Mrs Owen. A bad business, but I want to wish you well in your new life. We all have to move on.'

Gwen hands the keys to the Colonel and they shake hands solemnly. He locks the door behind them as they step out into the yard.

William and Harry carry the cases, the Colonel following as the family tramp up the lane for the last time. Robert drags, not understanding, but neither Gwen nor Jack turn their heads.

The Colonel's car is waiting on the verge, behind Harry's smart new Austin. A perfect gentleman, he helps Gwen into the passenger seat, while Harry herds the boys into the back

'Everything all right there in the back?'

'Fine, Uncle Harry,' says Jack, eager to hear the engine start.

'Robert?'

Nothing.

'Well then.' Harry is hesitant, not sure how to handle this. He needs Dilys' support, but she is waiting for them at home with the baby. 'Shall we be off?'

'Yes,' says Gwen.

They go, and there are people along the road: the parish of Llanolwen come to see them on their way. The Colonel; stalwart William George; Betty and Annie, plump and waving; Mrs George, supported on sticks, nodding grimly; the Lloyds, the Absaloms, the Devonalds, the Johns, Miss Evans, the Reverend Harries. They stand witness to her departure just as they had stood witness to her arrival all those years ago. But now they are not suspending judgement. She is one of them, protected by the communal spirit.

There is a vow of silence in their eyes. A promise. The

357

long silence that condoned and ignored and permitted all the horror will hold steady now and be both her shield and her burden, concealing her guilt, if she in turns conceals theirs.

The motor car rumbles on through the dappled shade of heavy trees, past the choking growth of hedgerows, swallows dipping under chapel eaves, the deep green of riverside meadows, the wire fences and concrete tracks and silent Nissan huts of a now deserted prison camp. Memories to be obliterated as a new world beckons.

She will never see all this again, but she will keep faith. The secrets of the past will be buried, the fear, the hatred, the love strangled at birth, the trust stifled. Far behind her, dust will settle on Cwmderwen, the woods will shroud the nameless dark corners. She goes, empty, leaving the brambles and nettles to conceal the truth forever.

29

A shaft of filtered sunlight played on the wall of Cwmderwen. Three months had made all the difference. The sun no longer merely touched the ruin of the old barn. It reached the house itself, at least in the middle of the day. The palest of cream masonry paint helped. It reflected the light, instead of devouring it as the exposed black stonework had done. Matthew Harries, whose lads had spent many happy hours chipping off the old rendering, and carefully repointing the stones, raised his eyebrows slightly when I'd asked him to paint it, but he agreed it was an improvement.

So were the bay tree and the tubs in the courtyard. The crocuses were open but the daffodils were delayed, way behind the drifts of solid gold around the gate of Castell Mawr. They had hazels and willows already budding into silvery green, but the shaggy neglected woods of Cwmderwen were all oak and ash and, as Carys had explained to me, those were always the last to come into leaf. Of course they were. But they would come eventually, like the clematis, still stick-like and unconvincing, which was set to grow around the door. A pretty green pump stood over the well – ideal for washing down the cobbles.

The impulse to wash down the cobbles was there, but I thought, I hoped, that no one visiting Cwmderwen would now look at the place and think of murder.

Except me.

Somewhere here, a poor German prisoner had been stabbed to death with a pitchfork, butchered by an insane monster who had abused his own children, raped his daughter and driven her to suicide. And on these cobbles, my Nan had finally blown out the brains of the man who had wrecked her life. It was as clear to me now as it was to all those others who had held their silence for sixty years.

The Owen family home. Knock it down, Dilys had said. A little too late for that, but I was doing what I could to plaster over the past. Who would recognise this place now? A tasteful little holiday retreat.

The dresser had gone, burned. Too much rot, too much warping. Besides, I couldn't look at it without thinking of that school book, hidden in it. Sam has had that translated too. Rose's words. A girl's hatred of her monstrous father.

Nice to know I was not, after all, tainted by Nazi rapist blood. No, instead I was descended from a sick violent incestuous child abuser. The blunt irony of history bludgeoned me with an inescapable truth; if I had the power to rewrite the past, save Rose from all her misery and whisk her away to safety and happiness, I would unwrite myself. If all that vileness of sixty years ago had not happened, I would not be. But I was, brought here by all the designs and accidents of my life, both the good and the horrible. I couldn't change the past, only the present, in hope for the future.

So I'd done what I could to make the place new. I had a

new sideboard and shelves. Shaker simplicity in blonde wood. The living room sparkled with pale china, mirrors, pewter. The carpet was cream, the furniture white. Impractical, I knew, but I wanted to force light into the place. Everything was modern. It might not be what all tenants would like, but I wanted to obliterate any illusion to the past.

I couldn't sell the place. Not yet. My back garden was largely down to grass, new turf that would take a while to settle. But at the end, where a useless old apple tree once stood, there was now a new sapling, a copper beech, which would one day be tall and stately against the oaks and ash. Around it were shrubs, stunted as yet, and golden stone slabs with a garden bench. It took muscles that I never realised I had, but there were some things I couldn't ask anyone else to do. Once that corner was established, no one would want to alter anything, dig anything up.

Behind the seat was a boulder. I'd spent three sweaty hours getting it there, rolling it down from the woods with the pickaxe. My little gesture, just to prove those tedious R.I. lessons were not a waste; Peter the rock. It seemed little enough, but something was required. Still too much bare earth, but that wouldn't last. When the tree was large enough, then perhaps I would sell. Until then, I was going to let it as a holiday cottage, recoup some of the vast fortune I'd thrown at it. Once I had seen the place littered with the detritus of other families, hopefully as happy as families could reasonably expect to be, perhaps the spell would be broken for good.

My phone purred.

'Sarah.' My mother. 'Glad I found you. I tried your flat,

then remembered you might be in Wales. How's it going?'

'It's good.' I left the pot of primulas I'd been prodding and walked to the old rusty gate, where phone reception was slightly better. 'I'm just making sure everything is ready for guests. The agency has got someone lined up for Easter.'

'Excellent. And how about you? No more trouble from Marcus, I hope.'

'No, he's telling everyone I was a bit too unbalanced, you know. I refused psychiatric help apparently, so he had no option but to cut me loose. That's fine by me. I don't mind.'

'Good! Of course, as your mother I reserve the right to kick him in the balls if I see him, but I'm glad you've been able to put it behind you. So what else is happening? Sam hinted that you might have something to tell me. Very cryptic.'

My eyes wandered to the dark shadows of trees looming behind the house. There were so many things I could tell her, but I suspected I never would. Undo all Nan and Dilys' good work? Anyway, there were better things to talk about. 'Sam's a tease. It's nothing important. I mentioned to him that I was quitting Frieman and Case.'

'No!'

'You're disappointed.'

'Not disappointed. Surprised, that's all. I thought you were all lined up for a partnership.'

'I was. Trevor was falling over himself to arrange it – or would have been if he could summon up the energy. He knows I've been the driving force in the firm. But he'll have to manage with Maya. I know it was a nice sensible career and I could have made something of it. But not the something I need to make.'

'So what are you doing instead?'

'I'm going to sing. I've got me an agent.'

'Sarah!' There was no doubt about the joy in her voice this time. 'Oh thank God.'

'Thanks to Leo. Do you remember him? One of Sam's ex's. The pianist. We met for a drink and I said I wanted to sing again, so he fixed me a couple of engagements at Murphy's. And an agent was listening, and one thing led to another—'

'Sarah, this is wonderful! I always knew you could make it.'

I laughed. 'Curb your enthusiasm. I haven't made it yet. I may never make it. But at least I'm going to try. And since I've blown all Granny Peterson's legacy on this place, I've got a job. Fundance Kidz. Inner city theatre, you know, that sort of thing. We ran a campaign for them last year and they liked my ideas so I'm going to be working on their publicity. Can't let all my hard-hearted commercial experience go to waste. The pay's lousy, but who wants money?'

'You won't starve, I'm sure. And I'm so relieved you're going back to music.'

'Blues, not opera,' I warned her.

'Sarah, I don't care if it's Bizet or Bessie Smith. You've got an incredible voice. Just use it. I was so afraid you'd given up for ever after that terrible accident.'

'Yes. Funny, all these years feeling guilty about some silly remark I'd made to Jemma before she died, and all the while I should have been feeling guilty about not following her advice. Anyway, I'm doing it now.'

My mother sighed down the phone. A huge sigh of relief. 'It's never too late to start again.'

'Like you did.'

'Well, yes. Have you forgiven us? Sam told me you and he went to see your father. How is he?'

'Fine. I'm not an angel; Mandy still drives me up the wall.'

My mother laughed. 'She has the same effect on me. I do wonder how he puts up with her.'

Marriages. All odd and inexplicable in their way. 'Mum...' I hesitated. 'Suppose Dad had ever hit you—'

'Oh no, stop there. Don't be ridiculous. Chris hit me? Where did you get such an idea?'

'No, I never thought he did. But supposing he had, or he'd hurt one of us, what would you have done?'

'I'd have been out of there like that, of course.' I could hear the snap of her fingers. 'What's this about?' Sudden suspicion. 'Is this about Marcus?'

'Good God no. Just a woman at work. I think she's abused but she insists on staying put. Why would a woman do that?'

My mother sighed again. 'I really don't understand it. You've got to talk to her, tell her...'

I let her advise me how to advise my fictitious colleague, as I gazed into the darkness of Cwmderwen's windows. Where had the advice been, sixty years ago? Never too late, my mother said, but it was for those who had been devoured here. At least I could go on.

When my mother rang off, I went back inside, cleared away the last of my mess, gathered my bags. I had brought Dilys' old album with me for some shamanic reason. Something to do with letting the spirits go, maybe. I opened it, to the page with the picture of Rose.

My big eyes looking back at me. If I wanted to know how

364

Rose would have looked, had she lived to be an adult, I need only look in the mirror.

But she hadn't grown up, my aunt grandmother. Like me, she sang, but her song was smothered. Was there ever joy in her life? I would never know for sure, because all that Rose might have become had been obliterated here. And here was I, a second Rose, the whole world open to me.

I flipped back to the first photograph in the book. The family studio portrait, circa World War I. A smart, dignified, proud little man with his sweet, genteel, slightly faded wife. The good-looking bright-eyed boy, later to succumb to TB, the plump frilled toddler Dilys, the slight, fair girl, Nan, hand resting on the harp, a gentle smile on her lips. She never smiled with her eyes, said Sam, but she was smiling here. Her eyes glowed with hope.

I shut the album. There was still hope, out there somewhere, and I was going to find it. Better, I was going to make it. Just one more stop before I sailed into the future.

Penbryn. March sunshine is glowing on the slate roofs below me; the cemetery is up on the hill, open and windswept, an elemental feel although the grass has been neatly clipped and the gravel paths are neatly raked. It takes me a while to find her, although Dilys told me where to look.

Rose Elizabeth Owen. 1934-1948. They shall reap in joy.

It is a small white stone, much like those to either side and all around. Quiet undisturbed anonymity, far from the gloom of that dark dell in Llanolwen. The clean wind sweeps in from the Atlantic, washing away all memory of grief. She was brought here too late, out of that place, but her child, the innocent fruit of misery was taken away to be loved and to grow healthy and whole, to be happy and have kids and make silly mistakes and find her feet as an artist in Ireland surrounded by middle-aged lovers. One little bud of hopefulness to be rescued from the catastrophe of Cwmderwen. What other justice can there be?

An elderly woman at a nearby grave, busy replacing wilted chrysanthemums, looks up at me and smiles with friendly curiosity. 'That's an old grave. Never seen anyone visit it before.'

I think of the photograph, nursed by Dilys, the long silent love. A grave is nothing really. But still, I am here now. 'We all live a long way away.'

'Ah. A relative of yours then.'

'Yes.' I place my daffodils against the stone. I am not going to explain more. Not to a stranger in a cemetery. Maybe not to anyone, ever.

There had been a time to speak out once, when speaking would have done some good, but it is long past. Better, for now, to leave the dead to their silent sleep.

If you enjoyed *A Time for Silence*, why not try
The Mysterious Death of Miss Austen...

6 July 1843

I have sent him her hair. When I took it from its hiding place
and held it to my face I caught the faintest trace of her; a ghost
scent of lavender and sun-warmed skin. It carried me back to
the horse-drawn hut with its wheels in the sea where I saw her
without cap or bonnet for the first time. She shook out her curls
and twisted round. *My buttons*, she said, *will you help me?* The
hut shuddered with the waves as I fumbled. She would have
fallen if I hadn't held her. I breathed her in, my face buried in
it; *her hair*.

To the ancients it was a potent, magical thing. The Bible calls
it the source of a man's strength and a woman's allure. How
strange that it should have this new power; this ability to bear
witness after death. Science tells us it is dead matter, stripped
of life long before the body it adorns.

I suppose he has had to destroy it to reveal its secret; he can
have no idea what it cost me to part with it. All that remains
are the few strands the jeweller took for the ring upon my
finger: a tiny braid, wound into the shape of a tree. When I
touch the glass that holds it I remember how it used to spill
over the pillow in that great sailboat of a bed. If hair can hold
secrets this ring must surely hold mine.

Now that the deed is done I fear what I have unleashed. This
is what he wrote to me yesterday:

1

Thank you for entrusting the letter from the late Miss J.A. to my keeping, along with the lock of her hair bequeathed to you. You are quite correct in your belief that medical science now enables the examination of such as has not perished of a corpse with regard to the possibility of foul play.

Having applied the test recently devised by Mister James Marsh, I have been able to subject the aforementioned sample to analysis at this hospital. The result obtained is both unequivocal and disturbing: the lady, at the time of her demise, had quantities of arsenic in her person more than fifteen times that observed in the body's natural state.

You have told me that the persons with whom she dwelt, namely her sister, her mother, a family friend and two servants, all survived her by a decade or more. I must conclude, therefore, that the source of the poison was not any thing common to the household, such as corruption of the water supply. Nor could any remedy the lady received – if indeed arsenic was administered – account for the great quantity present in her hair. It may be conjectured, then, that Miss J. A. was intentionally poisoned.

This being the case, I need hardly tell you that bringing the perpetrator of such calumny to justice, after a lapse of some six-and-twenty years, would be next to impossible. If, however, you are willing to explain the exact nature of your suspicions to me, I will gladly offer what assistance I can.

I remain your humble servant, Doctor Zechariah Sillar

It is a source of some relief to me to know that the disquiet I have felt these many years is not without foundation, though I burn with rage to see it written there as scientific fact. To him her death is nothing more than a curiosity; his interest is piqued and he offers his assistance. I have not even hinted that the guilt lies with someone still living.

Where would I begin to explain it all? Elizabeth, surely, is the first link in the chain. But how would he see the connection unless he acquainted himself with the family and the secrets at its heart? How could he understand my misgivings without knowing her as I knew her? To weigh it up he would have to see it all.

But it was not meant for other eyes. I am well aware of the danger of opening this Pandora's Box. People have called me fanciful. Indeed, I have questioned my own judgment. But the possibility that I might be right makes me more inclined to take this man into my confidence. He has the twin virtues of learning and discretion, and knows nothing of the family. If it *is* to be seen, there is no one I know who is more suitable than him. The question remains, is it the *right* thing to do?

3 January 1827

Jane's nephew wrote to me yesterday. He asks me to contribute to a memoir he wishes to compile. I will have to tell him that I cannot – and furnish him with some plausible excuse.

His letter has unsettled me. Quite apart from the scandal a truthful account would create, the way the request was framed infuriates me. I have thrown the thing away now but the words he used still parrot away inside my head: 'Although my aunt's life was completely uneventful, I feel that those who admire her books will be interested in any little details of her tastes, her hobbies, etcetera, that you might care to pass on.'

Completely uneventful. How can anybody's life be described as *completely uneventful*? He wishes, I think, to enfeeble her; to present her to the world as a docile creature whose teeth and claws have been pulled. The respectable Miss Austen; the quiet, pious Miss Austen; the spinster aunt whose only pleasures apart from her writing were needlework and the pianoforte. Meek, ladylike and bloodless. How she would have hated such an epitaph.

I suppose he believes that I would relish the task of serving her up to the public like a plate of sweetmeats. I hope he lives long enough to understand that one does not have to be young or married to be racked by love and guilt and envy. How affronted he would be if I revealed exactly how I felt about his aunt.

His letter has had quite a different result from that which he intended. I have decided to make my own record of all that passed between us; a memoir that will never be seen by him or any other member of the family. I will write it for myself, to keep her close, and as a way of releasing what eats away at me. When I am dead Rebecca will find it amongst my papers and she can decide whether to read it or toss it on the fire. My feelings, then, will no longer matter.

Chapter One

1805

When I first met Jane her life, like mine, was an indecipherable work in progress. I had no notion, then, of what she was to become. But in the space of a few weeks she rubbed away the words other hands had scrawled beneath my name and inked me in; made me bitter, passionate, elated, frightened...all the things that make a person jump off the page.

Godmersham was where I lived in those days, although I never would have called it home, for I belonged neither above stairs nor below. I was one of that strange tribe of half-breeds, a governess. Educated but impoverished. Well-born but bereft of family. To the servants my speech and manners made me a spy who was not to be trusted. To Edward and Elizabeth Austen I was just another household expense. My only true companions were books. Like friends and relatives, they fell into two categories: there were the ones I'd hidden in my bed when the bailiffs came – old familiar volumes that smelled of our house in Maiden Lane – and there were the ones I was permitted to borrow from the Austens' library. This held many favourites, expensively bound in calf or green morocco, with gilt edging and endpapers of crimson silk. Their pages brought back the voices of all those I had lost.

Jane arrived at Godmersham on a wet and windy day in the middle of June. I remember the first sight of her, still clad in mourning for her father, her eyes bright with tears as she greeted her brother. The hall was bustling with servants, eager to organise the newcomers, and I could tell from the way she held her head that she found it all rather strange and discomfiting. I saw, too, the way Elizabeth looked her up and down like a housewife buying a goose. *Feathers rather too sparse and shabby-looking,* I caught her thinking; *not really fit for our table.*

Elizabeth Austen had given me a similar look when I first came to Kent. She was heavily pregnant and surveyed me from her armchair, peering over the rim of a teacup that rested on her belly. Her face reminded me of a doll I had when I was a child, a doll with blue glass eyes and real hair whose cold, stiff hands used to poke my flesh when I hugged her.

'Well, Sharp,' she said, 'I hope that you will live up to your name. Fanny is a good girl but she's easily distracted. She needs to be watched not indulged. The boys have no need of you: they are being schooled at Winchester. You may be required to teach Lizzy and Marianne when they are older – *if* you last.'

By the summer of 1805 I had lasted a year and a half, during which time Elizabeth had given birth to a boy, fallen pregnant again and been brought to bed with her ninth child, a girl this time. I wondered if I would still be at Godmersham when this little creature was old enough to take lessons, and how many more babies would arrive in the meantime.

The day Jane came I was standing at the top of the stairs, high above the gilded columns and marble friezes, holding the older children at bay until the formalities were over. But Fanny, who was twelve and the leader of the pack, broke free and hurled herself at her aunt, knocking Jane's black straw bonnet backwards. I remember fragments of laughter drifting up to me with the smell of wet grass and horses that had followed her in. She wrapped her arms around the child and hugged her like a saviour. I felt a stab of jealousy, for Fanny was more than just a pupil. She was the reason for my existence.

Fanny had become the closest thing to a daughter I could ever have imagined. I used to think about it often in those days, what it would be like to have a child of my own. Just one. Not a great brood, like Elizabeth's, for I saw how it was for her, a clever woman turned idle by her own body. No wonder she was irritable with those who served her; no wonder she sometimes looked at me with spiteful eyes. Perhaps she wished that she had been born plain, like me. Perhaps she wished she had not married a devil-dodger's son who loved ladies as long as they knew their place.

'Who taught you to think, Miss Sharp?' Those were the first words her husband spoke to me when I entered his house. I had been there a week without our paths crossing, which not unusual in a house of such grand proportions. I was coming into the hall by the door opposite the frieze of Artemis and the huntsmen; he was standing on the second tread of the staircase, which made him almost my height but not quite.

'My father, sir,' I replied, smiling at the courtesy he showed in addressing me. I thought he called me 'Miss' because he had known of me before I became his employee. But I was wrong about that. The prefix was used only to convey his displeasure.

'Indeed? I cannot believe that your father was a follower of that Wollstonecraft woman, so I can only assume *you* are the disciple. I will not have you filling my daughter's head with such errant nonsense!' He was not looking at me as he said this. His eyes were on the window, through which Elizabeth could be seen walking with a gentleman whose identity was not yet known to me.

'I am sorry if anything Fanny has repeated has caused offence to you,' I began. He made no reply, still looking away from me. His face looked very red against the white wig. A little of the powder had fallen from it, riming one eyebrow like frost on grass. I *was* very afraid of offending him. His silence made me panic. What I said next was ill-judged; it came from my heart, not my head: 'Am I wrong in trying to give her thinking powers, sir? I'm sure you would not wish her go out into the world as a tulip in a garden, to make a fine show but be good for nothing.'

'Better a tulip than a trollop!' He muttered it under his breath but loud enough for me to hear. I thought I was about to be sent packing.

He was halfway to the door when he turned and said: 'All that I wish for Fanny is that she should have a sound head and a warm heart. Shakespeare, Fénelon and Fordyce's Sermons: that is all she needs in the way of improving literature. They were good enough for my wife and they are good enough for my daughter.'

I was very careful after that, but I wanted more for Fanny than her father had in mind. While she was debarred from all the possibilities open to her brothers, I was determined she should be every bit as well-educated. If marriage and motherhood were the only parts she was to be allowed to play she must develop abilities that would exact respect. Ignorant as I was of the married state, I believed that although Edward loved his wife, he did not respect her. How could he, when she was reduced to a role that differed little from that of his cattle and pigs? I vowed that Fanny would grow up to be a very different sort of woman.

The Mysterious Death of Miss Austen

by Lindsay Ashford,

Honno ISBN: 9781906784263

More from Honno

Short stories; Classics; Autobiography; Fiction
Founded in 1986 to publish the best of women's writing,
Honno publishes a wide range of titles from Welsh women.

Eden's Garden, *Juliet Greenwood*

Sometimes you have to run away, sometimes you have to come home:
Two women a century apart struggling with love, family duty, long
buried secrets, and their own creative ambitions.

The Mysterious Death of Miss Austen, *Lindsay Ashford*

No-one has ever been able to provide a satisfactory explanation for
the tragically early death of Jane Austen. A shocking new possibility
emerges in this intriguing novel...

Back Home, *Bethan Darwin*

Ellie has lost the love of her life and decamps back home to mum and
granddad where a knock on the door uncovers the past granddad
thought he had left behind in the Welsh valleys. *"A modern woman's
romantic confession, alongside a cleverly unfolding story of long-
buried family secrets"* Abigail Bosanko

All Honno titles can be ordered online at
www.honno.co.uk
twitter.com/honno
facebook.com/honnopress

ABOUT HONNO

Honno Welsh Women's Press was set up in 1986 by a group of women who felt strongly that women in Wales needed wider opportunities to see their writing in print and to become involved in the publishing process. Our aim is to develop the writing talents of women in Wales, give them new and exciting opportunities to see their work published and often to give them their first 'break' as a writer.

Honno is registered as a community co-operative. Any profit that Honno makes is invested in the publishing programme. Women from Wales and around the world have expressed their support for Honno. Each supporter has a vote at the Annual General Meeting.

To receive further information about forthcoming publications, or become a supporter, please write to Honno at the address below, or visit our website:

www.honno.co.uk

Honno
Unit 14, Creative Units
Aberystwyth Arts Centre
Penglais Campus
Aberystwyth
Ceredigion
SY23 3GL

All Honno titles can be ordered online at
www.honno.co.uk
or by sending a cheque to Honno